Woman
of a
Certain
Rage

GEORGIE HALL is the alter ego of the rebellious
author and woman of a certain age, Fiona Walker.
A theatre-loving, dog-walking, Eurythmics-lip-
syncing fifty-something, she lives in Warwickshire
with her partner and their teenage daughters.

GEORGIE HALL

Woman
of a
Certain
Rage

HEAD
of ZEUS

First published in the UK in 2021 by Head of Zeus Ltd

9 7 5 3 1 2 4 6 8

A catalogue record for this book is available from
the British Library.

ISBN (HB): 9781800240025
ISBN (XTPB): 9781800240032
ISBN (E): 9781800240001

Typeset by Divaddict Publishing Solutions Ltd

Printed and bound in Great Britain by
CPI Group (UK) Ltd, Croydon CR0 4YY

Head of Zeus Ltd
5–8 Hardwick Street
London EC1R 4RG
WWW.HEADOFZEUS.COM

For Sarah Anderson, my wise, sage and
irrepressible co-giggler.

I'm Eliza Finch: wife, mother of three,
Jobbing actor, cake baker, wine drinker.
Now fifty, I'm also cursed to be
A sweaty, sleepless over-thinker.
The truth is I don't feel any older
Although I know that's seen as risible:
Women my age grow braver and bolder,
And almost completely invisible.

PROLOGUE

The Dog Fight

Our dog Arty died a fortnight ago. She was sixteen, which is over ninety in dog years, the young vet told us kindly when he came to put her down. It was a very dignified departure. She was ready to go but the family was heartbroken. We all had a good cry that night, since when I've mopped my tears out of sight. Goodness, I miss her. She was one of those dogs who comes and leans against you when you're upset, all kindness and patience. Even if I was angry – which I am a lot these days – she'd stick around and let it wash over her, although that could be because she slept a lot towards the end and was stone deaf.

We put her basket, toys and bowls in the garage. Yesterday we went on her favourite walk by the River Leam to scatter her ashes. Edward had made a Nanoblock headstone and Summer read out a poem she'd written. There was a tricky moment when a jogger came past just as the wind was blowing the wrong way, but he took it in good spirit once he realised it wasn't a beloved grandparent. Just a dog.

Just Arty.

It took all my powers of self-control to spare the family the sight of me sobbing uncontrollably on the riverbank like an ageing Ophelia. Instead, I gathered them in a group hug that was more of a head-butting rugby scrum, said a final thank you and goodbye to our darling old dog friend, then let them scatter away from this embarrassingly motherly display of affection as we turned to walk back home.

That's when Paddy suggested we should go straight out and get a puppy. A *true* family dog, he emphasised, as though Arty wasn't enough of one. Summer was taking a sad-face selfie out of earshot and Edward had put his noise-cancelling headphones back on, so I ignored the suggestion, hoping he'd get the message and let it go.

But he brought it up again later when we were on the big television-watching sofa, children upstairs, a void between us where Arty would have been curled up.

'Come on, Elz. Let's go for it. Let's get a puppy.'

I told him I needed a little longer. I felt tearful and panicked, as though this strange new dog was about to attack us. He said that I wasn't being fair on the family, that Edward needs a dog (which is rubbish; he couldn't have cared less about Arty; he wants a snake) and that it would be fun to have a puppy around the place. He got his phone out and started looking up litters on Gumtree, saying how he'd always fancied this breed or that breed. When I accused him of making it sound as though Arty wasn't ever the dog he'd wanted, he pointed out that, as a Heinz 57 rescue dog, *nobody* had wanted her until we came along.

'Anyway, she was always more your dog than mine,' he

2

said, and I felt indignation spark because that was never the intention.

I still remember how heroic and noble we'd felt trooping to the National Canine Defence League to find our family best friend: Artemis, a strange mottled creature of indeterminate age, breeding and colour, one ear up and one down, one eye blue and one brown, with a long sausage body balanced on delicate Sheraton legs, a white plume of a tail and an overwhelming desire to love. Certainly, I was the one who fed and walked her most often, so perhaps it's true that I got an extra dose of devotion, but she had plenty to share round.

And here was my husband shopping online for another dog, preferably with a bit more love for him and less for me to balance things out.

'You'll feel much better if you cuddle one of these.' He'd held up a screen full of Cockerpoo puppies.

'I will not!' I snarled, and that's when the fight kicked off. Our dog fight.

Once I'd made it clear that I don't want another dog straight away, and he'd made it clear he does, we quickly ramped it up to ranting at each other, all sorts of nonsense, at the end of which Paddy accused me of not loving him any more. I was sobbing too much to deny it. At least, that's my excuse.

I slammed my way up to bed while he stayed downstairs. After a long cry, a self-pitying message left unsent to my best friend Lou and three podcasts I didn't take in, I went back down and found Paddy asleep on the sofa, the TV still streaming back-to-back episodes of *Game of Thrones*, all flying fake fur, plaits and blood. I'm not sure he took on board my apology as he zombie-ed up to bed; I'm not

3

sure he even really woke up to hear me say that of course I love him.

I always regret shouting the first thing that comes into my hot head when we fight. But I was still furious with him about the dog idea. And now I was angry with myself for jabbering out a tired surrender.

I lay awake until dawn, feeling like the world was about to end, although that's nothing new either. (Hello insomnia! What doom shall we showcase at 5 a.m. today? Ah yes, Paddy leaving because you said such unforgiveable things. Then there's your failure to make your children's futures safe. And if we need more, there's the old undiagnosed tumour worry again...) The only thing new was that Arty no longer crept up into the bed to try to lick my tears away. Kind, gentle Arty, who wasn't afraid of death, while I am terrified. If I die, I wondered, will Paddy be straight on his phone, swiping left and right to try to find my replacement too?

Arty's dead, the disloyal bitch, and I miss her revoltingly.

I don't want another dog.

Another life, that's a different matter.

1

Drive Time

Sorry! I mouth at Paddy who is reversing out of the drive to take Edward to school after a quick car shuffle.

Our younger son's taken against the transport that the council provides to convey children to his special school an hour's gridlocked rush-hour drive away. This morning's meltdown on the driveway was his fiercest yet, our new neighbours peering from an upstairs window. It's the third day in a row Paddy's been forced to take Edward in by car. Sitting beside his father, earphones on and waving goodbye, Edward looks as though the last half hour of screaming, biting and kicking hasn't happened.

Paddy raises his hand farewell, stone-faced, as wrung out by it as I am. We're still licking wounds after the dog fight and now this. He thinks I'm too soft on Edward; I think he shouts at him too much.

I wish I could have been the one to take him in, but I need to be at work in twenty minutes and it takes half an hour to get there.

I manoeuvre my car back up the drive, and leave the engine running while I dash in for my work bag and to brief Summer whose bus isn't for another hour. 'Can you remember to hand that form in to the office or we'll be fined, and *please* look for your lost jacket and art portfolio today? Cat *out* of your room before you leave the house.' I've been saying much the same since she was in Year Seven like Edward and she's now taking A levels with no noticeable improvement. I hug her. 'Goodbye. Love you.'

She shrugs me off. 'You need to do something about that parting, Mum. It's M40.' We grade my grey regrowth according to roads, from Unmarked Lane through B and A to the dreaded M.

'I'm going back to my roots, like Bob Marley.'

'That is oh so wrong!'

'God, was that racist?'

'Odyssey sang "Going Back to My Roots".' She and Paddy are big music trivia buffs. 'And yes, it's poor taste.'

'Don't hate me.'

'I'm a teenager; I'm morally obliged to hate you.' She smiles to show it's a sort-of joke, but we both know she says it like she means it painfully often.

'I hate you!' were, coincidentally, the first words I ever said to Paddy, although I was definitely joking. And laughing. And *staring* at the Adonis in a beanie who had just correctly identified that it was Supergrass who sang 'Alright', not Blur or Suede or one of the other Britpop bands breaking at the time. I'd had a tenner riding on Pulp, which was all the money I had left to buy food for the week.

6

It was 1995, one of those grey February days when it never seems to get light. I'd been shut in an unheated scenery workshop with fellow members of the Cat's Pyjamas Theatre Company since breakfast, devoting our precious Saturday to painting the set for a low-budget bit of fringe agitprop. (For set, read a pile of splintered packing cases, several of which disintegrated under the weight of a thin layer of emulsion.) Our director had disappeared hours earlier to source more and we'd turned on the radio to dance round, too busy squabbling over the identity of the band on John Peel's live session to notice him return. He'd brought his new flatmate with him, a man so tall, blonde and handsomely chiselled, he should have come with *Heartbreaking Bastard* stamped across his forehead.

'Paddy here's agreed to build us a stage set.'

'I love you!' were the second words I ever said to my husband. I still remember the way he looked at me, and my goosebumps doing Mexican waves. He was *that* hot.

I thought I had his measure. I specialised in broody bastards at the time, mascara-wrecking heartbreak being a badge of honour for most twenty-something single girls of my acquaintance, along with Red or Dead boots, hanky-hem tops, CK One and a copy of *Prozac Nation*. We knew the score: meet him and register mutual attraction, flirty date one, fall for him, mark the phone for a week and tell friends he could be The One. Flirtier date two, mark the phone for two weeks and pretend not to care he hasn't called whilst secretly feeling suicidal. *Very* flirty date three, borrow his toothbrush, straight into date four, falling fast now, *intense* flirtation, lots more sex, the meet-the-friends date, all good, a weekend away, falling at warp speed, so much sex I get cystitis. Ouch. Most bastards baled here, but a few toughed it out longer: upscaled sex, more friend events, another weekend away. Staring into each other's eyes, not quite ready to say it yet, me free-falling dizzyingly. Crash landing is inevitable. Perhaps the pregnancy scare will do it, or the meet-the-parents. Then there's all those wedding invitations with a handy plus one. Oh, here we go. Calls are coming less frequently. He has a lot of work on, he says. Then calls stop. Mark the phone and just *know*. Shout at the phone. Leave light and breezy answerphone messages full of unspoken pain. At last it comes: *it's not you, it's me; you're too good for me; I'm not ready for this; I've met someone else.* Cry a lot. Broken.

Don't get me wrong, I broke a few hearts back. But I always fell hardest for the bad boys.

Nowadays being ghosted is all played out digitally, as instant as tapping an X on a screen. Back then, in real time, exorcism was a slow and painful process. They were devils, those beautiful nineties bastards.

Except Paddy Hollander, it turned out, wasn't one. He might have looked like a stud for whom bastardy behaviour should be second nature, but he was steadfastly kind. As a favour for his new housemate, this sex-on-legs cabinet maker whose handmade sideboards were all the rage in Shad Thames, built us a set even the National Theatre would have been proud of. When he realised I had nothing to eat, this demigod in 501s went to Safeway and bought me three bags of groceries *and* decent wine. He was laid-back; he was generous; he was funny. His Shropshire accent was the loveliest imaginable, his brevity of words thrilling. The intensity of his eyes spoke volumes. I'd never met anyone like him before, not just because his upbringing was so different to mine, but also his values. He didn't play games at all. And he was heaven in bed.

Paddy always called when he said he would. He bought me cranberry juice when I got cystitis. He *liked* going to weddings. Even my parents didn't put him off. This time, when I fell, I landed in his arms, safe and loved. His leap of faith was no less trusting, this pragmatic Shropshire artisan who fell in love with a highly strung actress. Call it a trapeze act.

It's more than two decades since I first span round with paint on my face and saw the man I'd share all the years to come with. I have never once said 'I hate you' to Paddy again, no matter how many times he beats me at music trivia or turns his back to my tears or shuts me out from his demons.

But I don't say I love you as often as I once did.

And I don't feel as loved.

Hell. It's eight forty-five. I am going to be so late for work. Outside our new neighbour – twenty-something trophy wife and hair extension enthusiast – is loitering on the shared driveway demarcation zone, baby on hip. 'Helloooo! Laith can't reverse the Jag if you leave your car there.'

Tall Victorian townhouses like ours weren't designed for modern car owners. They have three (company, SUV and convertible, all alpine white) to our two (utilitarian rust pile and family banger), but they park theirs with precision neatness whereas I keep ruining the mutual turning geometry with my *The Sweeney* style arrivals.

'It was just for a minute while we got the other car out and I—'

'*This is becoming an issue*, Eliza.' Neighbour death stares me. Hip baby death-stares me too.

'Yes, absolutely. But I've got to go now, so—'

'We were told you were considerate neighbours.'

'We are! And my apologies that some of us have to get to work but—'

'I have a career too! I'm on a baby break.'

'And he is *beautiful.*'

'*She.*'

Fuck.

'Non-binary babywear. *So* on-trend. Clever you!' That throws her long enough to make my escape.

I need to drive like a maniac to get to work in time, cutting up cars on the A46 all the way there. 'Sorry, sorry, sorry!'

There's always one who takes it personally. Today it's a lorry that I nip in front of at traffic lights. Its driver leans hard on his horn and then tailgates me for two miles.

I dodge lanes, trying to lose him, but he's not dropping it. This could be movie car chase stuff if it weren't for the fact it's a Portaloo truck, its cargo of peppermint green sentry boxes wobbling each time we all brake.

Portaloo lorry driver is upsides now, yelling something at me. His cab's so high all I can see is a tattooed arm – barcode, Roman dates, Aston Villa lion – and chunky gold ring.

I buzz my passenger window down jerkily, shouting,

'Sorry!' over a traffic reporter chirpily telling me I'm in a three-mile tailback.

'I said you deserve to crash and die, mad old bitch!'

'Sorry!' I say it again automatically before realising what I've heard.

I flick a V, but I'm just insulting a row of green loos.

He leaves at the next exit and I try to put the encounter behind me. A death threat's hard to brush off before your first cup of coffee. 'Old' will take longer to process.

I've got more assertive as I've got older – positively crabby, lately – although I still try as hard as ever to balance bad karma. When I mess up, I'm quick to apologise. (Except perhaps in my marriage.)

It shocks me how unforgiving society has become, particularly men. Or perhaps it would be more accurate to say that I've now realised how much I once got away with. It's not just the digital age of trolls and memes; it's always been like this. Being young and female is simply more forgivable than being old and female. Over fifty, apologies carry less weight. Which could be why I repeat mine so much.

'Sorry. Sorry! Sorry, sorrrrry. SORRY! Sorry. So sorry!'

An American friend once told me that Brits apologise in the same way Yanks say 'you're welcome'. It's an oral apostrophe not a statement.

Today I *am* genuinely sorry. Sorry that I didn't make up with Paddy and was snappy with the children, that I had road rage driving here, and now that I'm doing my job so badly. I've narrated tens of audiobooks with calm assurance, but today I'm fluffing and lip-popping like a beatboxer.

'Sorry!' Fuck, fuck, fuck (that far more universal oral apostrophe, silent in my case). I keep botching the same small section of text. We're overrunning today's deadline. With time so tight, I've skipped lunch to work through. I'm light-headed and dry-mouthed, as well as hot and bothered from crossing my legs and holding on tight to avoid another dash up two floors because I've drunk so much coffee.

Now my phone is lighting up. It's on silent, but Edward's school's name is striping the screen.

'One minute. I have to get this.'

I step outside. It's pastoral care. He's refused to get in the taxi home again.

Is it pick-up time already? Thankfully, Paddy's on standby.

Poor Edward gets so illogically scared of things. We can't possibly understand the sheer terror of that taxi. Right now it's his Armageddon.

'Can somebody come and fetch him?' asks the care leader wearily. 'I appreciate Mr Hollander's number is the one down to call, but he's not answering his phone.'

'Yes, of course. We'll pick him up in the next hour. Sorry!'

'Thank you, Mrs Hollander.'

I try Paddy's number, but he's not answering *my* calls either. There's nobody else I can ask. My elderly parents aren't up to driving all the way there or handling Edward when he's like this, and my brother, who lives with them, doesn't find his nephew easy to deal with. Not many people do.

Our oldest son Joe is the one who understands Ed best, and I worry it's no coincidence that his anxieties have escalated since his big brother went away to university last autumn.

'I have to go,' I tell my boss, a hipster twenty years my junior who usually empathises with family pressures with man-bunned earnestness. I love him, and I can see how much it pains him when he must act tough, like now.

'Eliza.' He explains with quiet, puppy-eyed apology that if we don't get this job finished today, I won't get hired again. It's not the first family crisis that's called me away, is it?

Family always comes first for me. Edward comes first. But I need to feed and clothe them.

'One more minute and I'll sort this,' I promise.

I call Paddy two, three, four times. I text furiously. He should be in his workshop. His phone *is* his business. Where *is* he? If he's on that narrowboat again, I'll kill him.

In extremis, I get back in the small room with the screen and complete the task in half an hour. I'm boiling hot and too faint with relief and hunger to feel any sense of achievement, especially when Hipster Boss high-fives my sweaty palm and says, 'All you needed was a bit of pressure! I'll remember that next time.'

At least it looks like there will be a next time. I need this work.

Now I'm road-raging my way to deepest industrial Coventry.

I use the journey to talk to my oldest bestie, Lou, on Bluetooth. She's been going through a tough time and we speak most days.

'Please cheer me up,' she pleads. 'It's his weekend to have the kids and *she'll* be there.'

I start describing my Portaloo road-rage incident, but she's just furious on my behalf so I tell her instead about our big family theatre outing followed by supper tonight. Still a trendy Brighton clubber who can dance until dawn, Lou loves teasing me that I'm becoming a 'greyhead', the heartless term we coined for elderly audience members when we were studying drama at university together. She should see my roots.

Realising that I'm in the wrong lane and about to leave the motorway an exit early, I nip back across the chevrons and force myself in a tiny gap. There's an angry beep.

'Oh God, I've picked up another one.' I tell Lou as a snarly sports car with blackened windows closes in tight behind me, headlights flashing. I hold up an apologetic hand.

'Don't let yourself be intimidated!'

'It *was* my fault.'

I try to get out of his way, but he's right up behind me, switching lanes when I do. When I attempt to shake him off by squeezing between two big articulated trucks, he squeezes in too.

'Escape along the hard shoulder!' urges Lou who watches too many *Fast and Furious* movies.

'I am in an elderly French people carrier – he's in a penis extension with more horsepower than Royal Ascot.' But I eye up the hard shoulder just in case. A movement catches my eye. 'OHMYGOD it's a dog!'

'A dog is in the other car?' Lou is agog.

I veer across and stop a hundred yards ahead of the

poor creature I've spotted on the tarmac. The sportscar pulls in up ahead with a sinister rev, but I don't care. I'm already wriggling across the handbrake to climb out of the passenger's side to run back, my throat full of dinner-gong heartbeats.

It turns out to be a lamb, not a dog, almost fully grown, bleating in terror as great high-sided monsters thunder by. But that's nothing to the terrifying sight of a well-meaning middle-aged woman bearing down on it, at which it hot-hoofs it up a grassy cutting and starts running up and down a sturdy-looking fence, on the other side of which fifty doppelgangers are grazing with heartless disinterest. It must have broken out somehow, but there's no obvious sign when I scale the bank after it.

I'm not a big sheep fan but I feel duty bound to try to catch it and heave it back in. The fence is five feet of post and rail with mesh stock wire stapled to it. Planted in front is a row of some scraggy, prickly bush, no doubt there to discourage escapees, or indeed entry. The lamb darts about behind them while I get snagged, poked, walloped and partially undressed by the bloody things.

I step back to reassess.

The sports-car driver is out of his car. He's the sort of man the media excitedly call a 'silver fox', olive-skinned and grey-bearded, leaning back against its boot watching me, arms crossed in an expensive suit. I beckon him to come and help. He waves back. Or is that an offensive arm gesture? I can see the flash of white teeth. He's laughing at me. Bastard.

The lamb shoots past again. With reflexes I had no idea I possessed, I grab it and somehow get it off the ground.

It is unbelievably heavy. And wriggly. I reel around with it clutched to my chest. One of its legs kicks its way down my top and lands a blow right on my breastbone. I am going to lose my footing and tumble us both onto the carriageway at any moment. I've wasted sleepless mornings worrying I might have an undiagnosed cancer/ degenerative disease/dementia and instead this will kill me. My children will be motherless and humiliated. It will feature endlessly on those real-life traffic cop shows *The World's Most Ridiculous Road Deaths*. Portaloo lorry man's prophesy will be done.

The lamb kicks free with an astonishing bound that propels it over the rail and back to its friends. I fall against a prickly bush, winded.

When I've caught my breath enough to head back to the car, picking the thorns out of my arms, I realise with relief that sports-car man has gone. There's a note flapping beneath my wiper.

You drive like shit, Crazy Lady, but that was beautiful. Bravo!

I scrunch it up. Road-raging sexist pig. He could have bloody helped. Yet a part of me can't help feeling Crazy Lady is an upgrade from Mad Old Bitch.

And I'm proud of my rescue. It's made me feel good.

Back in the car on hands-free again, Lou is also completely cheered up by the happy ending, although she thinks it's a shame sports-car man didn't leave his number.

'Why would I want that?' I harrumph.

'To pass on to *me*. I need a rich lover with an Italian two-seater.'

'Not one with a temper like that.'

She says she's sorry it wasn't really a dog. 'You could have kept it.'

'I'm not ready for another dog,' I mutter.

'I'm not ready for a new husband either,' Lou says sadly.

I stop myself joking that I am.

Lou is one of the very few friends with whom I can confide dark truths with blackest humour. In the bad old days of airing our mutual marriage complaints I'd have told her about my dog fight with Paddy, even the shameful bits. But last year Lou's twelve-year marriage ended when she discovered her husband inside their babysitter and that's trumped everything. Even hating Trump.

We finish our call and I drive to the leafy haven that houses Edward's school. He's been in the library making PowerPoints about Marvel characters and is on very good form, polite and bright, talking non-stop as we set off: what a great day he's had and how many heavy metals there are on the Periodic Table. It's only when I try to address the taxi problem that he starts banging his head against the side window. I stop myself, ask him a few *Dr Who* trivia questions. He's soon happy again, and so am I because for all his anxieties and differences, a happy Edward is the very best company. He even keeps his headphones off and lets me turn on the radio – a rarity – and we sing along to 'Walking on Sunshine' and then 'Old Town Road'.

Back on the motorway, Summer calls, her soft, up-toned voice on hands-free making Edward cheer. She's lost her bus pass at school, she explains. The jobsworth driver knows her but refused to let her get on.

'Come and get me from Waitrose?' It's just across the

road from the grammar school. 'I've had a Gucci recipe idea for tonight.' (Gucci is 'classy' in Summer-speak.)

'You're babysitting,' I remind her, glancing despairingly at the car clock. Traffic ahead is at a standstill, the extra round trip will eat time and we must check Paddy's OK, plus I desperately need a bath before we go out. There's a distinctly sheepy waff in this car...

'I can cook at Granna and Grandpa's,' Summer says. She's looking after her cousins and brother there while we're all out.

Even though I know this is just a classic ruse to get me to spend, I don't want to argue, because Summer – who is a wonderful cook – is sounding unusually positive, and one day her teenage animosity towards me will end. Why not now?

'Give me twenty minutes.' The radio kicks in again as we ring off. James Blunt's singing 'You're Beautiful', a ballad the nation loved until somebody pointed out how posh he is, and therefore single-handedly responsible for social injustice, fox hunting and Joules.

It remains a wonderful song. I long to believe what he's saying. I remember the bearded businessman lounging against his sportscar. *That was beautiful. Bravo!*

'*You* are beautiful, Mum.' Edward turns to me, only slightly spoiling it by adding, 'Even though you're now too old to mate.'

Just for a moment fifty-year-old Eliza Finch, mother of three with grey roots and a grumpy marriage, feels beautiful. This sunny afternoon feels beautiful. The world feels beautiful. You've only got one beautiful life.

Car horns beep behind and I realise the traffic has started

moving again and there's a big gap in front of me. I let off the brake. I want to share the love, the beauty of the day. I turn to smile as a car surges past me on the inside.

A crisp-suited blonde businesswoman in a BMW gives me the finger and mouths *you cunt*.

'Cockney rhyming slang,' I tell Edward quickly, turning off James Blunt.

Aged four or five, I overheard a friend of my father's calling Edward Heath the c word. I could tell from my parents' frozen faces that this was a bad, bad word. I stored it carefully and only brought it out on very special occasions, mostly when my sister's hand-me-down dolls were misbehaving. Pippa called Sindy a cunt in the privacy of my room when they fell out over tiny shoes.

Some years later my little brother abducted my entire doll collection in an Action Man parachute raid, including a brand-new Bionic Woman with Mission Handbag. I was devastated. Jaime Sommers was my confidante, heroine and future self. I loved her.

We negotiated long and hard and one by one the hostages were returned, but not Jaime. He said that she'd escaped using her superpowers and he didn't know where she was.

I took it to the highest authority.

'Miles has stolen Jaime Sommers,' I explained to my parents. 'He's a cunt!'

It would be years before the discovery of her irreparably broken bionic body in the drawer beneath his bed. He'd accidentally snapped off both her legs and hidden the evidence.

It still hurts. But what hurts most is that I got into far more trouble for saying one little word than he did for taking my doll. Forty-two years later and I still haven't entirely lived it down. *Nobody* says the c word in our family.

Paddy Hollander Bespoke Cabinet Maker operates out of a converted oak-framed barn belonging to his cricket team captain. Paddy pays a peppercorn rent, which might explain why he sometimes treats his working day with a pinch of salt, unlike his bowling.

We find him chiselling a dovetail joint, listening to loud rock circa 1985 on the geriatric CD player, Simple Minds singing 'Don't You Forget About Me'.

He looks surprised to see us. It turns out he's left his phone in the car after he went out to buy some lunch.

'The school couldn't get hold of you, then I couldn't. We were worried,' I say, trying not to sound too irritated as I notice today's paper well-thumbed on the workbench. Then I feel ashamed of myself for seeking proof that he's not been working as hard as me. It's not a competition.

'We bought your favourite toffees!' Summer weaves towards him brandishing a canvas Waitrose bag. 'Mum said no, but I talked her round.'

Our daughter isn't quite ready to shed her antipathy towards me. Summer loves spoiling Paddy, and I feel guilty enough about the dog fight to succumb to bribery.

Paddy looks from the bag for life to me, the disagreeable bag he married for life. He's trying to read my face and I'm trying to hide a groundswell of emotion because Jim Kerr's singing that rain keeps falling down and I'm suddenly upset about the dog fight again, angry at Arty for dying and at Paddy for not understanding and at myself for saying such awful things when all I wanted was to be told we can wait, this will pass. And to hug him, because I might be spiky and oversensitive, but I give bloody good hugs.

I look away, frightened I'll well up.

'What time are we due at your parents' place tonight?' Paddy is asking.

'Oh, you've got *ages*,' says Summer, who is photographing herself draped on a handmade carver chair with an ornate curved back. She makes Edward take off his headphones and sit on the matching one beside it to pose like a King and Queen. I want to chivvy them all home, clinging on to my hope of a relaxing bath, but I must make peace with Paddy first.

Pinned up on his big noticeboard are tens of my old acting headshots, some curling with age, the many faces of Eliza Finch. Alongside these are a couple of equally outdated school photos of the three children and a legion of pictures of his dad's narrowboat. Paddy worships that boat. In a mosaic of ageing, she remains the same glossy red, her pretty face never changing. Perhaps that's why he loves her so much.

'Do you like the chairs?' he asks me.

'They're lovely. Is it a commission?'

He shakes his head. 'Not too Oberon and Titania?'

'A bit, maybe.'

'I'll put them up on Etsy if you don't want them,' he says vaguely and I realise too late that he's made them for our anniversary next week. Paddy always makes furniture. After twenty-two years we could seat an orchestra.

'No, they're beautiful. Truly.'

Some of his pieces are works of art, but it's weeks since he's sold anything. He's reliant upon word of mouth and online trading places and for someone as softly spoken and tech phobic as Paddy, that's a slow sell.

'People, gather round.' Edward is addressing his impromptu court, face and voice deadpan. 'My taxi driver thinks we don't know what he's saying on his phone in Urdu, but Louis has a translation app. He calls us the rich white retards. Can I have a toffee?'

So that's why he won't get in the cab. I'd trade every mad bitch and crazy lady to take that away.

'We'll get another driver,' I reassure him. 'I'll call the council to complain.'

'I've been called worse, Mum.' Edward unwraps his sweet, characteristically unemotional, but that doesn't mean the insult's not burning in his head. 'You should hear what he calls other road users.'

I can imagine only too well. It's still burning in mine.

Crone, frump, battleaxe, hag, harridan, bat, bag, witch, cougar, bint, biddy, trout. Who can think of a single positive word used to describe a woman over fifty? We're 'feisty', 'bossy', 'irrational', 'overemotional', 'hormonal', 'abrasive', 'difficult' and we're fucking pissed off about it, but that's nothing to the white molten anger if anyone insults those we love.

Nobody calls my son a retard and gets away with it. Edward's got more sense than any of us. He's certainly got a better memory. And he isn't remotely ableist.

★ ★ ★

As soon as we're home, I leave a message on the council's SEND answerphone, demanding an appointment.

As I do, my eyes search the hallway. Returning home without Arty hurrying to greet me still leaves me hollow. She's gone. The sentient being that loved me most is dead. And a part of me vanished with her. Somehow I feel less visible in my own home as well as outside it.

Arty was far more sensitive to my moods than the rest of the family for a start. She came to find me while they just stand and shout for me. She *noticed* me.

For a moment after I've rung off I stand alone in the kitchen and just miss her.

It's already half past five and I'm desperate for my bath, but there's disaster awaiting us in Summer's room, where her beloved feral-turned-house cat has been trapped all day. It's peed on the bed, thrown a hairball up on the family iPad, pooed mid-carpet and run along the shelves smashing all the blown glass figurines Summer's collected since the age of eight.

'I hated them,' Summer reassures me as I sweep them up with a dustpan and brush, mourning my lost child of swan princesses and unicorns.

Downstairs, the doorbell is ringing, an unfamiliar solo with no dog bark accompaniment. It still gives me a sharp pinch.

Paddy and Edward have, predictably, vanished like smoke.

I hurry down, dustpan in hand.

It's the new neighbour, minus baby on hip. 'I'm here to talk about the *car situation*. We've taken legal advice.'

'I'm *really* sorry, but we're going out and I must change. Maybe we can get together to talk about it over the weekend?'

'We're at our cottage.' She flashes a bleached smile. 'I'm just giving you the heads up that you'll be getting a letter from our solicitor. Personal friend and *shit* hot on this sort of thing. So I suggest you get advice.'

'Thanks. I'm dining with two barristers and a judge tonight, so I'll ask them.'

She laughs. 'Like, yeah!'

'Google Peter Finch.'

I hate, hate, hate myself for this. I'm in my sixth decade, still scared of mean girls and still bandying Dad's name about like he's a superhero or something.

'Is that what I think it is?' She's looking in my dustpan at a lump of cat poo.

Much as I'd like to ask her what she thinks it is and thrust it under her nose to examine more closely, I say a wimpy 'must go' and close the door on her. Slightly slammily.

When I turn back I find Paddy has witnessed my shameful dustpan-waving namedrop. His face says it all, eyes flinty and reproving. 'What was all that about?'

'I might have parked on their bit a couple of times,' I admit.

'How often?'

'Maybe five?' Double that.

'And you think your Dad is going to help how exactly?'

'Let's talk about this later, shall we?' I say it like he's one of the kids because I'm embarrassed. 'We need to get ready and I *must* have a bath.'

'I want a shower.'

'I'm first.'

'Well, be quick.'

'Fine.' I hand him the dustpan to deal with and flounce back upstairs.

Nobody can call it an armistice.

2

Me Time

'Are you nearly done in there?'

Naturally Paddy doesn't specify what I might be done with: armpit-shaving, pumicing, cutting my wrists, masturbating, a little voodoo, maybe?

Boringly, all I've done is put shampoo in my hair.

'Not much longer!' I promise, moulding the lather into a mohawk.

The bathroom, last bastion of privacy in a long marriage. I love my baths. Lowering myself in just now was absolution, only slightly marred by my husband's arrival on the landing moments later.

I can hear him pacing around outside the door. 'We need to leave in quarter on an hour. Elz?'

It took ten minutes to run this water. I've been in it less than two. Sinking beneath the surface, I listen to my blood rushing in my ears as I ride out the familiar spike of resentment.

In my early twenties, I smoked Camel Lights in the bath

and read self-help books until my toes wrinkled. How I indulged my body, its sex and psyche, a present perfect I only recognise in the past tense. While my bathing ritual now includes a brisk but careful self-examination to check for tumorous invasion, back then I was exploring new worlds of self-pleasure every time I washed. Occasionally, I'd share my watery domain with lovers, latterly offering this exclusively to Paddy. We regularly soaked the flat below. God, but I loved him.

I resurface, too hot, skin stinging, and realise he's still talking. '… have to pick everyone up, don't forget.'

We're going to the Royal Shakespeare Company no less. Middle-aged, middle-class Midlanders unite. Or Southerners in the case of Julia and Reece, here from London for the weekend to celebrate Dad's eightieth. Our lateness always stresses my sister. More accurately, her control freak husband loathes being made late, as opposed to arriving deliberately late if I'm performing on stage which Reece finds empowering. Our power struggle is in its third decade.

Regretfully, I'm not cast in tonight's *As You Like It*. Dream on, Eliza. But we are all on show: pre-theatre drinks at Mum and Dad's followed by the undignified cram of six adults into an elderly Picasso Grand Tourer (Paddy has vacuumed the car specially), rhubarbing in the foyer then the play proper, late dinner and back into the Picasso. A full five acts plus after-show talk entre nous. Undercurrents will seethe while we all pretend that Mum and Dad aren't on borrowed time, that being married to Reece isn't making Julia miserable and that our little brother Miles hasn't been living a lie most of his life. Then there's the running joke of the actress and the carpenter. Happy families. No wonder poor Paddy has been dreading it for weeks.

I so longed to make Paddy love me when we first got together that I put on this terrific performance of what I wanted him to think of me: witty, sexy, kind Eliza with her long legs and fawn eyes, all fierce good humour and apologies for having had life so easy thus far. It took him years to see through it. He says I've changed, but I think I've only just figured out how much an idyllic childhood screws you up. Especially when, half a century later, it's obvious that childhood is finally coming to an end.

The weather app on Paddy's phone is being consulted religiously. 'Eighty per cent precipitation. We'll need to take coats. Hurry up, Elz!'

Last night's row runs through my head again. Why do I say such bad things in vino veritas? No matter how hard I scrub my skin, the stain won't wash off. 'Use the shower in the other bathroom.'

'Summer's live streaming in there.'

'*In the shower?*'

'Fully clothed. Vanity unit. Five-minute fan bulletin, she said.' I sense him smiling and try to share the vibe, although the idea of our daughter having a fanbase still alarms me. Who *are* these people? Can they be trusted?

The hours Summer devotes to shaping her brows like Nike logos are not lonely ones; it's an artform she shares with a growing legion of Instagram followers and vlog subscribers, along with eyelash curling, up-dos and don'ts, life hacks and every minutiae of life in a teenage boudoir. They message her all the time, these younger girls from all over the world of whom she's sweetly protective. She's no doubt breaking the shock news that tonight, while babysitting her younger cousins, *@Summer_Time* will be offline – Grandpa and Granna's cottage sits in a signal and broadband blackspot that is so not #instagood.

Here at home where our web of worldwide action spins around the clock, the smile in Paddy's voice has gone. 'Google says the traffic is bad. Eliza, are you deliberately trying to wind me up?'

'No.' I apply a luxury conditioning treatment I rarely use because it must be left in for five minutes, lie back and tell myself I *own* these five minutes. I'm live-steaming in here.

'As you're taking forever, I might as well have a bloody drink!' From which we can deduce he expects me to drive even though it's his turn.

I quickly fib, 'I'm just finishing a huge gin, sorry!'

'Liar.' He knows it.

I can hear him lingering. We're at a pivot point. This could go either way. I let Paddy lead because he's kinder than me. That familiar note of pacification in his voice as he nobly offers to fix me the drink I don't have. We need me to be on fire tonight, the Eliza Finch talk show. And yes, I could murder a stiff G and T right now. But his need is greater. Besides, the door's locked and I *want to be alone*.

'You go ahead, love,' I urge. 'I'll be chauffeur.'

I listen for the outbreath of relief, the same sound Edward made when he realised that he'd be sharing a sleepover with his cousins this evening, not coming to watch the play. It saddens me how reluctant they all are to get a dose of culture. Even Summer – studying A levels in English *and* Drama – has plumped for nine quid an hour over the most loved-up of all Shakespearean comedies.

We oldies are dining out afterwards at Russo's on Sheep Street. My parents have eaten post-theatre supper there for fifteen years. Restaurateur Antonio and my dad are the ultimate double act at these feasts, our host oozing with old-school Italian charm, beckoning the prettiest of his yawning waitresses and telling them to look after Signor Finch and his family, that we are his favourite clients. Much wine will flow. Paddy prefers beer, but my father will convince him to neck chianti like water *and* try a pudding wine. My family still scare Paddy into behaving badly, even after more than two decades of marriage.

Let's quickly get up to speed on Peter and Fiona Finch, living out their years in 'splendid retirement in the prettiest cottage in Warwickshire', to quote Mum's Christmas round robin. When the fun-loving Finches moved up here from Bucks fifteen years ago to 'be closer to the grandchildren', Joe and Summer were just four and two, and my parents bought a house with a large annexe, fully anticipating that I'd pack up the kids, abandon my marriage and join them soon afterwards. Whilst my little brother has taken advantage of this option more than once, I'm not so easily defeated.

The first time Mum and Dad met Paddy, they didn't even try to hide their disappointment. They had admittedly just sat through Cat's Pyjamas' Theatre Company's terrible off-fringe production of *Mother Courage* in open-mouthed shock (nudity and raw fish were involved as I recall, although I can't remember why). Aware that I was smitten with our 'set designer' – although unaware that he had been sharing my bed for three weeks – they quizzed Paddy about Bertolt Brecht afterwards. I'm not sure if they were more put out by him asking which team he played for or me laughing uproariously. It was totally sexual at that stage, I'll admit.

Later, Dad took me aside after we announced our engagement and tried to talk me out of it. I could tell Mum had put him up to it; he was using all her turns of phrase and called me 'darling girl' twice. He even offered to help me buy my own flat. They *really* didn't want me to go through with it.

The awful thing is, I *had* been having second thoughts pretty much right from the moment Paddy slipped the Coke pull on my finger. We had very little in common, as Dad reiterated that day in his courtroom summing-up voice; we were from different backgrounds, had different interests, wanted different things out of life.

All we had was love. In *As You Like It*, Rosalind calls it 'a madness'. I was mad at my parents for questioning my love and the man with whom I shared it. I was mad about the man.

That lecture made up my mind. I was bloody well marrying Paddy.

Paddy's footsteps have retreated and I relax. I wish I'd remembered to bring in the radio. And my robe, an elegant Norma Desmond number still hanging on the back of the bedroom door. I'm hopelessly sieve-brained at the moment. Early Alzheimer's?

I stare at my toes poking up from the bubbles, their painted nails heralding summer, a pretty touch above the spider veins lacing my ankles, which this paranoid hypochondriac has already identified as an early sign of heart disease, not to mention hideously unattractive with a kitten-heeled sling-back.

Keep staring at the nails, Eliza. Ageing is such a boring self-obsession. The whinging tone of a woman past her prime is like chalk on blackboard, which let's face it is a sound only we over forties remember. We're time-travelling comrades battling the centrifugal force of a world that revolves around youth. Ironic to reflect that in the days it revolved around *my* youth, I hated my body far more than I do now even though it was exquisite for all its small-boobed, knobbly-kneed, too-tall imperfections. How many of us wish we could go back simply to shake our younger self and tell her to enjoy what she has? Not just her desirability and gravity-defying, cake-defying resilience, but the blissful ignorance of all the things that might end her days? At twenty-five, I felt immortal. Now I'm double that age, I'm ever more alert.

I've had a low, dull ache in my side since the row with Paddy, which I've already Googled and based on my lifestyle choices is most likely to be ovarian cancer, liver failure, diverticulosis, a hernia or IBS. Not long ago, I'd have put it down to period pain, but that no longer features on my list.

I now settle upon liver failure and think of the consequences: Paddy struggling to cope without me; Summer forced to take a motherly role when her life is just opening out; Joe's mental health deteriorating again; Edward falling through the gaps in SEN provision; the harsh *Daily Mail* style judgement raining down from all quarters ('Eliza was always a dipso'). These ten red-tipped toes will soon be pushing up daisies.

Think positive, woman. You can turn this thing around, stop drinking so much cheap Aldi red, buy yourself a few more seasons of *The Crown*. What a relief that you're designated driver. No matter that you make this promise to yourself at least once a month, this time it's happening. Your children need their mother.

In our child-free London years, Paddy would mix us both killer gin and tonics and sit on the flipped-down loo seat to talk through our days. Ours was a bright third-floor one-bed Victorian conversion near Alexandra Palace; traffic whizzing past outside, fluffy towels rolled up on wobbly Ikea shelves, Diptych scented candles; his and hers toothbrushes; extractor fan that sounded like the opening of *Apocalypse Now*.

In those days, dialling up the internet to search for things on Netscape Navigator was a rarity, and our 'the future's Orange' mobiles were switched off when we got home from work to devote ourselves to coupledom.

Paddy would take over my bath water while I started cooking. The bathtub was pear-drop pink vintage when we moved in. In hindsight, it was much more practical for small babies than the reclaimed roll-top we replaced it with. That deep, cast-iron slipper became the pregnancy chariot in which I first stared down at the strange silver-threaded hummock where my flat stomach had been, unable to apprehend how quickly life was about to change. Soon after the bump turned into small, starfish-handed Joe, a photo of the roll-top starred in our local estate agent's window, and we traded London for the mid-shires to become a two-bath, two-car household, settling on a tall Victorian doer-upper opposite a riverside park. Right here.

I was thirty-three when I first lay in this upcycled, re-enamelled tub, heavily pregnant with Summer. Smaller than the family bath a floor below and tucked under an awkward eave, the attic conversion was a hard-won haven after all the planning, builders and DIY. Our own en suite! No plastic dolphin toys, bath crayons or baby shampoo up here: Cowshed, the six-thirty radio comedy slot and – when breastfeeding duties were at an end – ice-cold white wine. Paddy would wander in and out, nappies in hand, laughing as *Dead Ringers* took off George W and Tony Blair while I applied Bio Oil to my stretch marks and felt more exhausted and contented than I'd ever felt in my life.

Fast forward five years and the stretch marks were being stretched again; I was even more exhausted and a bit less contented.

My waters broke in this bath. Two weeks before due date, Edward arrived so quickly that Paddy was still on his way back from the workshop. He'd been making a cradle shaped like a canal barge, the most exquisite thing imaginable. He'd made cradles for both the others – Joe got a steam train and Summer a carriage (rock on, gender stereotyping!) – but that narrowboat was special. That boat represented Paddy's childhood and the dad he'd lost.

★ ★ ★

My five minutes is up, but Paddy has abandoned his sentry post, so I let my hair float around me, gazing up at the ceiling. Silence. I'm profoundly grateful for this moment.

While Paddy has several man caves – his workshop, our much-extended garden shed, the cellar and his dad's boat – I just have this bathroom.

I can't remember when I started locking the door. Was it the kids I wanted to keep out, or Paddy? Perhaps it was the truth about me I wanted to keep in.

I stopped having baths altogether for a period in my early forties. Instead I cried briskly through early-morning showers as I weathered first my career crisis, and then Paddy's, mopping away my tears in less time than it took me to shave my legs. No wallowing allowed. I'd look across at this bath, knowing that if I paused to think more deeply into why I was really crying, I might drown in self-doubt.

At its peak, I learned to assuage the pain by inflicting it. I'd pinch my skin as I washed, take the razor too close to bone. It helped at the time, and hiding the cuts and bruises became the secret power of shame.

When I read about young girls self-harming, I feel an aching motherly pity and deep remorse at my actions. Middle-aged women like me should be old enough to know better than to turn our pain in on ourselves. It stopped when Paddy's mother died, and I knew I had to survive.

Bath time became my favourite private ritual after that, the door locked, my thoughts under close guard, an emboldening routine that softens the brittle shell enough to stop it cracking. This is my sanctuary; I might not be able to wash off what life throws at me, but I can absorb it. When Joe's teenage sorrows threatened to overwhelm him, I retreated here to plan a strategy, and when Edward's autism diagnosis was followed by Mum's cancer one, I was toughing it out in the Heavenly Gingerlily big time. Me time.

Paddy's back on door duty. 'We'll be at your parents' place no more than five minutes at this rate.'

That, I reflect silently, is the point. I'm going to make us late because I love you. Because every minute that I'm in here, you're not suffering there.

Paddy struggles at Finch family soirees, still uncomfortable with the small talk and big egos. He visibly shudders when Reece slaps him on the back and asks how the carpentry world is bearing up, finds it hard not to talk to my sister's boobs and is a shag-magnet for the elderly Jack Russell. Meanwhile, Dad talks down to him, Miles winds him up, Mum butters him up and the volume on Radio Three is never lowered.

It's become much harder for Paddy to humour my parents now that his have both died. Dad drinks claret like water, has had both hips replaced, a triple bypass and several recent car prangs of his own making, yet on into his eightieth year he endures with his loud laugh and lopsided walk. Mum's now in recovery but still sneaks the odd cigarette and she looks amazing.

★ ★ ★

We lost Eddie first, the gentle engineer, canal fanatic and amateur radio hound. A heart attack at sixty-four. By cruel coincidence, it was the same week my great-aunt died aged ninety-nine; Paddy never openly compared the two, but he must have, especially when Dad pointed out how unfair it was she didn't make a hundred. Eddie had been opening a lock on his beloved Shropshire Union Canal when it struck. A year later, Ruth was diagnosed with rapid onset dementia. That was a tough one. Paddy's sister did most of the day-to-day caring, then Ruth was in a nursing home for the last few years, but oh the guilt. She was a month off seventy when we lost her.

Paddy never makes a fuss. His grief imploded, quietly, and our love moved up a level.

'For chrissake, Eliza!' He's exasperated.

Paddy changed a lot after Ruth's death, his mortality closing in on him. On both of us. He needs me to be strong.

I remember to examine my breasts, then rinse off the conditioning treatment.

3

Family Time

It's a running family joke that no matter how organised I think I am, I always leave something behind.

'Aren't you going to dry your hair, Mum?' Summer demands when we troop out to the car. Her eyebrows are works of art, their current angle midway between horror and pity.

'You said letting it dry naturally was good for it.'

'Yeah, like when you're not going out?' She catches Paddy's eye and I note the customary father and daughter alliance.

'The thing is, Mum, it looks sort of *limp*?' Summer's on a roll.

'I have no *time* to dry it.' I miss Joe, the only one of my children who tells me I look great no matter how stressed out I am, even at Christmas when I'm wearing a novelty jumper, light-up earrings and a thin film of sweat.

I glance at Edward for backup, for the 'you are beautiful Mum' that so lifted my spirits earlier. But he's already sitting in the car, noise-cancelling headphones on, playing *The Legend of Zelda*.

'Five more minutes isn't going to make much difference, Elz,' says Paddy. In marital shorthand, he is saying: *It's Grandpa's eightieth; you should make more effort. You'll feel better about yourself.*

'You want me to dry my hair?' In marital shorthand, I'm saying fuck off. The luscious brown mane of the woman he married has thinned horribly lately, but I'm trying my best, hide it from him.

He looks away.

Summer's eyebrows re-angle themselves kindly. 'And put on some barely there make-up maybe? A dab of tint and a swish of highlighter is *such* a hot look at your age.'

I don't have the heart to tell her that, at my age, looking hot is something I do without warning.

For a moment I stand firm. But I love them too much to embarrass them with my face off. I can't bear to think that one day my beautiful girl will also look in the mirror and say, 'I bloody give up!'

While Summer's obsession with her looks masks teenage insecurity, my converse vanity is no less intense. This bare poker face is denying there's regret etched in its lines. Take me as I am, it demands. I dare you to see me for the fifty-year-old woman I am. Female beauty recedes like a slow tide nobody notices until it's too far out to spot. What's the point of dressing up invisibility? I still see the same face in the mirror I always have, yet when I paint it, I'm doing so from memory.

★★★

I loved my first foray into make-up, which was no less gilding a lily than Summer's thick brows and tribal contouring. It was the early 1980s, and teenage girls in my small town were trending Princess Di hair, blue 'Smurf shit' eyeliner, frosted lipstick and orange foundation that stopped at the chin-line. Eliza 'Finchers' Finch was straight in there: pie-crust collar, winkle pickers, Sun-In, plastic pearls and a crush on Nik Kershaw.

By the time we all crammed into James Dutton's granny's sitting room in 1985 to drink cider and watch Live Aid while she was away on a Corsican package holiday, I looked like the lovechild of Madonna and Boy George. Like the rest of my pack, I wore oversized crucifixes, Doc Martens and my father's tux. I'd crimped, backcombed, hennaed and crazy coloured; I'd pierced, painted, pouted and primped. My Top of the Pops crush had been upgraded to Morrissey. I could snog, blow smoke-rings and apply liquid eyeliner perfectly.

Fast forward again, this time to the end of the decade, and I was in a smiley-faced Shoom bandana and Wayfarers, cycling shorts and cartoon waistcoat, waving my arms around shouting 'aciiiiid' in aircraft hangars, liquid eyeliner sharp as calligraphy.

Did the camouflage ever come off? Maybe I just accessorised it better through proceeding decades of womanhood until I found myself wearing the battle dress of middle age. That's when we realise in shock that it doesn't matter what you dress it up as if your sex appeal's been lost in action.

'Back in a minute!' I rush inside, apply two handfuls of Extra Hold Volumising Mousse and upend my head beneath the hottest setting of the dryer. When I turn the right way up, head-rush clearing, there's a fittingly Bananarama vibe to the fright wig clouding my face. A touch of root mascara and I'm Venus with laughter lines. Unlike many women in my profession, I'm not brave enough to trade my facial expressions for a lie of youth via Botox and fillers, nor can I afford to have an on-trend white smile. (My Agent-Who-Never-Calls has told me to stop smiling at castings because 'those crow's feet and fox's teeth do you no favours, darling'.)

I bare them fiercely in the mirror, alone with a hot flush and a small fireball of anger, all too familiar company. I look around for Arty, then remember she's dead and catch my reflection's eye again. Don't get upset, I tell it. You're an old pro. You can still put on the Ritz.

And you want to look better than your sister.

Seizing the eighties spirit, I paint on my reddest lipstick, big up my eyes with black kohl and a slick of liquid liner, finally applying mascara, a high-risk sport without reading glasses. I clip on my fat pearl necklace, a gift from my parents for my eighteenth birthday (seven years too late for the Lady Di trend and not a great look with Acid House T-shirts and glow sticks, but I've always worn it defiantly and lovingly with everything).

'Creep,' I tell my reflection, this unfamiliar painted lady with mascara on her nose.

In the garage to reset the alarm, I edge my way round the boat trailer to Arty's old bed, straightening its cushion and telling her to guard the house while we're gone. Then I scarper before I can cry, chased out by the alarm beeps.

When I climb into the driver's seat, the others are too

absorbed watching something hilarious on Paddy's phone to comment on my mini-makeover.

'You forgot your coat,' Paddy points out as we drive off. Then, after a full minute, he says, 'You look lovely by the way.' And I don't care that it sounds like a line he's forgotten until the script's moved onto the next scene. He knows how much I need to hear it tonight and I'm grateful.

'You look great too,' I say automatically.

Then I notice that he's wearing a suit and tie. Oh shit. That means he wants to have sex later.

Having driven to The Prettiest Cottage in Warwickshire with the driver's window open because the air conditioning has packed up and I'm boiling, I'm regretting the mousse. My hair is now gonk-in-a-wind-tunnel sideways, solid as polyfoam.

My sister's immaculate electric Jag is parked face out next to my parents' Leaf and Miles's plug-in sports car, six headlamps gazing glassily at our gas-guzzler. My parents and siblings can afford to be pompously eco while I destroy the earth. I wish Joe was around because I need him to explain that thing about electric cars using lithium batteries and lithium being a limited natural resource, its mining damaging the earth's crust. I can never remember it when I try to repeat it. Sieve brain.

Behind me, Edward's still fighting trolls on a windswept hilltop.

Paddy's pretending to be relaxed despite bulging neck sinews and white knuckles.

My family are surging round the side of the house to

greet us, animated by our lateness. They're all in dark glasses, which is curiously sinister. They've been in the garden, Pimm's highballs down to fruit.

Summer mutters, 'Auntie Jules has *definitely* had work done. That face is *so* not moving.'

Beside me, Paddy is nobly trying not to stare at Julia's tits, which so are moving beneath her wrap-around dress. My parents look old and frail as they smile and wave. Between them, dressed all in white with a mahogany tan, hippy beads and dyed hair, our brother looks like Julio Iglesias.

'I won!' Julia's husband Reece is in the lead, breaking through the lavender border with the Jack Russell sex assassin, both small, bearded and overly aggressive. 'I said they'd be half an hour late. Greetings Hollanders! Great hair, Liza!'

No sooner are we out of the car than he slaps Paddy on the back and says, 'So how's the carpentry business doing, Patrick?'

My husband's low groan is only audible to me.

Let's examine why Paddy finds my family so overwhelming:

It's not the Finch height. We all inherited Dad's longshanks, but it's Reece who has the family exclusive on Short Man Syndrome. At over six feet, Paddy's taller than me in our bare feet.

And it's no longer the conspicuous wealth. His socialist principles and my guilty liberalism notwithstanding, Paddy's learned to appreciate the Finch largesse: M&S food, generous Christmas presents to our children, not to mention the odd grand bunged at us when we're short, inevitably keeping me awake with self-loathing while Paddy sleeps better than he has in weeks.

It's our competitive streaks he can't handle. The mental speed, one-upmanship, intelligence and cruelty required to hold a conversation in this family has always unsettled him. All that bonhomie masks deadly rivalry. We're nasty. Spending an evening with us is like taking part in a gladiatorial death-match panel show hosted by Stephen Fry and Joanna Lumley.

My father is both ferociously clever and annoyingly interested in *everything*. He can argue on both sides and rarely forgets facts. He lost his original Yorkshire accent at Cambridge, but he still affects a fabulous flat, rolling moorland roar when in full cry. He demands snappy answers, strong opinions and wit.

Paddy's shyness bores him. That Dad doesn't see how considered, skilful and kind his son-in-law is maddens me.

Until recently, I'd have described my mother as a huge cultural snob. To earn her respect, you'd need to have read all the books on the literary prize shortlists *and* heard the writers speak, and secretly think Mary Beard is a bit blousy. But since the cancer all-clear, she's developed a lust for life which has reinvented all that so fast we're struggling to keep up. She attends poetry slams, has had a tattoo and is going to see Kylie at Glasto. I'm just so grateful she's still with us, I'm happy whatever her passion, although the off-grid wanderlust came as a surprise.

Paddy remains cautious around her. Rightly so. Mum's currently scouting for a rainforest trekking buddy, and we can all guess which member of the family would survive longest in the wild. My husband's already regularly co-opted as her handyman, just as I'm on-call chauffeur and shopper, the practicality of village life increasingly challenging for the elderly. The post office stores closed a year after they moved here, no bus stops here any more. Dad's driving is terrible, Mum's only marginally better, and both refuse to do it after dark. Whilst in situ, beloved son Miles is spared driving duties thanks to nine speeding points, a two-seater and a new habit of being found one over the eight in the village pub where he's been adopted as both The Only Gay in the Village and its best karaoke singer.

My attention-loving little brother Miles has recently gone through a Damascus transformation of his own. One minute he was running a Midlands corporate events company with wife number four – penthouse in Brum and studio apartment in Barcelona – the next he's in Mum and Dad's annexe. What nobody predicted was that he'd burst out of the closet at the age of forty-seven, and with such enthusiasm to make up for lost time. He's OUT, baby.

It's badly affected his friendship with Paddy who finds it particularly hard to relate to this all-new Miles because the two of them used to spend hours together on the narrowboat talking engines and rugby and Miles never breathed a word about this other life he was leading. Now it's *all* he talks about, mostly to Mum.

A big-hearted people-pleaser beneath the flippant façade, Miles struggled to cope with Mum's illness and perhaps this self-revelation in all its blazing, spotlit honesty is his backlash. All her children reacted differently: Miles came out; I aged; Julia got even more controlling.

★★★

'You're driving so won't have one of these.' The Pimm's jug is whisked past me and my sister hands me a pint glass of still-hissing mineral water. Jules is big into hydration, but I mean, honestly…

'You look hot,' she points out. She's cool and crisp in designer linen, barely there make-up immaculate.

'I'm not hot, baby, I'm *smokin'*.'

'Sweaty.' She's examining me closely. 'Are you going through the…?'

'You're not still SMOKING are you?' Dad bellows from the other side of the garden where he's showing Paddy a new raised bed. Dad has this uncanny capacity to listen to about three consecutive conversations, but it's started to misfire now he's going deaf.

'No, Dad! Gave it up years ago.'

'Don't worry,' Jules tells me sotto-voiced, 'the change of life started when I turned fifty like you. I can prepare you for the worst.' Three years older than me and five years older than Miles, Jules has always acted as though she's the only responsible adult amongst us. Which she probably is.

'It's thirty degrees out here!' I laugh. 'It's so not the change.' It so is, but I argue with her as a default. I'm holding onto my younger advantage in this round.

'You need some loose change for the carpark, you say?' Dad bellows.

'We're fine, Dad!' I then drop my voice and growl at Jules: 'It's still peri-menopause.'

'Liar. Mine's still going on *three years later*,' my sister groans in a fevered undertone. 'It never bloody ends. Have you gone off sex?'

'Did you?'

'Oh, I went off that years ago. Otty would be an only child if it weren't for one too many strawberry mojitos at Ask Italian after *Mamma Mia*.' Her whisper gets even lower. 'You and Paddy were always far more sexed up. She raises an eyebrow in the direction of the rose arch where her husband has cornered Paddy to talk about music.

'Paul Weller over Ed Sheeran any day, yes? Shall I tell you why?' He launches straight on. Reece rarely leaves enough time for replies to his questions because he isn't interested in what others have to say.

Julia and Reece take my family's competitive streak to a whole new level.

Both barristers, their marriage is brilliantly argued, occasionally adjourned but never decided. Jules dumped him four times in their engagement year alone, once for every inch she's taller than him. She once drunkenly told me he has a huge dick for his height, but I've been close enough to those budgie smugglers on holiday to have my doubts. Reece nevertheless remains a family colossus in ego terms. His current mid-life crisis – his third if you count the affair and the failed hair transplant – is a full-on cliché involving a hipster beard, motorbike and a three-piece band called Bosh, average age thirty-five, in which he plays bass. They mostly do Blur covers. Reece is fifty-four. You only have to do the maths.

Paddy dislikes Reece because I do. He's loyal like that. And Reece is *very* hard to like, which must be why Jules stuck with him. Setting herself near-impossible challenges is her leitmotif.

My big sister runs a lot. Outdoors, on a machine, up and down stairs, along corridors. She's completed the London Marathon twice. I used to think she was in training to run away from her marriage, but she never does. Certainly not since having children, another much-delayed event, then Ottilie came along, quickly followed by Vervain.

The girls are lovely, now ten and twelve and bright as buttons. I'm a *very* proud aunt. And I refuse to fall into the trap of criticising someone else's parenting skills – at least, not unless I've had a drink – but aren't those names *ridiculously* pretentious?

Paddy thinks I'm overly sensitive around my sister. I disagree. Forget the Page Three tits and Court and Social career; I love her even though she's bossy and judgemental and married to a bastard, and our parents have always preferred her over me. We worship each other beneath the sarcasm.

'Do you get restless legs?' Jules is asking.

'Only when I want to run because you're banging on about the change of life.'

'Victorians used to call it the "climacteric".'

'CLIMATE CHANGE? DREADFUL BUSINESS!' Dad shouts from the back door as he heads inside for a 'precautionary visit' (him taking a pee before setting out anywhere has been built into Finch family life for decades).

'Maybe global warming is Mother Nature's menopause?' Julia whispers. 'Her last hot flush as her fertility dries up?'

'You are *so* cheering me up this evening.'

'Have you talked to your doctor about HRT?' she demands in an undertone, mouth barely moving. 'Mine said it was my choice, but I crunched the stats and what with Mum's cancer, and Auntie Vi dying of it so young, it's a no-brainer. Chances are you or I will be titless by sixty as it is.'

Thankfully this conversation's shut down because we need to set off to allow time to pick up Dad's hearing loop headset which he stresses about if he's not got at least half an hour before the performance. Jackets are fetched, children kissed and pep-talked, the Jack Russell removed from humping Paddy's leg. Taking a quick swig of my water, I realise that it is refreshingly cooling so I drink it all and get head freeze, but at least my body returns to a normal core temperature. It doesn't occur to me to pop to the loo before we leave.

Traffic crawls into Stratford agonisingly slowly, our eyes blinded by the evening sun. I'm pouring sweat because Mum insists I keep my window closed to safeguard her hair. Forced to crank my seat forwards so much to make room for Julia's legs that the steering wheel is hard against my ribcage, my right tit keeps setting off the windscreen wipers. She's having an animated call with a client whose husband has just turned up demanding the Sage espresso maker and the family labradoodle (did I mention she handles divorces? Potentially handy). Sandwiched between her and Dad, who is fretting we'll miss curtain up, Miles catches my eye in the rear-view mirror and pulls the face he's been mastering since he was six – all tongue lolling, foaming-mouthed, cross-eyed horror mask – and which in humourless middle age I now have to remind myself sharply is not a heart attack/asthma fit/anaphylactic shock. The brothers-in-law are in the back row, London-based Reece talking loudly over long-time local Paddy to recommend where I should try to park the car.

I drop everyone directly outside the theatre, taking my ticket and waving them away with a stoic smile: 'I'll see you in there.'

Yessss! Engage automatic door locks, open all windows, kick start the Annie Lennox CD and we're cruising past the riverside day trippers and theatregoers spilling out of the Dirty Duck, me and the battered Picasso. All too briefly, we are alone and could go anywhere.

Annie is singing 'No More I Love You's', which makes me want to run away even more. We could burst through the *Bladerunner* hoardings into wilderness, fly over the *Thelma and Louise* canyon, warp-speed *Back to the Future*. I could drive home and have the place to myself. I could drive to a whole new life, although realistically the car would probably break down before I got beyond the M42, and I'd miss the kids.

Besides which, Kismet has other ideas. A Range Rover pulls out of a parking space immediately ahead of me. You could fit a bus in there. Even my rusty parallel parking skills can nail this one.

My first attempt almost kills a Japanese tourist. I apologise profusely out of the window and he backs away with his hands up. 'Solly! Me no good English.' We both apologise to each other for a bit then give up because I'm causing a traffic jam.

I start to reverse again and he stands and watches, which is unnerving. At least he's not filming me on his phone.

Five minutes later, after hotly revving in and out at increasingly unlikely angles, the Picasso and I are snugly alongside the wall. The drinkers outside the pub applaud, as does my Japanese audience of one. I get out to take a bow, then get back in again to flip down the sun visor mirror. Make-up still miraculously intact, I sit quietly listening to Annie while I regroup embarrassment and anger into something less sweaty. She's speaking to me tonight.

A polite shadow bobs by the open window. My tourist friend hands me a parking ticket he's bought from the machine. I glance up in surprise and he gives a shy smile and makes a drink gesture. At least, I think it's a drink gesture.

Blimey. Still got it, Eliza. Must be the eighties hair.

'Gosh. Thank you. That's terribly kind. What a lovely gift. I'm afraid I'm about to go and see the play on the main stage.'

'Me no good English,' he reminds me. Did he just wink?

Apologising that I have family to join, I glance at the car clock. Fuck! It's three minutes to curtain up. Me no pause.

4

Play Time

My family are all in their seats. My bag gets searched, the flashlight lingering on three dirty tissues and a Galaxy wrapper.

The lights are about to go down as I – 'sorry... thank you... sorry' along our row. Excellent seats. Dad always buys the best. I'm right next to him in C34, just two grey heads between me and the stage.

Paddy shoots me a black look from C29, trapped between Reece and my mother. Julia – on Dad's other side – is scouring the programme for anybody she's seen in a BBC crime drama.

There's a swing dangling from the fly tower, a ravishing actor upon it, languidly sad.

'It should be you up there, Elz,' Dad says automatically as the musicians strike up. He says it every time, and I know he's trying to be kind, but I wish he wouldn't. Especially when it's a male character. I always played the male parts at university because there weren't enough real men and I was tall. At drama school there was a shortage of mad old ladies which became my niche. Now I'm slowly turning into one, nobody wants to cast me.

The lights lower, his hand folds over mine and I feel a warm, tingling sensation.

I need the loo. I *really* need the loo.

I always wanted to be an actor. The stage is in my soul. Mum and Dad are passionate theatregoers and took us along with them as often as possible growing up: Shaftesbury Avenue, the South Bank, the Barbican, Old Vic and Donmar, out here to Stratford, up to Edinburgh, down to Chichester. What an education! I'd look at these amazing figures strutting and fretting their hour and know I had to be amongst them. My parents never stopped banging on about qualifications, so I sat all my exams like a good Finch and studied drama at university where I blagged cheap tickets to anything I could see. Who else can boast they watched all seven consecutive performances of Daniel Day-Lewis playing Hamlet? It's still my top trump at dinner parties. I sometimes pretend to have seen the ghost of his father too, just to see the jaws around me drop.

Fast forward thirty years and I'm no longer such a good audience member. I suffer from acute, inconvenient jealousy the moment the action starts. I'm a competitive Finch, remember. We find failure very hard to swallow.

And after almost thirty years, I'm finally learning to accept that I am never going to be a successful theatre actor. From the day I left drama school I was proclaimed too loud, too masculine, too tall. Directors always cast their gazes and their Rosalinds elsewhere. I used to cite Janet McTeer and Fiona Shaw as reasons to keep going, but let's face it, they're Janet McTeer and Fiona Shaw. Eliza Finch might be a decade younger, but it's way too late to catch up professionally. At some point I might be brave enough to admit I was simply never good enough, but it's the 'what ifs' that keep you going in this profession and I won't give up hope of making this family sitting beside me proud.

Orlando is delivering his opening speech, complaining that his brother's being a meanie after the death of their father.

My jealousy is having a brief stage raid. I want to be *in* this production, not sitting down here between a woman sucking a mint and my dad who's hand in mine is warm and reassuring – and making me sweaty. I haven't taken off my jacket and my handbag's still on my lap. Shit! My phone is on.

I manage to fumble one-handed into my bag to put it on airplane mode, but not before half the contents fall out. Groping around underfoot for lost lipsticks, pens and purse, I feel up Mint Lady's ankle by mistake. I'm getting hotter and hotter.

Orlando's whinging at his meanie brother now, and there's a bit of stage-fighting going on. I've never liked all the macho stuff at the beginning of *As You Like It*, and personally think Rosalind a bit shallow getting the hots for Orlando when he's taking part in a wrestling match.

Mint Woman hands me back one of the crumpled tissues which has found its way onto her lap.

Please God let my bladder hold, I pray. There's at least an hour and a half of this to sit through until I can have a wee.

I'll admit to always being a tad weak-bladdered. Growing up, I used to nip out and widdle behind the coal bunker in our garden if both the Finch family's loos were occupied because I couldn't wait, not even for five minutes.

Then pregnancy and childbirth screwed my bladder up some more. It's perhaps true that I short-changed myself on the pelvic floor exercise front, and my high-risk coffee addiction means I live life on the edge, although it's always amazed me how long I can hold a wee in if I really try.

Until the first time I really tried and didn't quite hold it.

Now I'm not talking a full-on floodgates tsunami. No, it's the little leaks: those occasions you don't quite get the tights down in time, the jeans fly is stuck or some bugger's closed the loo seat without you noticing before you sit down.

And it's the dawning realisation that this small but embarrassing affliction is here for keeps, along with a host of other signs of ageing that conspire to make fools of older women: the sweats and mind fog that oestrogen leaves behind when it scarpers, along with the fattening tummy rolls and thinning hair, and the squinting scowl of laughter lines trying to see the funny side.

Which brings me to the little laughter wee. Lately, mine's gone rogue and the joke's on me.

I'm watching a comedy and I can't laugh.

★ ★ ★

It's the twenty-minute interval. I have spent seventeen minutes of it queuing for the Ladies and the three-minute bell is already ringing to get us back in our seats.

Right now, I have the best seat in the house, locked in my cubicle, celebrating that I made it without mishap. The RSC upholstery is safe. This woman can clench.

I'm still steamingly hot, yet I savour this moment a drip at a time. I have queued a long time for this.

Back outside, my fragrant air-bladed hands have a bottle of water pressed into them.

'You'll need this,' Julia insists.

'Wow, thanks.' Sadist.

I look around for Paddy, but he's already gone back in. As I follow the grey heads shuffling into the auditorium, the torch is flashed in my bag again. I spot a small jewelled ballet pump and realise, to my horror, that I've picked up somebody's shoe.

I just have time to tuck the cool water bottle into my top, gripped between my sweating breasts, before Dad takes my hand again. He falls asleep three minutes in. Dad's never one to let a bottle of interval Montepulciano go to waste, but it's taken its toll.

Mint Woman now smells of coffee. Good call, as long as her bladder's up to it. Did she hop to the foyer, I wonder? As soon as the action onstage is suitably distracting, I ease the ballet pump out of my bag and drop it as discreetly as possible underfoot.

The water bottle is fantastically cooling. Thank you, Jules.

On stage, Orlando and his new mate Ganymede (Rosalind

butching it up) are engaging in some pretty intense gender-fluid flirtation. The actor playing Rosalind is very good. Intelligent, empathetic, adorable. I totally believe her feelings, the spontaneity of her thoughts, and in her love.

As You Like It is all about love, and Rosalind and Orlando are head over heels in the stuff. It's intoxicating. How we all drank in that feeling the first time we felt it, that addiction, that *madness*. Not the mutually dependent banality it later becomes. The pure initial fix is something magical, so potent it knocks you off your feet, spins you round, turns you upside down. I once defied gravity with Paddy, who caught me almost before I knew I was falling.

It strikes me that I almost certainly won't get to experience Cupid's arrow through this heart another time. That G-force fall.

Watching Rosalind faint when she hears of Orlando's fight with the lion, I feel a couple of tears slide down my face. *That* sort of love. Theatre often moves me to tears, and more so than ever recently. The same's true of films, books, Long Lost Family and anything starring Olivia Coleman, even the old Kev and Bev ads. Maybe I'm just leakier all round these days.

Before I know it they're all dancing and rejoicing in the Forest of Arden, and I don't want the play to end. Beside me, Dad lets out a snorty snore that wakes him up, mutters 'Howzat!' then gapes wide-eyed at the stage, on which the god of marriage Hymen is represented by a giant baby-faced papier-mâché puppet. It really is *giant*. I'm not sure it quite works for me, to be honest, but it's an impressive piece of engineering. I sneak a look along the row at Paddy who's rapt. When Paddy's full attention is on something, he looks just like our sons, that wide-eyed Hollander wonder carried through from small boys to men.

Unable to stop myself, I think back to our argument. At its height I said something awful about his parents. I remember how angry he was, we both were, and I can't unsay it. A marriage is full of things you can't unsay or undo. They dilute that first intoxicating love a drop at a time, taking us from cloud nine through thin ice to deep water.

When the actors take their curtain call, my crumpled tissue is soggy and threadbare, and I'm too red-eyed and snotty and full of shame to look at Paddy. I clap and clap and clap instead. The lights go up and we stand up. I wait to shuffle out behind Mint Lady, grateful to notice the Cinderella of Row C is now wearing two shoes.

My sister catches me up in the slow mass exodus to the foyer. 'You've been blubbing. Don't tell me, emotions all over the place? A low-dairy wheat-free diet can help.'

'I'm sure Antonio can rustle something up on the soya and flax front,' I mutter, knowing I'll soon be pigging out on antipasti, arancini, wild boar ragu and tiramisu come what may.

'Oh, old Antonio's retired, I thought you knew,' she says, with the satisfaction of insider to outsider.

I'm in shock. Antonio *is* Russo's.

'He's moved back to the family home in Puglia and a nephew of his is running the restaurant now. Dad adores him.'

I feel a flash of possessive anger, of resistance to change. Nobody can replace Antonio. It's the end of an era. This young usurper will surely fail.

'I hear you might be getting another dog.' Jules switches subject as we wait for the others.

My all-over-the-place emotions dial back to anger. 'Paddy told you we're getting a new dog?'

'During the interval.'

'Well, we're bloody well not,' I snap, no longer feeling so teary and shame-filled.

Jules looks startled. I think I might have just accidentally spat on her a little bit.

While we're waiting by Door 3, I'll quickly divulge the bit of the dog fight I'm most ashamed of. It's colouring everything tonight.

It came right at the start, when Paddy was showing me adorable puppy pictures and telling me how much better cuddling one would make me feel. And all I could think about was how I'd watched Arty's last breath, a breath *I* had wished upon her by telling the vet to inject her, one final breath that stole away her companionship and love forever. And I miss her, I miss her, I miss her.

Paddy just didn't get it. I needed him to get it, this pain, to understand it was grief.

So I shrilly explained that I wasn't ready to replace Arty any more than he could just rush out and replace his parents.

Paddy looked like I'd just hit him.

I know. It was a stupid, stupid thing to say.

He shouted that it's not the same, not even close, and that I had absolutely no idea what I was talking about.

And he's totally right. But I was upset and hurting and so, *so* angry I just couldn't back down.

Paddy might not have heard my apology later that night, the rage and hurt still tight in my throat, but he is the one who is willing to draw a line, to say no more about any of this for now, to put it behind us.

But I don't think he can quite bring himself to forgive me, and I can't forget about it.

Out in the foyer Reece manfully takes charge of returning the hearing loop headset while Dad gets loud and flappy, rounding us all up to walk to Russo's. He's hungry and a bit groggy from sleeping off the interval wine. Mum and Miles have already started on the scene-by-scene critique as we're herded outside. Night's arrived, soft and warm as a shot-silk wrap.

'What did you think?' Paddy falls into step beside me. The unforgotten argument walks silently between us.

'That you're justice, with eyes severe and beard of formal cut.'

'What's that supposed to mean?'

I explain it's from the Seven Ages of Man speech we heard Jacques say earlier tonight, although technically I didn't hear a lot of it because the only thing going on in my head at that particular point was *don't wee yourself, don't wee yourself.* 'You know, "All the world's a stage"? By the fifth act of a man's life, he's "justice": a judge.' Please stop judging me, I want to add, but Reece is running backwards ahead of us all, holding up his phone camera and shouting 'smile!' so that he can crop, filter and label the moment to put on Facebook, and the real moment passes.

'Peter's the judge,' Paddy mutters. Before he retired, Dad was a circuit judge, very Gilbert and Sullivan in the wig and gown.

'Dad's in his eighth act,' I point out, putting my arm through Paddy's and elbowing the argument out of the way again. 'You're the one with the wise saws and modern instances.'

'Well, I am a carpenter.' He smiles across at me and straightens his tie. His gaze has more watts than usual tonight. Seduction is definitely on the cards. Do all men see sex as marriage's hard restart, something that needs to be done when the usual buttons stop working?

When Paddy wants sex, he puts on a suit, like it's a job interview.

He thinks I get off on all that James Bond stuff because years ago, when we were quite new together and went to a *lot* of weddings, the novelty of him in a three-piece did absolutely do it for me. As did the sight of him out of it, in his overalls, in jeans, in anything.

He's convinced it was the suit. I sometimes wonder if I should signal back that I'm also in the mood by putting on a hat?

The trouble is I'm hardly ever in the mood for sex nowadays. I usually need to drink at least a bottle of wine to even come close. Tonight, staying sober to chauffeur, my sex drive has been valet-parked so far from sight I'll need to hitch a lift to his party.

★ ★ ★

Everyone's starving and Dad walks so slowly, we could have eaten our weight in tapenade by now. To our frustration, he stops to look at properties in an estate agent's window, which is really just to catch his breath, but Jules is straight in bedside him pointing at a bungalow, trying to draw me into a 'wouldn't this be much easier for Mum and Dad to cope with, Eliza?' observation (she thinks that because I work part-time for Stratford's funkiest all-female estate agency – hosting viewings to supplement my income between narration jobs – my knowledge adds professional gravitas to her ongoing mission to downsize them). I hold up my phone apologetically, turning away to call Summer.

She tells me everything's fine, yeah-yeah-yeah-ing distractedly, desperate to get me off the line, the television audible in the background. Old-fashioned scheduling is all that's available at Grandpa and Granna's cottage and I recognise the Graham Norton Show theme. The hot priest from Fleabag is on tonight; I'll watch it on catch up. (Summer thinks I'm too old to enjoy the series; I think she's too young; we both hate the fact Paddy likes it).

'Is Edward asleep?' I double check. Please don't tell me he's still playing the Switch.

'Sort of.'

He's still playing the Switch.

But we're outside the restaurant now, and the rest of the family are going in, so I ring off. Glancing in, I see the familiar glow of candles on each table, the gingham cloths unchanged, along with the Italian flags and copper pans on the walls.

It's almost empty. Antonio's usurper is already failing, I conclude sadly as I wait to follow the others inside.

'Signor Finch, *buona sera*! *Signore*! *Avanti*!' an unseen voice incants as my parents are gathered inside. '*Benvenuto*!'

Ahead of me Miles rebouffs his fringe, Julia's tits are swiftly raised and Reece adopts his iciest prosecutor smile as Mum makes introductions.

'And this is my other daughter Eliza and her husband Paddy. This...' she loves a theatrical pause '... is Matteo!'

Antonio's successor is older than I expected and offensively handsome, Mediterranean skin a golden contrast to his peppery hair, his knockout smile in direct contrast to the unfriendly pout of the nubile younger woman glued to his side, dark hair wantonly piled up, Amy Winehouse-meets-Lolita.

'*Bellissima*!' He kisses my hand.

I stare at him, picture him cross-armed and leaning against a snarly bonnet on the hard shoulder.

I wait for him to recognise me too. His eyes smile into mine for a moment – they're extraordinarily intense, obsidian dark – then he moves on to pump Paddy's hand. Nothing.

The gonk hair and warpaint have ensured sheep-hugging Crazy Lady is under cover tonight. That and the magical invisibility cloak of being a woman over fifty.

Except I can't remember the last time a man looked me as directly in the eye as he just has, and I hadn't realised how much I missed it until now. Is this another one of the things women don't notice gradually disappearing with age, I wonder, that bold male focus drifting away from us to look at something more interesting?

Matteo exudes the timeless masculine confidence that comes with high-grade charisma, a man whose desirability knows no age limit nor harbours self-doubt. I haven't forgiven him, however great he looks. I'm equally affronted that Paddy's gaze is straight on the Lolita waitress, who Mum doesn't deign to introduce, but from the proprietorial arm the restaurateur puts around her before leading us inside, I'm guessing at a younger wife or girlfriend.

Our table is beautifully decorated with helium balloons, prosecco already poured, flutes raised as soon as we sit.

'To Peter! Happy eightieth!' Reece muscles in before anyone else and we obediently echo him.

It's far too hot and airless in here and the music is awful: Dean Martin singing 'Amore'. Even Antonio wouldn't stoop so low.

Fanning myself with the specials menu, I look around at the few occupied tables, a scattering of sated diners polishing off desserts while hungry fellow theatre-goers crack open breadsticks. Tucked neatly into a table for one in the corner is my Japanese tourist friend. He waves at me shyly.

I cheer up enormously. How thrilling! I think I might have acquired a stalker.

5

Meal Time

'Delithous, thanths.' I lean back to let Lolita collect my plate. I've eaten my arancini too fast and burned my tongue. 'Very hot. *Caldo.*'

Not looking at me, she moves on to gather Paddy's antipasti board, and I witness his eyes drift to her lusciously pert backside.

It's after eleven and he's looking distinctly glazed. He's not talking much which isn't unusual. Reece has droned on uninterrupted about his new motorbike and Dad has summarised rugby, politics and business with kind but soul-destroying condescension.

Miles and Mum are still talking about the play, their conversation exclusive. They're too far away for me to join in, but from what I can earwig, they've got as far as analysing Act Two.

Meanwhile, I'm stuck talking to our host, who takes waiting at tables so seriously, he waits constantly by ours, like we're a small, select audience at his chat show.

Matteo's outrageously flirty, his routine off-pat. He wants to know my favourite places in Stratford, where I like to eat, what I enjoyed about tonight's performance, listening intently, prompting, teasing and laughing, his questioning gaze direct. It's old-fashioned and compelling, threatening my sangfroid. That intensity.

He still hasn't recognised me as Crazy Lady even when I steer him onto the subject of sheep as a personal dare. He just gets very animated describing a delicious-sounding traditional lamb sauce called *Sugo di Agnello* that will feature in Russo's soon. Unlike Antonio, Matteo doesn't cook here. He's brought over his own chef and they're going to reinvent the entire menu for Puglian authenticity, the emphasis on ethically sourced meat and on-trend plant-based diets. The wickedly rich wild boar ragu and I are having this one final, farewell meal together.

My relationship with food has been a lifelong battle of greed over need. As an actress, the pressure to be slim is enormous, even as a character actress, even as a bloody voice artist. And whilst I know my job title is now gender neutral 'actor', at times like this I go old school on the basis that epicene rebranding hasn't made the problem go away. The narrowed eyes of directors and casting agents have been dismissing muffin tops since Sarah Bernhardt limped onstage.

I find it maddening that my metabolism keeps moving the goal posts. Thanks to the shock discovery a year or so ago that my waist was missing, I now eat less than ever and I am, like Anna in *Notting Hill*, permanently hungry.

Tonight, I'm taking these calories for skinny actresses everywhere. And actors.

I need the loo again but I'm holding it in because I'd have to go directly past my stalker's table. That means I'm still stuck with Matteo who has spun a chair around to sit on it, Christine Keeler-style, interviewing me like he's a volunteer at a nursing home. Have I ever been to Italy? Here's what he would show me, feed me, share with me if I did, and how they would *love* an English rose like me. It's a script designed to flatter which it does, but I want him to go away. I have a perspiring forehead I need to napkin-off unobserved, but there's no point hoping Paddy might step in and rescue me from all this one-on-one attention. He's never been the possessive sort. (Even on honeymoon in Thailand when I was briefly kidnapped by a taxi driver off his head on yaa-baa, he was extremely laid back about it.)

'And what is it you do, *bella*?' he asks. I long to whisper *I work for International Sheep Rescue, tell no one.*

'Eliza's an actress!' Dad says proudly (my parents don't do unisex) and Mum's focus on Miles flickers.

'You are in television, no?'

'Radio and voice work mostly.'

'Eliza was in *The Archers* for a while,' Mum explains. 'You know, the *soap*?' She always, always makes it sound apologetic.

I should point out here that Mum and I have a difficult relationship at times.

I love her deeply; she's kind and funny and through the worst dark days of her cancer treatment we clung to each other for dear life. But we are both jealous types, and she's never quite forgiven me the longevity of my career, for all its feast and famine. Mum was also briefly an actor (highlight: she handed Robert Stephens his cloak on stage at the Royal Court for six weeks in 1964). She didn't go back to it after having children whereas I did, only not as well as she feels she would have done. She's become the doyenne of damning with faint praise. My first role in a Radio 4 play was a huge thing for me and I bust a gut to nail it. After it was broadcast, Mum just said, 'You were fine, darling girl.' Nothing more.

It goes without saying Matteo has never heard of *The Archers*.

'They fired her, poor darling,' Mum sighs. This isn't strictly true. I was the Pargetters' bouncy nanny brought in to cheer things up after foot-and-mouth struck in 2002, and I was supposed to marry a local MFH in a Jilly Cooper-esque racy romance, but when I got pregnant with Summer they shelved it, then the Hunting Ban came in, after which I was spotted on Ambridge Green as rarely as Usha. I just faded out.

'Eliza also narrates lots of books.' Dad should really be my PR.

'You write books?' The Italian looks impressed.

'No, I record talking books.'

'To kids, yes?'

'They're mostly grown-up books.'

My brother whispers something to Mum whose eyes bulge.

'Don't say anything, Miles,' I warn him.

It sounds lovely, doesn't it, reading books out loud for a living? And it is often good fun, albeit a bit repetitive spending eight hours a day locked in a small room with nothing but a manuscript, bottle of water and lip salve, trying not to mispronounce things, breathe in too loudly or let your stomach rumble. They've saved the roof over my family's head. Which makes me feel all the more ungrateful that I'm getting a bit frustrated with the job. At first, I read out all sorts: biographies, manuals, cookbooks, historic sagas – and I loved that, but of late I keep getting offered the same work. I've been typecast.

'Eliza's just won *Narrator of the Year* for female erotic fiction,' Miles tells the table.

I could kill him.

He beams at me.

Beaming back, I raise my glass, one finger strategically to its fore.

'To our award winner.' Miles raises his glass around the table in retaliation, two fingers strategically V-ed for me. 'Congratulations, you dark horse, you. Next stop the Oscars.'

It's true I've read out nothing but priapic cocks and land-slide orgasms for over a year and I'm a winner. Apparently my panting is first-rate. If anybody asks what I'm narrating, I tell them it's women's fiction – guaranteed to be greeted with about as much interest in my family as *The Highway*

Code. Even Paddy doesn't know it's soft porn. Miles only uncovered the truth because he caught his ex-wife listening to one while she was ironing and recognised my voice.

I manage to hold my smile. *Narrator of the Year for Female Erotic Fiction* is my first professional accolade, an engraved glass open book shaped like lips which is hidden in my bedside drawer. I told Paddy I was just at the awards to make up numbers, and yes I felt bad for lying, but I had to protect him from all the aural sex I'm giving when our love life is U-Rated.

I glance at him but he's giving nothing away. My sister and Reece are making shocked little 'O's with their mouths; Mum clearly can't decide whether to laugh or cry, Dad's face is sweetly baffled and Matteo just laughs uproariously then goes to check progress in the kitchen.

'Tell me, Eliza, what's the method acting behind reading out mucky metaphors for the ladies?' I might have guessed Reece would be straight on it. 'Do you sit on the washing machine before recording to get in the mood? Fna-ha!'

My brother-in-law's sexism badly needs an update.

I match his tone. 'With all the online porn you watch, Reece, you should know it's easier than that to get in the mood these days!'

It's a guess, but his eyes flicker tellingly.

We're both grateful to see Lolita flouncing out of the kitchen with bowls of pasta.

My ragu, scalding hot like my starter, has none of the lovely sage-flavoured earthiness I remember from when Antonio made it. Within seconds, I get a bit of the meat stuck between my teeth. I can't dislodge it, no matter which way I contort my burnt tongue or discreetly fish around with a fingernail.

Paddy blows a discreet kiss and I wonder if he thinks what I'm doing is intended to be seductive, a bit of finger-sucking table play? He must be pretty drunk by now, given Matteo's glass-refilling efficiency.

He smiles across at me slowly. I'm not sure whether to be relieved or worried. My erotic professional secret, it seems, has full husband approval.

Turning my face away to try to discreetly dig deeper with the fingernail, I catch sight of Matteo holding out a credit card terminal to my stalker. Both are looking straight at me. I turn jumpily to Paddy, finger still in my mouth. It's Austin Powers' Dr Evil rather than erotic.

He's holding his smile gamely. There's a large lump of basil between his front two teeth.

These unfashionably ivory teeth of mine have seen a lifetime of devoted twice-a-day brushing, regular dental checks and more flossing than a primary school disco, yet they are ever-more determined to be food traps. Perhaps it's because I feed them less as I get older that they store spinach, seeds and meat for later?

My dentist has given me little interdental brushes to poke about between them twice a day and I'm regularly appalled by the rubble that comes out. One day I got a bit carried away and the interdental brush itself stuck between my teeth. Paddy had to help me remove it with a small pair of pliers and some olive oil. That's love.

★ ★ ★

My stalker has paid up and gone. I didn't look up as he left and I'm slightly regretting the missed thrill of fear. We have the restaurant to ourselves, chairs on tables around us, candles guttering. Matteo – jacket and tie now off, gold neck chain glinting – is doing his Christine Keeler chair thing beside Dad, amaro glasses charged. My sister and Reece are having one of those sotto arguments where their mouths don't move. Paddy's entertaining himself handing finished dessert plates to Lolita whose cleavage dips into his eyeline each time. (No matter how many times I've tried to explain to my husband what The Male Gaze is and why he should avert his, he's unconscionable when drunk.) Mum and Miles are onto Act Four. I've got a lump of sugar-spun toffee stuck alongside the pork.

Now that I can visit the loo without fear of abduction in a suitcase to Tokyo, I hurry off to lose another quart of mineral water, dig out the trapped food with my earring hook (handy tip that – the friend who passed it on swore it came from Judi Dench) and reapply my lipstick. The rest of my make-up is largely sweated off, but the gonk hair is holding up.

When I get back to the table, Dad's telling Matteo about the narrowboat. 'She belonged to Paddy's late father. We renamed her *The Tempest* when we bought her. She's magnificent!'

'*Che coincidenza*! Since I was a boy, I love these colourful barges on your canals. I always want one.'

'Then we must take you out in her, mustn't we, Miles?'

'Mmm?' My brother casts his languid smile across

the table, the one he uses when too drunk to follow the conversation.

'*The Tempest*! She's moored not far from here,' Dad tells Matteo. 'Miles has plenty of free time to take you out.'

'I would love that!' Matteo is straight in there. 'The painted boats, they are beautiful like your women, yes?' He smiles across at me and I raise a cynical eyebrow.

I notice Paddy has stopped looking cleavage-wards and looks thunderous instead. He is *extremely* possessive about the boat.

A sixty-foot narrowboat then called *Lady Love* (I know, ew), that barge was Eddie Hollander's pride and joy. Messing about on boats was a lifelong passion he passed on to his son. She'd taken the Hollanders the length and breadth of Britain's waterways by the time Paddy inherited her. The beautiful red barge was one of the few things the family managed to hang onto after everything else was sold to pay Ruth's care home fees. Which made it doubly heartbreaking that we later had to sell her to stay afloat ourselves.

Despite having no interest whatsoever in boats, my parents kindly stepped in and, name change aside, she's much the same as ever. They've hosted a few parties aboard. Paddy still tinkers at weekends. We've had a couple of holidays on her, although the kids prefer camping.

Miles was the one member of the family who showed a great affinity for canal life, loving the barge's vintage kitsch, Paddy's generosity with beer and the fact the radio always tuned to a test match or eighties retro rock. But his enthusiasm for hours pottering along the Midlands' waterways waned when he no longer needed an excuse to avoid going home to his wife. Only Paddy continues to do that.

Miles is now learning to fly a microlight as part of his sexy rainbow reinvention as Warwickshire's gay James Bond. He has a bet with Summer that he'll get his private pilot's licence before she gets her full driving one, and being a competitive Finch he's already clocked up his first solo flight and a minor air traffic incident involving a weather balloon.

At last, the bill is fetched. I've swallowed so many yawns I've given myself hiccups and I'm boiling hot again. I hold my breath and bet myself that if I hiccup in the next ten seconds I'll get to play Cleopatra at the National Theatre alongside Daniel Craig. I don't hiccup. Bugger.

Having finished their production critique at last – no turn unstoned, as Diana Rigg used to say – Mum and Miles are now the ones basking in Matteo's spotlight, and competing for attention.

'Of course, Shakespeare drew inspiration for *As You Like It* from the epic poem, *Orlando Innamorato*,' Mum shows off, 'written by a countryman of yours, Matteo.'

'In fact, you might be surprised to learn that Shakespeare set a third of his plays in Italy,' Miles tells him.

They look suitably discomfited when Matteo proceeds to reel off all thirteen titles, laughs affably and complains, 'And not one set in Puglia!'

Behind him, Lolita is throwing eye daggers at her boss/husband/lover while holding the card machine out at Dad.

I'm sweating from my eyeballs; I step outside to try to cool off and wake up. Paddy nips out after me, intent on a clinch. Oh hell, I'd forgotten about his sex mission. I'm far too hot for the overture to start. We can do all this at home. With luck, I'll sleep through most of it.

But he loves a spot of pavement necking and I don't want to spoil his good mood, so we indulge in a quick nostalgic kiss in the shadows of a neighbouring shop doorway, not realising there's a homeless man in there until we fall over his dog. It's a serious passion-killer. The man's asleep. I stoop to stroke the dog apologetically, a collie with odd eyes and one ear up and one down. Arty looks back at me, saying she's sorry too. Sorry I died. I fish in my bag for a tenner and fold it into the man's hand, ignoring Paddy's disapproval.

Back in the restaurant, Mum has got in a muddle with her jacket which Matteo is helping her put on. She's so thin it frightens me, that beautiful death dance between age and beauty. I step in to help, but she bats me away, insisting, 'Matteo can do it!' He flashes his big smile, calling her 'Bella' and 'Dolcezza' and she giggles coquettishly. I can see how much the attention lifts Mum, but it still makes me uncomfortable. In a surge of bad temper, I remind myself that beneath the overplayed charm, this foxy silver-tongued flatterer is a road-rage despot who wouldn't lift a finger to help a sheep in distress.

Catching me watching him, Matteo leans across, dark eyes smiling into mine. 'You OK, beautiful crazy lady?'

I don't let myself react, although my heartbeat goes from seventy to 110 like a Ferrari in a police chase. When did he recognise me? Right from the start? Bastard.

There was a time I'd have found the perfect witty put down in a breath – assuming I'd resisted the headstrong temptation to name and shame him – but I am tired, sober and humourless. I turn away, ignore Paddy's curious look and walk back outside without a word.

I want Antonio back. I want Arty back.

I want *me* back.

6

Bedtime

We're back home. It's the first time we've had the place to ourselves in years. And I don't want to have sex. Not remotely.

Paddy is happy drunk and pulling out all the stops. The mood lighting's on, the smoochy playlist selected on Spotify (I take a quick look and it's actually called *Music for Making Love*), the wine uncorked (he's no fool – he knows I need my engine priming) and the suit is staying on for now, doing its magic aphrodisiac thang.

My eyes do their looking-for-Arty thing even though I know she's not here. Why can't I shrug off the weight of homecoming sadness each time there's no big welcome?

How I long to feel as drunk and horny as Paddy. I swig wine as we do-si-do around the kitchen island.

His voice is seductively low... 'Tell me about these sexy books you read out.'

Yes, he can clearly see a positive in tonight's surprise revelation.

'Do they ever turn you on?'

'God, no!' (That's not strictly true. One I narrated recently set amongst Venetian courtesans had me so hot under the collar I had to slip off for a discreet loo break, but it's definitely not a mood we can recreate here, so I'm not about to tell him.)

Over the speakers, Ginuwine is singing 'Pony', the bass vibrating with burpy percussion as he promises to throw out his party guests and wreck my body. I'd rather have Dean Martin and his big pizza-pie back.

'Let's go up to bed.' Paddy gives me his hard, horny stare, only slightly boss-eyed from tiredness and Dad's largesse.

My wine catch-up is waking me up. I'm not ready for bed; I'm buzzing, I need to defuse. Avoid having sex.

'I know, I'll write a restaurant review on TripAdvisor!' I announce.

Paddy tries to talk me out of it, but I already have the laptop out on the kitchen table.

I like writing reviews; I try to find a positive in everything. It's karma. I've been on the receiving end of some scalding invective (the *Birmingham Post* calling my Celia in *Calendar Girls* 'flaccid' was a low point) and it's my way of making peace.

To balance the planet, for every bad review I receive, I post a good one.

Unless it's for Russo's.

I complain that I still can't feel my tongue after that arancini removed most of its surface, the wild boar ragu was stodgy, the pudding almost took out a tooth and the service was invasive and – checks online thesaurus – oleaginous. Which, let's face it, is a light grilling for an overbearing restaurateur whose nubile waitress has given my husband an inconvenient hard-on he refuses to give up hope on.

'You go up and get into bed,' I urge him. 'I'll join you up there.'

But he's not falling for that one.

I post the review before I've double-checked it because he's come round to read it over my shoulder and I hate that. The tone of bitter disappointment might be slightly darker than intended, but I have promoted it from one to two stars – doubled the score indeed! – so what you take with one hand...

Paddy has changed the Spotify playlist to one more age-appropriate. The Blue Nile are singing Saturday Night, a throwback from student days. If ever there was a make-out track it was this one.

I can't put this thing off any longer. We're going to have to have some sex. It's either that or I'll be up against that wall of angry husband back all night, sleepless with guilt and self-loathing, convinced Paddy's going to leave me/ start going to hookers/develop a rampant porn addiction because I'm not giving him what he wants.

I wish with all my heart that I could feel more enthusiastic about it, but the truth is I feel the same sense of dutiful weary dread that I do when the bed needs changing. It's lovely afterwards, but what an effort.

Making love with Paddy was once the best sex I'd ever had. That's not necessarily as good as it sounds because, while

I'd had quite a lot of sex up until he and I made it official, the standard hadn't been all that great. Orgasms had been a distinct rarity; I was much better at doing those myself. With Paddy, the average briefly shot up, but the numbers all too swiftly fell away again once the novelty wore off. After the kids, it would have taken EST to get these nipples hard.

But I liked sex with Paddy. I liked the performance of it, the power, the closeness afterwards.

I miss wanting sex with my husband just for the sake of it.

I hope whoever came up with 'the older you get the better you get' isn't watching us from up high tonight. There's nothing quite as passion-killing as waiting through both two-minute toothbrush timers, then flossing and rinsing.

We could do this afterwards, I know, but we've started now so we might as well get it done, more comfortable with this familiar bedtime routine than with sex, which we haven't done for months.

We both end up in our pyjamas, which is a bit strange, but at least it gives us something to work on to get the party started.

We try for a tentative kiss that tastes of toothpaste and inhibitions.

'Just popping for a wee first!' I say brightly.

In the bathroom, I fish around in the cabinet for the Vagisan. Tackling the desiccation of my once-welcoming pink bits is such an unsexy stage of foreplay, I've secretly taken it on myself. I know I should probably share what's happening to my body with my husband, but somehow the 'let's talk about vaginal dryness' moment slipped by.

We get down to business, lights off. I hurry him past foreplay and now we're away. He's doing long, steady strokes incredibly slooooowly, which I hope isn't for my benefit because it's very hot down here, and I think I might be getting cramp.

I wish, wish, wish I could get in the mood. Not feel panicked.

'Oooooh yes, ooooo yes that feels good,' I offer some encouragement.

Oh God, he's going even slower now.

I'm feeling emotional for all the wrong reasons. And sweaty. I want to love this. I love this man, don't I? Where's my on button gone?

Paddy isn't a great talker during sex. I think it puts him off. I really like it – a bit of 'you're so hot' goes a long way (although perhaps not when I'm literally this hot) – although the first time I suggested we jazzed it up a bit with some dirty talk, he sounded like a hostage being made to read out a kidnapper's demands. He got better at it, but his relief was obvious when parenthood brought with it a need to keep quiet. Now it's a force of habit.

Right here, right now, with him inside me, I hate the silence. It feels like a criticism. It feels lonely.

'Faster!' I beg, upping my performance to get things moving, fingers through his hair, across his back. I love Paddy's back, which is broad and freckled. He ramps it up gratifyingly, but I think that last glass or three of Barolo might have been a mistake. He goes a bit soft and slips out a couple of times, which we both pretend not to notice as we regroup.

Why, why, why can't I enjoy making love with my husband? Lou says she thinks about David Beckham and it works every time, but I'm no good at that. It feels like being unfaithful. (And I've always thought Goldenballs overrated. I mean, that voice! You'd definitely want him to keep schtum in the sack.)

Overthinking again, Eliza.

I reach down to coax him back into play, gratified by the response in my hand, less so by the strange groans he's emitting. Either he's got a sinus infection or there's some serious passion going on here. It throws me off my stride.

I find myself wondering if Paddy is thinking about our Lolita waitress. Jealousy hollows me out, but I talk myself round. This is about Paddy and me, a husband and wife making love. Leave the pouting temptress to her Matteo in the little flat above the restaurant, her worldly-wise Don Giovanni talking her through their mad, passionate Italian lovemaking: '*La tua pelle sembra seta, il tuo corpo e' perfetto, sei bellissima!*' (I speak no Italian whatsoever bar those phrases I researched how to pronounce when narrating the Venetian courtesan book – my favourite was '*il tuo corpo e'pazzesco, viene per me*', 'your body is insane, come for me', oh YES!) Afterwards, unable to sleep, Matteo will set out alone to drive like a maniac around the British motorway network, listening to Italian opera at top volume in his sports car whilst searching for something more fulfilling, something that makes him feel, something that reminds him what it is to be human.

Suddenly I am shame-drenched with desire. For the first

time in forever this old mothership is bursting up through the waves. The nipples are zeppelins, the libido flying out of its deep dark lair. I join in, greedy for more, deeper and quicker, that all-consuming need.

But Paddy's shrinking away as fast as I try to draw him further in.

'Sorry, love. Too much wine.'

I get a peck on the cheek and the big freckled wall of his back. He is mortified. I put my hand on his shoulder and it's gently brushed away.

The mothership sinks without trace, libido lost at sea. I lie awake, staring at the ceiling, because I know without doubt that it's my fault, it's me. I'm not sexual any more. Then, when I am, I'm a flailing madwoman.

It's me, it's me, it's me.

God, I miss having Arty to hug. I'm so unhappy. I want a hug.

Guessing Paddy needs a hug too, I wrap an arm around that big back, press my face to its warmth.

He shrugs me off.

I move as far across the bed as gravity allows and cry very, very quietly.

Somehow sleep briefly mugs me before the familiar eyes-wide of the just-before-dawn insomnia shift.

Oddly, my first waking worry is not that my marriage is in a bad place. No, my first conscious thought, along with a twinge of full bladder, is that rescuing a sheep is not a very valiant boast. I'm going to die of one of my multiple lifestyle-inflicted diseases without doing anything in this ever-decreasing mortal coil that stands out as courageous or selfless or even wildly reckless. Apart from rescuing one sheep. That I thought was a dog.

Everyone should do something to be remembered by, something to make them immortal.

Listening to the day breaking, craving more sleep, my mind whirs with all the life-changing challenges, dares and noble deeds I may never achieve.

With effort, I talk my insomnia off its ledge by reminding myself that I can get started on immortality after the alarm goes off.

Then the alarm goes off.

Hitting cancel not snooze because it's still set to the weekday early shift, I spoon Paddy whose hand reaches back to pat my leg, like I'm Arty. I want to say that I'm OK with the idea of getting a puppy if it makes him happy, that I want Paddy to be happy again. But I can't speak because thinking about Arty has made me choke up too much.

Eventually he starts snoring lightly, the moment passing.

Seconds later, I'm deep in sleep.

7

No Time

For the first Saturday in forever, Mr and Mrs Patrick Hollander have woken up alone in their home. At one time, lovemaking would be urgent and obligatory – after letting the dog out – but Paddy wouldn't try again so soon after last night's disaster, especially given I'm suffering a bad night sweat – a morning sweat? – when he delivers a cup of tea to the bedside, telling me he'll be working on the narrowboat all day if I need him.

'We'll bring you some lunch,' I offer, only half awake and wrung out. I peer blearily at the clock. It's not yet eight.

'If you insist.'

It would be counter-intuitive to bad-temperedly point out that I don't *insist*, I'm being conciliatory.

I wave him away sleepily. 'We'll drop in after Ed's swimming class.'

'I'd like that.' It pains him too, this conspiracy of niceness. He makes no comment on my glistening wet face, but he pulls open the sash on his way back out.

As soon as he's gone, I throw back the covers, peeling myself off hot sticky bedding and out of sodden pyjamas as I trail to the bathroom to shower, the pelting water clearing my head and reminding me that today is the day I'm figuring out a way to leave my mark in the world. Think positive! Eliza Finch is on a mission.

This cheers me up enough to make the effort to see off the gonk hair with caffeine shampoo, run the Venus over my stubblier zones and even anoint knees and elbows with shea butter when I step out. Let immortality start with self-preservation. Hot flushes are just nature's sauna.

The first few times I found myself drenched in sweat it was logical to blame cooking over a steamy hob, global warming, the increasing use of artificial fibre in Boden tunics, or just that I was 'hot and bothered' which, as is obvious, I am a lot. But it's happening too often to deny there's a connection to my age.

The hot flush and the night sweat mark the high noon and darkest hours of menopause, ringing alarm bells every few hours now the biological clock has stopped ticking once and for all. It happens without warning, sometimes just once or twice a week, sometimes multiple times in a day or night. From nowhere I feel as though I've been sitting outside too long on a scorching day or exercising to boiling point, and yet it comes from within me, this white-hot dripping heat. I've mugged up on it online, and as well as caffeine, spicy food and alcohol, one of the biggest contributory factors to hot flushes is stress and tension. Be happy, Eliza, or you'll have to keep sweating it out!

I've naturally also Googled all the other symptoms of menopause, and the checklist women of my age share includes vaginal dryness (tick), reduced sex drive (tick), low mood (TICK!), difficulty sleeping (tick tock tick tock) and problems with memory and concentration (or have I ticked that already?). Other changes include dizziness, headaches, gum problems and a metallic taste in the mouth, tingling feet and hands, itchy skin, hair loss and brittle nails, bloating, stress incontinence, allergies, body odour, palpitations, osteoporosis, dry eyes and weight gain.

Call me shallow, but that last one is a particularly cruel blow.

My positive outlook fades to black when my favourite pair of cut-off jeans fails to do up, the stretchier reserves only obliging after a struggle that leaves a pie crust of doughy flesh spilling above the waistband.

'No, no, no!' I march despairingly to the full-length mirror in which a woman with my head and the torso of David Walliams in red bra and cropped jeans is looking furious. One blowout Italian meal and my midriff's wearing a fleshy new stab vest. (OK, so there may have been a few barbecues and extra bottles of wine as contributory factors, but this is nevertheless an overnight discovery.)

Hardly surprising poor Paddy lost his ardour with his arms wrapped round this. I push together the bulges to either side of my belly button so that it moves like a mouth shouting, 'Somebody help me! There's a woman in here!'

I look round for Arty to share the joke. Remember. She's gone. Like my waist and womanliness.

I grab a pillow from the bed and scream into it, on and on, suffocating in my own noisy grief. The pillow smells of Paddy, which just makes me howl louder. If I used to think that finding myself drenched in sweat without warning was the most unpredictable menopausal symptom, I was wrong. Nor is it the inexplicable weight gain, the insomnia or low libido.

It's the emotional explosions, the illogical tantrums sparking from nowhere, the high-voltage upset at some injustice, then white-hot fear, or blistering sensitivity, occasionally melting into heartbreaking compassion. All this weeping and wailing is drying me out. I can't keep up with it, and each lightning strike leaves me in ashes, scorched and exhausted, nervously awaiting the next ambush.

Downstairs, seeing Paddy's toast plate dumped in the sink alongside my unrinsed wine glass, I feel a bit angry and teary again which I know is all about last night, but I blame it on the state of the house. There's not a surface without *stuff* on it. Bloody, bloody stuff.

I swear at each item of mess while snatching it up, repeatedly screaming, 'Fucking *stuff*!' I then curse my husband and children in turn, jumping out of my skin when a female voice behind me says, 'Sorry, I'm having trouble understanding you right now, please try a little later.'

Now I curse Alexa instead, and try to make her react to my increasingly blue language while I empty the overflowing kitchen bin, followed by the badly stacked dishwasher. She is resolute that she doesn't understand me, but our neighbour (the affable retired physics teacher on the right, not the shared-drive new-Nazi neighbour to the left) catches every word of 'fucking trumped up digital weather bitch spy DJ' as I stand by the shared fence trying to cram last night's wine bottle into the already full glass recycling box. He asks if I'm OK. I tell him I'm fine, just running lines for an audition.

'Sci Fi?' he asks hopefully.

'Jane Austen adaptation.'

I go inside and take a few deep breaths before calling my parents. Mum's hungover falsetto is strained. 'You're not picking them up yet, are you? Summer's making everyone breakfast pancakes. She is *such* a sweet girl! Messy, like you. But well meaning. Can you bring painkillers when you do come? We've run out.'

I ring off, embracing this rare window of opportunity before I need to set off. Inner happiness, Eliza. You have the place to yourself. Enjoy it.

I go into the garage and stand by Arty's old bed, feeling tearful.

Fail.

Nobody knows how much her love meant to me. Or that losing her has coincided with losing so much of myself.

Arty didn't judge me by anything but my kindness. My age never counted against me, nor its femininity. To her, I wasn't a mother, wife, co-worker, daughter, sister, object of desire or derision. I wasn't even her owner. I was just me.

I can't help myself; I can't stop missing her.

In search of distraction, I go back to the kitchen and check through my phone's messages. Joe's shared this morning's survivor's photo from his summer ball, a drone shot in which he's somewhere amid a crowd of students sprawled round a fountain blowing plastered, stoned kisses upwards. I send love hearts back and then retune the radio to catchy pop on the local station, dancing around the kitchen to 'Shiny Happy People' as I tidy, trying to remember what its ironic message is.

By the time the surfaces are clear, Joe's replied that he's at his voluntary job at a food bank. He's helping the impoverished of Exeter while I'm feeling sorry for myself and swearing at Alexa.

I ask her what 'Shiny Happy People' was rumoured to be about. The Tiananmen Square massacre, she tells me dispassionately. I was nineteen when that took place, the same age as many of those students who died fighting for freedom, and I still remember the shock of it, the first real sense I had of the scope of my freedom compared to others. Joe's that age now. Joe, who marches and debates and freedom fights whereas I no longer even shout at the television when *Question Time*'s on. It's said we get more right wing as we get older, but I feel increasingly out of touch, muted by the mantra I was raised with: never discuss politics, money or religion.

A jolly jingle cuts through REM and a voice announces that he has Graham from Solihull on the line with a *great* story for Saturday morning listeners. 'Heeeeello, Graham!'

'Yes, hello. Well I was driving home from work on the motorway yesterday when I saw a woman stealing a sheep out of a field...'

Mortified, I switch to Radio 4 which informs me that Greta Thunberg is today being honoured with Amnesty International's Ambassador of Conscience Award. Her small voice trembles angrily as she tells us we, the world's older custodians, have poisoned it. I turn the radio off, feeling personally responsible.

That's it. I *must* do something for good, something for change, and something to stop me disappearing into old age like a dissolving bath bomb, my fizz gone.

Figuring out how to do it will have to wait until after I put the bedding on to wash.

It saddens me that each generation now seems morally obliged to accuse its predecessors of selling out, of being poor caretakers, as though there must be a baddie to each goodie. Greta's little voice cuts me to the quick, not because the world isn't on fire, but because it's now burning so brightly it's no-platforming the wisdom that comes with age, its patience and its pragmatism, its regrets, its survival, its helpfulness.

Humans are, as we grow up to discover, all in search of a responsible adult. Right now, that's a teenage girl from Sweden.

At thirteen, I genuinely didn't think I'd live to see Greta's great age. Nuclear terror had us in its grip in 1983, those missiles ready to launch; reading *When the Wind Blows* gave me nightmares; watching women holding hands around a military base full of armed tridents made them come to life. My friends and I believed all life would be destroyed any day at the touch of a button.

Perhaps all generations start their moral awakening thinking the world is about to end?

Teenage rebellion is a rite of passage that I barely recognise in myself thirty-five years on. The Eliza who sent off her postal order to join CND was obsessive, tens of badges soon peppering her lapels with rainbow peace doves and cutesy messages like *Inspector Clouseau Says 'Ban the Beumb'*. My love of debating and campaigning lasted well into my twenties. I joined the League Against Cruel Sports and Compassion in World Farming, became a vegetarian, debated at school then student union, picketed with comrades and argued furiously with my parents about everything. I was an idealist without any set direction, catching onto campaign slogans: Say No to Cruise, Support the Miners, Free Nelson Mandela, Meat is Murder, Choose Life!

Fast forward thirty years and I'm still teased by the Finch family as the rebel with too many causes.

My children's generation has a new set of badges: avatars, emojis, memes and hashtags. While Ed fights it out for glory in virtual battlefields and Summer 'influences' her disciples to apply warpaint, it's Joe who has inherited my passion for real causes, but with far better focus. I'm grateful for his social conscience, but it frightens me too.

It stemmed from a very dark place: not nuclear but self-destruction. At fourteen, Joe was deeply depressed without us knowing it.

For once I'm not obliged to spend an hour bellyaching at Summer and Ed to sort and process their laundry. I grab all identifiable dirty clothes in Summer's pigsty and Edward's monk cell, stripping and changing the beds and collecting enough cups and plates to start a café. This rare bonus should have put me ahead of the clock, but I make the mistake of performing a Parental Safety Check of their cupboards and drawers.

OK, so it's technically snooping, but very low level. If I wanted to know about their inner lives I'd have to be a far better whizz at cracking online passwords. Filching through a few knickknacks is barely a security pat down.

To my relief there's no evidence of drug taking, binge drinking, knives or unhealthy pastimes, although Summer has a *lot* of my jewellery.

If it hadn't been for the parental safety check, we would have had no idea how bad things were getting for Joe at school five years ago. He was monstrously unhappy, something he only confided in a Moleskine notebook. Much as I hated myself for reading it, I was madder at myself for not seeing the signs sooner. That book was terrifying: he wrote about there being no point to his life, about the world being a better place without him.

Since then I've considered the quick drawer frisk a potential lifesaver – unless it's my husband's bedside drawers, which I daren't go near in case they contain grounds for divorce.

Joe has embraced his global causes as a reason to stay alive. And while he makes a point of not campaigning hard at his family, we're all right behind him: Summer's activist hashtags change with each season's trending humanitarian movement; Ed sticks more steadfastly to ending cyber bullying and saving badgers; meanwhile Paddy and I recycle assiduously and try ever-harder to like soya protein.

The least I can do is find a reason for action, not just lie awake at 5 a.m. worrying who will look out for my children when I die.

Morally liberated, I peg the wet washing out and put on another load.

I arrive late at The Prettiest Cottage in Warwickshire where Summer and Ed are deep into a tub of Cadbury Celebrations and a jigsaw with Dad, briefly metamorphosed from screen-obsession to wholesomeness by indulgent grandparents and a not-spot.

Mum's reluctant to let them go, having already been abandoned by Jules, Reece and the girls who are visiting Warwick Castle. I stay longer than I should, drinking tea and agreeing last night was super.

'Isn't Matteo *charming*?' Mum says breathily, like she has a crush.

'Mmm.' I want to take issue, but it will just draw attention to the fact he got under my skin.

'Paddy was very quiet.'

'Strong and silent is his thing, you know that.'

'Mmm.' She deliberately uses the same inflection I did.

Mum and I mainstream passive aggression together on bad days.

She takes a cup of tea through to Miles who is still sleeping off his hangover and I start gathering my children's things. The Jack Russell terrier follows me round, dropping his ball and nudging it towards me whenever I stop.

I stoop to take it, then unexpectedly well up. Arty did the same thing as a young dog.

'Are you having one of your weird sad moments?' Summer has come in and caught me with my face pressed in my hands watched intently by a small crouching terrier.

'Just dizzy,' I mutter.

She walks to my side, prising the ball from my grip to throw it, then puts her arm round me. 'I told Dad you're right about not getting a new dog just yet.'

'You did?' I'm beyond touched.

'I was talking to Mr Owusu about it this week.'

'Oh yes?' I say tightly. (Mr Owusu is a teaching assistant in Summer's art class, on whom she has a raging crush.)

'He suggested I should do a multi-media montage called *It's A Dog's Life*. I was thinking of something Britart retro, inspired by Tracey Emin maybe? We've still got Arty's basket, haven't we?'

I feel a fierce spike of anger at using Arty's things, her death, like that. I manage to quash it enough to tell her we'll talk about it later when we're not in such a hurry.

Her Nike tick eyebrows angle kindly. 'Can I skip drama club today? I'm knackered.'

'Not for the amount it costs each term. Here, see if you can spot your brother.' I find Joe's summer ball photo on my phone and hand it to her.

The ticks lower disapprovingly. '*OMG*, why d'you like it with a purple heart? Mum, a purple heart means you want sex.'

'It does?' I snatch the phone back. 'Why don't I *know* these things? I thought that was an aubergine?'

Summer explains the meanings of different colour heart emojis while we carry bags out to the car. Yet another hidden code of which I'm ignorant. I must no longer send purple, black or green hearts for fear of serious reprisals.

'She's winding you up, Mum,' Ed assures me as he clambers into the back seat, hooking his earphones on.

'Am not!' A Nike tick arches.

Mum hurries out with a shopping list. 'I almost forgot, Julia asked if you'll pick these up for her as you're going to a supermarket. You are all still coming to lunch tomorrow?'

'Paddy's playing cricket,' I remind her.

'But Joe's up for the day, yes?'

'Yes.' I glance down at the list and spot anchoiade, raspberry vinegar and girolle mushrooms. My sister is an Elizabeth David purist.

'We're delighted our oldest grandson will be here!' Dad has followed her out.

I tell them about Joe working his voluntary shift today. 'It makes us all feel like we should do something truly selfless too, doesn't it? An act of kindness without ego. We get very self-absorbed as we get older.' I eye the list again.

'I felt just the same at fifty,' Mum pats my hand, 'didn't I, Peter?'

'My God, yes!' Dad guffaws. 'All those charity committees you joined, the WI, voluntary driving and so forth. Always on the go.'

'I was thinking of something a bit more life-changing.' There's a growl in my voice.

'It's a phase,' Mum dismisses. 'You'll soon realise that nothing you can do will make a blind bit of difference. Family comes first. Very tricky age for a woman, fifty. It gets far lovelier after you've weathered this decade, just wait and see.' She takes the list from my hand, plucks the pen from Dad's shirt pocket, adds Co-codamol, Imodium, Rennies and Anusol then hands it back.

★★★

Nobody in the family ever mentions Mum's fiftieth birthday. It was August 1991, and the hints had been dropping fast.

She'd been dieting for weeks, had half a dozen new sparkly frocks and coordinating shoes in her wardrobe and casually left her address book out where we could find it. She expected a party.

Obliging and generous, Dad planned everything to a tee and had us all sworn to secrecy. Mum's passport was located, her summer wardrobe raided and packed, the dog booked into kennels.

We travelled to a jaw-dropping Tuscan villa, all mile-wide views with misty poplars. Just Mum, Dad, Jules and me (Miles was supposed to divert from a Euro-Railing trip with a bunch of university mates to join us but ran out of money somewhere in Germany).

Dad showered Mum with Florentine gifts: gold jewellery, leatherwork, *pietre dure*, ceramics and perfume. The sun shone. Crickets chirruped. A private cook came twice a day to conjure feasts.

Twenty-two, footloose and fancy-free, I got a nut-brown tan while reading my weight in self-improving fiction and flirting with Gino the pool man. After a couple of days, Jules stopped making expensive calls shouting at Reece – they were 'off' at the time – and joined me, also turning brown and flirting with Gino.

Mum got sunburn, then shellfish poisoning, then developed conjunctivitis and trapped a nerve in her back, which was so painful she begged and charmed an Italian doctor into prescribing opiates that could have knocked out a horse. On her birthday itself, spaced out on painkillers and prosecco, she shouted that she fucking hated Italy, and should have married Peter fucking O'Toole after all. Then she screamed that she was old. Then she fell in the pool.

At the time I thought my mother supremely selfish and ungrateful. Now I know first-hand that passing one's half-century is very tricky to navigate, regrets burning as brightly as the cake candles. She'd longed for a party, noise and hubbub to cheer her up and help her forget the newly empty nest at home, her beloved little sister who had died not long before, her lost career and lack of purpose. Instead Dad took her to *his* favourite place at ludicrous expense, where her two lazy daughters drew every eye, her body entered meltdown and she got a lot of handbags and painted pottery she didn't want.

No wonder she went on a charity bender afterwards.

I'm late dropping Edward at his trampolining club in Warwick (he isn't keen, but experts insist it's good for mental health), then it's a race across country to deliver Summer to her drama group in Evesham. Back up the A46 to pick up Edward then take him across to Stratford for his autism-friendly swimming class, about which he's also unenthusiastic. The leisure centre is next to a retail park with a supermarket megastore that I hurry round while he splashes. They have nothing on Jules's list, so I snatch up the nearest substitutes. I'm starting to sweat badly again, another hot flush bubbling up.

I collect Edward, still wearing his tinted swimming goggles with noise-cancelling headphones over them, deliberately blocking me out as punishment for expecting him to learn something that's 'an aqueous skill-set belonging to another species, and fundamentally incompatible with a Nintendo Switch'. I buy his favourite hot chocolate in exchange for the goggles, and we head to another retail park where there's a Game store, his usual reward for enduring the trampolining/swimming double act. While he's browsing, I dash next door to Boots for the drugs Mum asked me to get. An untrusting pharmacist fires lots of awkward questions at me about co-codamol addiction. My raging flush has alerted his suspicions, and no wonder; when I catch my shiny-faced reflection in the sunglasses stand, I look like a heroin addict going cold turkey.

Having sheepishly asked the pharmacist what he would recommend for, ahem, perimenopausal symptoms, I purchase a LadyCare magnet, Menopace, Pukka Womankind tea, and an arsenal of herbal supplements including one that boasts aphrodisiac qualities. I've also bought a battery-powered face fan. I'll be cool-headed and horny as Gwyneth Paltrow in no time, with added Boots points.

Ed has taken root in Game where he can't afford the second-hand Sonic classic he wants to buy and I refuse to sub him the twenty quid it costs.

'I WILL DIE HERE RIGHT NOW!' He throws himself down on his knees, covers his head with his hands and starts rocking.

This isn't unusual, although it's been a few months since it last happened and I was hoping that meant we'd turned a corner. I breathe deeply and resist telling onlookers 'he's autistic!' in the same tone characters in movies shout 'he has a gun!' (this is a tech store after all; I'm the weird neurotypical in here).

Instead, I crouch down beside my poor, stressed son, our

exit strategy tried and tested. 'You will not die, Ed. We are taking Dad his lunch on the boat. We will come here again next week. We're having lunch now.'

Up until Ed was eight or nine, it was obvious most bystanders blamed his tantrums on overindulgent parenting. Now he's bigger we're given a wider berth, just the occasional 'spoilt brat!' still coming our way. I sometimes dare myself to picture the scene when Ed's eighteen, broken-voiced and fully loaded with testosterone. Before that happens, I pray for his coping strategies to evolve, and I also pray for a better collective understanding of autism.

Ed's anxiety isn't just about the desire for gratification. While this moment started out with the same 'Can I have this?'/'No you can't' scrap so many parents have with kids in shops, its ramped up tenfold in nanoseconds because there's no sensory filter with Ed. He locks onto console games because they take him somewhere he can block out the confused unpredictability of real life he finds so hard to tolerate. Games have logical algorithms he can master, whereas human nature doesn't, especially his own.

Most Saturdays are not like this. He gets high on trampolining, grumbles good-naturedly about swimming and then we browse the games so he can decide what to save up for, then go home for lunch or visit Granna and Grandpa, always sticking to the same routine. Ed likes routines.

Most Saturdays don't usually involve waking up in his grandparents' cottage or lunch on the boat with testy Mum and Dad.

* * *

It's later than I'd hoped when we get to *The Tempest*'s mooring, by which time Ed's unhelpfully muttering '*Spin! Hammer! Fire! Jump!*' and '*Maaamma-hoo-ha-hoo, wow-wow!*' (he repeats game catchphrases when stressed). The marina café tables are all crammed with tourists; pretty girls with bare shoulders glance up from their phones as we pass, my son impersonating a small moustachioed Italian plumber. '*Mario time!*' '*Oh yeah!*' '*Hoo! Just what I needed!*'

There's a group of American tourists photographing *The Tempest*, and I'm forced to apologise when Ed burrows through them to step on board muttering, '*Super Mariooo Sunshine! Hoo!*'

Paddy looks up and glowers for a moment before realising it's us.

It makes sense to all but Paddy that the couple who have The Prettiest Cottage in Warwickshire would wish to keep their narrowboat moored in one of the county's Most Idyllic Spots, no matter how impractical. When they took ownership of *The Tempest*, Mum and Dad moved her from a humble canal-side marina to showstopping central Stratford's riverside where she's now a much-admired tourist attraction, often photographed and occasionally vandalised.

As well as being a piece of living industrial history below the waterline, an old traditional canal narrowboat like ours is a feat of lifelong craftsmanship above it, her interior as highly decorative as her colourful livery, a magical doll's house to peek into. Thirty years ago, after serving his apprenticeship with Shropshire's finest cabinet maker, Paddy refitted the inside of his father's narrowboat as a way of saying thank you for all the support his parents had given him. It took him every weekend for six months, a floating work of art and labour of love finished in oak, walnut and hand-veneered marine ply.

After Eddie's death, the narrowboat became a shrine. She may have changed ownership and name, but the lovingly planed, jointed and fitted woodwork inside the boat remains much as it was when Paddy first produced it as a young man, his bright future ahead of him like our children's are now. It's aged to beautiful glossy, mellow imperfection, the Hollanders' felled family tree carved and dovetailed into the boat's heart.

Today, as well as the tourists, Paddy has several enthusiastic gongoozlers (canal equivalent of trainspotters) watching him from the nearest café table.

He's out on the stern deck, T-shirt sleeves rolled up, looking manfully oily as he straddles the open engine inspection hatch, refitting something mechanical that he says is essential if Grandpa and Granny want to go out in her.

'Unlikely,' I point out kindly. Mum's refused to step on board since the Jack Russell jumped into a particularly ferocious river lock and everyone thought he'd drowned. He eventually bobbed up none the worse for wear, but the psychological damage was done.

One glimpse inside reveals spilling cupboards, upended cushions and all Mum's interior design touches buried beneath a mosaic of open toolkits.

'I'll tidy up in a bit,' he mutters.

'It's fine.'

We're horribly awkward, and yet I now feel oddly protective of him. I try to silently convey this as I give him his lunch, but he's too busy grumbling that I've bought him a Chicken Caesar wrap again to notice.

As a diversion, I tell him about my sister's exotic ingredients, aware that my voice is artificially bright, as though I'm performing a Victoria Wood sketch. I've always jumped through hoops to please him, even ones a square peg like Paddy can't easily follow.

When we first went out together, I played it indefatigably bright and bubbly, desperate to get laughs and be liked. I *really* fancied Paddy Hollander.

'Are you always this happy?' he'd ask with that slow smile.

'I'm like a stick of rock with the word "happy" running right through me!'

If he'd snapped that brittle act in two, he'd have found the word LIAR. It breaks my heart that he believed me. Nobody's that happy, Paddy. Surely you of all people knew that?

Now we're here.

While Edward grumpily takes his sandwich inside the boat to shade his gaming screen, Paddy and I stay in the sun.

'What's he upset about?' Paddy nods into the cabin.

I tell him about the twenty-pound game. 'How's your morning been?'

Paddy describes the function of the engine part he's refitting and I nod, not understanding a word, until he eventually says Joe FaceTimed him during a coffee break.

'That was sweet of him.' I'm pleased and a bit jealous.

'Yeah. Make up for not seeing me tomorrow.'

'You can always miss cricket.'

'Joe understands.' They're both keen cricketers. 'It's an important match.'

'I'm not sure Mum does.'

'She'll get over it.'

'She's miffed you hardly said a word to her yesterday evening. Or to Miles.' I feel mean as soon as I mention it, aware that it was just as much their fault.

He stares down at his wrap. 'Yeah, about last night,' he says, voice a tense undertone. 'I'm sorry I let you down.'

'Honestly, it's fine. I should probably have helped out more.'

'No, it was me. I could feel it happening but there's nothing I could do. Sometimes I just can't keep it up, Elz.'

I stare at him in shock. Paddy never willingly talks about our sex life, and this is practically in public! 'Ed's here,' I point out quickly.

'He's got his headphones on. This is important.'

'You drank too much wine, that's all.'

'I thought it might make me better at it, like it does you. You put on that big act when you drink. You're so good at it, making all the right noises, pretending you're loving it.'

'Are you suggesting I fake it?'

'We both know you fake it, Elz, especially when you're pissed. I can always tell.'

There's a loud thud in the cabin as Ed goes into the bathroom.

'I can't pretend like you can, OK? But next time I'm going to make a plan beforehand to help me get through it.'

'A plan?' Is he going to map out our bodies and the bed like a fitted kitchen, marking all inlets, outlets and perfect working triangles?

'It's what Joe does. He was telling me how well it worked for him at the ball last night. He tried it with a couple of girls he's never met before and lasted over an hour with each. It's like having a playlist at a gig, he says.'

I'm struck dumb. Can our son really have been sharing sexual tips with his father?

'Maybe it's easier to keep it up with someone new,' Paddy looks at me earnestly.

I'm so shocked I can hardly breathe. Surely I must be hearing him wrong.

'I think I need to try it with strangers, Elz. You've Only Got One Life, Joe says. I'm not getting any younger.'

Before I can slap him or hiss that I could have bought him a packet of Viagra Connect in Boots there's a furious rattling and screaming from inside the narrowboat.

Edward has got trapped inside the bathroom – the lock's faulty – which causes much panicked consternation and Mario catchphrases as Paddy fiddles around with a screwdriver.

'Why don't you just replace the fitting, Dad?' Ed fumes when he's finally sprung out.

'This is a very rare Victorian Ashwell's Patent Toilet Lock, Edward.' Paddy starts screwing the facing plate back on. 'It came out of The Barge Inn where me and your granddad used to drink.' (Only Paddy could get sentimental over a well-engineered loo lock.)

But Ed's not interested, making pointed yawning noises as he returns to his game.

'That one's no better at backchat than his dad.' Paddy flicks the brass catch between *Engaged* and *Vacant* to test it. 'He should try Joe's method.'

At last the penny drops (as if into a cranky old loo lock) as I realise: 'You and Joe were discussing how to keep up a conversation?'

'Hollander men aren't small talkers, even clever ones like our boys.'

Watching him, I experience a fierce, blushing rush of affection and remorse. I reach out to touch his face. 'It's my family who are bloody hard going. Miles was deliberately rude for a start. I'm sorry you two have fallen out.'

'It's nothing.' He ducks his head away. 'He prefers flying now.'

Whatever the reason, I can guess how much he misses having somebody to crew the boat with. I pat *The Tempest's* bulkhead wall. 'Let's take her out soon.'

Paddy looks thrilled.

Another agonised wail from Ed makes us both spin round. His console has run out of charge, and the cable has been left at his grandparents'. 'I am going to DIE RIGHT NOW! *Mamma Mia! Let's a-go.* MY LIFE IS OVER!'

8

Fixed Time

'Why are all boats "she"?' Edward asks as we drive out of Stratford, meltdown forgotten now that we're back on a routine course.

'Ship figureheads used to be female to protect sailors at sea,' I reply. 'They probably liked to think of them being goddesses or mother figures to look after them.'

'You are my mother figure,' he says, 'and our family's figure head.'

'Thank you.' I wait. There's usually an Ed afterthought.

'Although you're an atheist and not very good at steering so your boat it would probably be scuppered with significant loss of life.'

A bottle of lunchtime Petit Chablis has taken the edge off the hangovers at Granna and Grandpa's cottage. Miles and Dad are both having a siesta on sunloungers in the garden. Mum's inside listening to *Any Answers*.

Despite protesting that I really haven't got time to stay, I end up with a mug of tea thrust at me, so I help Mum wash up lunch and listen with more satisfaction than I should as she grumbles about Jules's family 'treating this place like a hotel! And Reece is totally impractical. Which reminds me, can you look at my computer? I'm trying to write to Melvyn Bragg about his sinuses again but it won't print it out. Miles has no time, and you are so clever with these things, darling girl.'

After turning it off and on again I'm clueless. Thank goodness for Edward who has it fixed in minutes, runs a virus check and finds a link to the vintage Sonic game he wants to buy so that he can show Granny.

Mum obligingly gives him the twenty quid, telling him, 'You boys are so much better with computers than we girls.'

'Mum!' I reproach.

'You're not a *girl*, Granny,' Ed points out pragmatically, pocketing the money. 'And actually, the best pupil in my IT class *is* one.'

I want to hug him.

'Don't say "actually", Edward,' Mum tells him off sharply.

'If you do think you're a girl, Granny,' the Ed afterthought strikes a grave note, 'it's probably because you are having a second childhood.'

Edward is very fixed in his ways, unwittingly selfish, anxious if his routine is altered, and characteristically autistic (he prefers 'Asperger's', but that was no longer a term our local authority's CAMHS team accepted by the time Ed joined their statemented pupils on one glorious united spectrum, a magic roundabout of difference). He was diagnosed in Year Three, six years ago. We were lucky it was spotted relatively early and although at first I hated the idea of him being labelled, he was so profoundly grateful to find where he belonged, autism is now his designer label.

In many ways, Edward strongly resembles his namesake Eddie, the Hollander grandfather he never got to meet, a fellow gent, geek and control freak, with the same Weetabix thatch of hair above a Ferris Bueller face, and that high anxiety which folds away into itself. Paddy disagrees, but I believe our son comes from the over-diagnosed generation whereas his grandfather hailed from an undiagnosed one, much as ours remains.

Edward might not show his best side when we're places in which he doesn't feel safe – let's face it, anywhere that's not home. And he might rather get lost in a screen than in table talk, but he is the most family-oriented and devoted of all of us and says he never wants to leave home. He's made me laugh and cry more than any other human being I've ever known. The battle to keep him in mainstream education was epic but I'd fight anybody to give Edward Hollander an equal chance in this world, not because he's autistic or disabled or labelled. Because he's brilliantly, uniquely, totally Ed and I love him.

Today, that love is severely tested by another trip to Game, but it survives intact.

We're home at last, and my menopausal mood-swing-o-meter is already heading into the red again. Where do Saturdays go?

I've driven almost a hundred and fifty miles today, which is not only a shameful carbon footprint, but I haven't yet spared a moment to think about noble, immortal acts to make life feel more worthwhile.

Now Summer's back from drama club and she and Ed both have lots of homework they must crack on with because we're out tomorrow. I put away shopping then tackle the washing mountain and start prepping the lamb meatballs for tonight (why didn't I just buy ready-made frozen ones, why?) While I'm chopping onions, I take a long call from Lou who's in floods because her ex has taken the kids on a mini-break with Babysitter Girlfriend – 'Daisy says she could hear them having sex through the wall!' – I listen in horrified sympathy, phone sliding round between ear and shoulder so I can carry on chopping because the kids are in the room and I can't go hands-free – she's said 'slutty little tart' three times and 'his fucking cock' twice – and this sauce needs to go on asap.

No sooner has the call ended than Paddy's back, mucking up the downstairs shower with black engine oil marks before dripping round the utility room in nothing but a towel and sifting through my ordered piles of washing, looking for his cricket whites, only to discover they're still dirty in his kitbag from last weekend.

'Why are they still in here?'

'Is that a rhetorical question or do you genuinely have amnesia?'

We start to scrap and I feel aggrieved for womankind, which could partly be me channelling Lou's mood. I tell Paddy it's not always my responsibility to unearth his cricket gear, although I'd have washed them if he'd put them out.

And then he tuts (he knows I hate tutting) and asks if I've remembered the cake for tomorrow's home match?

'You expect me to bake a cake for your cricket tea?' I'm shocked.

'You offered. And you told me to remind you.'

Certain I didn't, I reply that I'm no more fucking Nigella than I am his laundrymaid, and he points out that I've washed everybody else's sports stuff so it's a bit deliberate to leave his out and am I trying to make a point? I hiss, 'Yes, my point is that you're a bloody dinosaur!'

I miss having Arty to walk my fierce temper off.

Feeling martyred and telltale hot, I march out to the garden with the plastic recycling. As soon as I do, breathing in a cloud of jasmine, I have a crystal clear flashback of sitting out here last Sunday evening, the best part of a bottle of rosé up, consoling Paddy for being caught for ten and offering to bake a cake for his next cricket tea. Oh, my lousy menopausal memory.

Now I mutter dark oaths by the bins, trying not to cry, hating myself for the brittle, self-absorbed cow I've become. 'You need to pull your fucking self together,' I tell myself. 'Or non-fucking self.'

'Is it *Persuasion* or *Sense and Sensibility*?' asks a voice beyond the garden fence with a clink as our affable retired neighbour recycles a jam jar.

Inside, I start baking for Paddy. My emancipated soul burns, especially when Summer joins me to take over mixing lemon juice and caster sugar to pour over two cakes hot from the oven, her favourite task, then photographs her handiwork on her phone. Seconds later a luscious, lip-smacking shot is cropped, filtered, captioned *Making drizzle cake with my fam!* tagged *#baking #yummy #cake #homemade #instafood #delicious* and shared with thousands of followers.

'I love it when we bake,' she confides.

It's our closest moment of (hashtag) mother-and-daughter togetherness in weeks.

'Can I take the spare one into school next week? I think lemon drizzle is Mr Owusu's favourite cake.' She checks his Instagram feed, heavily populated thanks to a second career in photography that's given him a cult status at school. In amongst leggy models, broody musician portraits and abstract landscapes are some seriously high-end food shots. 'No, it's OK, it's pistachio and lime.' She likes the image with colour-appropriate heart emojis. 'We can make that next time!'

How is it possible that Paddy and I have raised a daughter whose virtual world revolves around a fifties Disney Princess idyll of old-fashioned femininity, from its shapely eyebrows to its sweet-scented gingham kitchen?

'Something smells good!' Paddy appears from the garage with a box of beer under one arm and his cricket pads and bat over his shoulder. He's still wearing his towel.

Has he been in there all this time, I wonder? He's looking a bit shifty. Best not to ask.

Ah, the sweet scent of domestic bliss.

Let's get this out there: Paddy and I are both products of traditional, gender-divided upbringings, inheriting a combination of latent chauvinism and conflicted feminism that can make for a bumpy ride.

When I was a teenager, I mistakenly believed feminism was for academics or activists who always seemed impossibly articulate and grown-up, superbeings like Susan Sontag and Gloria Steinem or scary placard bearers like Andrea Dworkin. I never doubted I was the mental and emotional equal to any man; it was feminists I felt inferior to. While they wrote earnest, uncompromising books for Virago, I devoured romantic bonkbusters and watched *Baywatch*. I borrowed *The Female Eunuch* from the library when I was fourteen, then speed-read it shamelessly, dying to get back to Shirley Conran's *Lace*.

It wasn't until my late thirties that I felt comfortable even calling myself a feminist, by which time Tina Fey and Joan Rivers had laughed me into it, the Spice Girls had zig-a-zig-zigged for girl power, and Caitlin Moran was mixing feminism up with TopShop and Wookies in a fifth wave that made up for not being able to quote directly from *The Second Sex*.

Paddy's upbringing was no less bilateral. Unlike my parents, both his worked, and both for the same employer: his dad maintained the machinery on the factory floor and benefitted from a union, a men's-only social club and a pension scheme; his mum served part-time in the canteen for pin money. Eddie divided his free time between his shed, lock-up, allotment, pub, club, football stands and his *Lady Love*; Ruth went to bingo with the girls from work. As with my parents, Eddie played no part in housework, childcare or cooking, but had complete autonomy over the bills and television remote control.

When Paddy and I said 'I Do' it was in the understanding that our marriage wouldn't be like our parents'. We're equals. We both toil just as hard for our crusts. I might currently earn more than my husband, but it's worked both ways during our marriage. And he's always been prepared to do his domestic half (happy would be pushing it); the problem is I like the way I do those things more, and so does he, just as I prefer the way he reverses the dinghy trailer into the garage or changes a tap washer.

I worry that we've passed our subconscious prejudices onto our children. Not so much Joe, a fluidly postmillennial male, but Summer is set-dressing her life to be far too perfect, and Ed has distinctly binary leanings. In an age when gender-neutral parenting is all the rage, were Paddy and I too brainwashed by our own childhood diet of Peter and Jane, Terry and June and He-Man and She-Ra to shake off the sexual stereotypes? Or am I just much better at baking cakes?

Saturday night is 'family' night. We eat the lamb balls (Summer leaves the couscous, Ed leaves the sauce, I eat my tiny actress portion, and Paddy demolishes everyone's leftovers plus two slices of bread and butter as a defiant class statement). Then we retire to sofas to watch rubbish game and talent shows on 'proper TV' (well, I watch them and answer/comment/criticise excitedly while the other three look at their smaller screens).

Throughout, my legs tingle and jump uncomfortably. This is new.

Paddy and I sit an unfriendly dog width apart. He drinks a lot of beer. I take this as justification to drink too much wine, reaching out to stroke a cushion in lieu of Arty.

Just as I start to well up, a book is placed on the sofa arm beside me: *1001 Amazing Facts*. I look up and see Ed flicking his knuckles, a repetitive stimming action he does when he's excited or anxious.

'For you.'

'But it's yours.' He won it in a Blue Peter competition along with an orange badge, and he treasures both.

'I want you to have it as an Act of Kindness.'

Ed's year at school have all been tasked with 'Acts of Kindness' this term, the theory being that Aspies have to learn traits like generosity, empathy and polite conversation which come instinctively to neurotypical people. He has a habit of choosing unlikely moments to enact these, but I'm absurdly touched that so many of these gestures are bestowed on me.

'It's to help you with television quizzes because your average is low,' he explains.

'Thank you, Ed. That's so thoughtful.'

Tonight's kindness makes me even more teary, which he doesn't understand at all. I hug the book to my chest which he doesn't understand either, so I look up an Amazing Fact about the number of bridges on the Trans-Siberian railway instead, which pleases him enormously (3,901 if you're interested).

After Ed slopes off to bed, Summer talks us into watching the first episode of *Killing Eve* Series Two. Paddy budges up to sit on Arty's ghost, arm swinging protectively round me at the sight of Villanelle in Batman pyjamas breaking a kid's neck. He knows this sort of thing freaks me out. I'm practically hyperventilating with discomfort for the rest of the episode, partly because it's way too sadistic for my taste, and partly because his arm is making me very hot. I don't want to shrug it off because we're both trying to make up for last night, and gestures like this are rare for Paddy. Plus, I keep jumping out of my skin in horror.

I've never been particularly comfortable with violence on screen, from the flying ketchup of eighties slasher movies to the flat-capped, gritty beatings of *Peaky Blinders*. My aversion worsened after I had children, and recently I've found it upsets me more than ever.

I question why we are so obsessed with human pain and suffering, what is it about us that we need to recreate man's violence against man for our own thrill-seeking entertainment, close up in HD? Must we celebrate unnatural death in order to feel alive?

The thought makes me both uncomfortable and terribly sad, and to wonder what is it about me that I cannot bear to watch something millions love, including my own family? Is it another middle-aged woman thing? Yet another hormone awry, robbing me of taking pleasure from something? Sex and violence. Please don't let shopping be next.

When the credits finally roll, Paddy and Summer want to binge watch the rest of the series, outvoting my plea for an award-winning literary tear-jerker on Beeb Two. My legs are running with jumpy electric twitches now; I cross them, fold them under me, stick them straight out on a footstool and then shake them about, which feels quite good until

Summer snaps at me that I'm deliberately spoiling the programme.

The wine bottle is empty.

'I might go to bed.'

Paddy's arm stays round me. 'Give it a chance.'

He likes protecting me.

My legs full of spasms, I stick it out until a creepy male character is stabbed in the throat with a knitting needle then has a dirty loo brush shoved in his mouth, at which point I wriggle out from Paddy's arm (he's too engrossed by now to complain), wish them goodnight and head upstairs. Free to waggle my legs around at will, the twitching eases.

In bed, I Google leg twitches to learn that Restless Leg Syndrome is a common side effect of poor circulation, itself a common side effect of low oestrogen, AKA female decrepitude.

The phone vibrates with a late-night message from my brother, a gif of Simon Le Bon on the prow of a yacht in the 'Rio' pop video (Miles and I were both massive Durannies), along with a line of smile emojis and *SOS! Bring life jackets tomz.*

He must be out in the garden to have a phone signal.

Yawning, I send a tired *What's Up?*

He replies with a screaming shock face: *Jules gave Ma and Pa the downsizing lecture. Now she's being a complete cow. Help!*

I'm not taking sides.

Don't be so Swiss, Sis.

It takes me a moment to work out he means neutral. Miles loves talking in riddles. His mind remains a puzzle

I've been trying to unravel since the day he arrived in the Finch family, red-faced and wailing, and therefore unlikely to make it into the *Thame Gazette*'s Beautiful Baby page, his six-year-old big sister Julia told me.

'Mummy wouldn't have needed this one if you'd been born a boy, Eliza,' she'd pointed out pragmatically.

'He ith going to be my betht fwiend,' said three-year-old me.

A promise I kept for the next twenty years until Miles broke too many girlfriends' hearts, crashed my car and bought himself a Club 18-30 holiday on my credit card. I should have spotted the signs of acute narcissism when my Bionic Woman became his first martyr.

My brother has sent a picture of Emmental cheese labelled *YOU*.

Holier than thou, I reply.

Haha! What do you call a small Swiss man?

Toblergnome. We spent much of our childhood reading joke books out to each other.

He sends a picture of Julie Andrews atop a mountain range in *The Sound of Music*.

Please stop interrupting my midlife crisis, I complain, adding green and black love hearts, pressing send.

I have friends who don't communicate with their siblings from one year to the next, yet my childhood remains so close to the surface it still colours everything.

Now he's sent rainbow love hearts and a grumpy gorilla meme that reads *You can't have a midlife crisis if you don't have a life!* to which he's added a row of crying laughing emoticons.

I decide to ignore it. They should make a menopausal

emoji, I reflect. A bad-tempered, red-faced, tearful sweaty one. Maybe I'll get Edward to submit a design to Unicode. Could that be my lifetime legacy?

Yawning, I re-open Google to finally search out noble acts and challenges that might make my life feel more worthwhile. Where shall we begin? A sponsored sky dive, community litter-picking, a silent retreat for conflicted feminists?

I join Greenpeace.

Slow start, but worthwhile.

Now I renew that long-lapsed Amnesty membership and sign half a dozen Change.org petitions. I'm on a roll!

Pop-ups remind me that I must share all this to social media to help spread the word, but I hesitate. To those who disapprove of public virtue signalling, it's anathema, to the woke it's never enough. And I need to do something more... Just *more*. Charity isn't immortality, even Gift-Aided. We need to give more of ourselves than money. More of our soul. In a secular society, this is our redemption, and it's all too often done with the regret of hindsight, like my mother's ambition to take on the mighty Amazon or Jules running marathons from a marriage she'll never leave.

My expectations are lower; I simply want to feel like the woman I was, to tap back into her I-can-do-anything lifeforce.

Younger Me had no bucket list, not even a To Do list, just infinite possibilities of self-improvement stretching out into the misty distance ahead.

Now that misty distance is shortening rapidly towards cataracts and cloudy urine samples, I worry about all the things I always meant to do – the travelling, the culture, the mind-blowing sex, the big career break, the kind acts, the immortality. Can I still live that life?

I'm too tired to decide...

I must have been asleep an hour or more by the time Paddy joins me. I drift up to semi-consciousness enough to feel him prise the phone out of my hands and lean across me to put it on my bedside table. He settles back to briefly spoon, his erection pressing into my back. He knows full well it won't get any action. He's just making a point.

9

Crunch Time

We've just collected Joe from the station, and I'm trying not to be too tearful and overexcited by this all-too-brief gathering of my three children. Any lapse of concentration could prove fatal because Summer is behind the wheel of the rust bucket, L-plates slapped on fore and aft, Nike eyebrows furrowed in concentration.

It's terrifying. We start out by narrowly missing a cyclist, then fail to spot the lights changing at a pedestrian crossing. June is flaming at max, and so am I, my flush triggered by hot upholstery and fear.

'It's thirty along here, Summer,' I murmur, eyeing the speedo.

'I *know*. Hey, tell us all about uni, big bro!' she calls out to Joe. 'Stop yakking about Sonic, Ed.'

Ed's voice, machine-gun fast, is midway through urgently describing his new game in painstaking detail. He breaks off with an overexcited, 'Yeah, how's it hanging, mate?'

I bite down on a smile, stealing a look over my shoulder

because it's such an un-Ed thing to say and he's trying to look cool for Joe. Although he's poker faced as usual, his gaze holds his brother's, a rare honour from the boy for whom eye contact can be as hard as one-armed press-ups.

'Life's good thanks, Ed,' Joe yawns away his own smile.

Understated in white T-shirt and jeans, hat brim tipped low over sleepy eyes, he's wearing three days' stubble, a chronic hangover and a new compass tattoo on his wrist that Summer's already announced she wants too but cannot have or Dad Will Freak.

Each time I see our son, the man he's going to be has taken him over a little more, a stronger version of the boy we're letting go. Joe possesses Paddy's inner quietness – along with the light eyes and hair – only with more self-belief. Describing student life with customary wry wit, his voice has the same husky lilt as Paddy's when he was younger.

My little interjections of 'I remember that!' and 'I was just the same!' bounce off them all. I must stop trying to relate everything to *me*. I'm just Mum, my previous existence the stuff of myths.

A car horn makes me swing back in a panic. 'You're in the lane for the superstore, Summer, keep left.'

'I am *not*! Don't lecture me, Mum!'

'I'm just giving you a driving lesson.'

'Correction, you are a responsible adult with a full driving licence *accompanying* me while I *practise*.' The car shudders as we tackle a roundabout in fourth gear.

After fifteen hours of professional lessons and with her test already booked, Summer needs this practice. Boy does she need it, being both a supremely confident yet slapdash learner.

Sticky with sweat, I try to get Robbie Williams' 'I Love My Life' going in my head for positive energy, today's low having started when Paddy left the house so absurdly early it scuppered any tea-in-bed rapprochement plans (the match doesn't start until two, but he said something about running errands for team captain Simon, from whom he rents his workshop barn so cheaply we're perpetually in his debt).

We drift right, on a collision course with a panicked-looking elderly man in a Honda Jazz.

'Watch out!' I don't love my life again yet and now I'm losing it, and my beloved children with it.

I reach across to snatch the wheel left to save our souls. She slaps me away.

We miraculously don't crash.

Summer drives on, fuming at fellow road users. 'That was *her* fault!... Why did he do that?...Get out of my braking distance, bastard!'

She drives just like her mother, bless her.

It still takes me by surprise that I continually relive my childhood through parenthood, the bittersweet parallel of witnessing my own mistakes repeated by my children no matter how eager I am to spare them the same pain.

Like me, Summer sees throwing away her L plates as her freedom pass, and she'll need the same L for Luck to pass first time. Woefully underprepared in Mum's Renault 5 (her advice before the test simply 'act like you know how to drive, darling girl'), I put in a performance of a lifetime that granted me a full licence. The thirty-three-year gumball rally that's followed may not always have been pretty, but I can boast a decade's No Claims Bonus.

What I'm not, and never will be, is a good teacher. My parents were just the same when we were learning to drive: Mum would grip her seatbelt release and the door handle and shriek 'slower, ye Gods!'; Dad would just fall asleep, usually after a boozy lunch. I disagree with anybody who says: 'those who can't, teach'. Those who can teach are angels, higher beings of patience and faith. Especially travelling at speed through a popular tourist destination without dual controls.

'Not too fast,' I advise as Summer navigates Warwick like she's in a car chase.

She brakes and then tuts at me. Tuts! She knows I hate tutting. I tut back. It escalates. We end up sounding like a pair of furiously dripping taps.

Then I hear Ed whispering, 'It makes ladies barren and mad, Auntie Jules says.'

'What's that?' I snap.

'Nothing.' His headphones go back on and I feel guilty for breaking up the chat.

I love my life, Robbie reminds me.

'I spoke to Dad yesterday, did he say?' Joe leans forwards.

'Yes, he enjoyed your tips on making conversation with girls.'

He laughs. 'Yeah, that cheered him up. He was seriously salty?' (Both Joe and Summer do that younger generation thing of turning statements into questions to be less confrontational. It has an adverse effect on me.)

'What is "salty"?'

'Grumpy,' Summer translates, telling Joe, 'The Elds have had a big argument.'

I had no idea she knew the scale of the Dog Fight. (And I wish she wouldn't refer to her father and me as 'Elds', which makes us sound like leathery animatronics from a fantasy movie.)

'It's your anniversary next week isn't it, Mum?' asks Joe. 'Are you planning anything special?'

'Let's focus on today first. This lunch is all about Grandpa.'

'Yesterday I told Dad he should take—'

'Bus lane, Summer!' I yelp as we sail inside a line of static traffic. 'Sorry, Joe, you told Dad he should take what? Was it "Mum to the Seychelles"?'

'A chill pill?' He exchanges a look with Summer in the rear-view mirror.

As we crawl along, I feel that throat-grip of worry about Paddy and the fissure between us.

'Why not have a night or two away together?' Joe's not letting it drop. 'You said you're not recording next week, and Ed's just told me he's away at PGL camp?'

'And don't forget I'm staying over with Alice midweek so we can rehearse late!' Summer adds over-brightly. (I always suspected there was something behind that plan.)

'Has Dad put you up to this?' I demand.

'Hardly.' Joe leans in between us, hat brim tipped back. 'You know what he's like? He sounded a bit down yesterday, that's all? Maybe you could both use a change of scene?'

I swallow the tight knot again and say nothing.

'Give it some thought maybe?' Joe's the family diplomat.

'Of course I will, but I do have more than one job to keep this family afloat and I am actually working next week.'

I know they think I'm having a little dig at their father, and I feel bad, because I am.

Then Summer mutters 'Edible undies party,' and they both snigger.

'That was *years* ago,' I huff, aware she's got me back on Paddy's behalf.

As an occasionally 'resting' actor, I've waitressed and temped, manned tills and reception desks, entertained at children's parties and spent one unforgettable summer sweltering in a fake fur bear costume as a local theme park's mascot, accompanied at all times by a minder to stop children throwing food at me.

Being an Ann Summers 'Party Ambassador' was, briefly, a terrific earner. Girls nights in, hen parties, birthdays, I'd turn up with a box of goodies and earn enough to keep my (then tiny) children in Mini Boden. Paddy was going through his bad patch, so I played down the sex toy side of things and let him think it was more of a beauty accessories line. In the end I gave it up after just a few months; the acting work had picked up and I'd already plundered most of my young mum network from nursery and primary school – plus continual exposure to a sisterhood pissed on prosecco and giggling over Rampant Rabbits was quelling my desire ever to have sex again.

The reason the children now know and tease me about the 'edible undies parties' is because years later Arty found her way into a box of leftover stock in the garage I'd completely forgotten was there. A half-chewed liquorice mankini thrown up on the sitting room carpet while you're all watching *Thunderbirds* is hard to ignore.

Of all my 'resting' jobs, the estate agency work I do now is the one I enjoy most, accompanying viewings for Warwickshire's funkiest all-female estate agency. It's flexible and pays for my wine. I already have a riverside retirement flat booked in at ten tomorrow and there's two more pencilled in afterwards. That's the Aldi Pinot Grigio sorted for the week.

One job I'm guaranteed never to do when resting is driving instruction.

Still trying to get out of the bus lane, Summer's distracted by Joe asking, 'Is Kwasi still working at your school?'

The car drifts tellingly as she starts gushing about his creative genius.

Joe and Kwasi Owusu – the digital image wunderkind who assists in Summer's art class and stirs her wakening heart – overlapped at sixth form college and briefly even played in the same band. It marked the start of Summer's crush, and it makes the situation at school doubly awkward because she first viewed 'Mr Owusu' as one of her brother's peers; although a year older than Joe and already out grafting for his art, he now seems a lot more grown-up.

'You should have seen his Generation Fluid exhibition in the Art House,' Summer's babbling, car veering towards the kerb now. 'It was like *so* groundbreaking. He's doing a shoot with Lady Charlecote next week which he's—'

'BRAKE, Summer!' The back end of a bus is coming up to meet us.

She does a very creditable emergency stop inches from a tailgate wrap poster for *Toy Story 4*. Woody looks down on us kindly.

'Quick reactions, excellent,' I congratulate, waiting for my heartbeat to drop below a hundred and fifty, and try to lift the mood with a '*Yee-haw! Giddy-up partner! We've got to get this wagon train a-moving.*' My kids were raised on *Toy Story*.

'*Reach for the sky!*' Joe gets behind me.

'Who sang that?' I hum the melody. Pop trivia always soothes Summer.

'It's *stars*. S Club 7. Reach for the *stars*,' she corrects, still glowering and adding her own Woody catchphrase, '*This town ain't big enough for the two of us.*'

I manage to stop myself singing the Sparks song. At least the hot flush has abated and soon we're heading away from Warwick and they're singing 'You Gotta Friend in Me'.

I say, in my calm, modulated instructor voice, 'You're going to turn right ahead where it's signposted Barford.'

Still singing, Summer takes no notice.

'You should start to slow down about here.'

Her phone is in the holder clipped to the air vent on the dash and rattles like mad when the car goes over forty. As she reaches out a hand to steady it, I realise she is singing *into* it.

Is she *recording* this?

'Slow DOWN! Mirror, signal, manoeuvre!'

'See what I have to put up with, people?' she tells the phone camera as she looks, indicates, brakes and executes a perfect turn.

'Slayed it, sis!' Joe encourages.

'You're doing really well, Summer, but this phone goes off.' I pluck it out and put it in the glove box.

'That's so *unfair*!' She's yet to learn this gets her nowhere, fourteen years after first coining the phrase. She still stamps her foot too, the speedo rapidly passing forty.

'Summer, don't go too—'

'I *do know* the speed limit, Mum? I passed my theory already?' To prove her point, Summer cruises at fifty. It feels ludicrously fast.

Behind us, in his noise-cancelling headphones playing with a puzzle cube, Ed is oblivious to the danger we're all in. Joe's also surprisingly chilled. He passed his test two years ago but hasn't got his own car and rarely ever drives, so I suspect he hasn't enough practical experience on the roads to appreciate that almost the entire Hollander family may be wiped out at any moment.

I drive faster than this along here, I remind myself. But irrational, over-imaginative terror has gripped me all too often of late, and I can work up a tragedy out of any scenario: I've become a nervous flyer when I used to love it; I fight panic on big theme park rides; I dislike being alone in crowded public spaces. On a recent trip to London, travelling in the Underground, I grew so obsessed that an abandoned Maltesers box on the window shelf behind me contained an incendiary device that I started to silently hyperventilate, first swapping seats, then changing carriages at the next stop and finally getting off at the station after that to wait for another Circle Line tube, on which I sat down to find myself beside an abandoned Quality Street box.

I never used to be this phobic, this illogical, and I know that it's connected to menopause, but that doesn't stop me being scared stiff that I might never get my reckless streak back.

And I may be a pathetic wimp compared to my elderly mother who wants to travel along the Amazon or my little brother learning to fly, but neither of those two have volunteered to sit next to Summer doing sixty miles per hour along a country road, I notice.

'If I'm going to beat Uncle Miles to a licence, I need more practice like this,' Summer says as we race through tree-dappled sunlight towards Barford. 'He's already flying solo. Did you hear that, Joe? Miles is flying solo!'

They're soon having an animated conversation about Uncle Miles, who they both adore and proudly support his new-found openness about his sexuality.

'Flying's like a metaphor for his freedom, yeah?' Joe insists.

'He must have always known?' says Summer. 'It's not like it's a choice.' She checks her mirrors and indicates to overtake a cyclist. 'It's so sad that Boomers like Miles still felt they had to deny nature and live a lie.'

'We're not old enough to be Boomers!' I interject but am ignored because a) I'm being shallow and b) they're already hot-swapping a timeline of Gay Pride, Stonewall, AIDS, Section 28 and same-sex marriage at such competitive, bright and brilliant speed that even though I've lived through it all, I'm not sure I know enough hard-and-fast facts to contribute, or that my terminology is up to date.

Summer's driving beautifully, albeit whilst banging the steering wheel saying, 'HIV's amplified media stigma vetoed too many men's freedom to be out without prejudice!'

How does she *know* so much, I wonder? At their age, I hoped George Michael and Princess Diana would shack up and have a clutch of ravishing children. I didn't even guess Elton John was gay until he came out. Not a clue.

Theatre's diversity came as a revelation for a girl from the provinces, and the friendships I made through my twenties taught me life lessons about sexuality and acceptance I've never forgotten. But it wasn't until we moved to Leamington that I realised how rare and urban my experience is for my age group, certainly among the fellow parents, village league cricketers, canal enthusiasts and even the arty-farty theatre lovers that form our social circle. Our leafy Regency spa town just isn't *gay* enough – the one exception being each August when it hosts Warwickshire's annual Gay Pride, a family-friendly jamboree in the Pump Room Gardens, its inclusivity lovely, but all too transient.

Given my insight, my brother's news didn't come as the shock it was to some, although I hadn't taken any suspicions very seriously through his lifelong smokescreen of gorgeous girlfriends and car-crash marriages.

We still don't really talk about it, Miles and me. As siblings, we have remained extremely childish into adulthood. When together, we're never the grown-ups.

Our children's generation, by contrast, are very grown-up indeed, and like nothing more than playing Eye-Spy Gender and Diversity Bias to pass a journey.

'I can't believe Dad cancelled Miles as soon as he came out as gay,' Joe says.

'I thought they fell out because Miles chose flying over barging?' Summer suggests, her loyalty torn.

'It's sad that Dad can't see how loudly his silence speaks against LGBTQ plus acceptance?'

I grumpily want to ask if 'pastsexual' qualifies for a letter but instead say, 'Your father is *not* homophobic!' Because he isn't. 'Look, your uncle lost interest in the narrowboat, that's all. We're all of us anti-hate in this family, even the "Very Elds". I've never heard your dad say a word against anybody gay.'

A pointed look passes between them via the rear-view mirror and Joe says gently, 'What you need to understand, Mum, is that anti-fascism has been repurposed? It's not enough to be anti-homophobic or anti-racist or anti-sexist these days? You have to be *actively* anti?'

'I marched for this stuff before you were born. And *please* stop saying everything like it's a bloody question!'

'Sorry. Let's not argue about it.' He pacifies, my tactful envoy for his shiny post-millennial generation with its sad social conscience and upcycled vocabulary.

'The struggle is real. Hashtag Mum's Triggered?' Summer always likes to have the last word.

'Hashtag, Watch your speed?' I mimic the inflexion. I like having the last word more.

They titter, although I suspect that they are laughing at me not with me.

I'm starting to sweat up again, the flush circling back round like a storm. On days when I get five or six in quick succession, I try to be positive by counting them cumulatively, like magpies – two for joy – but I nevertheless long to wail '*it's so unfair*'.

* * *

Life *is* unfair. We campaign against it when we're young, grumble when we're older, chip away at it in between. Then our children start talking down to us, think they've reinvented protest, accuse us of bigotry without context, and it's *not fair.*

I did it to my own parents, so I've had it coming, this middle-aged portal which transports us from passionate young things to reactionaries in the blink of the media's eye, in the same way it offers us 'retro' music and thinks we should start planning for our retirement. We don't just age, we are aged, herded together somewhere around fifty and tagged 'Over'.

If my children think I am no longer 'active' enough, they obviously have no idea what goes on in my head. This Over is an overactive over-thinker through and through.

Summer's mobile starts ringing in the glovebox while we're driving through the picturesque, traffic-calmed village of Barford. A moment later, I feel my stomach hollow as we fly over a speedbump she's failed to spot.

Like me, she assigns family and friends personalised ringtones; whoever 'Vossi Bop' is must be important, because she goes on to mount the curb and then stalls at the mini roundabout, embarrassment and road rage building. 'Who put that thing there!'

'Vossi Bop' stops. I tactfully say nothing – mainly because I'm still too winded by my seatbelt – and Summer restarts the engine. My hot flush has now been topped up by an adrenaline spike and I'm overheating so much my eyelashes have sweat beads in them.

I stick my head out of the window for a moment to breathe in some cool rushing air. (It feels good. No wonder Arty used to do it, ears inside out, tongue lolling out. But I don't try that.)

When I duck back in, hair on end, Joe and Summer are chatting about the family getaway to Cornwall later this summer. Apparently it's the poorest county in England, my holiday choice no doubt yet more evidence of our lack of active anti-fascism.

I could point out that they were happy enough to take all the cream teas, pasties and surfing on offer during last year's fortnight in St Ives with Granna, Grandpa, Miles and his wife (their last summer together, although nobody guessed at the time). But I don't want to risk touching on the new-found divide between their father and uncle again.

We slow behind a tractor with a faded, peeling LIBERTY & LIVELIHOOD sticker in its rear window, a collie smiling back at us over it.

I feel another pang for Arty.

And then I remember something Paddy said during the Dog Fight.

'I don't want a *new* dog!' I'd sobbed. 'Losing Arty was like losing a part of me, and I want her back! I don't want anything else. *Her* love, *her* friendship, *her* loyalty. She needed me and I miss her, Paddy. I miss her needing me.'

I wasn't just talking about Arty, although I didn't realise it at the time.

The pent-up anger that came out of him rocked me back on my heels. 'All those things you mention – friendship, loyalty, love even – they're based on trust, not need. Why does everyone in your bloody family mistake the two? If I trust somebody, I don't expect them to change the rules without warning. I don't bloody need that!'

This was quite a speech for Paddy, and one I took at face value. I thought he was talking about the change in me: hotter, fatter, angrier, less sexual and a lot harder to love. That change of rules. It cut me to ashes, and the argument turned nastier, my hackles high, my ego shredded.

Now I replay it with less red mist: *If I trust somebody, I don't expect them to change the rules without warning.*

He couldn't have been talking about Miles, could he?

10

Lunch Time

'Told everyone you'd be forty minutes late!' Reece is on bristly form, first in line to welcome us into the Prettiest Garden in Warwickshire. 'Joe my man! Join the chaps for a Bloody Mary and tell us all about life in your university backwater. Summer and Edward, the girls are hosting a croquet tournament and need another pair. Eliza, your sister's giving her all to a rack of lamb in the kitchen, and would appreciate moral support. Granna was helping but she's had to lie down with one of her migraines.'

Less than a minute of Reece being imperious and I want to lie down too.

Joe murmurs under his breath, 'You did remind Auntie Jules I'm vegan, Mum?'

Bugger.

Inside, Jules's hot flush makes mine look like a cold snap as she broils, chops, pounds and curses. 'Do not touch a fucking thing! I have this completely under fucking control!'

My sister's a fantastic cook, but a very uptight one. It's genuinely the only time she swears.

'Smells delicious.'

'Crustless watercress quiche with pear salad, then herbed lamb with goose fat roasties and buttered baby veg, polished off with Eton Mess. If anyone complains, I will fucking stab them. Could you check on Mum?'

I put off mentioning the vegan thing.

Upstairs, Mum's lying in her darkened bedroom listening to the radio, a funereal violin dirge with a piano plinking at annoying intervals. She likes to set a scene.

'Come in, darling girl.' She raises a frail hand. 'Is Joe here?'

'Yes, we're all here, except Paddy of course. How's your poor head?'

'I don't have a migraine; I needed to calm down. Your sister's being insufferable.' She sits up and pats the bed beside her.

'I'm sure lunch will be worth the stress.' I perch, not wanting to be played against Jules.

'Not that. It's this obsession with bungalows. She quite upset your father last night, banging on about our impending decrepitude, not to mention haranguing Miles for signing away his half of the company and the flat and not having a divorce solicitor.'

'It *is* her profession.'

'And your brother's profession is being entrepreneurial. He started working on something as soon as he got here, still very hush hush, but I know he's excited. That boy can make money in his sleep.'

'It's relationships he can't keep hold of,' I say a bit testily.

'He just hasn't met the right person yet.' Mum's loyalty will never waver. 'Oh, I know he can be cavalier and secretive – he gets that from your father.' There's a beat in which she looks quickly away, family secrets swiftly tidied from her thoughts. 'But he's generous to a fault, your brother.' She stands up, crossing the room to draw open the curtains and look down at the garden. 'Aren't my roses lovely this year? Come outside and I'll give you the tour. Do you want to powder your nose first?'

'I'm fine.' For once I don't need the loo.

'I would, darling girl. You're very sweaty.' Mum's voice softens. 'Your sister told me you're going through the change of life now too. It's ghastly feeling so out of sorts, but it does get better, really it does. I found I was the happiest I've ever been afterwards: I was no longer frightened of everything; I stopped wanting to kill everyone; I even forgave Maggie Smith for stealing my career.' She fixes me with a knowing smile. 'Briefly.'

I'm grateful for someone who understands the raw edge of my insecurities so well. Mum bowed out early, but she still plays What If.

I have a fridge magnet that says: *Somebody Else's Success Is Not Your Failure.* Mum gave it to me; she has one too.

It's true, but the older we get, the more we appreciate that for many women – especially those in highly visible professions – our youthfulness and sexual allure are all too often viewed as the only measure of our worth. As I reach each of the milestones my mother crossed twenty-eight years ahead of me, I understand her disappointment more.

While male actors my age graduate seamlessly from playing Hamlet to his uncle Claudius, with old Polonius up their sleeves for later, now that I'm fifty I have more chance of appearing as Yorick's skull than Hamlet's mother, a part too often reserved for women barely older than her 'son'. Talent is all well and good but if you're female, staying young is the hardest act of all.

Giving the kitchen a wide berth, Mum greets Joe like a prodigal, tells Dad that no, he can't have a second Bloody Mary and orders Miles to fetch her a glass of chilled Gavi and a spritzer for me.

'You and your uncle must sing for Grandpa later,' she tells Joe.

He catches my eye pleadingly but I do hard-eyes back because I know how much it means to Mum and Dad when they sing together at family celebrations, even if it's mortifying for the hungover drummer of student indie band Nuanced Perverts to be seen duetting old show tunes with his fake-tanned uncle on his sister's Instagram account.

After Miles returns with the drinks, Mum and I take a turn around her rose beds, admiring the pink pompom blooms of her Princess Anne alongside Margaret Merril's big white-petalled faces as she tells me in an undertone how ghastly she felt at my age, suffering in silence because 'my generation simply didn't talk about menopause, or if we did it was in euphemisms'.

'How *did* it affect you?'

'Oh, not too badly at all once the HRT kicked in. I didn't

know about the risks then, of course. What do you think of this peony? Too flouncy?'

I shake my head and smile. What Mum – who's always fashioned herself as a rebel – can't see is that she remains precisely of the generation she's complaining about, her empathy spoken in a shorthand of 'chin up', 'you'll get through this' and 'best not go into detail'.

'I remember my legs itched terribly,' she ventures in a whisper.

We are very alike, Mum and I, right down to our knack of lifting one eyebrow with impeccable timing. But we are women born into markedly different eras. Touring the rose beds, we manage to bond over brittle fingernails and agree 'getting jolly hot' is a nuisance, but there's no way we're going near depressive insomnia, low libido, dry vaginal walls or increased stress incontinence. Besides, she's more worried about my marriage. 'You would tell me if something was wrong, wouldn't you? We were all saying last night how miserable Paddy looked on Friday.'

My defensive fires crackle. 'That's his resting face.'

'Well, he needs to get it moving. He's turning into his father. Eddie never smiled much.'

'He smiled on the inside.'

'Wives need more than that, darling. We need a sense of excitement and adventure, of being adored and desired. Is he giving you that?'

I wonder if she's inferring sex, then decide not. More likely off-grid travel and Glyndebourne tickets. 'He's suggested going out on the boat soon.'

'Well, I suppose that's something.' She turns to deadhead

a few butter yellow Charles Darwins. Then she says, 'Everything feels so much better when you're out the other side of this change. You'll see. You'll want to challenge yourself, take risks you never did. It's like coming through fire to clear air.'

I'd like to ask more, but there's a loud shout of alarm from the table and we turn to see Dad's chair tipping over backwards, depositing him in a lavender bed.

'Oh my God, Dad's head's burst open!' Miles screams.

'Peter! NO!' Mum cries, yellow petal flying out of her hands like confetti as everyone hurries over.

'I'm absolutely effing fine!' comes a furious roar from amid a haze of blue. 'It's Bloody Mary.'

Dad's dripping with tomato juice, a celery stick on his forehead.

Mum bursts into tears. 'Do you want to kill yourself, you silly fool!'

'The lavender broke my fall, old girl.'

'Not the chair tipping over! The cocktail! I TOLD you not to have a second one with your blood pressure.'

Sunhats, linen, parasols, citronella candles and a family in full bloom, its stems bearing blossom, our latest generation growing up fast. Sunday lunch with Granna and Grandpa Finch is a tradition my children all hold dear.

For Jules, Miles and me, whose childhood meals were cooked in the same orange Le Creuset ware, and eaten at the same tables forty years ago in Buckinghamshire, it's the perfect opportunity to give each other a roasting.

Dad's fall puts lunch back yet further. Poor Ed who

needs clockwork meals is stimming back and forth in his earphones, clicking his knuckles and longing to be home eating a plain ham sandwich rather than unfamiliar dishes he's been briefed he mustn't be rude about.

And I fear that hungry, hungover vegan Joe may have to forage the hedgerows.

As I head inside to offer to carry food out, I call for Miles to help too, because cornering my brother for a word is also playing on my mind.

Guarding an Aga-singed watercress quiche that looks like a giant sun-baked cow pat, Jules points a flan knife at me and tells me to stay where I am and await orders.

She eyes her quiche critically. 'This looks wrong. Is it missing something?'

'Mayo?' I suggest, edging towards the larder in search of raw food to smuggle out.

'The twenty-first century?' suggests foodie Miles, tracking me towards the wine rack.

'Fuck off and open your own bloody restaurant, why don't you? On fucking Mars with Elon fucking Musk.' She checks the recipe book. 'Of course, a dusting of paprika! Can you fetch it from the larder, Elz?'

I dive inside gratefully, pocketing a bag of sultanas, some walnuts halves and an open packet of Jacob's cream crackers.

'Actually, I always fancied being a Michelin-starred chef.' Arriving at the wine rack behind me, Miles starts studying labels.

'Is that the next great business plan Mum was telling me about?' I tease, trousering a slab of Bournville and turning to find him looking at me with troubled eyes.

GEORGIE HALL

'Listen, I need to talk to you about Paddy later.' I pick up a red-topped spice tub that looks like paprika and try to make out the label without my reading glasses.

There's an instant uneasiness. He looks at the pot too. 'Is that right?'

'Yes! You keep ignoring each other. Joe's been trying to convince his sister their dad's a homophobe.'

'Well, he is pretty uptight about it,' Miles selects a brace of Dad's favourite claret, 'especially once I told him I used to have a tiny crush on him.'

'You did *what*?' I clutch a larder shelf in shock.

'I thought it would make him laugh.'

'You have romantic *feelings* for Paddy?' I'm in shock.

'God no, not now, not at all! This was over twenty years ago when you were first together, and only ever briefly and from afar. When I couldn't figure out if I wanted to be like Bowie or be *with* him, Paddy was a god of cool. I used to daydream that he'd turn up in that clapped-out truck of his and invite me on a road trip to Frisco.'

'Christ alive, Miles! You *told* Paddy this?'

'I felt much the same way about Sean Bean, Mark Wahlberg and Madonna. It was nothing!'

I can imagine Paddy's silent shock, not knowing what to say, my reserved husband who has adapted so much from his rigid upbringing to fit in with our metropolitan, liberal-minded family and its funny middle-class ways, but still has a default setting of man's man, his friendships resolutely down-to-earth.

Talk about changing the rules.

★ ★ ★

146

Paddy and Miles had nothing to say to each other when they first met. It was obvious Paddy thought Miles was a player, and like most of my family Miles was politely baffled by my strong, silent boyfriend. Or so I thought at the time.

My brother was Mr Festival back then, responsible for colourful marquees, tipi villages and fire-jugglers popping up all over stately homes before he figured out the big money was in corporate events. He was also already divorced and a father, having dropped law at Brasenose at twenty to wed his pregnant Aussie girlfriend, a fiery union that lasted barely two years before she fled back to New South Wales with their son.

He met Wife Two in an Ibiza club in his mid-twenties. We all liked her, but workaholic Miles was never in the same time zone and eventually she fell in love with somebody else. Wife Three was an Internet date, ten years his senior, desperately beautiful and desperate for babies. That happened way too soon, his second son born on their first anniversary. They'd bought a dream Cotswold country house, got madly into debt and argued non-stop. Eventually she threw him out. With no money to rent his own place and Mum ill at the time, he ended up living on *The Tempest* for a couple of months. That's when, sixteen years after first meeting, the brothers-in-law finally made friends.

Paddy was permanently on call because things kept breaking down on the boat and my brother was in a terrible state about leaving his young son, history repeating itself, and Paddy became his confessor. There's a timeless therapy to canal life and having faced his own demons on *The Tempest* more than once, Paddy knew her to be a great healer. Within weeks, Miles had swapped self-destructive bottles of Smirnoff for craft ale and was hooked on barging. Even after he moved to Brum to set up his new events company, the two friends cast off a few times a year to potter between waterside pubs. They were great foils.

We had high hopes of Wife Four – his business partner, refreshingly bright and level-headed, a fellow divorcee – but all too soon after wedding vows were exchanged on a Greek island, Miles was spending more time on *The Tempest*, questioning what he'd done.

When my brother came out as gay to the family over lunch on New Year's Day, Mum was the only one to claim she'd known long before Miles realised it himself. He caught all the rest of us all on the back foot, especially Paddy.

'It's not like Paddy's insecure about his sexuality,' Miles is saying in a hushed undertone. 'It was just a throwaway joke when he complained that nobody fancied him any more.'

'Paddy said that?' I feel like I've been smacked.

'Sorry, not very sensitive now I think about it, telling him boys as well as girls found him hot half a lifetime ago. Who wants reminding they're no longer the young stud they were? But we'd had a lot of whisky, lamenting middle-age and marriage. He was supposed to laugh.'

'Lamenting?' I stand very still. 'When was this?'

'March maybe?'

I was away working a lot then. Meanwhile, Paddy was getting drunk with my brother, saying he wanted somebody to fancy him and *lamenting his marriage*.

We can hear the cottage landline ringing, its old-fashioned *bring-bring* like a call from the past.

I feel the rage bubbling, ill-timed and illogical.

'Everything all right in there?' Jules calls, opening the larder door a fraction, but there's barely enough room for two in here as it is. The phone is still ringing.

'Fine!' I have Miles backed up against the wine rack. 'Just quickly explain what you mean by "lamenting"?'

'What's said on *The Tempest* stays on *The Tempest*.' He clams up, spotting the mad look in my eyes.

'That bloody narrowboat!' I snarl. 'Sometimes I wish I'd never set eyes on her.'

'I feel your pain.'

Briing-briing.

'Can I just have the paprika, maybe?' Jules suggests.

Miles is pointing both barrels of his claret bottles at me. 'Perhaps you should talk to Paddy about this?'

'THE PAPRIKA!' Jules forces her way into the larder with us. It's like a game of sardines.

'I am talking to *you* about it!' I rail at Miles. 'And now that you've revealed you and Paddy fell out when you told him he was once your secret crush, I need to know what you mean by lam—'

'That isn't why we fell out!'

'ENOUGH, you two!' Jules squeezes past Miles to snatch the paprika out of my hand. 'This stops *right now*. Button it till later. Think of Dad. Miles, go out and give everyone a top up and a witty anecdote to stave off hunger pangs. Sing, if necessary. Elz, come and use your artistic flair to help me reshape a crustless quiche that's been hurled into the sink.'

'Why's it in the sink?'

'BECAUSE YOU'RE NOT THE ONLY ONE GOING THROUGH FUCKING MENOPAUSE!'

Miles and I file meekly out the larder behind our older sister. The landline is still ringing. Jules plucks up the kitchen handset as she passes, says 'fuck off!' crisply and hangs up.

As Miles bolts gardenwards, I follow her to the sink, where she stops, fists clenched, and hisses through gritted teeth, 'I just can't handle failure right now!'

I take a look at the watercress quiche. It's not pretty. Now lopsided, the cowpat crust has cracked and ruptured to reveal green-veined innards.

'It's hideous!' Jules groans.

'We'll dust on lots of paprika and no one will know,' I insist.

Jules does some deep breathing, then pinches the top of her nose and says a couple of Buddhist 'oms' and a 'fuck it' before spinning round to face me. 'Do you find you keep getting things totally out of perspective?'

'All the time.'

'We're being gaslighted by our own hormones.' She fixes me with her doomsayer stare. 'The loss of oestrogen and progesterone directly affects cognisance. It's why so many women struggle at work through the change. Tasks they could do without thinking twice before their hormones dwindled become almost impossible. I'm only telling you this for your own good, Eliza. It can last a *long time*, and a *lot* of crustless quiches will get fucked in the process. The three most common side effects are: memory loss, fatigue and anxiety.'

My mind flits to the forgotten lemon drizzle and to falling asleep, phone in hand, worrying I'm no longer brave or impulsive.

'Brain fog is commonplace.' Jules is on a roll. 'All

the disturbed nights' sleep just make it worse. We miss appointments, miss paying bills, forget things our children need for school and make big professional mistakes. It can be cataclysmic if you have a critical, high-powered job like mine.'

'Lucky for me I don't,' I mutter.

'Feelings of failure and regret are commonplace too. Your inferiority complex is going rogue.'

'You used to say it's the only complex thing about me,' I remind her in a bimbo voice.

'Actually, it was Miles who said that. Why are you two always obnoxious to each other?'

'He just told me he had a crush on Paddy in the nineties,' I justify.

'We *all* had a crush on Paddy back then,' she dismisses, 'he was ridiculously good looking and never spoke. We thought he had hidden depths.'

'He *does* have hidden depths!'

'Most men do, Eliza.' She sighs. 'The depths to which they will sink to get what they want. Now help me get this thing on a board.'

We manage to portion it and shake on lots of smoky red paprika. Except it's not smoky, it's peppery. We both start sneezing violently, eyes streaming.

'This is cayenne, Eliza!'

'Oh God, I'm so sorry! Would a distracting garnish help?'

Rubbing our burning noses, we look down at the red-dusted cowpat and we start to laugh. Soon we're leaning against one another, hot eyes streaming with tears, stitches pinching at our sides.

'Stop!' I gasp. 'Or I'm going to wee myself!'

'Me too!'
And that sets us off again.

Jules will forever remain the undisputed champion of my silliest and longest giggling fits. We once had a running joke about hypnotism that lasted years. I can't even remember the original gist of it now, just that the words 'You are feeling very sleepy' would set us off, triggering hopeless, helpless laughter that actually hurt. Even today, if we catch one another at the right moment after the third or fourth glass of wine at Christmas and say 'And sleep', its effect is instant and leg-crossing. The first time Paddy saw it, he thought we were both possessed. He still doesn't get it, this laughing gas effect we can have on each other.

It's yet another one of the ways my family conspires to mystify and alarm him.

'What am I going to do?' Jules wipes her eyes with a tablecloth.

'Just serve the pear salad; they won't care.'

'You're right. Go out and distract them some more.' She heads back towards the larder. 'I'm going to add some blue cheese and walnuts and rustle up a quick flatbread.' A moment later, she's inside shouting, 'WHERE the FUCK are those FUCKING walnuts?'

I hurry into the garden where wine glasses are brimming and Miles has persuaded Joe to join him in song, Jules's historic guitar fetched from the conservatory complete with its Keep Music Live stickers.

Although I let the side down by being pretty tone deaf, we're a musical family, especially Joe, who runs some riffs while Miles makes his introduction.

'Ladies and gentlemen, kinder and canines! My boy Joe here and I are going to sing you a number you'll be familiar with. Join in any time you like.'

Mum and Dad are rapt, beaming proudly. I might be the professional actor, but it's my brother who has always been the star turn in our family, and Joe's his protégé.

Miles smiles questioningly at me, seeking a truce. I look away, unable to quite forgive the word *lamenting* or my suspicion that there's something I'm not being told.

'*Birds do it, bees do it,*' Joe starts.

'*Even educated fleas do it,*' Miles's tenor joins in loudly. '*Let's do it...*'

We all come in on, '*Let's fall in love!*'

Out on the lawn, my nieces giggle shrilly as they clack croquet balls through hoops. Beneath the table, the Jack Russell is sitting on my feet like Arty used to. He rolls over ecstatically when I ease off a shoe to tickle him as we all join in singing the Cole Porter classic (although we soon start to invent many of the things that fall in love because we don't know all the words). Could we get any more quintessentially middle class than this? Boater hats, striped blazers and a couple of black labradors maybe?

Dad's delighted, florid face sun-rayed with laughter creases. He and Mum hold hands while they listen, which makes us all feel sentimental.

I sing loudly that chimpanzees in zoos and courageous kangaroos do it, then break off to suggest to Reece in an undertone that he could check whether Jules needs help but he just reaches for the wine bottle and says, 'Your sister married me precisely because I'm not the sort of lentil-knitting sub-dom who checks on his wife in the kitchen.'

I stick my tongue out at the back of his head and realise too late that Summer's videoing me on her phone as she pans round the scene. I smile and wave to cover up, imagine Paddy laughing when he sees it later.

And all at once I feel a sense of loss that scalds my skin in a way that isn't a hot flush or a blush or even cayenne pepper. My absent husband laments his marriage… It's the burn of lost love, I realise, this feeling, an indignant longing.

Somewhere along the way, I've lost the woman he fell in love with too.

It's almost two o'clock. Paddy's match will be about to start. Maybe I'll wish him luck, a small gesture of rapprochement. I haven't done it in years, and it will be a part of the new, better me who will live a more redemptive, fulfilled and generous life. Lament no more, Patrick Hollander.

I hurry to stand at the highest point of the garden where my phone obligingly finds a signal and I call his mobile.

But it's not Paddy who answers. It's a woman, sharp-voiced with urgency. 'Eliza, thank goodness! We've been trying to get hold of you on your parents' number.'

'Who is this?'

'Dinah Price, Simon's wife. Paddy can't speak on his phone right now, I'm afraid. There's been a bit of an – incident. Is your lunch finished? Are you free at all?'

'Oh God, what's happened? Is it an accident?'

'I'm rather afraid there—'

The line drops out. I now have no signal. When I hurry

inside the cottage to call back from the landline, it goes straight to voicemail.

'I have to go out!' I tell Jules.

'What, *now*?'

When I explain, she's straight onto logistics. 'Best you drive over there, I agree. Call them back on the way. Leave everything here to me. I'll tell the others and play it down until we know more, let them enjoy lunch. I can drop the children home, pick up those books for the girls you keep promising me. Here's a bottle of water, you *must* stay hydrated. Oh, and I meant to check that Joe's still vegan? I made him Portobello and roasted tofu, but there's plenty of lamb if he's reverted.'

Even amid a menopausal menu crisis, Jules is clearer headed than I am at my caffeine-high best. Kissing her gratefully, I hurry out to the car.

It's only when I'm out of the village racing through open countryside that I realise I've left my handbag in the kitchen and my mobile beside it.

11

Over Time

Beyond the boundary, the church clock strikes the quarter hour as I run to the pavilion. A thin crowd is there to watch the first few overs, waiting batsmen dotted along benches shaded beneath the veranda or sitting round picnic tables out in the sun. I target the first familiar face, a ruddy-cheeked tail-ender. 'Where's Paddy?'

'Been in a fight, has he?' he chortles, pointing inside. 'Hope you're not afraid of the sight of blood! There'll be more if Dinah doesn't get her kitchen back soon, haha.'

The club room smells of hard-boiled eggs and bleach. Trestle tables gleam with striped oilcloth; empty cake stands lined up for the feast to come. A trail of dark red splatters on the floorboards leads me to the utility recess between the changing rooms and kitchen, euphemistically known as the 'physio suite' because it contains a couple of exercise balls and an ancient massage table on which my blood-soaked husband is sitting, two brightly-aproned Florence Nightingales in attendance.

My cry of alarm makes him look up, startled. Although most of his face is obscured by an ice-pack, I can see one eyelid is swelling darkly, a fresh cut dissecting the eyebrow above it.

'Christ, what's happened?'

'That was quick, Eliza!' Dinah greets me with relief. Mid-sixties, elfin and well-bred, she's wearing a Keep Calm and Make Tea pinny and a matching don't-panic smile. Beside her, in a spotless on-trend barista's apron, a much younger blonde is holding an ice pack to Paddy's face like a giant powder puff.

'What happened?' I rush to his side. I feel fiercely protective. 'My poor love, what *hit* you?'

He looks at me intently. 'Googsgersganigis.'

'Sorry?'

Dinah steps closer. 'He's bitten his tongue, poor chap.'

'He said it looks worse than it is,' the blonde with the ice pack explains.

Paddy nods. 'Gugugozegeed.'

'Just a nosebleed,' Icepack Blonde tells me.

'Paddy, it's a head injury! You need checking over.'

'Try not to panic, Eliza,' Dinah says tartly, 'the club's first-aider has reassured us it simply needs cold compression.'

'Where's this first-aider now?'

'Right here, aren't you, Patrick?' Icepack Blonde strokes his arm. 'He refused to let us take him to A & E.'

'Gauguin gluggy gruyere.'

'Of course you don't want to go there!' Icepack reassures him, dabbing away. I wish she'd stop stroking his arm like it's a plush toy.

'Out of the question now there's so few of us left to do

the tea.' Dinah's steely. 'The wicketkeeper's new girlfriend fainted at the sight of him and another helper put her back out trying to stop her fall. They've both had to go home. Which is why I'm so glad *you're* here, Eliza.'

'Igaigongegiza oogun!' from Paddy.

'"I said *don't* get Eliza to come",' Icepack translates brightly, turning to look at me in that glazed way younger women do, not seeing me at all, just my age range. 'It's funny, because Dinah was saying only last week that it would take a miracle to get Paddy's wife to ever help with a match tea.'

Dinah smiles tightly. 'And here she is!'

I gape at her. Surely she didn't get me here today just to help with tea?

(And if so, did she punch Paddy to do it?)

In my experience, the wives and girlfriends who make village cricket match teas generally fall into two categories, Royal and Casual.

Royals are a cake-baking, Archers-listening, whites-washing dying breed. They're old-fashioned, well-meaning, rallying stalwarts who stay until the last ball's bowled but never expect to join the players in the pub. Nothing is too much trouble for the team. Royal Teas are traditional affairs, full of foolproof Mary Berry classics. Dinah is exemplary at them.

Casuals are the sugar rush, a sun-worshipping, app-filtered younger brigade. Decorative, excitable and eager to impress, many only last a season or two, treating the teas like Bake Offs, well aware that the fun starts with the first round in the pub after the last over. Icepack Blonde, I suspect, is a Casual Tea.

I belong to a subcategory, Absent Tea.

Remembering my sister's warning about being gaslighted by our own hormones and getting things out of perspective, I try to stay calm.

'You're surely not intending to bat?' I ask Paddy.

'Igakkingorff!' His eyes plead with mine.

'Who are you telling to fuck off?'

'Actually, he said he's batting fourth,' Icepack corrects.

'That's ridiculous!' I protest.

'Exactly what I said,' Dinah backs me up. 'Simon won't drop a player of Paddy's calibre from the batting order unless at least one limb's severed, but surely he should be in eighth or ninth? It hardly sets a gold standard when one's fourth man is looking so—'

'Heroic?' coos Icepack, and I swear Paddy looks pleased with himself. 'We all love your husband.' – she tells me – 'He's so rugged, isn't he?'

There's a definite alpha-swagger to the way he waves her nursing ministrations away and makes to stand up. 'I've gogago and gange.'

'He's saying he's got to go and ch—'

'I worked that out, thanks!' I push him back down. 'You're not going near that changing room until I know how this happened and that you're not concussed, Paddy.'

I think I must have pushed a bit hard because he's clutching his mouth in pain.

'Igotits ingace gy eyailate!' he tells me, eyes martyred.

I look to Icepack for help, but she holds her hands up. 'Something about "tits in the face" and "jailbait"?'

Groaning, Paddy looks away.

'Nobody knows how he got like this, Eliza,' Dinah tells me gently. 'All I can tell you is that Simon couldn't get hold of Paddy to confirm he was playing today, then he turned up ten minutes before the match, covered in blood.'

Somebody's covering up a lie. Paddy definitely told me he was running an errand for Simon this morning. I can feel the hormonal red mist rising, my overactive imagination whirring: is my husband our cricket team captain's henchman with a violent flipside I've never witnessed? Is that the reason his phone gets 'left in the truck' so often at the workshop? Do these mysterious 'errands' involve money laundering, drug running, human trafficking? Does the man who laments his marriage spice his life up with danger?

'Ge truck Gailgate! Gargoot in gy gace!' He grimaces in pain.

I spot a bottle of water nearby and hand it to him.

'Ganks.' He drinks some with relief.

'Does that feel better?'

'Guch.' He speaks very slowly, 'The gruck gailgate hit gy gace!'

As he says it, a small roar goes up outside, local outrage mixed with grudging applause.

'Jonesy's been caught!' someone shouts into the club-house. 'Third man's going into bat, Paddy! Standby! And put a bloody helmet on. This fast bowler's like a trebuchet.'

This triggers my memory, the fog lifting. I hurry after him as he heads towards the changing room. 'You got hit in the face by the truck's tailgate?'

'Yes!' He looks at me over his shoulder. 'Getting gy kit gag out.'

'I knew something like this would happen! It's been sprung like a mantrap since he fitted the new hydraulics. He keeps saying he'll adjust it. Now this. 'What if it had been one of the kids? Edward?'

Looking annoyed, he disappears inside. Icepack Blonde puts a hand on my shoulder, pink Shellacs digging in. 'I'll make you a cup of tea shall I, Eloise?'

'And we'll start on the match tea!' Dinah cries, beaming at me. 'You are the saviour of the day, Mrs Hollander. I might even overlook all those cakes you've promised us over the years!'

'What do you mean, *promised*?'

I've sneaked out behind the pavilion to update Jules, using Paddy's phone and a borrowed powerbank, my voice low. 'I can't figure out how to escape. I have spent *years* trying to avoid being in this situation. They suck you in, groom you, control you until you can only think in scotch eggs and banoffee. I've been trapped in there for an *hour* wrestling cling film and folding paper napkins. *And* Dinah seems to think I never bake the team a cake. How can she forget all my red velvets? I've got Paddy's truck keys and I'm playing a lemon drizzle straight between her eyes.'

'Do be careful of that truck,' Jules warns.

'I'm not going near the tailgate. Poor Paddy. It must have caught him smack in the face.'

'And you thought he'd been beaten up by Warwickshire's underworld mafia!' Jules hoots. She loves that bit.

I decide not to reveal that Paddy's whereabouts between eight and two today are still unaccounted for. 'He's already forty-two not out and cracking fours like he's swatting flies.'

'Your husband's the last of his breed.'

'We *have* bred more,' I remind her, although I secretly doubt any are as tough as Paddy.

'And we're going to drop the ones you prepared earlier off on our way back to London, although Joe tells us he's stopping off with a friend there overnight?'

How hurt I'd felt when he told me that he wanted to catch up with the old schoolmate who's now at UCL rather than staying over with us. But at least I've guilt-tripped him into booking an evening train so we'd get a proper farewell before he goes to France.

Then Jules says, 'We'll take him down with us. Much nicer than the train. He's thrilled with the idea.'

I'm not, especially when she adds, 'We're just finishing the washing-up then we'll set out.'

'Already?'

'Mum and Dad want to go up for a nap.' She lowers her voice. 'Lunch got very testy. The food went down a storm but Dad did one of his "your mother and I can't take it with us" inheritance numbers. I'll tell you about when I drop yours off. You will be back?'

'How can I?' I groan. 'Match tea is at least half an hour away. Dinah's checking her sandwich points with a spirit level and protractor as we speak. I just want to run for the hills.'

'So do it! Lay the lemon drizzle at her feet and politely tell her to shove her bloody teas. Then scarper. For both our sakes. I think Miles might have taken what you said in the larder a bit too literally.'

'What did I say?' But she's already rung off.

I lean against the wooden wall for a moment. I'm ravenous, but I haven't dared sneak so much as a triangle of coronation chicken in medium sliced white while Dinah's policing her feast. Remembering my larder raid, I dig through my pockets, pulling out a bag of sultanas and helping myself to a few. I feel a rib dig of anger as I replay Miles telling me that Paddy had complained nobody fancied him.

Applause from outside as the runs count up. The LMCC's battered hero is exactly where he wants to be: at the crease, batting for glory, somewhere I can't demand to know where he's been and why he lamented our marriage. *Lamented*.

Hell hath no fury like me marching across to the pickup truck and pulling open the driver's door.

The lemon drizzle cake isn't inside the cab, but there are crumbs everywhere, the plastic container it had been stored in discarded on the back seat.

I'm no detective, but I think we can safely deduce that Paddy ate the cake, and that he did so between 8 a.m. and 2 p.m., his location unknown. He may also have eaten previous cakes I baked for his cricket club's teas, possibly every one of them.

Well, the LMCC is getting a contribution from me whether they like it or not. Let them eat cake!

Grabbing the container, I empty the contents of the packets in my pockets inside and carry it back into the clubhouse.

'Where have you been, Eliza? The urn needs checking!' Dinah doesn't look up from arranging cream horns, little golden phalluses that make me think of the Ann Summers parties I hosted back in the day.

'Rustling up a deconstructed raw vegan cake!' I decant my larder booty out onto the vacant Emma Bridgewater stand, where it rains down prettily, Jacob's crackers and all. Then I break up the Bournville to scatter on top.

'Deconstructed is somewhat *outré*,' she says sternly. 'Eliza, are you feeling all right?'

'Menopausal,' I admit. 'Very, *very* menopausal, Dinah. Isn't it just PURE *UNADULTERATED HELL?*'

'Gosh.' Dinah's left eye quivers. 'Is it? One hardly remembers.'

'It's the anger I can't handle, Dinah. You must remember that? The ANGER that makes you want to *KILL*? The Lady Macbeth "unsex me now" anger, our hot blood boiling within.' I lift the knife by the malt loaf and start hacking slices from it. 'I can take the hot flushes and low libido and forgetfulness, it's the murderous urges that do my head in. DIE, DIE, *DIE*, SOREEN!'

'Maybe you should go home and lie down, Eliza?' Dinah suggests faintly.

'Are you sure? I don't want to let you down.'

'I think that's best.' She manages a twitch of a smile.

'I'll come and help another time,' I promise. 'Bring another raw vegan cake!'

As I head back to the rust bucket, Paddy scores his half-century to a roar of approval. He holds up his bat, supremely pleased with himself.

Fifty not out.

I know the feeling.

12

Killing Time

New Neighbour and Death-Stare Baby watch eagle-eyed from their half-landing window as my sister reverses her eco hybrid beside the rust bucket so neatly it could have been airlifted in.

'We can't stop,' Jules apologises when she gets out, hooking my forgotten handbag over my neck and shouting, 'Just a leg stretch!' as the girls race into the house with Summer and Ed.

'Forgive me not getting out!' Reece waves from the passenger seat, *Alto's Adventure* glowing on his phone screen. 'Just sending some urgent messages!'

Jules starts telling me in an undertone about Dad's can't-take-it-with-you speech. 'He was squiffy, which didn't help. It was mostly the usual *King Lear* stuff about coffers, chattels and inheritance tax. Only this time *The Tempest* was mentioned.'

My pulses jolt.

'The boat?' I clarify carefully.

'Miles thinks that Italian restaurateur, Matteo, might want to buy her. They're supposed to be meeting up to take her out soon.'

My blood pressure is pumping bars.

'General opinion seems to be there's no point keeping her for Paddy to polish at weekends when Mum and Dad hardly ever go out in her any more.'

I want to rage that Paddy does more than polish her, but Joe's alongside now, hooking an arm around my shoulder. 'Don't stress, Mum. Letting go of the past can be therapeutic.'

'That boat means *everything* to your father. Did you argue?' I demand.

'It's not really my place, Mum.'

I bite my lip hard. He's right. His grandparents can do what they like with her. I'm just being a materialistic shrew.

Jules pats my shoulder. 'Thought it best you knew. I'll round up the girls!' She heads for the house.

'You OK, Mum?'

I'm chewing imaginary wasps with the effort of holding back a tirade about *The Tempest*. It's not Joe's problem. Added to which, New Neighbour is still watching us, hip baby swaying, reminding me of the time I carried Joe there, that solidly warm weight of early motherhood. How can it be twenty years ago?

'Fine! I'm absolutely fine!' *MILES WANTS TO SELL THE BOAT, ARRGHHH. PADDY WILL FREAK.*

He gives me a sideways smile. 'Can you talk to Summer about Kwasi maybe? It's a big deal for her?'

'It's a big crush.'

'A bit more than that?'

The driveway sways. 'Please don't tell me they're having sex?'

'I doubt it.'

I close my eyes. Now this.

'He's a cool guy, Kwasi,' Joe is saying. 'Swears like a drain, but clever and kind. He would never do anything to hurt her, I'm sure of it.'

'He's a member of *school staff*.'

'Talk to Summer? She thinks she knows it all, but she needs you, Mum. And *don't* say anything to Dad. He'll just be old-fashioned and irrational? Summer has thin skin right now, and Dad's in a major black mood if yesterday's FaceTime was anything to go by?'

'He felt bad that he wouldn't see you today,' I remind him, anxious needles in my temples at the thought of how much darker that mood will be soon.

'At least he was spared Uncle Miles's singing,' he grins back. Then from nowhere, he says, 'Mum, I think he might be depressed.'

And as he goes into the house I straighten in shock because of course it makes sense.

Mental health issues run in our family. They do in everyone's, of course, in the same way that we're all on Edward's colourful spectrum, it's just some of us are in the shade longer than others. When Joe suffered his bad bout of depression as a teenager, cognitive therapy, talking and time helped enormously, and he is now refreshingly open about it. Not so his father.

Paddy had some very dark days in the year after Eddie's

death. He refused any sort of help, or even to acknowledge it was happening, and being shut out completely was almost unbearable at times, as was trying to keep the family ship together.

Those were months fraught with worry, mistrust and rejection; it became like living with a stranger. When the clouds finally lifted, I was too grateful to probe. I do know it wasn't his first depressive episode. (I only learned about it afterwards, and not from him. It happened in London before we met, in the early nineties, when he was living with the old schoolmate who later became his business partner; he's the one who let it slip.)

Seeing it first-hand is quite another thing, the sheer impenetrability of a deep depression, of despair's black rockface.

Meeting Paddy – now or quarter of a century ago – I defy anyone who doesn't know him to imagine his demons. He's the man you want in a crisis, the survivalist hero who saves the day with an easy smile. All those years ago, to my twenty-something self, Paddy Hollander was the strongest-minded man I'd ever met, my sanity. He still is.

To see him depressed is like seeing him bleeding out and knowing there's nothing I can do to stem the flow.

I've been so obsessed with my own hormone-depleted anxieties lately, I haven't stopped to consider how he's doing, how he's coping with a wife who can't sleep or feel desire or sit still or stay cool, with a career that's stalled again, with our children flying the nest.

He can't fall down the hole again. He just can't.

★ ★ ★

Jules has re-emerged from the house, knees buckling, with her chin steadying two boxes of books Summer's donated to her cousins. She sends Joe in to grab a bin bag of outgrown clothes. 'Tell the girls to come out too! We have to go!'

When we transfer the boxes to Jules's car boot, I spot a collection of familiar things from the cottage already in there: two oil paintings, the antique bronze stag we used to call Bambi, the Wedgewood fish platter and our maternal grandmother's Georgian silverware. I make no comment. Given how generous Mum and Dad have been to me over the years, it would be churlish to kick up a fuss about the way Jules treats each visit like a bric-a-brac rummage, happy to encourage Dad's premature estate dispersal.

'They won't really sell *The Tempest*, will they?' I ask.

'Miles was pretty persuasive.'

'But Mum and Dad know how much she means to Paddy.' If Paddy is depressed, this is the last thing he needs. Almost as awful, I can clearly hear myself saying to Miles earlier: *That bloody narrowboat! Sometimes I wish I'd never set eyes on her.* And him saying *I feel your pain.*

Is this my fault?

Jules lifts the family eyebrow. 'Miles has a stake in *The Tempest*, don't forget.'

I say nothing, feeling stupid because although I remember some sort of trust being drawn up when Mum and Dad bought her, I was too relieved to take much notice of the legal side.

I'm trying not to panic. 'Why can't he just leave things as they are?'

'Possibly my fault.' Jules pulls an apologetic face. 'This divorce of his will be bloody costly, so I suggested he turn as many assets as possible liquid, then the cash can disappear to reduce a settlement claim.'

'You *advised* him to do this?'

'I didn't know *The Tempest* is in an absolute trust until today.'

'I have no idea what that means.'

'It means that he can sell her to recoup his share. You signed the papers, Elz. Did you actually read them?'

My idiocy has bells on, roller skates and a megaphone. Paddy will be devastated, and it's all my fault.

'Why not buy her back?' she asks with the glibness of somebody for whom this would be no more financially challenging than an M&S food shop. My sister has never been told the full story of why Mum and Dad bought *The Tempest*; I'm not sure how much Miles knows either.

Ruth Hollander blamed her husband's narrowboat for his heart attack, insisting Paddy must take *Lady Love* away from Shropshire straight after the funeral to do with as he wanted as long as she remained out of her sight.

I don't think he let himself grieve until that long, solitary trip navigating the canals between his childhood home and Leamington, then he found he couldn't stop. For months, he'd drive to the mooring and just sit in her, listening to music, whole days passing. He couldn't talk about how he was feeling at all. His work started suffering, orders massively overdue for custom-made kitchens, the finish sloppy. It was heartbreaking.

Paddy still blames himself for the business going under, but there was more to it than that. The recession had a huge effect, then his silent partner wanted his investment back. I took every job I could, but it wasn't enough. We missed four mortgage payments. Five and we were out.

That's when Mum and Dad stepped in. The money they paid for the narrowboat bought us much-needed time to get back on our feet again. To this day, Paddy thinks they came up with the idea themselves. I made them promise to play it like that, to say that they had always wanted a canal barge and they were emphatic that Paddy must do nothing different after the transfer of ownership, that she was his in all but name.

Then they changed her name. *The Tempest.* (A joke entirely on me, their Miranda who married for love. *You may deny me, but I'll be your servant, Whether you will or no.* Held to ransom.)

Now a storm is well and truly brewing.

'Miles won't go through with it,' Jules reassures me in her dispassionate legal voice accustomed to breaking it to rich wives that they're losing the second home in France. 'He probably just wants a jolly day out on the boat with a handsome Italian.'

'You know the *real* reason behind all this, don't you?' I fume. 'He wants to have a go at Paddy.'

'Because he's dropped him as a friend?'

'He has not!' I hiss. 'It was Miles who ghosted *him*. It's typical of him to discard old allies and ride roughshod over the things that matter most to them. He's been like it since childhood. I should know. Jaime Sommer lost both legs because of him.'

'Good God! Who's Jamie? Was this recently?'

'Miles can't be allowed to sell a piece of family history down the river, Jules!'

'Please don't get upset,' she shushes me. 'I appreciate it's tricky timing with your marriage in such a bad place—'

'IT'S NOT!' I shrill, then hiss, 'What is it with you all thinking that? Mum said it too.'

'You're going through menopause, Elz. Every marriage feels like hell on earth. Plus, I was in the larder with you and Miles earlier, don't forget.'

And now I want to cry because she's right; Paddy's not the only one lamenting our marriage right now.

'An American study recently found that two-thirds of all divorces initiated by women are by those in their menopause years,' Jules tells me wisely. 'We finally want to break free from domesticity, drudgery, breeding and being taken for bloody granted. Meanwhile all our middle-aged husbands want – and expect – is regular food and sex. Without these on a plate, some become greedy wankers.' She glances over her shoulder at Reece in the car, tapping on his phone screen. 'I'm worried for you, Elz. It's lack of communication that tests marriages most through menopause and forgive me, but Paddy makes semaphore look wordy.'

'We *have* talked about what's happening to me.' (Me shouting mostly. Quite often in tears. Especially during the Dog Fight.)

'Some men can't handle it. I see it with older divorcing clients all too often: the resentment, the demonising, the self-justified infidelities.' She glares over her shoulder again. 'After his wife's pregnancies and early motherhood, her menopause is the point in a marriage her husband is most likely to seek sexual satisfaction elsewhere.'

I feel like I'm about to throw up. 'You don't think Paddy could be having an affair, do you?'

'Gosh no! Not Paddy.'

'Because if he is, if he risked everything we have to shoot his load into another woman, if he did that to his children, to me, I'd kill him with my bare hands!' For a moment everything tunnels and spins in a vortex of mania, and then it clears.

Jules puts a supportive hand on my arm. 'Statistically women are more likely to commit murder or kill themselves during menopause than at any other time in life.'

Without warning I'm enclosed in a sisterly hug that smells of Jo Malone London Orange Blossom and willpower. 'I'm always here if you need me, Elz.'

I'm in shock. It's the first time Jules has spontaneously hugged me since Bucks Fizz won the Eurovision. 'We'll get through this, kid,' she whispers. We're both uncomfortably hot and thick-waisted, and I'm wearing a crossover handbag with large fashion studs so it's a bit like being trapped in an iron maiden, but it nevertheless feels good. She releases her grip and pats me down vigorously, like an airport check. 'That feels better, yes?'

'Thanks.' I nod, stunned.

'We must go.' She looks at her watch and shouts, 'GIRLS!'

They've been trying on Summer's unwanted clothes: Ottilie is in a crop top that says *Sorry Not Sorry!*, Vervain in baggy camo combats looks like she's been radicalised by Sporty Spice, and Joe's gender-bending in ridiculously tight rainbow trousers that look very Mick Jagger. Even Ed's posing long-sufferingly with a pom-pom-fringed cowboy hat.

'What would you give to have that again?' Jules sighs. 'That spontaneity?' Dewy-eyed, she heads to the car.

Joe offers me a farewell bear hug. I hug him back tighter than ever because I'll miss my wise sage unbearably. Ed's already disappeared back inside, cowboy hat left on the door knocker. Summer's also racing to the house, mobile aloft, talking to someone on a video call.

'She wants to catch the first England match in the Women's World Cup,' Joe tells me. 'You are invited to join her for the second half.'

'Why not the first half?'

'Ed's running you a bath. Something about an Act of Kindness? He thinks you're stressed. And that you smell,' he deadpans, then grins.

'God, but he's good; you all are. I'll try to talk to Summer about Kwasi,' I promise, 'and I'll look after your dad too,' I add, eager to absolve myself of the death threats, compassion crashing around in their wake at the thought of Paddy being sad with life.

'Yeah, pass on my love to the grumpy old man.' He grins, which I think's a bit unsympathetic in the circumstances. 'And please watch Uncle Miles's back, yeah?'

I feel my smile get stickier.

'Seriously, Mum.' Joe makes a love heart with his hands then presses them together in namaste. 'Attention-seeking is a classic signaller for low self-esteem. He's masking it, but it's there.'

As he lopes off, I realise my mistake.

It's not Paddy that Joe thinks might be depressed. It's his uncle, the all-singing, all-dancing, barge-thieving marriage-lamenter, Miles Finch.

13

Tea Time

I used to think I could intuitively read people, that I possessed a unique actor's insight into the psyche which enriched my 'nothing is wasted' emotional range and made me a good listener. I was wrong; I'm no better than anyone else at seeing past the surface on which we project our own imaginations. Hence, I see my brother as perpetually playful and scampish, instead of the complicated character he is. And I see Jules as shiny and invincible, not fissured with cracks through which she screams when she cooks or runs from on her garage treadmill. Equally, I attribute all sorts of complicated and conflicting maelstroms of emotion to Paddy beneath that taciturn exterior, but perhaps, like my sister says, a husband's main desires are as simple as food and sex?

As for my children, I have to continually remind myself that I thought I had all the answers when I was their age too, but now I've gained the wisdom to know that I don't, it's best not to ask anyone under twenty too many direct questions – especially when talking about relationships (or 'ships' as Summer calls them).

The bath was a stroke of genius. I am soothed, my head cleared of emotional rubble thanks to the podcast Ed set up for me; *Mighty Marvel Geeks* is perhaps more his bag than mine, but helpfully distracting.

I find Summer's lined up the spare lemon drizzle cake to share when I join her to watch England vs Scotland and I guzzle two slices as I plan my mentalist mother moves to broach the subject of Kwasi Owusu.

The trouble is, Summer's on her phone non-stop. Every time I try to say anything – 'that was a good move', 'more cake?', 'do you want to talk?' – she ignores me, so I up my game by planting subconscious references to art and photography. 'I wonder if anyone's done a digital art installation about football for their A level?' She snorts with laughter at one of the comments on her feed and likes it.

'I thought you wanted to watch this together?' I grumble.

'I *am* watching. And commenting.' She glances up at the big screen. 'You missed a sick first half. They're playing safe now.'

I'm not a football watcher normally. There's a hundred other more useful things I could be doing on a sunny evening and I long to be walking Arty by the river so that I can think through how to broach the boat fiasco with Paddy later.

'Go England!' I cheer as our plucky girls rebuff Scotland's valiant attempts to turn the tide. Then 'Go Scotland!' because Granny Finch was born there.

'You are *so* on the fence?' Summer takes a selfie of us

together in which she looks gorgeous and I have three chins and redeye.

Briefly in possession of her attention, I pass on a subliminal hint: 'I think it's best to keep an open mind, don't you? I prefer to see both sides in football, as I do in love.'

She adds lion filters on the photo of us, labelling it *Go Lionesses!* before firing it into the ether to gather hearts. 'I didn't know you were such a girl footie fan, Mum?'

It's certainly a different experience to watching men's international matches with Paddy – the only football I usually ever see. The game on screen today is much less aggressive, the camaraderie magnificent, the Essex facelifts equally so. But I'm much more of a tennis fan. I like my sport like I like my sex as the old joke goes: one on one with no dribbling.

As a competitive Finch I know I should embrace team sports. I love camaraderie and cooperation, but I don't like rules. Or balls. Or communal showers.

If I'm honest, I'd trade any televised international tournament for a new Sally Wainwright series. Her characters probably struggle to talk to their teenage daughters too.

While *@Summer_Time* updates her followers with more *#womensworldcup* thoughts, I compose a hasty text to Miles, but my clumsy fingers and autocorrect conspire against me as usual, turning *We need a chat about The Tempest asap, Ex* into *We need to chat about the tempestuous asp sex.*

Before I can tweak it, Summer turns to me, eyebrows strangely off-kilter. 'Mum, can I talk to you about something?'

Surprised – surely my subtle mentalist hints can't have paid off? – I absentmindedly press send. 'Of course, anything.'

She gazes at the screen. 'Promise you won't tell Dad what I'm about to tell you?'

The football-and-cake was a ruse, I realise, feeling even more gratified – *#mumstheword* – although worry grips me. 'If you don't want me to.'

She blurts, 'I have these feelings for somebody and I don't know what to do?'

'Romantic feelings?'

She nods, tears rising. 'We get on so well, laugh all the time, only now I can't *breathe* when he's near me, and I think about him all the time, and I want to *die* I'm so unhappy because he s-s-says nothing can happen, and now he's leaving?' She starts to cry and I cuddle her close. She's warm and soft and vulnerable, physical contact between us so rare it's bittersweet.

I am deeply relieved he is leaving, however hard it is to feel her heart breaking against mine. 'It's OK, darling. I'm so glad you told me. It's all going to be all right.'

'No it's not! He's going freelance and global! Look!' She holds up his Instagram feed, but her thumb's slipped and I can only see a picture of my own relieved face and numbers counting down to the words *You Are Now Live.*

'Is this streaming?' I ask worriedly.

'Ooof! Man!' She cancels it, hugging the phone to her chest, wet eyes huge. 'What do I do?'

'Can you delete it?'

'Not that! *Him.*' She leans in against me again.

This, I realise, is something I need to handle very,

very gently. Because I know how much it hurts; she's not the first seventeen-year-old to be gripped by a teacher crush.

'Summer, I have to ask, how far did things go?'

She sobs harder. I feel deeply darkly anxious.

'*Nothing's* happened between us. We had this super high-key argument last week cos he thinks I'm involved with somebody else who he disapproves of, but I'm not! He says I'm too young for love and I have to concentrate on my A levels?'

I like this boy.

'And he says he'd be no good for me because he grew up around Salford drug dealers and some of them are still his friends and he swears all the time and wants to screw the art establishment by becoming the digital Banksy, even if that means trolling and getting arrested. His anger is his art? He'll be iconic, he's so lit.'

I downgrade like to a respectful desire not to be his mother-in-law.

'But now he's firedooring me! Today he messaged saying he's dropping me from this cutting-edge project he's got coming up? That I helped organise as part of my coursework? It's so unfair! He says he doesn't feel the same way about me, but I *know* he does? He's *sacrificing* us! I can't let him go, Mum.' Her voice breaks. 'It hurts too much.'

Her phone is vibrating between us with notifications of comments and likes. I wrestle it away and place it on the sofa arm beside mine.

'It's nothing like it was with Jack,' she sobs into my arm. (Her only 'proper' boyfriend thus far, and amiably diffident.) 'This is soul-destroying.'

'It's totally normal to have a crush like this at your age, darling.'

'It's not a *crush*? It's LOVE!'

'The same love that poets have when they create their most beautiful work,' I reassure her. 'A love that hurts like a wound but passes with time. The love we call unrequited. That love?'

She cries harder. We stay like this for a long time. Her phone vibrates regularly from the sofa arm.

Eventually she pulls away, wiping her nose with the back of her wrist. 'Don't tell me I'll grow out of it,' she sniffs. 'Because I won't?'

'Maybe not, but you'll get better at avoiding it.'

'My friends think I'm completely delusional?'

'All love is partly delusional,' I point out. '*Merely a madness.*'

'*Yet I profess curing it by counsel,*' she quotes back, smiling tearfully. 'You don't think I'm being an idiot?'

'There's more to it than that.' I take her hand. Summer can be whiney and immature, but she's fiercely bright beneath the glossy armoury, struggling to match real life up with her expectations. 'Life is a muddle of near misses and sliding doors, especially early on. It's human nature to use our imaginations to take every journey. And it hurts, I know. I was in a similar situation to you once.'

'Trust me, you *never* felt like this.' Then she eyes me beneath lowered Nikes. 'Like, seriously?'

I nod, thinking back to my own teenage obsessions that blistered my heart raw, one in particular, the forbidden low-hanging fruit of a flirty teacher. I'm shocked to find myself mourning the craving I felt for him, its dangerous intensity. I envy Summer her passion, however agonising, and her honesty. At her age I would never have admitted to a living soul – least of all my mother – the slavish devotion I harboured for 'Mr Vella,' I say aloud, enjoying the way his name still fires my pulses.

Maxim Vella.

Or was it Maximo?

Ah, that first man crush. Not a popstar pin-up or spotty contemporary, but the older man we lie in bed imagining touching us, teaching us carnal pleasure, like a Jackie Collins' hero or Johnny in *Dirty Dancing*. Only *real*.

Mine was a foreign language student teacher who had my heart completely in his grasp for three terms.

'He was French,' I tell Summer. Or was it Spanish? 'He helped run the choir that I was a part of.' Or was it a drama club?

Floppy dark hair, olive skin, white smile, passionate about his subject. Did he have an earring? I'm sure he did.

God, but I loved him.

I would have died for him.

His big limpid brown – or possibly blue – eyes looked straight into my soul.

Now, when I try to picture Maxim Vella, I just see George Michael smouldering at me from a poster on my bedroom wall.

'Mum, you've gone sweaty again? Are you having one of your hot moments?'

'He gave me a lucky silver charm, I remember.' He gave one to each member of the group in a show we did. I wore mine on a chain and it gave me an allergic rash. 'He was generous and funny, and loved to make me laugh. He left after a year to take a job overseas.' I smile sadly across at Summer, acknowledging time's symmetry. 'I thought I'd never get over it either.'

She's affronted. 'This is *different*. I *won't* get over it. He'll always be out... *there*.' She waves at the television screen, as though Mr Owusu is planning to play international women's football. 'On every stream I have? You had no social media back then, no Internet even?' (She could be saying 'no electricity and sanitation'.)

'The dark ages of analogue love,' I concede, aware that her phone is buzzing away beside me, a self-contained universe of false expectation. 'There was no button for liking or following or haunting, not even a colour emoji heart to express our anguish. I'm guessing black, am I right?'

She shoots me a dirty look, then cleans it up with a fresh glimmer of interest in my ancient history. 'Didn't you ever wonder what happened to him?'

'Not really,' I lie. I've Googled everyone I've ever fancied/ snogged/dated, but Maxim Vella's name draws a blank. Now I find myself trying to imagine what he might look like today. To my alarm, it's restaurateur Matteo's intense focus that appears in my mind's eye, demands to know why I didn't recognise him all along? *I am your fantasy figure, bellissima. Always, you choose the same type, si? You want more passion, more admiration.*

I shake my head to make it go away. 'I've no idea where Matt – I mean Maxim Vella – is.'

'Well, I'm not going to let that happen? I'm going to become a super-famous influencer?' Her eyes are bright with defiance. 'Then Kwaz will photograph me for the cover of

Time or *Vanity Fair* and see the real me, not the schoolgirl? There'll be no stigma.'

'When do you plan on this happening?'

'Maybe in my gap year?' She looks at me levelly, daring me to question it.

I match her straight face. 'Think he'll be shooting *Vanity Fair* covers by then? How does that fit in with trolling the art establishment?'

'We flex careers now, Mum. One monetises to facilitate the other. He is the next Tuschman. I just have to be the next...' She closes one eye, thinking, 'Emma Watson?'

It could be worse – I thought she might say Zoella or Kim Kardashian – but my heart still sinks. 'You still want to be an actor?'

'It's a family trade.' She's defiant. 'I've already got a fan base and screen experience.'

'That's not acting.'

'That's not the point. Nobody wants you if you're nobody. Recognition legitimises all art. If you'd made it big and been famous, Mr Velcro might have looked *you* up.'

'Vella.' I hold my indignation in check. 'And "making it" is not just about celebrity, Summer, it's also about creative fulfilment.'

'Reading out rude books for a living?' she sneers, one Nike tick raised.

'I won a Narrator of the Year Lippie, I'll have you know! You can tell that to *Vanity* bloody *Fair* when they profile you.'

'Why would I even mention you? You talk about yourself enough for both of us. Congratulations, mother dearest, yet again you have made this all about YOU. You and your teen crush and your pound-shop acting career and your regrets.'

'I'm sorry, I was trying to—'

'I'm not *you*. I can't make up for your mistakes, Mum. I know what I want and I'm going to get it! So instead of complaining that you were once all that, why don't you do something about it? Dare yourself again? Get your own life back! Stop trying to live mine.'

Pop, pop, pop, I hear the anger bubbles rising and boiling. I always fall for it, the Summer stealth attack on my ego. It's a mother/daughter game we play in which she undermines me to make herself feel better. And I inevitably get pompous and priggish. (I really should remember all this; I did it to my mother after all.)

'Maybe I WILL!' I shout. 'Maybe you can all fuck off and I will do what I WANT for a change: I'll wear double denim and drink Malibu for breakfast and look up all my exes; I'll stage a one-woman show called *Hot Crush* all about Maxim. I'll get an eighties perm and drive a yellow open-top car and make your father dress like Patrick Swayze and we'll scorch round Hyde Park Corner with the stereo pumping out M People.'

She's gaping at me. 'Mum, what's got into you?'

'I am NOT just *Mum*! I'm Eliza Finch. *She's* got into me, Summer. You told her to! This girl I once knew, a girl just like you who was fearless and ambitious and wanted to kiss all the wrong boys. She's still right here! All the time I've missed her, it turns out she was hiding inside me. And even though her hormones are dying, I'm not letting that bitch go. We're on a comeback tour!'

★ ★ ★

If I'm honest, I faked it a bit with the cricket tea ladies earlier. That red mist was very drama school. I was angry, but not blindly so. Not the sort of angry that says things she'll regret, Dog Fight angry.

Angry like I am right now. But Summer's looking at her phone screen, eyes like saucers, finger swiping frantically. '*NO*! I thought I turned live stream off. It's been streaming EVERYTHING!'

'To whom?' I snarl, not really caring.

She's laughing and squealing. 'Oh. Em. Gee! It's already got over five hundred likes! They are *pouring* in. That's sick!'

A shadow falls across the sofa. 'What's sick?'

It's Paddy. He must have come in through the back door, far earlier than expected.

'Is something wrong?' I ask, pulses still thundering.

'Opposite.' His speech sounds normal again. 'Away team's batting collapsed before we'd bowled half the overs. What's sick?'

'Mum's stats. She's been telling my followers about falling in love with her teacher called Max Umbrella and finding her true eighties self again. It's hilarious!'

'Maxim Vella,' I correct, jumping up, 'and it was over thirty years ago. How's your face?'

It looks remarkably intact, just a red mark across his cheek, a split eyebrow and hint of a black, swollen eye. He's far too high from thrashing the opposing village eleven to care. Having batted a personal best, he then helped bowl them out in record time, a man of the match extraordinaire. I even get a kiss, a bit Charles-and-Di polo match, maybe, but it matters. Victory has lent him that extra shot of testosterone wow factor and he fills the room with straightforward masculinity.

Spotting the remainder of the cake, he wolfs it, telling us he's not stopping, just showering and changing before going for a celebratory curry with the lads.

I watch the cake crumbs on his lips. 'How do you like our lemon drizzle?'

'Delicious. Totally wasted on a cricket tea, like all your cakes. And you.' He gives me a wry look. He knows I'm onto him.

I'm still jittery and it makes me rash. 'Must have been hungry work running that errand for Simon this morning?'

But Paddy's gaze has drifted to the female footballers on screen. I want to snap his attention back from all those firm young thighs.

'What was it? The errand? Paddy?'

'Nothing important.' He keeps watching.

Summer's still scrolling and laughing, 'This is insane! Hashtag Mummy Hot Mess. They think you're totally wacko, Mum. In a good way.'

'They should've seen me stabbing a fruitcake and shouting my head off in the cricket pavilion.' I grit my teeth and watch Paddy for a reaction.

She shoots, she scores. He turns to look at me, incredulous. 'Nobody said anything.'

'I'm afraid I might have shocked Dinah and – what's her name?'

'Bianca.' It suits Icepack Blonde perfectly. 'You're OK now though?'

'Fine! Just the usual – what did your follower call me, Summer? Hot mess?'

'Think chaotic, slightly psycho and a suicidal failure,' she explains in case I think I'm forgiven for being self-obsessed, 'but kind of compelling?'

'And exceptionally good at baking cakes,' I snap.

Paddy eyes me warily, and I find myself wanting to ask if Icepack will be at the curry night. But that would sound psycho.

'Is Bianca going on the curry night?' asks the Hot Mess, not caring.

'Probably.' He looks baffled. 'Why?'

'Just wondering.' If he asks me to go along too, I will, I decide. Part of the new, better me. Or old me on her comeback tour?

He doesn't ask, just casts a final glance at the athletic women celebrating on screen before he leaves the room.

As he pounds upstairs, I hear Summer whoop, 'OMG Kwasi *liked* it! He's literally never liked any of my Insta stuff ever. Man!' She's practically crying with joy, gazing at her phone. 'Seven hundred likes! Maxim Vella is *trending*. He has a hashtag! There's a shout out to find him. Our fam livestream is going viral.'

'Who exactly heard that conversation?' I ask anxiously.

'Mostly teeny fans who think it's sweet that old people still try to remember stuff like that. It's all good, Mum, look.' She holds up her phone to show me rows of comments with love hearts, kittens and namastes, grey-haired granny emojis amongst them.

'I am not sweet or *old*!' But to Summer's followers, everyone above thirty is 'Over'.

'You and Mr Paella were like Romeo and Juliet with shoulder pads!'

'Vossi Bop' rings out on her phone. In an instant, she swipes to answer it, already on her feet and heading for the door at speed. 'I know! Yeah, she's totally extra and up herself but that was fire, facts. Same. Embarrassing, yeah, no cap! Yours too? Yeet! Yes, Leibowitz! No lie! I'm not missing next week by the way, just saying. You owe me this...' She moves out of earshot.

Most of this is as lost to me as ancient Norse, but if it is Kwasi, I sense I may have pushed forbidden love closer together not further apart by being 'totally extra'. I close my eyes, wishing I hadn't made it all about my youth, not her present. When will I stop living in the past? When will now feel as good as it did then?

I love Paddy and our children. That should be enough. It's not like I have a sex drive to take out on tour any more. Not even a menstrual cycle.

Switching off the television, I slump back down on the sofa, pulling a cushion over my head, longing for blank.

Instead, in my mind's eye Matteo is swinging his chair around to sit astride it and fix me with his deep velvet gaze. *Now you know who I remind you of, eh?*

High above, Paddy is singing 'A Change is Gonna Come' in the shower.

It seems it has.

14

About Time

My ten o'clock viewing is late.

The flat is in a converted mill overlooking the Avon, a luxury retirement block on Stratford's Waterside. The wife of the couple living there has passed away recently, her widower moving in with family. It's full of pictures, knickknacks, mementos, and hundreds of books, all neatly tidied so the space can be inspected.

My all-female estate agency's mantra is 'happiness sells houses, cleanliness clinches the deal!' so I've put fresh freesias out in a vase, a squirt of bleach down the loo and opened the doors onto the balcony with its café table and jaunty geraniums perfectly angled. The scene is set. It's a tempting one, although I don't yet qualify – the criteria for living in this riverside spot is that buyers must be over fifty-five, the subtext is 'exclusive and cultured'. Leaseholders can even rent private moorings outside.

This is the sort of place Jules wants Mum and Dad to move to. But they love The Prettiest Cottage in Warwickshire with its long-established garden and freshly re-rooted prodigal son.

Perhaps unsurprisingly, Miles didn't reply to my *tempestuous asp sex* text last night. I start composing another while I wait, demanding to know what he thinks he's doing suggesting Mum and Dad sell *The Tempest*.

Is my brother as depressed as Joe suggests, I wonder?

I delete what I've written and type: *I'm worried about you. Call me. Exx*

Jules has a theory that the children of long-married, mutually devoted couples always struggle to find happiness in their own relationships.

I have a less rose-tinted view of our parents' relationship, but I can see how this explanation also fits Miles and his ceaseless quest to anchor the wanderlust with love.

As for me, marrying my working-class hero meant rebelling against my parents' ambitions for me and I've always found great happiness in going off script, but I worry that Jules's theory is finally chiming true. I can sense the fracture between Paddy and me widening.

By the time he rolled in from his team curry last night, I was asleep in bed. Waking up in the early hours, I stared up into the darkness worrying about my marriage withering, about what Paddy will say when he hears the narrowboat might soon be sold, about Mum and Dad not coping, Summer hating me, my latent anti-fascism letting down my generation and why I still miss Arty so much I had to swallow knives of grief to stop myself sobbing.

During this morning's routine, Paddy was so hungover

he said nothing at all. At least, I think that was the reason for the silent treatment. I didn't ask; I was too tired.

Yawning, I go out on the balcony to call the council's Special Educational Needs department again about Ed's school transport.

I'm told the colleague I need to talk to is on holiday but I take their direct email and message straight away from my phone with a brief explanation of the issue with the taxi driver, copying in Ed's school Head and Paddy on his work email. I then text Lou to see how she's doing, attaching an Edina Monsoon flapping GIF. She sends back a Bitmoji of her likeness laying into a punchbag. Friendship shorthand is a lifesaver.

Think positive, Eliza: *happiness sells houses.* I head back inside to plump cushions. All I know about the prospective buyer is that he's called Mr Wright, he's looking for somewhere to move into with his new wife, and he's 'proceedable'. The name makes me smile: somebody has met her Mr Right at last.

When I check the brochure to make sure I have all the amenities off pat, I spot that the lease requires residents to be over fifty, not fifty-five.

That makes me eligible, I realise with a jolt as the buzzer goes.

Fifty bothers me, really bloody bothers me, in a way no other landmark age has. Celebrating it felt like passing through a door I can't ever go back through. My thirties and forties flew by without me ever feeling any older. One minute I was late twenties, worried I'd be left on the shelf, then WHOOOOSH: I'm fifty. I've gone through the door and nobody left behind can see me.

It's scary this side, like walking along Sniper Alley, trying to work out where the fatal shot's going to come from. And even if I do make it to the far distance, all that's waiting is old age.

(I read a quote recently that if our forties are the old age of youth, our fifties are the youth of old age. It didn't make me feel remotely better about being fifty.)

I buzz in Mr Wright and take up position by the lift.

The tall, stooped figure who steps out of the doors, creased suit reeking of stale cigarette smoke, is probably mid-sixties and vaguely familiar. He has the dishevelled look of a once-handsome man subsiding into old age through the back door of a pub, although the glitter of a gold signet ring and well-worn Lobb brogues hint at erstwhile grandeur.

'Mr Wright, I'm Eliza from the agency. Welcome to Lace Mill,' I offer my hand to shake, which he ignores.

'Where's the girl I booked the appointment with?' he demands, revealing yellowing camel teeth. 'Blonde, legs up to here, huge' – he leaves a deliberate pause – 'smile.'

'She's on another appointment so I'll be showing you around today.' Now I've heard the gravelly voice, I recognise him as one of the tipsters who once co-presented televised horseracing.

'I suppose you'll have to do.' He looks me up and down dismissively, my beige shift dress and nude court shoes kept just for viewings, perfect for blending into a magnolia wall, my split ends tucked into a neat chignon, plus the pearls, of course, because we're a class agency. His gaze lingers on these. Or it could be on my bust. Hard to tell given he's wearing the sort of half-tint glasses that went out of style in the eighties.

'Will your wife be joining us, Mr Wright?'

'Fiancée, and hardly,' he tells my pearls/chest. 'Marta's still in the Ukraine. Bit of a visa cock-up. The agency are sorting it out.'

'Mail-order bride' is now on a loop in my head.

'Come in and look round lovely Flat Seven!' I hand him the brochure and run the spiel about the history of the building, the working days of its watermill, the high-class conversion, the shared facilities for the discerning mature buyer.

'Let's cut the crap and see what's here, shall we?' He marches off.

I wonder how young his Ukrainian bride is; I'm not sure she'll be allowed to live here under the age restrictions. Best not say anything while I'm on soft sell.

'Isn't it a wonderful view?' I gush as I follow him into *the generously proportioned double aspect master suite.* 'Imagine waking up to see something as breathtaking as this every morning?'

'I've prettier things to look at.' He casts me an amused, appraising look that makes me step back from a chilly blast of déjà vu.

Thirteen years ago, in an apartment not unlike this one, overlooking a canal by Birmingham's Brindleyplace, I admired the view.

'How would you like to wake up to this?' asked the man I was there with.

'Very much.'

'Play your cards right and you could.'

By which, I thought he meant that I'd soon be acting in the Birmingham-based drama we were there to discuss. He thought I was giving the green light for what was about to happen.

Had #*MeToo* been trending in 2005, I'd have honestly said #*NotMe*. Mild flirtation and plenty of innuendo, yes, but at a time when male producers, directors and playwrights regularly demanded actresses strip off at auditions so their figured could be 'assessed', I'd never had to. Nor had I been asked for sexual favours in return for a part as others I knew had. Not until that day in the waterside apartment with a television director on whose decision my biggest career break rested.

That day marked my singular professional encounter with... what do I call it? #*TimesUp* lite? Compared to the experiences of other women I know, it was trivial. But it changed me.

My Agent-Who-Never-Calls had miraculously put me forward for the pilot episode of a new daytime drama, a legal soap about a barristers' chambers in Birmingham, full of human interest, diversity, clichés and at least five 'I *object*, your honour!' per episode. I *knew* that world; the role could have been written for me: Alicia Swan, a ball-breaking thirty-something brief. Her name even *sounded* like mine.

The director was from my parents' generation and I'd

passed the screen test with flying colours (an impersonation of my sister which they loved). Now he wanted a chat about the character moving forwards, so we'd met up in a coffee shop in the city centre. If the series got made, he explained, he'd like Alicia to take a more central role. We talked about human rights, legal aid and McLibel.

He said he'd made some notes but, oh bother, he'd left them behind. His flat was nearby. We could pop there together.

It wasn't until we were alone together, view admired, that I understood. All the enthusiastic talk coming out of my mouth was nothing to his desire to come in it.

Mr Wright is now in the en suite where I have pointed out the convenience of 'his and hers basins and body-jet shower for that spa-clean feeling'.

'Washing your arse when you're too old to reach it, you mean!' he barks. 'Care to demonstrate, Elsa?'

'Eliza.' I smile fixedly. *Happiness sells houses!*

'So are you going to show me or not?' he snaps impatiently.

'I'm sorry?'

'How the shower works. I want to see the water pressure.' He casts me a sly, amused look.

I've been accompanying viewings for years and nobody's asked me to do this. What is the professional protocol on this, I wonder? Am I allowed to tell him to back off? Or am I over-reading it?

Nobody's asked me for a blow job on a property viewing either, but what happened thirteen years ago still makes me question everything.

★ ★ ★

The randy television director had been in the industry a long time, and I trusted him. I didn't even question what was going on when he poured two glasses of wine.

His flat was a bland, rented pied-à-terre with piles of newly-bought books and DVDs everywhere, and as we sat down in two armchairs I enthusiastically told him that I'd do whatever it took to make the character of Alicia Swan work.

'Then come here.' He'd beckoned me towards him, manspreading. 'Use your head, darling.'

At first, I was incredulous. 'What are you suggesting?'

'We both know.'

Still not really sinking in. *Surely not that?*

'Use. Your. Head,' he repeated with a twinkle of the eye. 'Call it lip service.'

'I'm not like that!'

'Like what?'

'I'm a professional.' More embarrassment, reluctant to offend. 'I really *do* want to work with you.'

'Then show me how much.'

'I have a husband and two kids.'

'I have a wife and three and I'll raise you a grandson. We're both grown-ups, Eliza.'

Angrier still. 'I didn't come here for this. This is a total abuse of your role.'

That's when he crossed his legs and arms, looking extremely pissed off. Then he started to laugh, a hollow, incredulous chuckle. 'Oh Eliza, *please* don't tell me that you think I was coming onto you?'

Mortification kicked in. Or adrenaline. Hard to tell. 'I thought maybe you were.'

The chuckle stopped. Hard eyes. 'Don't flatter yourself.'

And in those three words, he had me beaten. It wasn't *use your head* that haunted me in coming weeks and months. It was *don't flatter yourself*.

Why was I so polite and British? We laughed it off. I apologised. (I can't believe I actually said sorry.) I was *burning* with shame. We talked some more about the role, as though nothing had happened. Then I left.

The encounter chipped a fragment out of me, riving a hairline through my ego so small it's hard to spot. But I'm sharper with men now, more brittle, less trusting. And I don't flirt.

Mr Wright is admiring the high-pressure water flying every which way out of the shower, steam rising. 'More than big enough for two in there, eh?'

'Absolutely!' One arm soaked from turning it on, I stay as far away as possible.

'You can turn it off now!' he calls from the hot mist.

I can hear my phone ringing in the bedroom, The Proclaimers singing 'I'm Gonna Be', chirpily announcing they would walk 500 miles. It's my brother's ringtone.

'Hurry up, Elsa!' demands Mr Wright.

'It's Eliza.' Stretching into the shower to twist the tap shut, I get even wetter, the front of my dress soaked, my hair flattened.

Guffaws of laughter greet the sight. 'Miss Wet T-shirt has nothing to fear from you, eh?'

Rage and humiliation fizz in my veins. 'I'd appreciate it if you didn't make comments like that.'

'It's only a bit of fun. Marta's thirty-one. Need I say more?'

Sopping wet and indignant, I snap, 'Perhaps it's best if you continue looking around alone while I dry off on the balcony?'

'I could,' he shrugs, 'but I'm not buying this place, darling. It's for oldies.'

'Over fifties, yes.'

He scrunches up his nose like there's a bad smell. 'Tell blondie in the office to give me a call if she gets something more up our street. And I want her to show me round, not matron. I'll see myself out.'

I wait for the sound of the lift doors closing, grab one of the hand-embroidered cushions and scream into it with all my force. Like elephants, angry women never forget.

My Agent-Who-Never-Calls reported that the team behind the barrister drama had decided I was too old for Alicia. Perhaps the actor who was cast used her head, but the pilot was never commissioned as a series; I like to think it would have been had I been playing her.

I haven't been put forward for a television role since. My dented confidence turned in on itself for a long time. *Had* I misread the situation?

Don't flatter yourself.

For a while I was so angry about it, I wanted to rush back to that flat and slap him, tell him to fuck off, tell him that I was taking it to a tribunal. And I wanted to tell my thirty-five-year-old self that every woman who has struggled to lose baby weight, to conceal the tiredness of motherhood, to compete for work against fresh-faced, childfree juniors understands what it feels like to doubt herself, and standing up for herself takes guts, but she has to. We all have to stop apologising, Eliza! Otherwise nothing will change.

I never told anybody what had happened, not even Paddy. I was frightened he might think I encouraged it, and – shamefully – that he'd think less of me if he knew the director's reaction.

I flatter myself I'm much stronger now. But men like Mr Wright still put me in the blackest of moods.

Out on the balcony, I return Miles's call. It goes straight to voicemail. I don't trust myself to leave a message. I'm fit to explode, my pulses slamming. I wish I still smoked.

Bracing myself, I call the agency to apologise that I failed to sell the mill's appeal to Mr Wright. The buxom blonde senior negotiator – who isn't on another appointment at all – admits that she'd suspected he was an arsehole from the get-go. 'He was leery the moment he came in. We thought you could handle him, being…' She hesitates.

A consummate actor? Clever? No-nonsense? Ballsy?

'Older.'

I look up at the sky and watch a jet-streak fading. Somebody is sitting out on the balcony above me, listening to a wartime drama on radio, air-raid siren wailing, bombs raining. I try to cheer myself up by imagining one landing on Mr Wright, leaving nothing but a pair of smoking brogues.

★ ★ ★

Miles rings back while I'm still fantasy-bombing on the balcony and I answer with an unladylike hiss, 'What the fuck are you playing at?'

'I thought you were worried about me?'

'I am. You're certifiably mad suggesting selling *The Tempest*.'

'It was Jules's idea.' Whether seven or forty-seven, our little brother's lightning quick to shift blame. 'And Mum and Dad aren't remotely interested in her and never have been. A buyer has fallen into our lap and I could use the cash.'

'Can't I buy your share? How big is it?'

'Fifty per cent.'

I want to cry. Mum and Dad are so generous to all of us; I could never have asked for something like that after everything they've already done.

'Paddy's *heart* is in that boat,' I whisper.

'Then it's a good thing we sell her,' Miles says brightly. 'He might get it back.'

'What's that supposed to mean?'

'You figure it out.'

'What's *that* supposed to mean?'

There's a long silence at the other end. I watch some canoeists paddling close to the mill and my anger evaporates. 'Miles, are you depressed?'

I realise he's hung up.

We're also always slamming the phone down on each other, Miles and me. Paddy calls them our childhood hang ups.

I can see how infantile it must look, the cliché younger siblings still squabbling in middle age. We once stopped talking for a whole six months after an argument about car keys.

One of us always calls back eventually. I am marching along Mill Lane in blistering sunshine when The Proclaimers start singing again.

'You told me you wished you'd never set eyes on that narrowboat,' he points out petulantly.

'You know I didn't mean it.' I try to keep my voice calm, wondering how best to probe the state of his mental health.

'Like when you called me a cunt?' He laughs. That childhood insult I can never live down.

I'm even more certain Joe's right: when Miles doesn't like himself, he's hard to like.

Sympathy fraying, I'd quite like to call him one again, but there's an elderly couple walking towards me along the narrow pavement. A hot flush starts to surface. There's no shade to be had, brick walls hemming me in the heat. 'Don't let's forget I called you that word because you *stole* something that didn't belong to you and hid it rather than admit it, Miles,' I whisper angrily. 'You have never *apologised* for that.'

'Sorry.'

'Thanks.' I nip through Holy Trinity's south gate to shortcut across its churchyard, the tree shade so blissful I pause beneath a lime to breathe in the sweet scent of its first flowers, hot flush raging.

'Now can I sell the narrowboat without you going all Lucrezia Borgia on me?'

'No you can't! This is a *lot* more serious than a Bionic Woman toy, Miles.'

'You even remember what doll it was!' He laughs again.

'*And* Mission Purse. I still haven't forgiven you.' Remembering his possible depression, I check myself, switching approach. 'It's Paddy's and my wedding anniversary this week, Miles. Please don't do this to us now.' I stop myself again. If he's feeling vulnerable and lonely, the last thing my brother wants is me boasting about my long marriage.

'I don't think it's *fair*,' I say eventually, chest and neck flaming.

Just as I start to think my brother must have hung up again, he says, 'Hide her then.'

I'm not sure he means what I think he does. 'Hide the boat?'

'Yes, take *The Tempest* and hide her, I dare you.'

We grew up issuing impossible challenges to one another, Miles and I, dare, dare, double dare being our childhood mantra, and the cause of several visits to A & E. I once won a year off cleaning out the family goldfish for phoning up people with unfortunate surnames listed in the telephone directory – 'Are you Jo King?', 'I'm looking for Mike Hunt?' and so on. That same year, he broke his arm tightrope-walking for my secret stash of mini Mars Bars.

'Tell you what,' I can tell he's warming to the idea of a challenge, a whoop in his voice, 'if I can't find her by your anniversary, my share's yours.'

'You're not serious?' Despite myself, I'm wondering

where I could stash a sixty-foot narrowboat for seventy-two hours.

'Call it my anniversary present. Except it won't be because you can't do it. You've wimped out of life, just like your husband. And involve Paddy, the deal's off,' he taunts in an East End gangster voice. 'This is between me, you and the Bionic Woman.'

'Don't be such a cunt, Miles!' I cut the call, realising too late that I am standing within earshot of a guided tour.

One of the group, a large, loud-shirted, middle-aged American man, gasps, 'Lady, this is a churchyard! Please desist with your profanities. I thought Brits had better manners. Your Bard is buried inside that holy place!'

Rage is still ringing in my ears, sweat hot-washing my body, but I try to stay calm. 'Actually, Shakespeare got Malvolio to spell the c-word out in *Twelfth Night* as a gag, and the gravediggers were pretty foul-mouthed in *Hamlet* so I don't think he'd mind.'

'Do not let down your gentle sex and beautiful country, mam! See how shocked my dear wife is?' He points out a small, red-faced woman about my age, sweating much like I am. 'I demand you apologise to her right now.'

I catch her eye and share her pain. 'I'm so sorry if I've offended you, although not as sorry as I am that you have a sexist, narrow-minded husband. It must be hell. If you'll excuse me, I want a word with God about his sense of humour.'

As I hurry into the church to escape, growling, I hear a man's voice close behind me. '*Bellissima*! You are unwell I think?'

That's all I bloody need.

'I'm fine!' I turn round furiously.

Big brown eyes meet mine, heroically kind, searching for signs of plague. It's Matteo, the restaurateur.

'Eliza, you are ill? You feel hot? Faint? You want to sit down?'

'I'm perfectly well,' I reiterate, tempted to add *I'm having a menopausal rage and statistically I might kill you if you hang around.* 'Please just carry on with whatever you were doing.'

'I come here to see Shakespeare's grave,' he explains. 'Russo's is not open on Mondays, so each week I try to educate myself about my new hometown.'

He's dressed expensively in belted cream chinos and a crisp white shirt with one too many buttons undone to show mahogany skin, gold chain gleaming rebelliously.

'It's over there,' I point up the aisle towards the distant chancel, before diverting into a rear pew, grateful for the cool and quiet

But Matteo settles beside me with a contented sigh.

My murderous thoughts darken, a desire to shout 'fuck off' repeatedly to anyone and everyone dangerously present. (Sorry, God.)

'I should warn you I hate all men right now,' I tell him.

'Me also,' he agrees with a devilish smile. 'This is a beautiful church, yes?'

'It's OK.' I fan myself with the brochure for the mill apartment. I'm not much of a believer, but I send up a small prayer that he goes away before I hit him.

'You have sad eyes, Eliza. I notice them last week. Like *levriero.*'

'Who?' I imagine a tragic Italian actress, all deep brooding thoughts and spider lashes.

'Greyhound. Beautiful dogs. I want a dog very much.'

It's not wildly flattering being compared to a sad-eyed hound, but I can't argue with loving dogs.

When I stop fanning, he glances down at the brochure. 'You are also looking for somewhere new to live?'

'I show people round properties.'

'May I?' He takes it to examine. 'I am looking for somewhere myself. This is by the river, yes?'

'It's for over-fifties.'

'That is perfect. Grown-ups. I like to be near water. You can keep dogs here, yes?' He opens the foldout, then his eyes light up. 'I can moor a boat! The *chiatta* your brother is selling, maybe?'

It takes all my willpower to hold more profanities in check. Be professional, I remind myself. Happiness sells houses! 'It's a lovely apartment. Super location.'

'You show me round it sometime?' He looks up at me.

'By all means.' Or view it with a less murderous guide maybe.

'My family want me to grow roots. I can keep this?' He holds the brochure up.

'Be my guest. The agency's number is on there.'

'Thank you. My wife, she love the idea of living in England. She like your humour very much.'

I didn't spot his pouting Lolita crack so much as a smile last week. 'Where is she today?'

'She is dead, Eliza.' I have a brief, involuntary vision of his child bride lying on the restaurant floor in a pool of blood.

'Five years ago,' he goes on, his expression briefly unguarded before he looks away.

'I'm so sorry.'

'A new beginning in this country is a good thing for me.' He gestures at the church's ornately carved wooden ceiling. '*La vita è un viaggio. Chi viaggia vive due volte.* Life is a voyage. Those who travel, live twice.'

I like this concept very much, but I don't say so. I'm too full of rage still.

'Show me the resting place of your famous playwright, *bellissima.*' He stands up and offers his hand. Not taking it – mine's far too sweaty – I straighten my creased skirt, grateful the front of my dress has dried from its shower dousing.

I've seen Shakespeare's grave more than once, but I'm still on agency time and oblige given his interest in the mill apartment.

'You look different today,' he says as we walk up the aisle together. 'I almost didn't recognise you.'

'It's for the job.'

'You are a very elegant woman, Eliza, like your mamma. *Sprezzatura* as we say in Italy. *Mozzafiato.* My memory for faces is not so good these days,' he sighs. 'My kids tell me I have prosopagnosia, you know? Face blindness? But I never forget one as beautiful as yours.'

He smiles full beam at me which feels inappropriate, partly because I am in an ugly frame of mind and partly because we're in a church and he's just told me about his dead wife.

We arrive at the grave – a modest stone set in the chancel floor in front of the altar, one of five Shakespeare family graves lined side by side beneath the stained-glass East

Window. I always find it curious that William's is the only one with no name engraved, just a warning cursing anybody who tampers with his bones.

'It's thought graverobbers took no notice and stole his head,' I whisper to Matteo. 'Literally skulduggery.'

'No?' He is wide-eyed at this. 'Where is it now?'

'Nobody knows.'

'*Ammazza.*' He takes a picture of the stone with his phone. 'I can't wait to tell my Sara! She loves stories like this. She is at the beautician all morning.'

Sara must be the pouting temptress, I realise.

I head back into the main church and Matteo falls into step beside me. 'You know these young girls: the nails, the hair, the make-up, the clothes. She costs me a fortune! Now she tells me she wants eyelash extensions. Is crazy! But she is so gorgeous I could eat her, so who am I to complain? Look at this!'

We pause to admire the font which has a snazzy crowned lid decked with flowers and candles. I catch him watching me across it.

'You have them?'

'Eyelash extensions?' Can't he see mine are short and mascara-lumped?

'Children! I have four.' He beams proudly. 'Sara is my youngest and my only daughter. My boys are men now.'

Not a younger lover at all, but a proprietorial daughter. Feeling disgracefully judgmental, I remove Matteo Mele from my perv chart.

I tell him I have two sons and a daughter. It turns out Sara is just a few months older than Summer. 'My beautiful *cucciola*. So grown up now.'

Paddy re-enters the perv chart for ogling her so much.

'She's lovely.' Tarty.

'She is very like her mother.'

'Who must have been beautiful,' I oblige.

'She was. We were married twenty-four years.' He looks away again, his sadness palpable.

We head across to look at the shop, full of Shakespeare busts, scented candles and quote-striped tea towels, this church being Bard mecca. Matteo loves it all, hands soon full of leather bookmarks and snow globes to send home to relatives.

Watching him, so loose-limbed and hot-skinned, born of sunshine and sea, it strikes me that he doesn't seem to belong in a landlocked, historic town like Stratford upon Avon, serving pasta to tourists, let alone in a retirement flat.

'Have you been married long, Eliza?' he asks, eyes bright with interest.

'So long the UK won Eurovision the same year. I wore a cowboy hat and Paddy had curtains like that.' I point at a picture of a floppy-haired Leonardo DiCaprio as Romeo, transferred onto a mug priced at an unholy four pounds.

'Paddy, you say?'

'We'll have been married twenty-two years this week.' He's watching me closely again.

'Your husband... Forgive me, I don't like the man.'

Whoa! Where did that come from? 'Why?'

'He left a bad review for Russo's on TripAdvisor. Very negative.'

Inside my head is crashing into gear, remembering my sex

avoidance displacement activity. What did I write? And why does he think it was Paddy?

I hold my estate agent smile. 'Oh, I shouldn't let it worry you. He'd drunk too much.'

'Clearly.'

As he heads to the till, I hold up my phone and hurry outside.

'If you'll excuse me, I just need to make a call! Good to see you!'

In the quiet shade by the north transept, I hastily check TripAdvisor on my phone. The review is indeed written on Paddy's account, his username unhelpfully Patrick_ Hollander66. Oh God, it's much worse than I remember. And astonishingly badly typed. 'Diabolical' is repeated three times, each with a different spelling. I try to sign in to delete it, but I don't know his password.

The laptop at home must have been logged onto Paddy's Google account, I realise. Why didn't I check?

I'm in so much trouble, and that's before I even mention Miles and the narrowboat.

When I head alongside the church to the riverside, Matteo's sitting on a bench by the path, the property brochure on his lap, his phone to his ear, chatting in Italian. Spotting me, he rings off and leaps up. 'Eliza! I make an appointment to view the apartment tomorrow! Uncle Antonio, he knows the mill and is *molto felice*. You are my lucky charm, eh, *bella signora?*' He hands me a mug in a paper bag. 'To say thank you!'

'You shouldn't have.' The TripAdvisor review is burning my soul.

'I like this very much.' He taps the brochure, sitting back down.

I stay standing.

'The accommodation above Russo's is *piuttosto piccolo,*' he tells me, 'and Sara and her cousin – my chef Massimo – they want their friends to visit, to listen to their music, stream their movies. I prefer people my age around me, you know? Sara, she say her old papa cramps her style. Daughters are harsh critics, eh?' His smile creases up at me.

I laugh, feeling better about mine calling me a self-obsessed hot mess.

'You like your mug?'

Perching on the bench beside him, I open the bag expecting Leonardo DiCaprio's curtains. Instead it's bone china and decorated with a beautifully painted initial E, picked out in feathers, birds and flowers. 'It's lovely, but I really can't accept this.'

'Take it.' He smiles again, head dipping into my eyeline. 'The E will make you feel goooood.'

'You sound like an eighties raver.'

'*Bellissima,* I *was* an eighties raver: Roman Techno, Berlin's Love Parade, Ku in Ibiza.'

'Me too! Sunrise parties. Second summer of love.'

'Here we are sharing a bench like old people.' He starts drumming on his knees and beat-boxing 'Back to Life' by Soul II Soul.

For a moment he has my sense of humour in a vice and I

feel my rage vanishing. I join in, singing until I'm laughing too much to go on because we sound so dreadful.

'The world needs a third Summer of Love, *si*?' He gives me a long, dark-eyed look.

I drop my gaze first, fixing on the pendant hanging from the gold chain around his neck.

'You admire my *cornicello*?' He leans closer to show it off.

I laugh again because it sounds silly.

'It protects against *Malocchio* the evil eye. *Cornicello* means little hornet. It was a gift from my grandfather when I was born. See the two Ms engraved here for Matteo Mele?'

It glows against his olive skin, far too brazenly Italian for a Warwickshire riverbank, just as the light tufts of salt and pepper chesty hair around it seem too intimate, his aftershave too heady, the gaze which meets mine when I look up way too intense. It takes all my effort to drop it.

I slide back on the bench. He slides back too. We're both pressed up against opposite arms, staring at trees, wondering what just happened.

'I have to be somewhere,' I say quickly, remembering my urgent need to figure out where I can hide *The Tempest*.

'I'll walk with you.' He stands up and offers me his hand.

'There's no need.' I spring up unaided, but in my haste the mug falls from my lap, smashing into two.

'Oh no!' I yelp. 'I'm so sorry. I'll buy another.'

'It's OK.' He picks up the pieces and tosses them in a nearby bin. 'I bought the last E.'

'I'll change my name.'

And we start laughing again because some strange

chemical is whizzing around our arteries that isn't an artificial high but feels like one.

It's far more dangerous. I hope it wears off soon.

15

Two Time

'I am a Mele not a Russo,' Matteo tells me as we walk along the river path into Stratford. 'Mele means honey; our ancestors were Puglian bee-keepers. My wife, she loved researching our families' history but – boh...' He smiles sadly.

He's Antonio's nephew through his mother, he explains: 'Mama is his little sister and she married a Mele. We're tall and handsome; Russos are short and sexy.' Matteo oversaw restaurants opening in Tokyo and New York before agreeing to come here to help create a bigger British franchise, the Stratford move made partly for Sara's benefit – 'she loves your country, wants to study here, but I do not think London is safe for her' – and because his children say he mopes in big cities. 'The more people, the lonelier the grief.'

He moves on quickly, talking instead about his young chef Massimo. 'He wants a Russo bistro in every British market town, a television show and a Ferrari.'

'Like yours?'

'Beautiful car. It is on my bucket list to drive fast through cardboard boxes like your British cop shows.' He glances across at me, waiting for my laugh.

'Short bucket list if you run people off the road like you tried to do to me last week.' My sense of humour is already under threat. I'm sweating up like a racehorse and my feet hurt in the court shoes.

'*Macché*! You too, *cara*. In Italy we say *Chi si fa pecorello, I lupi la mangiano*: make yourself a sheep and the wolves will eat you.' He gives me a sideways smile.

'Here, we say beware of a wolf in sheep's clothing. So why didn't you help me that day? Why stand there and watch?'

'You looked so beautiful I was *paralizzate*, how you say, frozen to the spot?'

I feel my goodwill towards him retract. 'You were angry at me.'

'I regret it. Today, I would cross any road to save a lost lamb for you.'

'I'll hold you to that.'

After a pause he says, 'Maybe not Milanese autostrade. Not unless we were lovers.'

'I'm married,' I remind him.

'And I am Italian,' he reminds me.

I laugh to show I get the joke, then have no idea what to say.

We walk on in silence. Inside my head is not silent at all: bells, whistles, sirens, rave anthems, Munch's 'Scream' and Vivaldi's *L'Amoroso* are all vying for attention.

We step out of the way to let a group of dogwalkers pass, a stream of wet-nosed, waggy-tailed fur. My heel turns on the grass and Matteo puts a hand on my arm to steady me. I'm aware of it there as I rebalance myself. Then it moves down to enclose my fingers. A Trump-on-May move; proprietorial, old-fashioned masculinity.

I remove my fingers from between his as the dogs sniff their way past.

'I want my greyhound,' he sighs. 'You have a dog, Eliza?'

Feeling it would be insensitive to mention Arty's recent death after he's talked about losing his wife, I just say, 'Not at the moment.'

He takes my fingers again and squeezes them. 'Everybody needs a dog, *cara*.'

He helps me back out onto the path, and we walk at least five metres along it before he lets go of my hand.

PDAs have never been Paddy's thing. The last time he held my hand in public was before Edward was born. I grew up with touch as a norm: cuddles, ruffling hair, stroking arms and backs. Touch. It's like breathing. I can't live without it.

In Paddy's mind, touching is a private thing. The Hollanders didn't 'do' physical affection.

For years our children compensated my need for cuddles, and Arty was there to step in when I was shrugged off by embarrassed teens and sensory-challenged Ed. While my sex-starved husband took my every affectionate touch as a cue for some rare bed action, Arty craved the straightforward touch of kinship, of affection. Instead of reaching out to touch Paddy, I'd stroke her.

I miss her warmth every day. I miss touch.

A courteous man taking my hand to help me step back on a path should be no more sexual than patting a dog.

Which makes it awkward that I find myself turned on by it.

As we walk on, Matteo tells me, 'I downloaded one of your books.' We are passing the RSC. Painful timing. 'Last night, I fell asleep listening to your voice.'

I'm not sure what to do with that information. But I'm relieved when he reveals it's an early one, a quirky historic novel that required minimal panting.

He asks what I like to read, a question guaranteed to keep 99 per cent of Finches talking nineteen to the dozen. I'm a beg, borrow and steal reader, grateful to my parents for the bedrock of classics that mean I'm not afraid of literary fiction, although I'm happiest with a comforting chunk of whodunnit. Matteo's reading taste leans heavily towards spy thrillers – 'I *live* those books! You must try. I will buy you one!' – and when we move on to films he's funny and enthusiastic and, like me, a big devotee of old Hollywood classics.

We've been so busy talking we've walked through Bancroft Gardens, crossed the canal footbridge and are already in front of the Gower Monument, Shakespeare cast in hot glossy bronze sitting high on his plinth, pigeon guano on his bald pate. At each compass point around the statue are four further bronzes of characters from his most famous plays. I hesitate by Henry V holding his crown aloft, gluttonous Falstaff the sexist dinosaur to our left, Hamlet the young overthinker to our right.

Behind us, the moorings in Bancroft Basin are striped with colourful narrowboats.

There's no wise wizard Prospero in the Gower tableau, but *The Tempest* is floating so close by, we can almost see her.

'Here's fine,' I tell Matteo, as though instructing an Uber driver to drop me off. 'You get back; I think it's about to rain.' My next appointment isn't until after lunch; I'll sit it out on the narrowboat and form a masterplan.

'I've nothing urgent,' he says with that wide smile. 'The marina is just across the road, no? The boat your family is selling is there, I think? I would love to see her.'

'I'm afraid I've got to dash straight to another appoint—' A flurry of digital camera clicks nearby distracts me. Somebody is photographing us, big black lens pointed our way like a weapon. A hand waves at me above it.

Lurking behind Lady Macbeth, smiling excitedly in a white bucket hat, is my polite Japanese stalker.

He takes a few more pictures of me, then he hurries over, miming eagerly, and before we know it Matteo has been handed the huge bit of digital gadgetry and is obligingly taking a shot of stalker and me lined up together by Henry V.

'Matteo, I'm not very comfortable with this,' I mutter as Mr Speak-no-English holds his hands above his head imitating the bronze prince with his crown.

'Don't be mean, *bellissima*,' Matteo calls from behind the big black lens. 'The man, he just wants a picture with a beautiful English rose in Shakespeare's Stratford. Smile for me, baby! Arms up. That's it! Beautiful!'

He thinks he's bloody Mario Testino. But he's so funny and enthusiastic, I throw a few poses, the silliness catching.

Our Japanese friend turns to me with the same drink

mime he made last week. Then he points across the canal basin at the floating café barge.

I shake my head vigorously and point at Matteo, who is shouting, '*Bella, bella!* Love that pose! Now point at Shakespeare, yes? This light is terrific!'

His breath quickening, my stalker launches into another mime, pointing to Matteo and then pointing his pinky finger up with a wide smile and nodding a lot, as though questioning the Italian's endowment. It might be a cultural thing, but it's a worrying one.

Overhead, the sun is battling to hold out against a single black rain cloud, a downpour imminent. When Matteo finally hands back the camera to a flurry of 'Thank yous!' with prayer hands, he replies in Japanese, saying something that sounds like, '*Doy! Tashi mashty.*' Show off. They're soon having an animated conversation with more drink gesticulation and pinky finger pointing – at me this time – and then Matteo puts his palms up, shaking his head.

'I'll be off!' I start to back away.

'I come with you,' Matteo says. When the tourist starts after us, he stops him with a mash up of Italian, English and Japanese, the only words of which I recognise are 'Harry Potter!'

Perhaps it's best to have his company until I put distance between myself and my camera-toting admirer. I set off as fast as my court shoes will let me, waving my stalker farewell, Matteo soon striding alongside.

'You speak Japanese?' I'm already out of breath.

'Badly, but I pick a little up in Tokyo.'

'What was he saying?'

'He asked my permission to buy you a gift as a tribute to your acting talent.'

This strikes me as odd, although I'm quietly thrilled to have been recognised. 'I wonder what he's seen me in?' (I've done some recent film extra work and a furniture warehouse sale TV advertisement.)

He chuckles. '*Bellissima*, he thinks you are Emma Thompson.'

Ten-year age gap aside, I elect to find this flattering. 'Why did he need *your* permission to buy me a gift?'

'He thinks we are secret lovers.' He holds up his pinky finger.

'I hope you put him right on both fronts.' I realise I am now talking like Emma Thompson.

'My Japanese is not so good. Now, show me this narrowboat.'

I once starred in a thirty-second television advert for an orthopaedic foot care brand. My character was a podiatrist in a white lab coat who gazed caringly over the big toe she was examining to reassure the public that, whatever the problem, we had a product to help everybody 'enjoy life feet first!'.

The advert didn't run long – the slogan ill-judged for the elderly target market – yet it remains one of my more visible career roles, and it's the only time I've ever been recognised and stopped in the street, my advice on bunions, cracked heels and ingrowing toenails in high demand throughout

2014. People sometimes got quite shirty and accused me of duping them when I apologetically explained that I was an actor not a foot expert. I still occasionally get cornered by a member of the public eager to whip off a sock and show me a verruca. I now tell them I've been struck off the Chiropody Register for gross misconduct.

'There she is!' I point out *The Tempest*, hoping I can now make my excuses to escape back to the agency and drop off the flat keys.

But Matteo's already striding along the jetty boards, beckoning for me to follow.

'*Che bello*!' He admires sixty feet of glossy red narrowboat, picture-postcard traditional from her harlequin-painted cratch to her tiny curved stern. Moored at the end of a row of six directly in front of the marina café bar, she is by far the most decorative and historic.

'All my life I wanted one of these! Since *Travelling Man*, you know?'

'Is that a book?'

'Television series you make here in the UK. In the eighties.'

I apologise that I didn't know it.

Matteo explains in the same breathless detail I might recount discovering *Kids from Fame* or *Dynasty* that it was one of the crime shows that Uncle Antonio lovingly recorded on his rented Sanyo video machine to share with his family back home. For its two series, it was an institution in his corner of Puglia.

'The hero, Lomax, he is a loner living on a *chiatta* and searching for his lost son.' Matteo talks enthusiastically, his description peppered with Italian adjectives as he tells me of their adventures, from escaping arson to dodging an assassin's bullet.

'On a narrowboat?' I try not to laugh. Here, I can guess why it perhaps lacked the enduring cult status of Bodie and Doyle's occasional whizz across the Thames in an outboard inflatable, given that getting through a canal lock takes upwards of ten minutes.

'It was very dramatic, very dark,' Matteo insists. 'He was pursued everywhere, always under surveillance.'

The prospect of trying to hide *The Tempest* from my brother until Wednesday makes me sympathise with Matteo's TV hero. Miles would delight in giving chase.

Hearing a digital camera shutter, I glance round anxiously, but it's a young couple taking pictures of the photogenic rainbow that's arching through the sky over the sunlit boats as the shower finally breaks.

'We can go inside?' asks Matteo, stepping on the well deck, pulling up his collars against the raindrops.

It would be easy to lie and say that I've forgotten the combination codes. But then it occurs to me that I could use this opportunity to put the Italian off her, and by the time I've thought it, I've hesitated too long to lie convincingly. We're both getting very wet now. The tourists are all cramming inside the café bar to get out of the rain.

I step on deck too.

'There might be oily engine parts lying about,' I warn. 'Paddy was trying to get her going at the weekend. She's pretty unreliable these days.'

Inside, the forward cabin is immaculate, sunlight still spilling in through the little rain-specked portholes onto the oak panelling on one side, clouds as dark as dusk the other. Like an ageing stage diva in need of flattering light, she suits this sort of chiaroscuro. Raindrops hammer on the wooden roof.

'She's beautiful,' Matteo breathes.

Damn. How dare the family ark look so *gorgeous*? She was a tip two days ago.

He's working his way through the boat, ooohing and ahhhing at the saloon with its cosy tartan furnishings and reclaimed elm, pausing to admire the little wood-burning stove in the corner, then on to that showcase galley kitchen with its one-lidded red range cooker, Belfast sink and full stave oak surfaces, all hand-finished with trademark Paddy Hollander class. This barge has been spared no detail in her English country nostalgia idyll. If they thatched narrowboats, she'd have it.

My mother might not be interested in barging – to my knowledge she's never spent a night on board – but interior decoration is her passion. The old narrowboat had a distinctly masculine vibe before Mum stepped aboard with fabric swatches, everything tastefully chosen to complement her son-in-law's exquisite woodwork. In return, Paddy crams as much of the soft furnishings in the cupboards as possible in case he gets them dirty. But today, everything's back in its place.

'You live the high life on here, eh?' Matteo's opened a galley wall cupboard to admire its black iron hinges, and I'm taken aback to see a case of champagne in it. Moet, no less, not the Aldi one bulk-bought by my parents. It must be Miles.

'Cancel all your appointments, *bellissima*!' He spins

around. 'We will get drunk! I love this boat! I want to toast her.'

He's high on narrowboat, like he's snorted Colombia's finest off her gunwales.

'Don't shut the door, the lock sticks!' I pursue him to the bathroom, which these days is more City-boy wet room than the stoop-and-sloop thunderbox it once was. 'I promise you don't want to get stuck in here,' I warn. 'Especially when the pump-out toilet backs up. The catch seizes, see?' I flick it a few times while the door is open and it obligingly seizes up.

But he's heading into the master berth, another showstopper.

'Oof!' I fall over a pair of discarded Italian loafers.

He's lying on the bed. 'I love it!'

It's a great bed. A hand-carved two-poster in which, many moons ago, Paddy and I made love. A lot. Well, quite a lot.

'I *want* this barge...' He gazes at me intently.

I look away, appalled by his desire for something I've resented for so many years, yet feel honour-bound to save for Paddy.

'She's a museum piece,' I mutter, pulling a cupboard door open and closed repeatedly to try to demonstrate its creakiness, but it's freshly oiled and perfectly engineered. Hanging inside is a black, feather-trimmed basque, I realise in surprise, slamming it shut. 'She's got to that age where everything breaks easily.' I tug violently at a drawer which glides open to reveal what looks like fluffy handcuffs along with a tub of something called Love Lube. I bang that shut too. 'Something younger would be much more practical.'

'I like maturity in boats and wine, *dolcezza*. And what else...?' He waits expectantly.

I'm too distracted thinking about what I've just seen to play along. (It'll be *women*, that worn-out cliché. Save it for my mother, Don Juan.)

'People…' He smiles.

I frown, opening the drawer a fraction to confirm I wasn't imagining it, then close it. I wasn't imagining it.

What I surely must be imagining is that this ebullient, playful Italian man remains draped on the bed for my benefit, smiling up at me like an aftershave ad in *GQ*.

And God help me, for the first time in years, I can feel that tick, tick, tick of attraction. It is so, so, so wrong.

Moral compass aside, my libido has lost its magnetic north. It would be too simple to say I've stopped finding men attractive in the way I once did, but they are rapidly becoming blurred out. The opposite of beer goggles if you like. Maybe one's libido gets cataracts?

I'm worried that it's just my possessiveness that makes me admire Paddy's handsome features so often. Am I objectifying him? His physical presence still strikes me afresh, and often, yet I don't desire him physically. My deep-frozen sexual drive's not beyond our reach, I hope. The thaw will come. In the meantime, I don't want anyone getting their mitts on him.

Is that supremely selfish? It feels like it. Especially right at this moment.

'This bed is soooo comfortable, yes?' Matteo is still smiling up at me, laughter lines drenched in ambient light. 'You try?'

It sounds like an offer, although I'm certain it can't be, not in broad daylight with a married oldie. Predictably, I'm hotting up once more, but not in a good way.

'Yes, I've slept in it,' I tell Matteo matter-of-factly. 'Along with Paddy and our dog.'

'You said you have no dog.'

'We're currently between dogs.'

'A sad place to be. You must get another quickly.'

'You sound like my husband.'

'I hate your husband,' he reminds me, stretching his hands behind his head.

It's a badass move. I can feel my neck colouring, sweat trickling, and other bits of me revving up for once without the aid of Norah Jones and red wine. Please not here, in the boat, with this cliché of Italian flirtation, beneath which might be a man who's chivalrous, witty and artistic, who speaks Japanese and in praise of older women, but who has no idea how this married one ticks. Tick, tick, tick…

'It was me who wrote the TripAdvisor review,' I blurt. 'Not Paddy.'

'You are very noble to try to take the blame, but I still do not like him.' He extracts something from beneath the pillow that's caught against his wristwatch. It's a leather whip with long tassels, the sort designed to be drawn teasingly along excited skin. 'Does he use this on you or the dog?'

I've never seen it before. The floor feels like it's tilting, my legs wobbly. I sit down hard on the bed. Matteo bounces slightly, leather thongs fanning.

I can't ignore this. First a cupboard full of unfamiliar champagne. Then lingerie, fluffy cuffs. Now this. I want to blame Miles, but I can't believe lacy BDSM is my brother's kink, whereas my Christmas baby-doll/negligee/garter set was an under-the-tree staple from Paddy once upon a time…

What has Paddy been up to? And with whom? And why oh why do I suddenly feel a reckless need to flatter myself with revenge?

I look at Matteo, femme fatale to fall guy. 'Trust me, you don't want to know.'

'You are upset?'

'Not at all.'

He's still holding up the bloody whip. 'I can see it in your eyes.'

'I'm just worried that I'll miss my next appointment.'

I spring up gratefully as my mobile buzzes into life with Dad's ringtone – 'Papa Don't Preach' – and hurry up the steps through to the little boatman's cabin to take the call, shutting the door behind me with a 'must take this' apology.

Dad is bad-temperedly impatient. 'Miles tells me you're in a tizzy? Truth is, Eliza, I'm getting too old for messing around on boats, and the trust splits the asset equally between you both; your sister never wanted part of it, so she's taken the Tofanari bronze and Granny's silver instead.'

Thirty pieces of silver for a traitor, I reflect murderously. Jules kept quiet about her level of collaboration.

'If Antonio's nephew wants to buy it, I say we sell it to him. Friend of the family and all that.'

'*Her*, Dad. The boat's a she.' I lean against the stern doors, longing for fresh air, a familiar heat coursing up through me. Not again. But they're padlocked on the other side. Behind me, I can hear Matteo moving back through the boat, whistling. I hope he doesn't unearth any more of Paddy's kinky treasure.

'Your mother and I know you need the money, lass,' Dad's voice always slips into its original Yorkshire when he's being overprotective. 'We're going to use the proceeds to buy you something you're soon going to need very badly indeed.'

A private detective to investigate my philandering, Love-Lubing husband perhaps? Please God not a divorce.

'A pension!'

I've always avoided financial planning, partly because I never have any finance to plan, and partly because I never believed I needed to worry about it just yet.

Jules is ISA-ed and insured upto her laser-corrected eyeballs; Miles probably has more offshore investments than the Murdoch family; I have an overdraft, a Post Office Savings Account book dated 1981, two paper Premium Bonds and a *lot* of unchecked Lottery tickets (which makes me potentially far, far richer, let's face it).

There's no time left for me to save. Or grow old. And I can't shake the image of the kinky undies in the boat cabin wardrobe. What champagne-fuelled spanking orgies does my husband get up to on here when I'm not around? To think *I* felt guilty bringing Matteo on board to admire her bulkheads.

I listen out for sounds of him still moving around inside *The Tempest*. The whistling has stopped, but just as I think he must have gone, I hear footsteps again, fast and shuffling, not like his previous loose-hipped saunter.

Dad's waffling on about my national insurance contributions. I cover the phone mic and poke my head out.

The bathroom door's open, obscuring my view along the corridor, but feet hurriedly retreat off the boat.

'It's not as though Paddy has a retirement plan,' Dad is saying. (Aha, here we go.)

There's no point reminding him that Paddy cashed in his modest pension to try to keep the business afloat. It would be equally futile to point out that my parents said they would look after Eddie's boat indefinitely when they stepped in.

'It's to your credit that you are so loyal, but Paddy isn't earning anything like enough to keep this boat going. Or you, come to that.'

'I'm cheap to run, Dad.' Why does my father always make me feel silly and naïve, I wonder? I'm fifty years old, yet he adopts exactly the same there-there voice now as he did when he used to read *The Owl and the Pussycat* at bedtime. 'At least can we hold onto the half share?'

'Your family needs more to keep it afloat on a rainy day than that wretched vessel. Old age overtakes us horribly fast. And for some it doesn't come at all. Just look at poor Eddie. It's a gift to grow old, Eliza. Bloody well take it.'

Death, I think about a lot. Old age, less so. It's such an abstract thing, a lucky dip of variables and an unavoidable curse of survival. Our genes might give us an advantage, boosted by lifestyle choices and modern medicine, but in a world where a whip-slim teetotal septuagenarian can find themselves far more physically enfeebled than a century-old Scotch-swilling cake lover, it seems to me there's no predetermined course.

Unlike my terror of death, I don't yet feel old age close by, nor can I bring myself to acknowledge it needs planning and funding. Actors have no fixed retirement age after all, and playing old ladies was my college forte, so my career might even take off. And whilst I find it a fraction harder to bend down to paint my toenails than I did a decade ago, it's still hard to conceive of a day I won't be able to do it at all.

It's easier to dwell on death. You know where you are with it. Dead. And I want my corpse's toenails painted crimson.

There's always time for that breakthrough role, I vow silently as Dad summarises my limited pension options, his tone lecturing now, annoyed that I don't sound more grateful. I'm only remaining silent because I don't want him to know how close I am to crying, his least successful child. I want the call to end.

It shames me that at my stage of life I'm still so phobic about money. Like death, I hate it; I fear it, it shames and obsesses me, particularly at five in the morning when I free-fall panic that we can't give our children the opportunities afforded to their cousins, that Edward might require care into adulthood we can never hope to pay for, that one of us will get ill and be unable to work.

Breathe, Eliza.

This boat is worth far more to us than money, I remind myself, although right now I'd willingly throw myself overboard. I'm in full flush, boiling hot and claustrophobic, the diesel smell from the engine beneath the floor gagging me. Tears bubble up, get swiped and bubble again as I feel my mood swing so fast I'm G-forcing menopausal outrage long before serotonin can get involved.

'Look at the hand you were dealt, Eliza: good health, bright mind, private education, fine looks.'

The silver spoon he welded into my mouth from birth is choking me, still trying to feed me honey to help the medicine go down. There are few parents as indulgently domineering as a self-made one, in my experience.

'You were bloody lucky to be born middle class, you know that?'

'What's class got to do with it?' I break my silence.

'It's not a swear word, Eliza.'

'It's become one, Dad.'

'Well, that's a great shame. You'd think differently if you'd had my upbringing. I worked bloody hard to give my children the opportunities you've had. You should be grateful you have a bit of class to fall back on, lass.'

Apologising that I have a client appointment to keep, I blow him kisses and hang up.

It's probably not very classy to unzip my dress and peel it off my arms so that I can unhook my bra to fan myself with it, but I'm too ablaze with anger and flush to care.

Yet again, I'm piggy in the middle between my family and Paddy. Fitting that my hot skin is mottled the colour of gammon.

I'm a middle-aged, middle-child Middle Englander. To cap it all, I'm middle class. Middle's my middle name. Could I be any more mediocre? Or, as Summer would say, 'meh'.

There's something offensive about all this safe and cosy

middle-ness. I'm guilty as hell about it, but that's just a side effect of my middle-of-the-road Liberal thinking, I'm told.

Occupying the middle ground of age, class and thought is now a byword for whinging privilege and humble-bragging, our freshly squeezed middle ranks protesting about climate change, pay gaps and library closures whilst still cooking on oil-fired Agas, politely never admitting what we earn and reading 99p Kindle books. We're halfway between futureproof and out of touch. Many of us also belong to the sandwich generation, caught between the needs of dependent children and elderly parents, our much-loved snowflakes and boomers. Generation X marks the spot, and yes I'm slap bang in it, madly muddling along (menopausally).

When the poetry line 'They fuck you up, your mum and dad' is quoted, Philip Larkin is rarely credited with wisely going on to point out that our parents were fucked up by their own first, 'By fools in old style hats and coats.'

My grandmother – a woman always hatted and hand-bagged – continually berated Mum and Dad for spoiling us: 'They'll grow up discontented.'

Maybe she was right. We're Thatcher's oversized children, milk-snatched milksops too evolved to make do and mend yet left behind by swipe-right selfies. In striving for the perfect life-work balance, we overplay both, left seething and unsatisfied behind Facebook walls of carefully curated perfection. Nobody likes a grumbler, especially one who owns more than one Ottolenghi cookbook.

We dare not leave this mean median mode without punishment. While a self-made working-class hero might be applauded for climbing to grandeur and a fallen aristo retains an air of decadent rebellion, we know our place: social mobility is far too risky. Jump rank – like the ultimate middle-England Middletons stepping from fitted carpet to red one – and we're getting above ourselves; fall down on our heels and we're ungrateful wastrels.

The Finches are determined to keep me afloat. Don't rock the boat, Eliza; sell it.

I just want to rock the bloody boat.

I make my way hotly back through the bedroom cabin, bra rehooked, dress round my waist. Matteo's gone so I take another quick peek in the wardrobe. There are several bits of lingerie hanging up, all *Carry on Girls* meets *Eyes Wide Shut* confections of wispy lace and garter. I check the labels. Nothing bigger than a ten. She's slim then, with cheap-thrill taste. I have a brief vision of Icepack Bianca stroking Paddy's arm and saying they all love his ruggedness, then dismiss it. This is far more secretive.

My film of sweat chills, a hollow toxicity brittle in my bones. I rezip my dress and open the drawer with the fluffy cuffs. I stare at the Love Lube tub, imagining his big hands clumsily unscrewing the top like he does his Swarfega at home, only intent on far more personal pleasures. Is this my husband's secret shag nest? Oh Paddy, what has come of us?

Thinking I can hear somebody moving in the galley, I look up. 'Who's there?'

Silence. Just café chatter outside.

Then the sound of a champagne cork popping at the front of the boat makes me quickly close the drawer.

'*Bellissima*, come have a drink with me!' Matteo calls out.

I swing the bathroom door shut as I march through to the galley, but he's not in the saloon. There's a large box of chocolates on the galley's oak work surface.

'Come outside! The sun's out again.' He's on the well deck.

I grab some kitchen roll to wipe my teary, sweaty face.

Outside, Matteo's filling two champagne flutes.

'You opened the Moet?' I gulp some fresh air. I don't care if he smashes every bottle against the side of the barge and renames her *Boaty McBoatface*; but there's no way I'm drinking the champagne my husband bought for his size ten floozy.

'Of course not. I buy prosecco from the café bar.' He passes me a flute. '*Salute!*'

'I'm driving.' I hold it away like a grenade, quickly pulling my dark glasses down from my head.

He's looking at me closely. 'Are you OK, beautiful girl?'

'Fine!' I lie, taking a swig to show I'm in high spirits. I appreciate its chilled kick. And being called beautiful always helps in times of crisis.

'I put the whip back where I found it,' he assures me in an undertone.

'Thanks.' I swig some more prosecco. It's so wonderfully cold, I want to press the glass to my neck and chest, pour its contents over them even. (Does Paddy throw Moet over his size ten lover in here, I wonder?)

'How much do your family want for this boat?' Matteo steps closer.

I step back, now unable to shake the image of Paddy enjoying his Love-Lubed, sex-loving innamorata doing the things I don't. I briefly envisage torching the boat with them kink-festing in it, using the cash I could get from selling it to Matteo as tinder. I double the amount my parents paid for her to buy myself time.

'Too much.' He sucks on a knowing smile, then shaves 40 per cent off.

The owners of the neighbouring narrowboat have just arrived to take her out and give me a cheery wave. They give Matteo a curious look and I hurry back inside.

He follows. 'It's a lot of money, *cara*.'

My mind's still in the wardrobe with the peek-a-boo basque and crotchless panties. *You've driven him to this*, a voice nags in my head. *A man has needs.*

'Say yes, Eliiiiiiza. You know you want to.'

You're barking up the wrong tree trying to butter me up with all that sexy-voiced cajoling, Matteeeeeo, I want to shout back. *Just ask my husband. I don't succumb to sweet talk. Or anything much.*

'It's not my decision,' I tell him blandly.

'But you can convince them, eh?' He's standing far too close.

My champagne flute is almost empty. I no longer feel sick or hot, just *very* odd. The anger's still sizzling, ever familiar, but there's a highly charged undercurrent that's all new, its sexual charge shocking me. This self-flagellating shame, envisaging Paddy with another woman, desiring another's body, is giving me headrush. It's horrid, visceral and the biggest fix of emotion I've felt all year. It shouldn't be, but it's turning me on.

Things are happening to this body that haven't for months: nipples out, check, pulses hammering, check, pelvic floor quivering, check. The inner tingle, check. No need for Vagisan right now, it's slip-sliding away by its own making.

I'm absurdly and inappropriately horny. And still very angry.

I march to the opposite end of the saloon to stop myself hitting something – or on someone.

Watching me, Matteo offers another thousand and a case of Villa Sandi, which he assures me is far superior to this prosecco as he comes to refill my glass.

'It'll have to be a better offer than that.' I knock it back feverishly, buying more time. I think I might be panting slightly.

He steps closer. 'Come here. I'll whisper it.'

I brace myself, craving punishment for my wicked thoughts. *Don't flatter yourself.*

I should state here that I'm categorically *not* up for adultery. No man other than my husband has had sight of my vagina since Edward was delivered and that's not about to change. But speaking as a woman who has watched men of my generation refocus on women of my daughter's, I'm curious whether I have any sex appeal left at all, and if I do, then who exactly does it appeal to?

Friend Lou led a recent social media rant when fifty-year-old suave French author Yann Moix was quoted saying women his age are 'invisible' to him and therefore impossible to love, the body of a twenty-five-year-old being far more desirable.

I stayed silent, ashamed to find myself agreeing with

him. My body *was* better at twenty-five. And I wouldn't have let creepy old Yann anywhere near it, so no worries there. Like every middle-aged male whose celebrity or wealth fools him into believing he's only as young as the woman he feels, there's a limit to how long he can press home the advantage to press that young flesh. It's a meat trade in which he'll have to keep paying more for cheaper cuts. His soul knows it.

Lou was scathing when someone online suggested that maybe men 'age up' in proportion: that a fifty-year-old woman becomes the fantasy of men over seventy-five: 'Face it, all men are the same,' she raged. 'Hot Teen appears in their drop-down box as soon as they type "h".'

(I typed h in our laptop to test this and got 'historic narrowboats' and 'HSBC login'.)

But is the reverse true? Do older women secretly all prefer the bodies of men half our age? On a purely visual level, say in one's direct eyeline at a hotel pool, maybe. But not to love, no. It was painful enough the first time. They hog the mirror for a start.

Lou openly admits to occasionally lusting after young men ('all legal: uni age, entirely an academic exercise') but I can't get there. At least not since I caught Joe's handsome, flirty friend Tig masturbating furiously in our walk-in wardrobe, his face buried in my best party dress. I felt criminal even running it back in my head afterwards; I'd known Tig in nappies. OK, so it didn't stop my subconscious screening one or two late-night flights of fancy – at least until he came out as gender-confused – but those were entirely beyond my control.

Then the hormones changed guard, and even my fantasy

world was gone. Whoosh. No time for end credits. Sex drive top-shelved.

There's still a latent pulse, that tug which tells me my basic instinct is deep inside, that an orgasm is waiting. But it's like a reminder for a car valet. Easier to do it myself. Then I forget and don't bother.

That's still no excuse for finding myself in a canal barge with an amorous Italian whispering in my ear, no defence to justify this loyal wife of twenty-two years risking a quick mid-morning flirtation to prove that this isn't a joke at her expense, that she still has, if not what it takes, then the chutzpah to take it.

Matteo is breathing warmly on my neck. 'Eliza...'

It should be funny, the just-one-Cornetto flirtation, but it isn't because the cliché just got serious. The warmth of his fingers around the bare skin of my arm. The closeness. His unswerving male gaze. The aftershave. The tick, tick, tick.

'*Bellissima* Eliiiiza...' God, I love the way he says my name. It's so Mediterranean. No, that's no excuse either.

'That first time I saw you,' he breathes, '*Ero pazzo di te*: I was crazy for you.'

'You were crazy *at* me.'

'You drive like an Italian. You look like a goddess. You save dumb animals. Oh, *mio cuore*! Then you come to my restaurant burning brighter than every candle, and all night, forgive me, I wanted to do this.'

He kisses me.

* * *

Forget aphrodisiacs like oysters and asparagus tips, forget silk underwear, luxury hotels, mood music and massages. Please, God, forget PornHub.

It's all in the kiss.

Klimt had it gold-plated for a reason. The intimacy of lips on lips.

Holly Golightly and Paul Varjak kissing in *Breakfast at Tiffany's*.

Molly and Sam in *Ghost*.

Han Solo and Princess Leia in *The Empire Strikes Back*.

Zack Mayo and Paula in *An Officer and a Gentleman*.

Denys kissing Karen Blixen in *Out of Africa*.

Jack and Rose in *Titanic*.

It's watching the big-screen kiss when I still get that inner flip, when the pulse finds its way through the maze again. It's my most enduring of sexual triggers. And when it happens, I know it's not gone forever, this roar inside; it's just lost its way a little bit.

Too many middle-aged women are quoted as saying 'I'd rather have a cuddle' if asked about their sex lives. But wouldn't some of us rather kiss like Bogart and Bergman in *Casablanca*?

Unless it's with the wrong person.

Caught by surprise, I let the kiss happen, ignoring the voice in my head shouting, *scream, hit him, handbag him!*

I'm so used to Paddy's lips – not lately, admittedly – that my first reaction is 'this is so bloody weird'. Like an out-of-body experience. Matteo's seriously hot-blooded, one of those men who kisses like he's trying to suck venom out of a snakebite. It's all so surreal, I want to laugh. And, oh shame, I kiss him back. That just makes me want to laugh more.

I feel *alive*. I'm still a woman.

Then I hear Paddy's voice call 'hello?' and I stop laughing.

16

The Nick of Time

I'm awake at 4 a.m. So far so normal. Crying a bit. Keeping it quiet. Standard.

I am going to run away. I've planned it all meticulously. Less usual.

Paddy is sleeping in the spare bedroom.

But it's not about the kiss; he doesn't even know about the kiss.

When I was thirteen, my mother had an affair with our next-door neighbour, a writer called Howard Cozens. I came home early from school and caught them in a clinch on the patio. Not a restrained *Brief Encounter* embrace; no, tongues and everything.

They spluttered an excuse about running lines for a play they were rehearsing – Mum had taken to am-dram with gusto, Howard was a leading light – but when I saw the show a few weeks later nobody kissed beyond a peck. Howard's hand had been up Mum's top...

The more I tried to make sense of it, the angrier I got.

Dad was still a barrister back then, away lots of weeknights. This impostor – conveniently home by day while his GP wife was out curing the sick – had taken full advantage. I went on the hunt for evidence and found a fat pile of letters stashed in a cliché shoebox in my mother's wardrobe, bemoaning his miserable marriage and eulogising Mum's tits. He'd written *pages*. My singular thirteen-year-old instinct was to see off the threat. I burned the lot. Then I glued together an anonymous note – a proper cut-and-paste newspaper ransom, entirely harvested from that month's *Jackie* magazine – which I posted next door at dead of night in a brown envelope, carefully marked *Mr H Cozens, Private and Confidential* so his wife wouldn't accidentally read it and be hurt: *I know What you'VE been UP to. It sTOPs here, OR EVERY-one else Will Know TOO.*

I assume he read it, although it was never mentioned. When the play run ended, the aftershow party took place at our house and I policed it vigilantly, marking Mum to ensure she and Howard remained a respectable distance apart. I even waited for her outside the loo each time she went in it, which Mum got fed up about because she was in there a surprising amount. Or so I thought at the time; not so surprising now that I've also had three children and developed a bit of a wine habit.

Let's track back to yesterday...

The Italian has a prosecco bottle in one hand, champagne

flute in the other and his tongue in my mouth. I have my arms around his neck and the giggles.

Paddy is outside, his shadow falling across the open doorway. 'Hello?'

With classic French-farce timing, I dive right, Matteo left. How he hides a bottle, two glasses and a semi so fast I have no idea but by the time Paddy bounds in, Matteo is on the sofa with this month's *Canal Boat* magazine on his lap, looking coolly casual and I'm panting guiltily by the galley peninsula, so hot and sweaty it's entirely normal.

'I didn't expect to find you here.' Paddy puts a kitbag on the work surface. 'It's an unexpected treat.'

How can he not realise? In my head, I'm playing a scenario in which Paddy punches Matteo, then I defend my actions by bringing up the basque/Love Lube/cuffs and punch Paddy.

'You remember Matteo from the restaurant? I bumped into him after my ten o'clock viewing!' I over-play it as they shake hands in a very Macron/Trump way.

'I tell her I must see this beautiful boat I hear so much about!' Matteo enthuses, still keeping *Canal Boat* magazine clamped in place. 'It's *stupendo*, my friend!' As the handshake crunches tighter, Matteo flashes his eyes at me behind Paddy's back, indicating my arm, and I realise his lucky golden charm is now dangling from my jacket sleeve. It drops, bouncing off my shoe.

'Thanks. I've been doing quite a lot on her recently.' Paddy turns back to me and smiles. It's his shifty smile.

I smile shiftily back, putting my foot over Matteo's *cornicello*. Ohgodohgodohgod, this is hell. 'Anyway, what are you doing here?' I ask.

'Just passing. Had to see a client.'

I eye the kitbag, wondering what's in it. Fetish gear? Is he meeting her?

'Tell me more about this beautiful boat!' Matteo effuses and I'm grateful for the covering fire as Paddy does just that: *The Tempest*'s authenticity and rarity, her long working life, her meticulous restoration and conversion, the care lavished onto her, the extras. Soon they're male bonding over talk of combustion engines, gearboxes and prop-shaft couplings.

'Tell me,' Matteo asks, 'did you ever see *Travelling Man?*'

'Did I ever?' Paddy looks positively boyish. 'Got the DVD box set at home.'

He has?

Matteo is beyond thrilled such a thing exists. Soon they're running an episode-by-episode analysis. Both agree that a scene involving a crop helicopter and Chirk Aqueduct was a classic. They're so absorbed they don't notice me kick the gold *cornicello* charm out of sight.

'Dad and me came across the original narrowboat, *Harmony*, on the Grand Union a couple of times,' Paddy tells Matteo. 'Even bought her lifebuoy ring as a memento. She's a floating art gallery down Somerset way now.'

From the Italian's face, my husband could be saying he dived the *Titanic* wreck and brought up Madeleine Astor's diamond choker. I'm in shock, but I barely have time to adjust to all this male bonding before it comes unglued.

'If you throw in that lifebuoy with the deal,' Matteo slaps Paddy on the arm, 'I might even buy this boat for the crazy price your wife named.'

Now Paddy looks like he wants to punch him, which is getting more on script.

'Perhaps you should leave me to talk to Paddy about this?' I tell Matteo in a mad, gritted-teeth way, wishing more than anything that I hadn't let him kiss me.

'Of course!' He winks (*winks!*) and leaves with lots of '*ciao!*', '*a dopo!*' and a 'call me!' phone mime directed my way, leaving me with the distinct impression I've just been played by a pro.

Or am I flattering myself?

Here I am awake, seventeen hours later, rerunning highlights of the Hollander domestic that followed.

We fade up on the interior of a narrowboat. It's midday. Sunlight streams through the portholes as Paddy and I face each other.

'My family want to sell this boat,' I tell him, freshly kissed and boozed wet lips trembling like Sue Ellen Ewing's.

'Have you no fucking idea what she means to me?!'

At this, I start pacing around and wringing my hands in time-honoured guilty soap-wife fashion. 'I do, Paddy. I do.'

'What were you THINKING, agreeing a price?'

What was I thinking of? How hot I was, mostly, and not in an adulterous and desirable sense.

To help us along, my phone rings at this very moment with 'Ain't Misbehavin'. It's my mother's ringtone and we both know it. I reject the call.

'I might have guessed your parents would do this to me.'

'Don't blame them, blame me! This is my fault.'

At this, my husband kicks the sofa, which I think on reflection was a subconscious reflex against my mother who had it reupholstered in flowery toile de jouy.

We both watch as a prosecco bottle rolls out from beneath it.

'Your loyalties have never been fucking clearer,' Paddy whispers through gritted teeth, and I know with a thudding heart and dry mouth that it's my cue.

'And what about YOURS, Patrick Hollander?' I march into the main berth and try to pull open the drawer containing the Love Lube and fluffy handcuffs but it's stuck fast. When I try to open the wardrobe, the handle comes off. Finally, I feel under the pillows for the cat-o'-nine-tails and lift it up like Crocodile Dundee. 'Explain THIS!'

If it had been a soap opera, it would have gone to a commercial break at that point, not carried painfully on.

I don't want to think about what happened next. The clock's taunting me. 4.15 a.m. Dawn's already breaking outside, the birds chorusing, my heart digging up its own worms.

Did my mother ever lie awake at this hour worrying about her marriage, her vanishing options, whether she'd ever feel alive again? Was Howard Cozens part of that? She never had to stress about money or work in the same way I do, but maybe that just left more time to panic about her diminishing value, to feel despair at the short, bright window in which women are seen as physically attractive in our culture of small screens and shopfronts, from seventies Miss World contests to today's Insta selfies. When we age, without warning the net curtains drop on that window of opportunity. The glass ceiling is only one of the dimensions women must break through. We have to stay visible.

Somehow I managed to host two more property viewings yesterday, fetch Edward, do the online shop, cook, message Lou and even return Mum's calls with ever-cheerier messages as we played answerphone tennis until bedtime. She knows something's up, she always does.

Today, I am going to run away. To do so, I must get up at usual o'clock and act as though everything's fine.

Now, illogically, my mind keeps bleating *I need my Mum*, but I can't stop myself remembering Howard Cozens' moustache engulfing her lips and his groping hand up her top. I've survived years by not thinking about that day.

Which means I've never examined it from an adult perspective. Now it's playing on a loop and at last I can understand why Mum looked at me with a glint of terror whenever we had cross words for months, years, afterwards. She thought I was going to betray her. But I just wanted to protect her. Protect *us*. I never breathed a word.

Big relief all round when Howard and his wife moved away soon afterwards.

As far as I'm aware, I'm the only one in the family who ever knew about Mum's fling. I've no idea how long it went on or whether it went below the belt. I prefer to think of it as a theatre company romance. I've seen those happen too many times to count. We all lose perspective when confined together working intensely on a stage show. It's why the Curse of *Strictly Come Dancing* strikes marriages so often. Those are horribly public. Most, like Mum's, get boxed up and stored away somewhere so we almost forget they're there.

★ ★ ★

Let's return for Part Two of the floating Hollander fight. We fade up on the bedroom cabin of a narrowboat just after midday. I'm holding up a cat-o'-nine tails accusingly. 'EXPLAIN THIS!'

'You weren't supposed to find out like this,' Paddy splutters.

Whilst still livid about my prosecco-swilling boat dealing, he's also now looking suitably chagrined, and seizes gratefully on the broken wardrobe handle which he starts to reattach.

I'm looking tearfully at the cat-o'-nine-tails. 'Who whips who?'

'I don't know! I just thought it might get things going again.'

'What things?' I glare at his crotch, imagining Size Ten Mistress administering to its secret fantasies. No erectile dysfunction when *that's* getting a BDSM play-whipping.

'It was supposed to be a surprise, OK?' He glances angrily over his shoulder. 'You didn't seem too keen on the chairs, so I switched plans.'

I gaze at him in shock, then down at the whip. 'This is an anniversary present?'

'A night away in the boat, I thought,' Paddy opens the wardrobe to test the handle, revealing the lacy lingerie, 'just the two of us.' He grits his teeth. 'Except you want to bloody sell her.'

'You got all that for... *me*?' It's taking a while to sink in.

'Well, *I'm* not bloody wearing it.' He slams the door shut. 'It was Miles's idea, wasn't it?'

'Skimpy undies and sex shop toys?'

'Selling the boat.'

'I tried to talk him out of—'

'You just brokered a deal!'

'Accidentally.' I put the whip down, hot with shame. That kiss. No, don't think about the kiss! This is about *Paddy's* secrets and fetishes, not my headrush error.

'Like you "accidentally" celebrated it by opening a bottle of champagne?' he fumes. 'That was for our anniversary too, by the way.'

'Where did you get it all from?' I open the wardrobe again, faced with crotchless peekaboo finery. 'Please don't tell me it's that sex shop on the A46 where the Little Chef used to be?' Was that where he disappeared to before yesterday's cricket match? Cruising the aisles of Warwickshire's adult superstore before coming here to set the scene for seduction?

He can't look at me. 'It wasn't there.'

'Did you buy it online then?'

'Does it matter?'

'It does if you mistakenly think your wife's still a size ten,' I point out. 'We get free returns if it's Amazon Prime.'

As I examine the labels on the underwear again, a memory triggers: The Dreamgirl peephole chemise, The Feisty corset, The Lucky Night body stocking. I know these names. They all come from a script I learned long ago, a performance perfected for a small elite audience of women.

And when I realise where my husband acquired them, it makes me want to cry.

'Oh, Paddy.'

★ ★ ★

Discovering that the sexy kit in *The Tempest* came from a box of leftover Ann Summers stock in our garage should have been laughable. But it wasn't. It was torture, a hung, drawn and quartered brain-freeze:

On one hand, relief. My Paddy has not been perving around sex shops, leaving his parked car on show to the commuters of Leamington. Celebrate!

On the other hand, guilt. He must have felt so confused when he found that box, so betrayed I never told him about my brief stint selling sex toys to yummy mummies.

On one foot, anger. He hasn't bought me lingerie, he *found* lingerie. He didn't even CHECK IT WAS MY SIZE. And what's with the whip and cuffs?

On the other foot, sadness. It doesn't make me want a carnal canal mini-break with Paddy; imagining he was having sex with another woman was the turn on. QED, I am the pervert.

I should have known that box was still knocking about, just one little brick in a great wall at the back of the garage that I never find time to sort through or throw out, and which drives Paddy mad because the boat trailer and dinghy only fit in at a tight angle. There are *lots* of boxes. As well as storing the usual things like old toys, camping equipment and Christmas decorations, a significant proportion are mine, some dating right back to my rented flat era. If investigated (which it seems Paddy has), they mostly contain hundreds of books and plays which I can't bear to throw out, along with theatre programmes and friends' letters and holiday souvenirs, and the box of party shoes I could never hope to wear again, drunk or sober. A boxed-up me that no longer exists. Paddy doesn't hang on to little mementos in the same way I do; just big things like barges. He's pulled out one of my bricks, a brick that could bring the walls down.

And when I pointed out that I knew where all this came from, Paddy's pride was like a smoke bomb. He didn't want to talk about that. There was something much more urgent to discuss, after all. That thing *I* didn't want to talk about: the pressing matter of a boat sale, a wheeler-dealer Italian and a bottle of celebratory prosecco – not to mention the mystery chocolates.

Back to the narrowboat for Part Three, we fade up on the galley at ten minutes past midday.

I am looking at the box of chocolates on the work surface. They're from the new luxury chocolatier on Bridge Street, a handmade selection in a huge, heart-shaped box. The printed label reads *TO EMMA FROM A BIG FAN*.

Paddy stands tall in the saloon, a totem of enraged dignity. 'I suppose he got you those to sweeten the deal? Well, you can tell Mateus Rosé or whatever he bloody calls himself that it's off. He can keep his dirty hands off her. We'll take out a loan, buy her back.'

'I won't go there again! It almost cost us the house last time.'

'This boat's like family to me, Elz.'

'Like the one you abandon to spend so much time on her?' I am wildly resentful of the boat at this particular moment, of Paddy's possessiveness over her, my brother hustling her, the Italian hankering for her.

'I planned this week's trip to enjoy her together,' he pleads.

'So it's all about her! What if I don't want to tag along, trussed in a crotchless playsuit?'

'This is bloody typical of you right now.'

I cross my arms. 'Tell me, Paddy, what's "typical of me"?'

'Negative, argumentative, jealous, selfish.'

'Keep going.'

'It's like you bloody hate everything: me, this boat, your work, the kids, going out, staying in, sex.'

'Let's roll that back and pick out the priorities, shall we? Mine: you, work, the kids, not necessarily in that order. Yours: this boat and sex. IN that order.'

'When's in hell's this thing going to end? What happened to the bubbly Eliza I married?'

'Maybe that bubble popped.'

'And maybe I'm running out of fucking patience too! I've had bloody enough of this.' He storms off the boat.

At this point, still mildly tight and wildly self-dramatising, I take another look in the wardrobe and confirm I've been married to a man for over twenty years who still doesn't get what turns me on, or know my cup size. Nor does he know what menopause really entails.

I'm not sure I always know any of these things myself. I wish I could talk to him about it all without getting embarrassed or frightened. I wish we could be intimate again without it being just about sex. I wish I still believed in myself as an object of desire. And I wish I hadn't kissed Matteo to taste the difference.

I am at least grateful for one thing.

Paddy has made it clear exactly what he wants, what will make him happy. And I want to give it to him. Because there's one thing my husband forgot to add to the list of the things that I hate right now: losing.

The dawn chorus is driving me mad, like the neighbours having a party I'm not invited to. I get up to have a pee, and as I'm about to climb back into bed, I realise somebody is moving about in the kitchen below. Is it Paddy?

I creep onto the landing to listen, but I can hear his deep sleep breathing through the spare room door. Worried that it's Ed getting in a panic about his Outward Bound trip, I head downstairs, but nobody's in here.

Then I see breakfast laid out for us all, one of Ed's Acts of Kindness, the cereal packets ranked in height order, a few garden flowers in a vase. A perfect family surprise. Not like my surprise.

I sit down by my heart-covered Emma Bridgewater *Mummy* mug and try not to cry.

Plugged into its charger on the peninsula worktop, my phone chirrups with an incoming WhatsApp alert. It's Lou, insomnia night-shifting too, sending a picture of a tearful Lichtenstein heroine which she's captioned *3 out of the 4 voices in my head tell me I need to sleep!* I message back four screaming emojis and *My voices now. Help!* Then I switch my phone to silent.

It lights up with her call in seconds. It's not the first time we've done this, although we usually only tell each other we're knackered in dopey whispers.

'Are you as knackered as me?' she asks.

'I'm going to run away,' I tell her in an undertone, opening Ed's Golden Nuggets cereal box to help myself to a couple.

'What the actual fuck? No way you're leaving Paddy!'

I don't go into too much detail – the fluffy handcuffs will never be spoken of outside the marriage, and I'll take that ill-advised kiss to my grave – but I do tell her that my family want to sell *The Tempest*, and as I go on to explain what I intend to do, I realise how much it helps to have an ally onside, even if she is a hundred and fifty miles away in Brighton. Lou gets why I need to do this, and do it alone.

'"Be the heroine of your life, not the victim"!' she tells me. 'Nora Ephron.'

'"If you want the rainbow, you gotta put up with the rain",' I quote back. 'Dolly Parton.'

I creep back up to bed, where I find Ed curled up in Paddy's usual spot, playing with the spines on his ancient stegosaurus toy. He hasn't done this for years. I get in and big spoon him, whispering, 'Are you too excited about your trip to sleep?'

'Sort of,' he says in a drowsy monotone. 'Why were you talking to yourself downstairs?'

'Just Lou.' Please don't let him have heard, I pray. 'Breakfast looks amazing,' I say.

But he's already asleep. Moments later, I am too.

My alarm is going off. It's 6.45. Ed's already up and away, stealing downstairs to put the finishing touches to his Act of Kindness. Alone on the bed, I want to pull the pillow over my head and make today go away. All the meticulous insomnia planning I did in my head is lost in the fog.

But I must get up, because I'm going to make things better. I'm doing it for my marriage and my family. And for the Bionic Woman. Above all, for myself.

What was it Summer said? *Dare yourself again.*

I very dare me.

17

Time Out

'I've been offered a last-minute narration job!' I tell Paddy and the kids over the Act of Kindness breakfast. 'The actor they booked has a throat infection,' I pretend to read an email on my phone (it's just Dunelm offering me 20 per cent off garden cushions). 'They need me to start today.'

Being a good liar doesn't sit easily, although you could say professionally it comes with the territory. I *always* feel bad lying, and avoid it as much as possible, like salt and refined sugar. But like those naughty crystals, white lies can make things taste a lot better.

My fierce grandmother used to tell us 'every lie is five minutes in hell!'. I've earned at least a weekend there this year alone.

'It's recording near Leicester over a couple of days, so they'll put me up in a Travelodge,' I tell them all, aware I'm already guilty of too much detail.

'But it's your anniversary tomorrow,' Summer points out, looking at Paddy.

'We'll celebrate it another time.' I look at Paddy too, but he refuses to catch my eye. 'I'll need to set off this morning if you can run Edward in?'

'Right.'

'I'll make sure you are on the school-trip phone tree,' I promise.

Ed's watching me. 'What's the name of the book you're narrating?'

'*The Secret of Dunelm Manor*,' I manage to wing it. 'Have you packed enough thick socks?'

He nods seriously. 'Also emergency rations, compass, whistle, bladeless multitool, fidget toys and dinosaur.'

This morning he's setting off on his Year Seven outdoor activity trip to paddle, climb and whiz along ropes in the Welsh Marches. How foolish we were to once imagine that being on the spectrum meant he'd hate such unpredictable, wet, strenuous stuff far from home. Instead, he relishes the regimen and routine, the safety checks and meticulous run-throughs, fantasising himself a Sci Fi hero in training. They're away until Friday and he's been counting down the days all term.

Summer's busy messaging her @*Summer_Time* followers on her phone promising exciting news and live streams later.

'You are dropping me at the bus stop, Dad?' She doesn't look up. 'I'm on a tight schedule.'

She's also away, spending a couple of nights with her best school friend and bandmate. They claim they need to rehearse for their upcoming debut tour of three local village fetes and a fun run, but I've long suspected an ulterior motive, possibly involving hair dye.

This is why Paddy planned our surprise getaway, I

realise sadly. Now he'll be home alone. Phone still in hand, I stealthily change the online shopping delivery from this evening to this lunchtime.

His face darkens when I break the news that he'll have to come back and wait in for it, but it's worth it to be certain he'll be here. I need a head start, and while I hope I can rely upon this evening's cricket nets, the pub, then Xbox to keep him busy, I don't trust him to stay in his workshop by day.

I remember to go on to Google Maps and stop sharing my location. Best not linger on the cosy cluster of circular avatars at home: Einstein for Edward, a big-eyed selfie for Summer and a silhouette egghead for Paddy. Quick scroll out to Joe's cartoon drum set in Exeter. Feel better. We're family. Wherever we go.

I'm doing this for all of us, I remind myself. But most of all for me.

I go outside to wave everyone off and I'm granted a rare gangly hug with my son during which I force myself to look at his father over his head. 'Take care. I'll call.'

Paddy nods, umbrage pulsing off him like gamma rays.

'I don't want to go, Mum,' Ed says in a low whisper. 'You might need me.'

'Of course you must go!' My heart thuds and I stroke his hair, wishing his anxieties were easier to predict. 'I will love you, miss you and wait for you, OK?'

He goes rigid. '*It's a-me, Mario! Thank you so much for playing my game!*' Then he peels away and clambers into the car. '*Let's a-go, little guys!*'

'He'll love it when he gets there, Mum,' Summer reminds

me as I swipe a stray tear. Grateful, I make to hug her too. But she steps back swiftly, heaving a huge backpack and her guitar into the boot, and I half wonder if she's running away too. We're on the shakiest of truces, my hot-mess mothering only forgiven because my double denim Mr Vella outburst has so far received almost two thousand likes, shares and comments including Kwasi and a social influencer called Zenny All who everyone follows.

She asks if I have any cash. In a panic of over-compensation I give her forty pounds. She's thrilled. Bribery pays off. I get the hug.

The moment Paddy's truck turns out, with me waving like I'm seeing them off to battle, New Neighbour appears, hip baby death-staring. 'Have you had the solicitor's letter yet?'

'Not to my knowledge. And I'm working away this week.'

'What is it you do again?'

'Hired assassin.'

Her face remains frozen, but from nowhere a shrill laugh. 'What do you charge? I'll hire you to kill my hubby!'

'I'm offering 20 per cent off for Father's Day.'

Her voice tightens to a confessional bleat. 'He won't let me order a new kitchen. The one in there's four years old and glossy white. The quote's ready to go. Inky blue and copper, bespoke, a *dream*. Too expensive, he says.'

From the gods comes an olive twig…

'I bet Paddy could do you the same kitchen for half the money,' I pimp shamelessly. '*Warwickshire Life* once called him *Leamington's Tom Howley with enough backbone to take on Smallbone.*' No lie. It's verbatim. My mother said it was ghastly grammar.

'I heard his company went bust. What went wrong?'

'Family tragedy. We don't talk about it.' Not a complete lie. 'By the time he'd bounced back, his business partner had taken the money and run.' He did. 'Paddy Hollander Kitchens are,' best breathy designer voiceover, 'rare objects of desire. Ginger Spice has one now she's upper class.' (OK, that's a seriously manipulated truth – Paddy made a kitchen for a barn conversion Geri Halliwell once briefly rented.)

'You are *kidding*?'

'You can see it on her Instagram feed.' I make to look it up on my phone, then stop. 'Oh, no, of course it's on Geri's *friend and family* Finsta. She doesn't share shots of the house on her public profile now she's rah.' I'm overacting wildly. Five minutes more in hell, Granny.

But her eyes have brightened through the freeze face. 'Do you have a card?'

I hurry inside to dig out one along with an old brochure. She flicks through it. 'I'll get him round straight away.'

Paddy's erstwhile backer got mullered by the credit crunch when redundancy from his analyst's job ended his high-flying career. He needed his investment back at the worst possible time: orders for handmade kitchens had flatlined, Paddy's mind elsewhere as it spiralled through the grief of losing his dad, then his mum's diagnosis, my professional work drying up, the children a non-stop triple act.

Paddy and his friend fell out over it big time, which I still feel sad about. He'd been Best Man at our wedding, a loveable rogue whose generosity had helped Paddy out of trouble more than once. And it was his money to take back, but Paddy so badly needed a demon, and there he was.

Word is he bought a farm with another old mate just over the Welsh border from his childhood home. Last we heard, he was making craft gin there. I hope Paddy makes it up with him one day, just as I wish he would patch it up with Miles. Old friends matter at our age.

I text Paddy as soon as I'm back inside: *If neighbour calls about a kitchen, DROP EVERYTHING.*

Now it's a quick change from the comfortable-but-professional layers to getaway camouflage: crop jeans, Breton top, boat shoes, hoodie, the fifty-something middle-class uniform guaranteed to render me even more invisible. Let's leave the pearls on for luck.

Edward and Summer have taken the only functional backpacks. I cram my things into a flight case with an extending handle and wheels which is all a bit *The Apprentice* for such an intrepid mission but will have to do. Then I catch myself adding the novel I'm halfway through and stop. What am I doing? This isn't a holiday. I'll be packing family board games and favourite films and box sets next.

As I head downstairs, I try to remember the name of the eighties television series my husband treasures and that Matteo was so obsessed with he still longs for a canal barge. Damn this menopausal memory! I go into the sitting room to scour the DVD collection – shelves beautifully handmade by Paddy – and right at the top, where we keep *Trainspotting* and *Kill Bill* and all those nineties action movies I always forget are so violent until I agree to re-watch one, is the one I'm looking for, *Travelling Man*.

As well as a traditional red narrowboat, there's a picture of its lead character, Lomax, smouldering on the box, played by eighties British heartthrob Leigh Lawson, AKA 'Twiggy's husband'. I know his name because it says so, and I know he married Twiggy because my middle-aged brain, whilst unable to retain a shopping list for more than an hour, can retain ancient celebrity trivia indefinitely.

I want to know how *Travelling Man* captivated the two men so much.

I accidentally slot Disc Two in, but it hardly matters. I only need a sense of it, and I select an episode called *Moving On*, which seems fitting.

It opens with a vintage Granada Television logo then straight into a scene set in a rural Black Country pub in which a local (played by an actor I'm certain was one of the *Play School* presenters and is trying hard to look sinister) arm-wrestles a man with a bad Australian accent and a mullet. Edgy synth chords say this is serious. An open Zippo lighter flame burns Aussie Mullet's hairy elbow when he loses. They make some sort of deal for a fiver (which they both agree is a lot of money) and then the title sequence starts, all terrifically eighties, a little sliding mosaic of video clips forming into the shape of a canal boat. The music's unexpectedly haunting and mellow.

Action switches to a derelict house. A long-lens camera is clicking, an unseen photographer spying on Lomax wandering around in a leather jacket looking very Roxy Music video.

My God, Leigh Lawson was scrumptious! And curiously Italianate, now I look closer. In fact, add on thirty years and a beard...

Stop it, Eliza. You're just punishing yourself. I go to a drawer to fetch some paper to write a note for Paddy, then find myself in front of the television again.

Lomax is swigging on a can of Top Brass lager as he motors gently along a sunny canal on *Harmony*, her red paintwork gleaming prettily in the sunlight, a far less showy old vessel than *The Tempest*, but the resemblance is clear.

I've seen enough. I mute the sound and sit down at the coffee table with the paper and a pen.

It takes me fifteen minutes and a lot of tear splotches to compose just one sentence of my farewell note: *I was going to get you a puppy for our anniversary, my love, but you're my best friend and I hope I can remind you why*. I can't think what to write next.

I stare tearily down at the page again. While I'm determined to do this, to run away, I don't want Paddy to think it's forever.

I hope we can still celebrate tomorrow. I'll call to say where. I sign off with an extravagant *Exxx* wondering if I'm tempting fate.

I add: *PS: Dress up*.

I head upstairs and tuck it between the bedcover and his pillow because I can't risk him finding it before bedtime. Then fetch the *Avon Navigation Guide* out of the en suite where it's deemed essential loo-side reading by Paddy.

In the sitting room, the old episode of *Travelling Man* is still playing silently: Lomax and *Harmony* the barge are now deep in a fierce canal lock while two men with mullets throw firecrackers down her chimney. I watch in alarm; I hate locks. And mullets.

I hunt for the remote, give up and instead head into the kitchen to pack some emergency rations – on-their-date sausage rolls and a few apples. Crouching down to cram them in the front pouch of the *Apprentice* case, I realise the TV remote is in my back pocket, along with several pens and an old dog toy. I hurry back to eject the DVD.

On screen, *Harmony* is now crossing the Chirk Aqueduct, a ten-arch stone construction that carries the Llangollen Canal across the Ceiriog Valley. Not far from where Paddy grew up, it's giddyingly high.

The shot switches to a crop-duster helicopter buzzing towards the great waterway in the sky, piloted by the actor with the bad Australian accent from the first pub scene.

This is the scene Paddy and Matteo bonded over, I realise.

I unmute it.

Lomax is halfway along the aqueduct and minding his own sexily brooding business listening to some Donizetti while Aussie Mullet – looking very *Top Gun* in aviator shades – starts taking aerial swoops at him in the helicopter. It looks incredibly dangerous. And very real. No stunt doubles here; Leigh Lawson's acting his heart out up there.

He's overboard! Where's the bloody lifebuoy ring? The very one that now hangs on our cellar wall here in Leamington Spa is missing from her stern.

I hurry closer to the screen as Lomax scrambles up out of the water onto the aqueduct wall – nothing between him and a seventy-feet fall, not even a rail – and, running backwards, gets swiped by the crop duster again. That helicopter is crazily close. As it circles away, Lomax dives in and swims after *Harmony*, still chugging along in forward throttle, and finally clings onto her stern as she heads into the tunnel.

I'm breathless. Forget Harrison Ford; Leigh Lawson is a stunt god.

I eject the DVD with shaking hands, quietly terrified.

Today, I plan to steal a narrowboat and hide it. I'll check the buoy and life jackets are on board first. And I'm going nowhere near any aqueducts.

I have something to prove here.

Although I'd hesitate to describe Paddy as a sexist, he did come preloaded with a lot of assumptions when we met, not least that women aren't as practically-minded as men, particularly when it comes to boats.

While it's true that his mum Ruth's interest in her husband's *Lady Love* didn't extend much beyond brewing up and making sandwiches in the galley, I wanted to skipper.

This tested the fledgling romance. Paddy had explained that barges don't handle like cars, don't have brakes and that while they travel very slowly, heavy old birds like *Lady Love* are steel-hulled and very hard to stop. What he hadn't explained was the strange groaning, shouting and lecturing sounds the men on board would make every time I got it slightly wrong and how bloody off-putting that would be.

After I'd battered her sides, run her aground and eventually got her wedged broadside across the canal whilst being talked down to all the time, I resigned my captaincy. And while I've returned to the helm many times in the years since and pretty much mastered the steering, it's not my idea of a relaxed day out.

Something I have never done in my life is taken her out single-handed.

Until today.

I am on my way to Stratford, Annie Lennox cheering me on with 'Sweet Dreams'.

The rust bucket's hands-free Bluetooth is a cheap, voice-activated gadget we bought from Aldi and it is notoriously glitchy.

Mum calls as I drive – I have to bark *'answer call!'* to make it respond – and we manage a quick exchange of hellos and my plea of 'of course I haven't been avoiding speaking to you, Mum,' before another call comes through, the phone screen telling me it's Ed's school. 'I have to take this, but don't hang up, Mum, I can put you on hold. *Hold call one! Answer call two!'*

'Hello? Eliza?' Mum is still there.

'Hold call one! Answer call two!' I command more bullishly.

'Mrs Hollander? I'm so sorry to bother you, but we can't get through to Mr Hollander.'

'What's happened?'

'Year Seven are on the coach, but Edward's been violently—'

'Hello? Eliza?' It's Mum again.

'Sorry, Mum, hang on a bit longer. *Hold call one! Answer call two!'*

'Hello? Eliza?'

'Mrs Hollander?'

'It's gone to conference call, sorry!'

' – all over the upholstery, I'm afraid, Mrs Hollander. He can't possibly continue on to PGL. We have a strict rule that all children who vomit must be isolated for twenty-four hours.'

'But it's only travel sickness, surely?'

'My daughter's right!' Mum leaps to my defence. 'Did you remember to give him a Kwell, Eliza?'

Bugger.

'You can't get hold of his father you say? Because I'm on my way to – Leicester.' Oh, the scalding shame of the lie. 'Where is the coach now?'

'On the A46 near Snitterfield. In a layby. How soon can you get there?'

I am minutes away from it. I want to scream. I have to go there. My great runaway is already limping home.

'That's near me!' Mum says brightly. 'I can pick Edward up in five minutes. We'll spend the day together, then I can drop him home with Paddy later.'

'Are you sure?'

Her voice drops to a reassuring growl. 'I am *dying* to get away from your father and Miles. That's why I've been calling you: I'm furious they want to sell the boat. I've only just offered her to the BBC as a *Shakespeare and Hathaway* location.'

'Oh, I love that series!' cries the school secretary. Moments later they're comparing favourite episodes over my dodgy Aldi Bluetooth.

I cut them off, sending up a silent prayer for Ed to be OK.

My mission is back on.

★ ★ ★

I've parked the rust bucket in Long Stay, rather than near the marina. As I cross Bridge Road, I keep a nervous eye out for Paddy, who I wouldn't rule out driving straight here after dropping Edward. Also for Miles. And the police. Is this a criminal act? It must be. What I'm about to commit is, I suspect, technically theft. I'm feeling distinctly paranoid.

Luck's on my side. The council tree surgeons are out in force in the little garden that runs alongside the marina, chainsaws firing up to lop branches. It's incredibly noisy, the air full of dust and leaves, tourists staying away from this side of the historic bridge, nobody sitting outside the café.

I've brought dark glasses and a baseball cap which I cram on as I make my way stealthily into the marina.

The narrowboats to either side of *The Tempest* are locked up and unmanned, none of Paddy's bargees in sight to raise an alarm when his missus makes a quick getaway on a collision course with their precious hulls.

No time to lose. I unlock the boatman's cabin and dump my *Apprentice* suitcase, hurry to the well deck to turn on the water and gas. Emma Thompson's chocolates are still in the galley, making my throat tighten as I think how foolishly I behaved yesterday.

Back at the stern, I pull up the engine cover hatch. Check oil, coolant filters, fuel and water. Switch the batteries across to charge, check the pump's switched to on, close the hatch. There's a full tank of fuel as well as plenty of gas and water to see us through a few days if necessary.

I'm shocked by how much adrenaline is thrumming

through me. Also by how unnervingly good it feels. In a slightly nauseating way.

The control panel is beside me. Key in ignition. Turn to HEAT and wait a few beeps. Turn to START and hear her roar. Let key return to RUN.

So far so good.

Cast off mooring ropes. Bow first, then stern then centre. Trickier alone – Paddy's bloody knots! – but not impossible. No gusting wind to push us about today, thank goodness.

Throttle in gear. Tiller in hand. AirPods in, Annie on – 'I Need a Man'.

I don't think so.

We're off.

I'm running away on *The Tempest*. I'm going to hide her until my wedding anniversary. My brother will lose this bet. As long as he doesn't catch me first.

18

Time Travelling

Stratford upon Avon, mecca for Shakespeare lovers and swans, is also important for its waterways, marking the point where the Midlands canal system meets the River Avon.

It's the Stratford Canal that's closest to Paddy's heart, its fifty-four narrow locks, four iron aqueducts and a single long tunnel being clever feats of industrial engineering enabling twenty-five miles of manmade transport vein to wend its watery way north through the Warwickshire countryside to King's Norton in Birmingham. It's part of a big circular cruising route known as the Avon Ring, along with the Birmingham Navigations, the Worcester and Birmingham Canal, then two rivers which return boaters to Stratford, the Severn and Shakespeare's Avon.

I prefer the rivers to the canals; the Avon's been navigated for centuries, but never tamed. It floods fiercely at times, its George Eliot mills isolated like ships in great water meadow expanses. Fringed with rushes and overhung with willow, it's a beautiful, savage thread of nature that knows its own bloody-minded path, not caring if it steals through great landowners' estates, farms, villages or forests. In watery terms, it's Heathcliff.

Annie stops singing as I pull away from the marina. It's Mum calling my phone, a disembodied Siri voice tells me.

My AirPods – a birthday gift from Jules – are far smarter tech than the rust bucket's Aldi Bluetooth, but I'm no smarter at using them, and I press the right once too often, only hearing '... we've just got an ice cream and he feels much better! We're about to...' before I cut her off again.

At least Ed is OK.

I cannot let my focus sway. I take my AirPods out and put them in my back pocket.

Here's my plan: I'm taking the River Avon because nobody will expect me to. It's harder to navigate, teeming with pleasure cruisers, restaurant boats, sightseeing day trippers and canoeists, more anonymous than the narrow canal with its well-trodden towpaths, multiple road bridges and army of gongoozlers. (Not to mention aqueducts.) It's also got far fewer locks to negotiate. The few that are on it are admittedly fierce, but there's bound to be people around to help in hot June weather like this. The secret is to look as though I know what I'm doing whilst not drawing attention to myself. As Mum would say, 'Act like you can do it, darling girl!' I thought it all through in the early hours: I'll wear a sunhat and dark glasses and adopt a Brummy bargee accent, and I've already draped a couple of picnic blankets over the old girl's cabin sides to obscure her name.

I plan to message Paddy later to let him know what I'm doing, but not until I'm too far away to catch. I have no doubt he'll try to find me – as will Miles as soon as he gets wind I'm taking him up on his dare – but they'll think I'm on the canal. And even if (when) they work out I'm on the river, both will bank on me staying close to the town. Which is why I've rejected my first plan to hide *The Tempest* in one of the overgrown, tree-fringed inlets a few miles downstream, a familiar stretch of river we've nicknamed Heart of Darkness because it's so wild. Paddy will know that's exactly where I want to hide out. What he'll never expect me to do is go a bridge too far.

Downstream from Stratford, there are just two road bridges that cross Shakespeare's Avon in almost seven river-cruising hours, both historic and narrow-arched, Binton Bridge and Bidford Bridge, known collectively to the family as the BBs or Bastard Bridges. Both are notoriously tricky if the river's fast and not much easier if not. I have never steered *The Tempest* through either of them, these two stone river-monsters that Hollander family lore places on a danger par with anacondas and dysentery.

Today, I plan to go beyond both BBs. The thought makes me clutch my pearls and pray.

My finishing target is Harvington Lock, which sits in an isolated spot close to a riverside garden where we were guests at a rip-roaringly riparian fortieth birthday donkeys years ago. Our hosts – a gregarious couple we'd met through our children's school PTA – rowed a bunch of guests out to show us a derelict old mill on an overgrown river island with its own dry dock, the perfect hideaway for a narrowboat. According to Google it's still there, only more derelict.

I messaged the couple first thing this morning with Mrs Peel cunning: *Are you still living in that gorgeous spot by the mill? Know someone who might be mooring nearby this week and loves spooky ruins if it's still there? Eliza (Summer's mum) x* To which they immediately replied: *Hello lovely Eliza Summersmum! Long time no see! Mill just as was! Tell friend to pop in for a snifter! Will give tour! Here all week! Xxx* and I felt a rush of gratitude that there are still people in the world unembarrassed of exclamation marks and words like snifter, which helps add to the sixties *Avengers'* vibe.

To get there, as well as navigating the dreaded BBs, *The Tempest* and I must make our way through six river locks.

First, let's exit Stratford inconspicuously. Just getting out of the marina has drawn a bit of an audience on the bridge, but I've done this bit enough times to manage it reasonably smoothly. I try to fantasise I'm Lomax, unflappably cool, not for a moment betraying to the onlooking crowd that I am stealing this boat.

'Drive on the right!' I mutter under my breath to *The Tempest* like we're exiting the cross-Channel ferry as we chug into open water. Except in Calais there isn't ever an *All A-Bard Open Top Tour Boat* unexpectedly in my path, bunting fluttering, half its passengers videoing me. And my steering's better.

'Sorry!' I miss it by inches.

My heart is thumping so hard I can barely hear my own voice.

Crossing in front of the lock that leads up to the Stratford Canal, the river is a-bob with hired rowboats and pleasure craft. Swans are pimping for food from the gallery, the metal footbridge over the entrance to the lock weighed down with tourists. I'm again photographed and videoed as we glide past. Somebody shouts out 'Hey, lady!' I also think I hear 'Mum!' but I'm putting that down to guilt.

I rev away, baseball cap rammed down low, avoiding swans and fellow boaters downstream.

Theatre straight ahead. Must put on a good performance, audacious as a player on a regal Elizabethan row-barge.

Up ahead is my first lock, the daunting Trinity. Braced with industrial iron girders like the ribs of a giant dinosaur to hold it square between silty banks, its descent is a hulking, black-hulled open grave of engineering. How do I do this alone? My heart's banging in time to the engine rattle but I'm determined to nail this challenge.

Then I spot a sight more welcome than a free checkout in Lidl on a Saturday: an open lock.

Unlike canal locks, which we must close after us when we leave like field gates, on rivers we're asked to leave them casually open when we go out – the Avon's water will never drain out through cavalier caretaking, after all – and the joy with which I greet a little white riverboat emerging from the lock is up there with spotting a parking space in central London. I cruise straight in, the water high in readiness. Just need to nudge up to the lock side, hop off, tie her up and get cracking.

★ ★ ★

All canal and river locks are essentially the same, big or small. Water is higher one side than the other. The section between is sealed off by 'gates'. After entering, we need to close the gates behind us and either fill it or drain it down to the level of the waterway in front before opening the doors ahead to continue. To do this, we need to lift 'paddles' in the gates to let water in or out, like running and letting out a bath. Each gate has a mechanism ratcheted up by ingenious winches and pulleys that we operate with a key called a 'windlass' – as in a windblown girl, not a clock-winding one. All canal boats carry at least one windlass, and tackling a lock's not a bad workout.

If you can get *off* your boat to do it.

Crack, crack, crack. The bow hits the stone lock wall repeatedly. It takes me forever to get the right angle. Locks intimidate me: green-slimed, brick-lined pits into which I must descend to go downriver.

When I finally leap off – wringing sweat, the ropes tangled, my knots fumbled – my gratitude that nobody was watching my bad captaining switches to anxiety that there's nobody here to help. Just geese. Tens of Canada geese honking up. They're as territorial and aggressive as football fans spotting a rival shirt in their stand.

I'm a woman under siege by wildfowl as I heave the gates shut and use the metal windlass to clatter the paddles down.

Sweatier still. Breathing hard. Legs pecked.

Why am I bloody doing this again? I move to the front gate paddles now and raise one. *The Tempest* bucks, pushed forwards hard by the force of river releasing, ropes straining. I cross to the other side to crank open the second lock paddle. Gush, swoosh, woosh.

Listening to the water, I suddenly need a wee so badly I'm tempted to hurry behind a bush, but the geese are back on the attack, honking furiously. And the boat's doing something weird.

Shit, shit, shit! She's tilting.

I've tied the ropes too tight to the moorings, trussing her up high as the level drops away. Blood pressure rocketing, I leap to the rescue, knowing she could capsize this way.

She rocks hard when I release them, the decks soaked. Now she's going down, coffin lowered into grave until, at last, the level from lock to river downstream matches.

Tie her off again, open the lower gate, cross over the footbridge to the other, open that, pausing to catch my breath. Behind me, the geese honk furiously as a runner goes past, panting and pounding. I don't turn, watching transfixed as two swans take off downriver, running and flapping clumsily on water before air's elegance lifts them up and away. Swans mate for life, I remember. Like barn owls, sea horses, wolves and Hollander men.

Hearing a thump from the boat, now deep in the lock, I peer over in a panic but she's still in one piece down there, so I cross back again, untie her, then brace myself to climb down the ladder inset in the lock wall to get back on deck. It's wet, slimy and rusted.

Why am I doing this? I want to go home.

I close my eyes going down, frightened I'll fall. I'm awash with sweat. Paddy would have the narrowboat's stern perfectly aligned to step on easily. By contrast, I splat onto the roof, turning my ankle and swearing a lot before scrambling back to the tiller, cranking the throttle forward and exiting into dappled sunlight.

Cue instant happiness. Fast as drugs in a vein. Is this a menopausal mood swing, or simply joy? I love coming out of locks, claustrophobia traded for the wardrobe doors to Narnia. How beautiful is this? Crinkled silk river ahead, park to our left, weir right. The geese are gone and I have swan outriders now. I feel like Leda. Except, now I think about it, I'm pretty sure Zeus disguised himself as a swan to rape her. Odette maybe? Nope, she died when Siegfried danced with the wrong bird. Bloody men.

You can do this alone! I remind myself. You don't need Paddy pedantically at your ear, telling you how to do it all.

The weir roars to my right. I can feel its force tug us as the barge powers slowly away from the lock, the willows giving way to a view up to the converted mill with its luxury retirement flats where I was conducting viewings just twenty-four hours ago. I have the strangest sensation of living a parallel life, looking back in at myself.

There's somebody on the balcony of that same third-floor flat. I recognise the blonde bombshell hair of one of the senior negotiators. She must be hosting another viewing. She's leaning on the balcony rail, looking straight at *The Tempest*. Surely she won't recognise me?

Oh God, she's waving and calling.

Keep calm! *The Tempest* is simply drawing the eye again, I reassure myself. Sure enough, another figure has joined her to admire the old narrowboat. Raising a bargee hand and lowering my head, we chug on. Slowly.

Ahead lies the Seven Meadows Bridge, the second of

Stratford's road crossings which carries traffic over the river on the town's western edge, open countryside beyond.

More shouts from the mill. Was that my name? I glance reluctantly up again. The second figure on the balcony is waving too, a man in possession of sharp tailoring and an intense gaze I recognise even from this distance. Matteo Mele.

He cups his hands to his mouth. '*Bellissima*!'

Refusing to react, I lower my hat peak and look away. Let him think he's got the wrong woman. Here on the river, I am not Eliza Finch the fifty-year-old actor who pants out bad prose, nor Eliza Hollander, over-huggy mother and neglectful sex-phobic wife who thought she was long past succumbing to a stranger's persuasive panache and prosecco. Forget conflicted daughter and competitive sister, grieving dog lover and menopausal motorist; I'm acting against all my types.

I'm being unpredictable and I love it. I haven't felt like this in twenty years. Today I could be anybody, achieve anything, my future full of possibilities. I could be the next Emma Thompson.

The modern bridges are up ahead, foot then road, the first cool stripe of shadow soothing my brow as we pass under, then a longer one marking the start of the adventure proper.

My phone is buzzing like mad with messages, and 'Ain't Misbehavin'' plays out twice, but I ignore it.

This is more than boat theft – I'm taking my life back.

19

Maritime

When I was thinking through this narrowboat hijack last night, there was a bit too much angels-singing salvation going on in my head to see any ulterior motive, to acknowledge a hot, sweaty need to be alone that I've felt building in my soul like drums of late.

Being alone at home doesn't count. There's always something to do, to fold, to file, to cook, to tidy. I can't relax; I need to be *doing* something. Aloneness isn't just about solitude, I realise, it's about independence of thought, that single-mindedness which sets itself apart and navigates its own course. And I like it far more than I expected. Maybe now I get why Paddy needs this all to himself so often. All this wind-in-the-face slow-motion river travel is pure oxygen. It's doing everything and nothing at the same time.

Yet I can't help feeling as though I've stolen my husband's secret pleasure along with the boat and it makes me feel sad that we can't share this together; that the theft of it is part of the joy of it.

Without him here to exert greater knowledge and prior claim, I realise how much I love being at the helm of *The Tempest*. She might be as slow-moving and stubborn to steer as my sex drive, but this gentle powerhouse stands for much more than conjugal rights and wrongs.

I need to do this my way, even if it might have been much better for my marriage had I simply admitted the truth to Paddy this morning: *Miles is paying back a childhood debt by daring me to hide* The Tempest *until tomorrow in exchange for his share, so I'm going to call his bluff and do it to show how much I love you.*

At which Paddy would want to take over, our anniversary turned into a *Romancing the Stone*-style mini-adventure in which he's all wily and practical, hand on the tiller on a manly mission, and I'm dappy and flappy in high heels, recoiling at dirt.

Or even more likely, he'd flatly refuse to buy into the idea that Miles could be stupid enough to gamble *The Tempest* to honour a four-decades-old Bionic Woman-doll grudge match.

Is Miles that stupid? Am I?

I am a middle-aged woman in possession of a weak bladder and coffee habit, which is why I may be barely past the ring-road bridge, but I'm already going to have to stop the boat to go to the loo. Also, 'Ain't Misbehavin'' has rung out for the third time and I'm worried Mum's in difficulty with Edward, so I want to call her back.

I nudge the boat alongside the reed bank and drop the engine to neutral, then hurry below deck, but the bathroom lock has jammed again and I can't get in.

Then I notice the luxury chocolates have gone, which is odd.

Grabbing the navigation guide from my case, I go back on deck to call Mum.

'Thank goodness!' she wails. 'I've lost Edward! I'd just bought him a lemon sorbet from Shakees – it always settled your stomach after you were car sick – and was putting one of those silly sachets of sugar in my coffee, and when I turned back he'd gone!'

'How long ago was this?'

'Half an hour, maybe? I've been trying to find a policeman.'

My head is racing, panic gripping. 'Where is Shakees?'

'It's the ice-cream barge, you know the one.'

'You're in Stratford?'

'Yes. In Bancroft Gardens. I lost Edward here.'

'Near the lock bridge?' I ask, realisation dawning. When I heard a voice shouting 'Mum!' I never imagined it could be my own son.

'I'll never forgive myself if he's been abducted by a paedophile ring,' Mum cries, ever the dramatist.

'You say the most encouraging things. Hang on, I have his location tracker on my phone.' I put her on speakerphone and pull up Google Maps with shaking fingers. It centres on my watery location. Right on top of my avatar is Einstein. 'I think I've found him, Mum.'

I go back inside the boat and knock on the bathroom door. 'Edward?'

Silence.

'Edward?'

'*Hoo! Just what I needed!*' comes a muffled Mario catchphrase, then more recognisably Ed: 'I'm not coming out.'

'Are you trapped in there?'

'*I'm fine! Oh you, it's all you baby!* The door jammed again but I'm – *Niiiiiiintendi! Wahoo!* I'm fine. You need me here with you. It's not safe. You could drown.'

'Mum, he's here with me,' I tell my mother.

'How can he be? You're in Leicester.'

I have to tell her the truth too, I realise. I might as well have posted it on my Facebook status.

At least Mum is gratifyingly onside, dropping her voice to a spy whisper. 'I'll keep Miles distracted. He has a flying lesson later, so he'll have his mind on that. You do know how to sail the thing?'

'I hope so.'

'*Act* it, darling girl. Good luck.'

We ring off and I hurriedly address the bathroom door. 'Don't worry, Edward, I'm going to get you out of there.'

But I can't get the Ashwell's Patent Toilet Lock to come apart. Soon, several tool kits lie open around me. Nothing is working. It's stuck fast.

'How did Dad do it so easily?' I complain, but Edward doesn't answer because he's put his headphones back on, so I have to shout.

'I think it was a three-millimetre flathead, stork-billed pliers, tweezers and a miniature tension wrench,' he explains wearily. 'Possibly also a bradawl.'

'What would that look like again?' I gaze down at the rows and rows of screwdrivers, spanners and drill heads.

'Honestly, I'm fine in here,' he insists. 'I have my survival kit and my new Sonic game. You need to get this boat moving, Mum, we're far too close to Stratford to be safe. I'm going to put my headphones back on now. If you need me, you know where to find me.'

I'm not sure he's really thought this through.

I'm not sure I have either, but I do know Ed's right and we're far too exposed this close to the road. And that I love having him with me, even if I do need the loo.

A good friend I met at NCT when we were both pregnant with our third children – increasingly rare, especially amongst older career-bruiser mums like we were – had a wonderful truism passed down from her mother: when our firstborn child drops its feeding spoon, we sterilise it thoroughly before handing it back; when our second child drops its spoon, we run it under a hot tap; when our third child drops it, we wipe it on our jeans.

And she was right. With experience, comes a warm glow of confidence that knows children are robust little survivors. I loved the idea of being a mother for the third time. I embraced it.

Except that Edward didn't drop his spoon because he didn't hold it. Mostly he ignored it or pushed it away. Occasionally he threw it, maddened by this world of taste and texture and the 'let's see the choo-choo train going into the big mouthy tunnel' noise that expected him to behave like his brother and sister had at that age, something he would never be able to do. Realising he's never going to be like the other two has been painful and frightening at times; the ups and downs of adapting to his needs remains a work in progress, but my continued humble joy at the sheer power of mother love owes no small part to my third-time lucky charm, to the boy who dared us to 'do' different in our family.

And Ed is turning into the ultimate robust little survivor. He endures a far harsher environment than the rest of us, adapting to a world that wasn't designed for him. He's resilient and resourceful and funny, even locked in a narrowboat bathroom, promising he'll save me if I drown.

Ed knows he could never save me. But he has learned that making me feel loved is more important. And he is exceptionally good at it.

Weir Brake Lock, AKA the Anonymous Lock, AKA Gordon Grey Lock.

On this stretch of river between Stratford and Evesham – known as the Upper Avon – all the locks bear two names, the first referring to its location and the second a benefactor or volunteer who was a part of the grand navigation restoration in the sixties and seventies. Because one generous donor was initially too modest to come forward, then later did, this one has three. Make your mind up, Gordon.

The Avon Navigation Guide informs me that it's the biggest, best and last of the new locks and was built in thirty-eight days by boys from Borstal, along with its weir. Mental note made to mention that to the husband and sons who have been promising to reline our pond for almost a year, although perhaps best to wait until all this has calmed down.

The Guide advises: coming downstream, take care to bear to your left into the lock channel.

The Tempest and I oblige like pros, following in the wake of a little white twenty-two-foot pleasure cruiser, fresh off its moorings. We fork past the lock island, overshadowed by the earthworks on the bank where they're building a new marina, gates straight ahead. Again, they're open, the cruiser already tucked in neatly to the left, its occupants beckoning impatiently for me to follow, classic examples of the 'Regatta Set' Paddy grumbles about on the open river. The husband is even wearing a blazer and a captain's hat.

'Plenty of room!' he commands. 'Do you know what you're doing?'

'Careful you don't hit us!' demands his wife, looking down her nose at my bright paintwork.

'I won't,' I mutter, clinging onto Mum's 'Act it!' advice.

Most river locks are wide enough for two boats, and the turbulence reduces drastically if you double up. Method acting now, I crack the old girl's boards a bit less, tie up better, turn my windlass with seasoned speed and focus cheerfully on the possibility of a waist reappearing if I keep this exercise up.

'Out on your own, are you?' the Captain shouts up as he lowers into the lock.

I weigh up the advantages of admitting there is a child trapped in my narrowboat loo, but I don't want to blow my cover. *Act it.*

'Yup.' I smile easily.

'Jolly brave,' says his wife from the opposite side.

'Friends slow you down. On one of these, that's bloody

slow.' I indicate *The Tempest* and wait for them to get the joke. They don't. Like beauty and romance, ironic wit isn't something people look for in middle-aged women.

Or maybe I'm just telling the truth.

The urge to be alone is one thing, but middle age can be a fiercely lonely stage of life. We still have friends, don't we? We trust they're out there. We just don't see much of them. Busy, busy, busy lives. As we grow older time runs away from us, exhausts us. Writing *Must catch up this year!* in Christmas cards is an annual ritual. Except hardly anybody sends those any more, and we all feel a bit lonelier for it.

We realise we see more of work colleagues, our children's playmates, their parents, our parents, our hairdressers – and if you're middle class, the cleaner too – than we see of old friends. Even a catch-up phone call takes careful planning. We pepper social media updates with positive reactions instead and increasingly rely on the big occasions as the rhythm of long-established friendships changes from regular small doses to landmark binges: fortieths, fiftieths, sixtieths, reunions, retirement parties, silver anniversaries. For each generation, they come in groups. Then fewer seem to come. Is it our FOMO or their JOMO?

And while our children appear happy to conduct their friendships online, my generation still craves sentient companionship. I recently worked out that of all my Facebook friends in the 'old guard' – those I've known longest or been through more with than most – I'd physically met up with just one in the past six months.

A measure of friendship is to make it real again. To do that, we need to live in real time, not the fast-forward blur we all pretend is normal. Sometimes I find myself desperate to press pause.

Instead I got menopause.

As the pleasure cruiser motors away from the lock, *The Tempest* and I dawdle to reclaim the river's peace. I should check on my stowaway again, but my phone keeps buzzing, making me jumpy and I want to press on through the Heart of Darkness.

Before I can push forward the throttle, I hear a shout out of sight on the footpath that leads past Weir Brake lock from Severn Meadows Road. Was that 'Eliza'?

I scour the bank nervously, grateful for thick rushes and willows as high as a fortress wall. There's silence. I must have imagined it.

Pulling my hat lower, I try to think through my character as a lovelorn Brummy bargee, but the more I do, the less I want to act. I dared myself to take this journey because I want to make things better, and because I used to be braver and kinder before I started losing hormones and sleep, and I need to remember that humanity. I have no desire to be somebody else; I want to be more like me.

To do that, I need to take a leaf out of Ed's book and block out the sensory overload.

I switch my phone status to Airplane – there is no 'Boat' – and slot my Bluetooth AirPods in. It has to be eighties, and it has to be rebelliously, singularly Annie: 'Would I Lie To You?'

I am at peace. And oh, oh, oh, the riverbanks. The reeds are green fires burning bright, copper aflame. Weeping willows wash their hair. As the bow wave of the riverboat vanishes around a bend and we reclaim the water all to ourselves, the lap is too seductively in time to the music, my resolve weakening. I wish Paddy was here.

Annie sings on as we putter along the satin sash of water towards a lapis fan of sky.

'It's Alright (Baby's Coming Back)'...

It's hard to emphasise how slowly narrowboats travel.

Most of us can walk faster.

But ramble, jog or cycle along the banks of any navigable river in Britain and I defy almost anyone to feel as peacefully at one with it as puttering along in a barge, this other-worldly steampunk waterway snail with her house on her back, time-travelling between industry and idyll at her own sweet pace, a glistening ribbon of river ahead.

As the old truism goes, it's only on the occasions we slow down in life that we get to look around and realise how unique it is. On a narrowboat there's no choice.

The undulating skirts of willows and reeds drop away to reveal a scattering of houses that drift by to our right, close-cut lawns immaculately striped like ironed damask on which retirees gongoozle from sunloungers and dogs bark. Developers snap up the old dormer bungalows along here to bulldoze and replace with architect-designed, zoned lifestyle homes. The gardens all flood, especially along the short stretch where the River Stour joins the Avon. I suppose living by a river is like a marriage to a man who bottles things up: you know every now and again it will be hell as it pours out, but the rest of the time makes you forget.

'*Thorn in My Side*' is succeeded by '*Don't Ask Me Why*'...

Luddington Lock, AKA Stan Clover Lock. Lucky for some...

My *Avon Navigation Guide* helpfully informs me this was built by prisoners from Gloucester Gaol and that I can empty my loo waste here (chance would be a fine thing). Bonus is that Shakespeare supposedly married Anne Hathaway at the village church on the riverbank, although the current one's a nineteenth-century replacement because the original burned down – which might be God's way of saying he should have written more parts for women over fifty.

As I draw closer, I see my Regatta Set friends coming back, bow wave high with irritation. Realising they're shouting something at me, I pull out an earpiece.

'GHASTLY *bloody* wedding boat moored up bang in front of the lock,' he warns as they draw level. 'Not *budging* until the photos are all done.'

'Typical bloody youth!' she quacks furiously. 'Could be waiting ALL day!'

Away they whirr, chins forward.

I chug on. A wedding boat at 11 a.m. on a Tuesday? Really? I celebrate their quirkiness.

It's true, the lock gates are totally obscured by a wide-beam restaurant cruiser with ribbons and flowers decking her bow. The name *Lady Charlecote* glitters in gold Tuscan font on her side.

Luddington Lock is a well-favoured turnaround point,

reached in the time it takes to serve two courses of a wedding breakfast. She's come downriver from Stratford and winded (that's boat-speak for turning 180°) before reversing past the weir barrels to tie up against the lock island while the guests get out to stretch their legs beneath the trees and pose for photographs.

I moor on the opposite canal bank, bashing the portside just a few times, then watch them over *The Tempest*'s roof, the sun in my eyes. It's a small, glamorous wedding party – no more than ten, all very young and fabulously dressed – and the photographer is an equally stylish neo rocker with skintight jeans and a Lenny Kravitz afro, familiar enough for me to wonder if he's well-known. He's a shouty sod, his voice so rock-stadium loud it penetrates even my AirPods. I pull one out to confirm the accent's Mancunian. 'Come on, show me some fooking affection newlyweds!'

Bloody hell. It's Kwasi Owusu.

I secretly observe the object of my daughter's desire: the self-styled digital Banksy is, it seems, wedding photographer for hire.

'At least *try* to look like you fancy each other, people! I'm losing the will to fooking live here.'

I put my AirPod back in – Annie launches into 'Missionary Man' – thinking things have certainly moved on since ours called for 'Bride, groom and bride's family, excluding cousins!' in St Luke's Gardens.

When Paddy and I married in Chelsea Register Office in the nineties, I wore lime-green silk matched with purple heels and a raspberry cowboy hat which I thought was wildly boho (photographic evidence suggests 'eye-watering' would be a safer description). My mother and Ruth outdistanced each other with lethally wide hat brims, and my sister's on-trend fascinator looked like a satellite dish (which is what she would have needed to make contact with Reece, delayed trekking on Mount Toubkal at the time, their 'on' about to go 'off'). Later, Jules refused to catch the bouquet even though I aimed it directly at the dish, and instead it ricocheted into the arms of my Best Woman, Lou, resplendent in orange and red Karen Millen, accessorised with a hangover matching mine. Lou and I looked like Opal Fruits when we stood together, bright smiles guarding a secret early-hours Smirnoff-fuelled debate as to whether I should go through with it...

The men all wore morning suits and rose buttonholes, my groom a picture of handsome blonde convention, anxious smile gleaming. I remember fleetingly thinking that if there's just one day a man can be a peacock, surely it's his wedding, so why can't we share that glory equally?

But there's only one Paddy in the world. Beneath the hired grey trousers and black tailcoat was a totally unique man. He is true to himself, no matter what he wears, as constant as the North star, a point on which my life always knows the way. I just wish I'd taken the time to appreciate it that day, but I was too busy eyeing the exits.

'There's no respect for tradition these days,' grumbles an old bargee moored behind me as we watch the wedding party across the water.

The newlyweds are posing for shots beyond a thick veil

of weeping willows, the flat-faced beefcake groom strutting around, shamelessly on-trend with a skinny-fitting petrol blue suit and *no socks*. His bride – a ringleted pillar-box redhead – keeps striking a Statue of Liberty pose with a champagne flute that's more Tank Girl than blushing virgin. Her meringue's bodice is corseted with punky geometric bows at the back, I notice – no doubt also one of this year's trends – and she has a conspicuous tattoo at the nape of her neck. There's something a bit odd about their body language, also about the ultra-fashionably dressed guests drifting around disinterestedly. It's all show. Maybe that's what marriages have become, I think sadly: *'I now pronounce you man and wife; you may take a selfie.'*

I'm grateful to still have Annie singing in my ears about original sin.

Heading inside the boat, I sing along as her mother tells her she can fool with her brother but not a…

'"Missionary man"!' I join in, looking round for something new to use to try to crack the Ashwell's Patent Toilet Lock. The need for a wee is increasingly urgent. I remove an AirPod and knock on the door. 'Are you OK in there Edward?'

Silence.

'Edward!'

'Mum, please don't sing,' he says in his monotone. 'I am fine. I've measured the porthole and in the event of an accident caused by your inexperience navigating riverways in a narrowboat, I could fit through it, although I'd rather stay in here and play my 3DS if that's OK, because I've almost reached the fifth level with Sonic. And before you ask, I'm not hungry because I've eaten two ganache truffles and one with toffee in it. And do you know these chocolates are for someone called Emma?'

'Yes, Dame Emma Thompson. A fan mistook me for her.'

'That's so random.'

'Actually no, Edward,' I say in a firm maternal voice (not unlike Emma's), '*Random* would be a wedding boat holding us up, on which Summer's art mentor is the photographer!'

'What's random about that? She's mentioned it enough times. Isn't that why you chose this route?'

'Of *course* I plotted it specifically to say hello to Mr Owusu,' I seethe grumpily. 'I've even brought spare champagne to toast the happy couple!'

Edward is too literal for sarcasm. 'It's irresponsible to handle rivercraft while under the influence of alcohol, Mum.'

'Especially when there's no toilet facilities available,' I agree bleakly.

'Have you finished talking?'

'Yes.' Pulling my phone from my pocket, I furtively check location tracking again. This isn't the 'cutting edge' project Summer was talking about, surely? A *wedding*? I'm relieved to see that her avatar remains over her school.

I found it hard to think of my teachers having a life outside the classroom. At Shand Abbey Girls School ('We're Shags Forever!'), I was shocked to my core to learn that timid geography teacher Mrs Gorse loved sky diving in her spare time, Mr Nimmo the sexy piano tutor's synth band had appeared on *Opportunity Knocks,* and my favourite

English teacher Miss Ruskin – a dryly witty Dorothy Parker type – was an active member of The Sealed Knot who loved nothing more than re-enacting the Battle of Edgehill dressed as a buxom royalist.

Teachers were our sacred deities, our surrogate family, our first celebrities. To see them out of context often confused our small world construct. (Many of us feel the same about our parents' working lives or private pastimes, mystery worlds we never see.)

A crush burns straight through context, seeing only what it wants to see, screening out all obstacles. While some see a polite, besuited part-time art teacher, Mr Owusu, others see loud and ambitious young photographer Kwasi – and a few of us still remember K-O the cool kid whose sheer raw talent, as well as his accent, made him stand out. Add enough filters of bright shiny love, and he's elevated above it all to a legend, a god amongst gods.

Back outside, the wedding boat hasn't budged. I jump back off *The Tempest* and pace around the moorings anxiously, wondering if anybody has noticed she is missing yet.

I want to get her much further along the river before I message Paddy, however hard my conscience is pricking (not to mention the pressing need for the secret behind springing the door lock, both to liberate Ed and my bladder). I'm still worried that Matteo recognised the boat. What if he really did run from the mill to Weir Brake Lock to try to shout for my attention? What if he alerts Miles? What if Mum does?

Don't panic. They have no idea you're here.

In my ears, Annie is repeatedly telling me to 'believe' and she's right. I struggle with religion, but sometimes it does help to give it a passing nod, especially at my age.

Spotting the wooden board for All Saints' Church, I take the freshly-strimmed track next to it and find myself alongside a pretty little village graveyard, shaded by yews, Annie now reassuring me 'There Must Be an Angel'. Weird timing.

Out of respect for the dead, I close Spotify and pull out my AirPods. Now I can hear the wedding boat music – a kitschy jazz – along with chatter, laughter, shouting and swearing. I can't make it all out, but I distinctly hear two 'fook!'s from Kwasi. He never did strike me as having the temperament for wedding work – or teaching, come to that. He's all livewire and unedited energy. As an earlier adopter of swearing myself, I feel his pain.

Especially with this bladder at capacity. 'Fuckety, fuckety, fuck, fuck, fuck!'

I resist an urge to cross myself. I'm an atheist after all. But I do quietly apologise to the dead around me for what I'm about to do as I look around for a discreet spot to have a wee.

There's a piece of string threaded through metal ground pegs by the path stopping walkers from getting too close to the graves, but I can still read their inscriptions. Many are couples buried together, I realise – Ronald and Jane, Tony and Gill, Alan and Margaret – they could be friends of my parents, enjoying an afterlife dinner party. It's strangely reassuring.

I move further along and find I'm parallel with a freshly flowered grave from a recent burial, just a few lilies on the mound of earth. I stretch over to read the words stamped on the temporary wooden cross where the headstone will soon be placed.

Seeing my own name, I almost black out.

From teens to early twenties, I imagined my own funeral a lot, and in much detail. Always a burial, pretty churchyard, hearse pulled by black horses, lots of flowers, veiled mourners, The Smiths playing live in tribute, readings by Jeremy Irons (Yeats) and Julie Christie (Rossetti), tributes led by John Gielgud ('the British Theatre has been robbed of its brightest rising star'). And, naturally, my exes all lined up side by side (numbers swelled by Rob Lowe, Patrick Swayze, et al) wailing, '*Why* did I let her go? How could Eliza *die*?'

Now I don't like imagining my funeral.

Funny, that.

Elizabeth Fitch, 1919–2019.

Not my name at all, but a 100-year-old near-namesake. Twice the woman I am. What a survivor!

Now I look more closely, I can see there's a rectangular shape where a headstone has been removed, presumably taken to a mason to be inscribed with her name alongside an existing one. I hope that means Elizabeth will be joining her husband at the dinner party.

While it might not be a sign from above, the doppelganger name has popped up goosebumps of compassion. I want to lay some flowers for her, and while I still badly need a wee, I can't possibly widdle near my namesake's resting place. At least not until I've shown my respect.

Gripped with once-in-a-lifetime religious fervour, I sprint back to the lock to cross the footbridge, surprised to find the handsome bearded groom smoking furiously midway. (Black tobacco; very existential.) With him an oriental girl in a sharply tailored suit is holding the wedding bouquet in one hand and an oversized vanity case in the other, talking too fast. I catch 'we have to do this his way' and 'we all know she's *way* too frickin' young for you'.

They look at me blankly as I try to get past.

I give it my best Richard Curtis eccentric-woman-at-wedding cameo, indicating the boat festooned with blooms and foliage, some of it already fallen into the river. 'I was wondering if I might beg a flower or two for a friend's grave?'

'Be my guest.' The girl thrusts the bridal bouquet at me then borrows the groom's cigarette for a drag.

'You can't give me these!'

'I caught them, lady, and trust me I'm not the marrying kind.' They exchange a smirk. (Do I sense drama of the sort with face-slappings unbefitting of an English country wedding?)

'Thank you! They're beautiful.' I beam at her, then at the groom. 'And congratulations!'

'Ha!' He reclaims the cigarette, taking a final drag before flicking it into the water. (Paddy would go apeshit at littering Britain's waterways, but I'm torn by the fact they've just handed me a hundred quid's worth of floristry.) Then he leans towards me, whispering in a thick, Eastern European accent, 'My new wife, she run away whenever I kiss her.'

'Gosh. How tricky on your wedding day!' I laugh politely, tempted to suggest he ditches the Gauloises habit. Then I look down at the flowers again, hand-tied peonies as garishly red as the bride's hair. Elizabeth deserves these. And I can pay with some words of wisdom. 'I was a bag of nerves on my wedding day too,' I tell the groom quickly, 'but something my father said to me proved entirely true: "A wedding's just your ticket to love; it's marriage that's the journey".'

They both swallow snorts of laughter, which isn't quite the reaction I was hoping for. I feel even more outdated.

'You really should put some socks on. You're asking for foot odour like that.' Waving my flowers gratefully, I beat a hasty retreat to rejoin Elizabeth.

When I got married, I felt an almost overwhelming urge to run, both in the build-up and on the day. I was sick with the urge to race off, dizzy with it. The only thing I can compare it to is vertigo, but I'd never suffered it at that point so I didn't recognise it; I thought it was stress.

Then I had children and, BOOM. I experienced real vertigo. I was sick with the fear of falling, dizzy with it, heart palpitating. Since motherhood, my vertigo has blighted holiday sightseeing more than once, yet it makes no sense: as a child I thought nothing of scrambling from clifftops to isolated Cornish coves, as a teenager I climbed up the Eiffel Tower, in my twenties I sunbathed on high London roofs.

When I read up on vertigo to try to understand the illogical fear of open heights, it came as a shock to learn that it stems from a desire to throw yourself off.

Which must mean I really wanted to run away from my wedding.

I can't deny, I feel a bit dizzy right now.

* * *

I lay the bouquet on Elizabeth's newly covered grave and recite some Shakespeare from *A Midsummer Night's Dream*. Might not be her cup of tea at all, but she's dead so she won't care.

'If we shadows have offended,
Think but this, and all is mended,
That you have but slumber'd here
While these visions did appear.'

With a silent apology and a quick check to make sure nobody's around, I seek out a quiet spot behind a yew to have the wee and the relief is blissful.

As I grope for a dock leaf to use as loo paper, a cold sensation on my backside makes me headbutt the tree trunk. It's a smiling labrador, wet from the river. A voice out of sight shouts, 'Horatio!'

Horatio and I exchange a look of understanding before I hoick up my trousers double quick, wondering what possessed me to match button flies with a D-ring belt.

'Hello!' the dog walker and I hail heartily as I march back towards the riverbank, still trying to do up the belt.

Kwasi's voice drifts across from the lock island. 'Will you fooking get back here! Your wife's waiting and she's getting well pissed-off!'

With the restaurant boat blocking the lock, I've no choice but to wait too, and share her sentiment. This is *not* going as planned: I have a family stowaway locked in the loo; I'm behind schedule; I haven't bought a change of trousers.

Shirley Valentine's midlife trip to a Greek island turned into forever; Elizabeth Gilbert travelled the world to find herself in *Eat, Pray, Love*; a glamorous American played by Diane Lane restores her mojo and a villa *Under The Tuscan Sun*; Sue Townsend, the late and great creator of Adrian Mole, wrote a book about a woman of a certain age (and rage) who went to bed for a year.

I have elected to escape in a narrowboat for *just one night* and I'm already feeling crowded, delayed and inappropriately dressed. It's all too disappointingly familiar. As is my sudden urge to give up, go home and snuggle up with Arty and the biscuit tin.

But Arty is no longer alive. I miss her more than ever.

Several boats are waiting below the lock as the wedding party continues laying siege to the island, jazz plinking from *Lady Charlecote*'s windows, glasses clinking.

The bride and groom have been reunited for a group shot beyond the willows. Both are drawing Kwasi's wrath. 'All I'm asking you to do is look at him like you fancy him! And you, mate, need to be more of a fooking gentleman!'

The redhead says something inaudible, to which the groom yells, 'Is enough! I take no more sheet from little beetch!' and struts off to smoke another cigarette while Kwasi draws the bride aside for an urgent pep talk, his arm around her. (Now I know post-millennials are far more fluid about these things than older birds like me, but I'd struggle to look fooking happy if Paddy didn't step up to the plate himself to apologise/rationalise/do the pep talking at this point, especially on our wedding day.)

I can hear Kwasi laying on his flattery with an f word. 'You're my fooking Dora Maar, our Linder, the next Juno

Calypso and a fooking goddess! These pictures will be mint!' Even from here, I can see his shoulders rolling and white smile flashing.

(I've always admired that brand of youthful self-belief which dances from foot to foot as though on hot coals like so many wild young men do. It's Edward who is our family dancer, bopping around when he's overexcited about gaming.)

Pausing by the narrowboat's porthole bathroom window, I peer in to see him cross-legged on the floor, his headphones on, studying his 3DS intently, Emma's chocolate box open beside him. When my shadow darkens the room, Ed looks up and lifts his console to take a photograph of me, for which I pose with a reassuring smile and a double thumbs up. *Act it.*

Should I be kicking the door down to set him free, I wonder? Isn't that what Emma Thompson would do? (Although an Oscar-winning Dame of the British Empire, Cambridge graduate and human rights activist is hardly likely to abscond with a boat she can barely steer for a childish dare. And even if she did, she'd call a locksmith to free her son before continuing.)

Sitting on a bench, I take out my phone and contemplate it for a moment, feeling defeated and angry, ready to switch off Do Not Disturb and call Paddy to fess up and beg help.

Pride won't let me do it. I slot my earphones back in for female empowerment instead. Thank you Annie: we're straight back with 'There Must Be an Angel'. We could all use one of those.

A movement on the lock footbridge catches my eye, a flurry of white. But this is no angel.

'Dad!'

I look up, pulling an earphone out. Surely it can't be? How could I miss it?

My daughter is in a big white dress with big red hair.

Summer is *the bride.*

'When I saw *The Tempest* I was like OHMYGOD! I love you, Dad!' she's shouting down at the boat (it seems she missed seeing me too, this motherly master of disguise in dark glasses and hat). 'Where are you? DAD?'

I stand up, pulling out the other AirPod and losing the disguise.

'Start the engine, Dad!' She hurtles blindly towards *The Tempest*, mascara tears running down her face. 'I need to get the fuck out of here!' Then she slams on the brakes in shock as I step in front of her. 'MUM!'

'What's going on, Summer?' Her face is very different, but I can't think why, the make-up immaculate as ever.

She pushes past me, eyes white-rimmed and fierce. 'Where's Dad?'

'He's not here.'

'No matter, we need to get going NOW!'

I hesitate, glancing at the bathroom porthole. Ed's face is peering out. Calm voice, Eliza. 'We're not going anywhere until I know what's happening, Summer.'

She dodges past me. 'I'll start the engine!'

'Who is that bearded man with no socks on?' I hurry after her, feeling light-headed. 'Please tell me you haven't just *married* him? And how in HELL did you get that tattoo?'

She has a phrase inked across the top of her spine in a swirly font.

'I'll explain later.' She's already jumping onto the bow, her netted skirts wider than the deck. 'The lock gates are opening, look!'

Which is when I realise that amid much whooping and light piano jazz, the restaurant boat is on the move, and the lock is being speedily reset by half a dozen wedding guests, no longer stylishly aloof but cranking and heaving and loudly ordering the waiting boats back so we can power straight in and out. I recognise a couple of faces from Summer's sixth form crowd.

On the island, the bearded groom has Kwasi in a headlock. Or it could be the other way around. Hard to tell. They're slow-fighting in the faintly Greco-erotic way vain men do when they don't want their veneers knocked out.

'Hurry up, Mum, while he's not looking!' she pleads as she gets *The Tempest*'s engine spluttering into life.

'You're seventeen, Summer!' I'm close to tears as I cast off the mooring ropes. Are drugs involved, I wonder? Child grooming? 'Marriage is illegal without parental consent. Who is he? How long have you been planning this?'

She gathers her skirts higher to make room when I step on deck. 'I never met him before today!'

I'm horrified. 'Is he doing this for a British passport?'

'Just for money, Mum!' she snaps. 'Whereas I did it for love like the tat says.' She turns her back to me, lifting the red tresses so I can read: *The more I give to thee, the more I have.*

It's from *Romeo and Juliet*, the balcony scene when love is blind and boundless and infinite. Like Lady Capulet, three acts later, I want to scream: 'Accursed, unhappy, wretched, hateful day!' but Summer's clambering up onto *The*

Tempest's roof from which she power-salutes her friends piratically, shouting, 'I gotta ride!'

They cheer.

'You are heroes!' Her energy is infectious. She looks down at me. 'And so are you, Mum. You have *saved* me. Let's go!'

At which point I'm clearly expected to max the throttle and whoop like a superannuated American mom in a high school drama, whereas I'm British and middle-aged with a Special Needs agenda. 'We must tell your brother what's going on. He's shut in the bathroom.'

'I'll deal with that.' She doesn't stop to ask why (Ed used to lock himself in bathrooms a lot as his 'safe' space when he was little, so it's considered quite normal still). 'You get this rig moving.' Jumping down from roof to deck, she crams her skirts inside and a moment later I hear, 'Ed, it's me! We're about to go through the lock. There might be some shouting, OK? Have you got your headphones on?'

From deep inside the boat comes a faint shout. 'Go away! I'm on level six.'

She bursts back out through the doors, ivory silk puffing. 'You heard him.'

And I suddenly realise why her face is different. The Nike ticks are missing.

'Summer, your eyebrows have gone!'

And in that moment, I see my younger self so clearly – that impulsive younger self I wish I'd let run free a little longer...

★★★

Somewhere in early middle age, fate stopped dealing me wildcards. More accurately, I stopped picking and playing them, taking fewer risks and trusting no strangers as I held my high-handed full house together. Family comes first. My reckless side retired from the game.

At what point, I wonder, did I start resenting my younger self so much for not gambling more on youth? I now regularly catch myself criticising her, wanting to shout at twenty-something-Eliza: 'MAKE MORE OF IT, ELZ!', 'STOP DOUBTING YOURSELF!', 'YOU LOOK GREAT IN STRETCH SATIN!', 'LIVE FOR THE MOMENT!'

Maybe growing old isn't about resenting our younger selves; maybe it's mothering her. And if that's the case, is fifty too late to act on one's own advice (stretch satin aside)? After all, my Older Self will be looking down on me in years to come, I hope. I can hear her calling now, the yet-older version of me. She sounds like my mother, acerbically encouraging, 'ACT LIKE YOU CAN DO IT!'

I'm claiming my Odyssey: I'm rescuing a runaway bride, a life-changing action (like the ending of *The Graduate* but without Dustin Hoffman. Or am I thinking of *Love Story* and Ryan O'Neal?). It doesn't matter. This bride is my only, beloved daughter. We are getting out of here.

By the time we leave the lock quite a crowd has gathered behind us to watch. Still on the roof, striking a self-consciously dramatic pose, red ringlets swirling, Summer shouts back, 'I will never forgive you!' Whether this is directed at her no-sock groom or Kwasi, I'm not sure. On the island, the fight between them lurches on, now reduced to a grunting slow bear dance, shirt cuffs and ties loosened, the latter shouting, 'Fooking let go of me!'

We race away from them all as fast as *The Tempest* can safely manage – we could swim faster, but it's satisfyingly noisy with a big bow wave.

I'm at full boil, a stealth bomb hot flush pooling sweat in every crevice as I navigate past the boats waiting to come into the lock.

Behind us, a man's voice shouts from the lock side, a rippling romantic tenor with a strong accent rising clear above the chatter and whoops there. 'Turn around, my darling! Please turn around! *Ritorno*! Come back!'

I look to Summer for reaction, but she's gazing over her shoulder with a puzzled expression. 'Who's that?'

'Hey, Bella!' comes the throaty Mediterranean key. 'Eliza! *Ritorno*!'

'Is he a friend of yours, Mum?'

I spin round so fast I let go of the tiller.

Matteo Mele is waving frantically from the lock side. 'Hey, crazy lady! You're beautiful, you know that!'

My red blush floods down to meet the hot flush coming up in a head-to-toe moist glow.

Summer scowls. 'Who *is* he?'

I grab the tiller to set us back on course and mutter, 'Never seen him before.'

20

Up Time

As we putter steadily away from Luddington Lock towards the Avon's meandering, high-banked camouflage, our departure is still being cheered and recorded on multiple phones, quite possibly including Matteo's. So much for not standing out. This journey could soon be viral.

Not that I care. It's all about Summer now.

My runaway bride is sitting on the barge roof, big silk skirt plumed round her like a parachute. Having pulled off her punky headdress, she's started to remove long red satin corkscrews of hair in sections, until soon just a tight ballerina bun is left which she releases into its familiar pale brown snake. She's stunningly, wonderfully Summer again – and all the better for arched female Finch eyebrows in place of the Nike ticks, although I elect not to tell her that just yet given how low and close together both are.

'Hideous snakes!' She tosses the lot down into the boatman's cabin then peels off her false eyelashes. 'How dope are my friends helping like that?' She admires her gel nails, long as ice-lolly sticks.

I know I should stay calm, agree, maybe point out that her mother's not a bad getaway driver either, instead of wiping my hot wet face against my arm before wailing, 'Summer, I demand to know the truth! What were you *thinking of*?'

'You're right. That's the *last* time I do the man I love a favour.'

'Like getting married?'

She slides off the roof and lands in front of me. 'Mum, you are so deluded!'

'*Me*, deluded? You're the teenager running away from her sham wedding!'

'Fake one, you mean.' She spins round so I'm forced to witness the skin-inked Juliet quote again. 'Help me out?'

'Just when did you get that monstrosity?'

'Not the tattoo – that's just a transfer, it'll wash off – the bodice clips!'

And for the first time I see that the dark fastenings along the spine of the dress which I mistook for punky bows earlier are bulldog clips gathering in inches of loose fabric. It's a classic magazine-stylist technique to make a garment seem fitted to the model.

'Today's wedding wasn't real?'

'Surely you realised it was a *photoshoot*, Mum! I *talked* about it! I told you I was helping Kwasi – I mean Mr Owusu – plan it as a diversity polemic, but then our original bride dropped out at the last minute which is why I had to step in with that misogynist personal trainer as groom.'

'So you didn't marry him?' My brain can't keep up.

'Reader, I almost killed him! And Kwasi too! I totally hate men right now.' She looks at me furiously over her shoulder. 'I can't believe you thought I'd marry a stranger, even for a moment, even supposing I legally could. Are you actually *mad*?'

I wipe my sweaty face with the other arm. 'Yes, Summer, I *am* actually mad. If you're lucky, in thirty years' time they'll have found a cure and no woman will ever have to go through this hell. We may well, however, still hate men.'

Note to self: stop overreacting and taking things so seriously. Why is my over-fifty default set to Worst Case Scenario? How could I even think for a minute that my bright, bolshy daughter would marry somebody to give them British Citizenship? (It's true that thirty years ago, stony broke and overexcited after watching the movie *Green Card,* I did briefly consider it as a way of raising cash myself, but that was largely to do with Andie MacDowell's rooftop garden, and it turned out to be much easier to get waitressing work at Café Rouge.)

It must be my plummeting oestrogen that's made me this paranoid. I'm more frightened of my children's power to hurt me than I care to admit. I have a refugee mentality, running from a youth culture I find increasingly oppressive and alien. I trust no one. Not even my own daughter.

It's no country for middle-aged women.

Summer has ditched her first professional modelling assignment, and she's very angry about it, so angry that she hasn't yet asked why her mother is piloting her grandfather's boat downriver or why her brother is locked in the loo trying to crack level six of his Sonic game.

'This dress was picked out for a six-foot Amazonian,' she complains, looking down at the ivory silk meringue which is still taking up most of the small aft deck. Following her gaze, I notice rough tacking stitches that have taken up the hem by several inches. She twists the skirt round her waist until it's back to front and wails, 'This thing is wack! It's supposed to be detachable. I can't rip it; it's been lent by the boutique in town. I am *never* getting married. You have *no* idea how hot and uncomfortable I am right now, Mum.'

'I could hazard a guess.' I have a perspiration waterfall running between my breasts and a neck like a smallpox rash.

'I need scissors.' She squeezes back inside the cabin, still talking, although I can only catch snatches over the engine. I pick up that today's photoshoot – an advertorial for the restaurant boat – was originally due to take place before the river got busy, but the client got cold feet when the bride turned up with hay fever, a cold sore and a penis.

'She's Warwickshire's premier drag queen. The whole idea was to gender challenge, but the boat owners said they thought drag was too cabaret, and the groom refused point-blank to kiss his bride, so I was conscripted as a last-minute replacement, after which Kwasi threatened to punch him if he *did* kiss me!' she shouts as she forces her way back towards me through the tiny boatman's cabin. 'I should have figured he'd blow up. The moment he's behind a camera it's like Dr Jekyll and Mr Hyde, y'know?' She brandishes a pair of kitchen scissors in a way that would tempt me to step back if it didn't mean falling overboard. 'Well, it's all over; I'm done with him; my love is *dead*. He's rude and hypocritical and always spoiling for a fight. I can't believe I missed Year Twelve Mindfulness for this.'

'You played truant?'

'It's a study leave morning, Mum! I'm talking about something really important here and you're just listening out for trigger words. You have no idea what it's like being objectified like that, being held to ransom by the contradictions of possessive masculinity.'

'Oh, I think I do. I am a woman too.'

The all-new eyebrows crease together disbelievingly.

'This is totally different!' She disappears back inside.

I'm increasingly frustrated by younger women, a Mind The Age-Gap divide that I fear is more about belated self-recognition than direct criticism of bright young things. I mistrust their self-absorption, that analysis-as-small-talk intensity they possess, the sense I get that when anyone under twenty – or thirty, let's be honest – speaks to me, she doesn't really see me because I am (and I hate this word) 'irrelevant'.

Did I once behave like that, I wonder?

I don't believe it's an exclusively mother and daughter thing, although that magnetises it. Our mothers are often the first women we objectify, ignore and deride.

Looking back, I struggle to remember middle-aged women through my late teens and early twenties, apart from Mum and her circle or my friends' mothers, and then only fleetingly. I was devoting myself wholeheartedly to acting, partying and romance, to my gang and my bastard boyfriends. Older female role models faded away amid this grown-up world of self-interest and male interest.

My invisibility thirty years later underlines the divide. I belong to a group I once ignored and dismissed, and nothing much has changed.

'The "groom" is some hench from Kwasi's gym who wants to be a model, and a total creep.'

Summer is still talking about the photoshoot, now in the boatman's cabin carefully snipping away the wedding dress waistband's tie fastenings. 'How ridiculous was that fight between them?'

As she cuts herself free, she explains that the project had zero budget. 'The trouble is, Kwasi needs commercial work on his portfolio if the agencies are going to hire him. He's edgy and brave, which they'll love, and he's not afraid of playing the gender spectrum. Most guys his age are running so scared of toxic masculinity, they're insipid.' She reappears on deck, the dress now an above-the-knee shift, perfect for bopping the night away to a cheesy wedding DJ soundtrack. 'He had to fight his way out of gang culture as a kid, so he's hardwired to be super-aggressive as well as super-talented? Having to zip it in a classroom doesn't suit his psyche? He teaches some total brats.'

I use the ironic eyebrow, but she doesn't notice. Her eyes are full of tears, the tough act wavering. She turns away and I hear a gulp and a sniff.

'Oh my poor love…' I reach out to put a hand on her shoulder, expecting her to shrug it off as usual.

She's turned round and is in my arms so fast we almost fall overboard. 'I am so, *so* glad you were here for me today, Mum! I have no idea how you knew to be there, but I love you for it. You are just amazing! Beyond amazing.'

Letting go of the tiller, I hug her tightly back. My child is in my arms and she is little again, clinging onto me, in need of the rock of mother love, believing I was there just to save her.

She peels herself away with an audible squelch. 'Mum, you're burning up!'

'Actually it's starting to ease off.' I reclaim the tiller.

'I'm going down to check on Ed. Have we got anything to drink on here?'

'Of course!' We need to celebrate this rescue and reconciliation. Dressed as she is, it calls for only one thing: 'There's a case of champagne in the galley.' (I love saying that. I never get to say things like that. Now we're back on task, a classic road-trip moment.)

But she wrinkles her nose. 'I was thinking green tea? I could do with a chat about it all.'

'Of course!'

'Why are you taking *The Tempest* downriver, by the way?'

I want to tell the truth, but she's so vulnerable. She needs this journey to feel safe and idyllic and healing for now, not a crazed dash to save the boat her father loves so much.

'Spur of the moment idea to go and see Susie and Nigel.'

'OMG, really? I hope Roobs is there. It would be so good to have somebody I can *really* talk to about Kwasi. This is turning out to be such a cool day after all.'

I blow on my sizzling forehead, quietly disagreeing.

★★★

Up until my friends and I married and had children (those of us who chose to) we confessed all to each other on a regular basis, usually over wine glasses brimming with something cheap, white and oaked. Ours was the Bridget Jones generation, and we were already at full speed when our flagbearer slid down a fireman's pole into print. *Her* big pants were *our* big pants. We *owned* that space: the sex talk, the bastard talk, the ex-talk, the 'is it love?' talk. From graduating to gestating, it was open house on our relationships.

Then, one at a time, we decided it *was* love, and stopped talking about it. The wedding band encloses a secret world; we'd never dream of confiding the same intimate details about our husbands that we had about past boyfriends. Pride's at stake, and when he's a keeper, you keep your secrets with him.

The river between Luddington and Binton Bridge is hypnotically quiet and lush, the first stretch of that Heart of Darkness overhung by endless willows and hemmed with the highest, wildest reed banks. For almost the entire stretch, *The Tempest* shares the water with no more than wildfowl, our most interested spectators a few cattle cooling their feet in one of the watering spots where the pasture fields slope down to meet the river.

Drinking weak black builder's tea and sporting a pair of huge butterfly sunglasses she's found in the boat (so OTT they must be Mum's), Summer has climbed back up on the roof to sit in the sun, eager to educate me about Kwasi. The childlike vulnerability has gone and she's using her TED Talk voice: quick, staccato bursts, as though neatly chopping each sentence into equal lengths for emphasis. She does this when she's lecturing me and Paddy about our elderly ignorance of all things youthful and groupthink.

'Being shouty and rude is his trademark as a photographer, it hides his insecurities and creates amazing energy but it wears everyone down eventually.' Today's blow-up between them has been brewing a while, she explains, his behaviour increasingly childish as their fiery friendship counts down to his return from teacher to peer. 'He's conflicted; the first-generation Nigerian culture vibe is so gendered. He's the youngest of seven; his parents are old school, in their sixties and hate each other, whereas you and Dad are at least pre-diabetic and know who Kylie Jenner is. Plus you still love each other.'

'We try.' I try not to think about last night, sleeping in separate bedrooms. Or wonder who Kylie Jenner is.

'Kwasi has different ground rules to me. He refuses to define what we are. He says we need distance, but it's like he's always searching for an identity in which I'm an ethical part, our unique space? He says that our divisions are deeper than class and race, that my radical inclusionism is overcompensating for my privilege, which is almost certainly your fault when you think about it.'

'Why is it my fault?'

'You've got the *Guardian* app, Mum, get with the zeitgeist. I'm also a communaholic, according to Kwasi, whereas he internalises. And he is being *totally unreasonable* about my ex.'

'About Jack?'

'It's more complicated than that.' Her eyes flash and again I decide it's safest not to ask. Communaholics tell all soon enough in my experience. (I used to be one, after all.)

'Do you think he'll come after us?' I ask instead.

'After I just trashed his shoot? He's ghosted me for less. We're lousy at making up. We're so alike. That's why I love him.' She blinks angrily, tears close at hand again.

This is safer maternal ground. Ah yes, that self-delusion I remember only too well, when yet another forbidden eighties heartthrob failed to live up to my love-struck expectations I'd have undoubtedly burst into defiant, dramatic sobs.

But Summer's tougher. 'He totally deserves what just happened!' And swearier. 'He's entirely fucking linear!' And lacking empathy. 'Can you believe Kwasi's so paranoid, he's convinced my ex has flown here to England to fight him for me?' And less faithful. 'I have never made a secret of the fact I have another man in my life who still cares for me, so what's his problem?'

Alarm bells are ringing. 'Are you talking about Jack?'

'That's not important, Mum. The fact is, Kwasi saw a picture of him on my phone, and since then he thinks he sees him everywhere. He is super-jealous. He keeps picking on old guys in Stratford, accusing them of being him.'

Flashing blue lights join the alarm bells. Has she got an ex we don't know about? Where would he fly in from? And... '*How* old are these old guys exactly?'

'Really, Mum, it's not what you think.' She rolls over onto her front, head propped up on her elbows, pure Lolita.

'How old?' I'm not letting this drop.

'Thirties, maybe?' She watches a pair of canoeists in dark glasses and space-age Lycra overtaking us, floating centaurs entirely focussed on their strokes. 'Dad's right. Love's all a game of poker, isn't it? He says we start out with two hearts and a diamond and all end up wanting a club and a spade, ha ha.'

'That's just an after-dinner joke he's heard at a cricket do and it's wrong.' Says the woman taking a trump card down the Avon to hide it up her sleeve.

'No, Mum, he is right,' Summer insists. 'It's poker, all bluff and no buff. Show them your hand and they're uploading your ass shots as avatars. And before you ask, not mine.'

My naivety at seventeen was Pollyanna-like by comparison to Summer's cynicism, but mothers remain just as tenacious. 'Who is this ex? Somebody you met overseas? When? It has to be on a school trip because we've only been to Cornwall and the Peak District!'

'He's nobody.' She looks away angrily. 'Really, *really* nobody.'

'Thirties is far too old. That's an *abusive* age gap, Summer.'

'I am old enough to know what I'm doing! Kwasi needs to respect that Joachim started me out on the journey to physical love. As far as Kwasi's concerned I am *so* not giving up my friend and mentor.'

'Jesus!' I scream. 'Who *is* this man?'

'How many times, Mum? He's nobody! You do realise, he's –' she looks at me over her dark glasses '– made up?'

It takes a while to understand what she's saying. ('Made up' as in happy, a lover of cosmetics or…) 'He's not real?'

'Pure fantasy, Mum.'

* * *

Sometimes we tell a lie that gets a bit out of control, yet seems to fit the circumstances much better than reality.

When I was about seven or eight, I was having a bad day at school. Nothing epic, just one of those sad, glum days that stem from lots of petty things: a hideous new short fringe haircut, not being allowed to stay up to watch *Top of the Pops* the night before, Miles nabbing the plastic toy in the Frosties packet that morning, my best friend off sick, spam fritters for lunch which I was *ordered* to finish. All that and rain. One of those days it's all too easy to lose our sense of perspective and humour. Like most days when we're fiftyish and menopausal.

So when the class bully broke my favourite pencil, and I burst into tears, it was a cumulative thing. But they were big, blubbery, shaming tears that for some reason wouldn't stop. On and on I cried, and the more I did, the more ashamed I was of being unable to stop, and the harder I cried. The teacher was lovely. I got to go into the staff room to calm down with hot chocolate and tissues and kindness.

When I finally stopped hiccupping and sobbing, she asked what had upset me. And when I thought about that pencil and that bully and how much she had wanted a reaction from me and how much I'd gratified her by *over*reacting, I couldn't say it. Instead, I blurted, 'My dog's died!'

It seemed more in keeping. The teacher seemed to think so too.

I hoped that would be the end of it, but oh no, the sympathetic questions kept coming. I felt compelled to give this dear departed pet a name, a breed and an age and cause of death. Soon Patch the red-and-white Cavalier who liked playing with sticks and hated blue cheese really felt like a part of my life and I really *missed* him. I even cried a bit more.

As soon as I got home, Mum cornered me furiously in the kitchen and asked what I thought I was up to, telling all those lies about a dog? The school had phoned her to sympathetically explain that I'd got a bit upset about poor Patch being run over.

Cue more tears. And I told her about the class bully and the pencil and the crying getting out of control. I added that I really *did* want a dog and I promised to look after it and walk it and groom it and feed it. I told her nothing but the truth.

She was a *lot* less sympathetic than the teacher.

We didn't get a dog.

It turns out make-believe Joachim has been very useful in training boys who take an interest in Summer to be less selfish and sex-obsessed. 'Because every time one is being a dick – or wants to send me a shot of theirs – all I need to do is remind him how respectful and expert and grown-up Joachim was with me, and that I'll take no shit from thirsty smols like them.'

'And you've never come clean that he's made up?'

'Why should I? He's the dragon they want to slay, the Daddy they have to live up to, my get-out-of-jail card? This way they can never hurt me.'

I get the point, a part of me wishing I'd thought of that when the nineties bastards were around, however deceitful.

'Kwasi has a big problem with imaginary Joachim.' She rolls over to sit up again, crossing her legs. 'He is super-disapproving and jealous. Which is how I know he secretly loves me too, like Mr Darcy with Elizabeth.'

'Jealousy doesn't equate to love, Summer. Maybe he thinks the age gap's way too big?'

'It's only three years! Dad's four years older than you.'

'Not with Kwasi. With – Joachim, is it?'

'Kwasi is in no way ageist.' She shakes her head. 'Mum, you have no idea how gold he is, how non-judgmental, how rare that is. You are so out of touch. Kwasi is an angel compared to most guys I know. Some of the stuff my friends put up with would make your hair curl.'

'So tell me. Bring me up to date.'

'You'll just interrupt all the time. Force your outmoded opinions on me. That's why I can never talk to you.'

'I won't interrupt.'

I appreciate that Summer's current eye-rolling disapproval of me is a well-worn rite of passage – just as mine was with my mother (although Mum claims she didn't have one with Granny because teenagers didn't have hormones or control issues until after the 1950s) – but it can be unbearably painful to endure. Summer longs to be older but never *old* like me. Her burning feelings for Kwasi are a part of this ageing-up, I'm certain, seventeen being a pivot point in life when the decade ahead and all its adventures can't come fast enough, unlike my point in life where just ten years can mark the rapid decline of flexible joints, continence, eyesight and teeth.

I have to believe Summer will one day stop questioning

me, that she won't always disregard what I have to say. But right now, I must stay silent, just to prove that my willpower is as steely as my unbending love for her.

As *The Tempest* slowly follows the Avon's meanders, I hear my daughter telling what it's like growing up in the shadow of lovelorn millennials swiping right in place of dating, and of young girls who learn what consent means before they know how to tie shoelaces. Of everything being sexualised by thirteen, of hating their bodies, of boys who think porn is the norm, of the endless quest to be perfect, to be liked, followed, on-trend, of FOMO and being scared AF of not getting it right. I've agonised about much of this with fellow mums, read the reports and witnessed her sermonise about it before, but it's tough to hear first-hand, delivered from the front line in a quick-fire monologue. For the first time in recent memory, Summer doesn't have a phone in her hand, meaning her entire focus is on what she's saying and who she's saying it to, a single individual, not a cloud of digitised reactions.

Sharp-witted and straight-talking, Summer thrives on analysing herself and her peers. She doesn't need me to relate to her, just hear her out. My opinions would only get in the way, and I don't offer any – even though I was just as dogmatic at her age, when life was still something improvised after childhood's set prologue – because today, for once, I have the time and space to listen; for once I'm not trying to hurry her along or multitask or think what to say next to exert authority or prove I'm still relevant; for once, life outside this moment in time doesn't feel very important at all, not even the fact I'm stealing a boat with my children as unwitting conspirators. I am her audience of one.

She explains that Kwasi was always different. That the first time she met him – at one of Joe's parties in the basement at home – she lied about her age so he'd talk to her for longer, that she was blown away by how clever and left field he is, how they kissed in the kitchen but Joe caught them and warned Kwasi off. He's not laid a finger on her since, has only ever been supportive and kind, but they burn for each other. She tells me her feelings for him have been like a forcefield protecting her in the past few years, and that by not fearing screen culture, she's owned it, that she wants the younger girls who follow her vlog to feel that same strength and control. Standing up on the roof of the barge, she promises me that, as an actor, she will perform '... outside the boundaries of sexual stereotyping and you will be totally proud of me, and women everywhere will feel less objectified and Kwasi will realise *what he's just lost!*'

Her hyperbole has no brakes, but I keep holding my tongue because I've vowed to, and because if I don't, this wiser older actress who has been physically objectified from the first step of her career path to the big red STOP! sign over forty, wouldn't be able to resist making comparisons, giving opinions, making it all about me. I can't redirect her life, can't live it for her. And I like listening without my mind busily thinking what to say next. As I tilt my face up to the sun, I devour what Summer has to say, however idealistic; I am proud of her enthusiasm, her kindness. I like it that she's not remotely self-conscious when she lists the many human rights causes she will support when she's a global icon. I remember how good it felt to think as boldly as she does, to know that life is there for the taking. Maybe this time, it is.

She even breaks into song – 'This Girl is on Fire' (it was too much to hope for 'Climb Every Mountain'). She means every word, dancing up and down the boat roof, encouraging me to join in.

A little Regatta Set cruiser overtakes, the captain taking off his hat in Summer's honour and calling out, 'Bravo, young lady!' The other passengers clap.

She bows and moves on to sing Beyoncé's break-up anthem 'Irreplaceable', pointing her fingers fiercely and telling an imaginary ex to put all his stuff together.

In the spirit of trust, I feel I should tell Summer the truth about this boat trip, but I don't want to break the spell. Instead, I ask her to go down and check that her brother is still OK.

'Why *is* Ed on here anyway? I thought he had PGL?'

'He was travel sick on the coach.'

'He was really looking forward to it!' That flash of anger is back in her eyes. 'You didn't think to drive him there?'

'They have a post-vomit quarantine policy,' I snap back. 'He's isolating.'

'So you thought you'd bring him along with you to see Nigel and Susie? No wonder he's up to his old tricks, locking himself in the loo. You are so selfish, Mum.' She flounces down into the cabin, and I reach for my AirPods for a much-needed Annie boost. 'Little Bird'. Ah, that's better. I'm putting my wings to the test, too.

I kept a diary on and off throughout my teens in which I dedicated many tear-stained paragraphs to how annoying my mother was being, how little she understood me, how much

I hated her narrow-minded, smug *old*ness. I'd occasionally leave the diary out where I knew she might stumble across it, sometimes helpfully open on the relevant page.

She took to replying in the margins like a teacher. I remember one entry, written after some petty domestic grievance, where I had scrawled in angry capitals I WILL NEVER EVER BE LIKE HER! She simply underlined it and wrote: *You will.*

Re-emerging after a few minutes, looking less mutinous, Summer mouths that he's *very happy* and *now on level seven*. A moment later, Annie suddenly sounds distant, the engine closer, and I realise she's picked up my phone to disconnect the Bluetooth.

'We can have music, yay!' She starts flicking through my Spotify downloads, selecting The 1975's 'The Sound', which is only there because I once mistook it for a seventies playlist.

Her phone's still at school, I remember, as she raids my bag for a mint, lip salve, hairband and Factor 50 before climbing back up on the roof to sunbathe and exclaiming, 'Look at those miniature cows!' She points at a riverside watering spot where a tail-twitching black-and-white group are clustered tightly under a midge haze, muscles quivering to shake the odd fly off.

'They're ponies.'

She lifts her glasses. 'Why do you always have to contradict me?'

'Because they're ponies. Or do you think they want to identify as bovine?'

'Don't even go there, Mum,' she rests back on her elbows. '*Nature teaches beasts to know their friends. Cymbeline.*'

'*Coriolanus.*'

'*Cymbeline!*' she growls, turning her head away.

I'm sure I'm right. Now it will drive me mad until I can Google it, as will the fact I can't show off that I once toured in a *Coriolanus* production reimagined in twenties gangland New York, our leading man a newly RADA-ed Old Etonian who went on to star in a huge movie franchise dressed in a trademark tux. He was very polite and shy, never joined us in the pub and had slight BO. I was cast as Gentlewoman – doubled with Unruly Crowd Member/Roman Soldier/Volscian Mobster plus stagehand and understudy – one of my sad little stage career highlights – but this isn't about *me*.

Another narrowboat putters by, all eyes on Summer who waves and blows kisses.

I bat away the desire to be waspish, but it stays buzzing close by as my menopausal mood swing flies back and forth between love and fury.

'Do you need to get back to school this afternoon?' I ask Summer.

'Please, no! I'd like to stay with you, Mum? Can I?'

'Of course.' My daring mission is turning into a day out with the kids. All we need is Joe wakeboarding up to complete the trio.

I consult the *Avon Navigation Guide* to remind myself what's coming up next, my mouth going dry at the prospect of the first of the old bridges, Binton, followed shortly afterwards by the notoriously deep and fierce Welford lock. The guide reassures me I've several furlongs of water to navigate first – riverways, like racecourses, are measured in old eighth of a mile lengths.

Above me, Summer is rolling up her dress to expose maximum thigh to the sun. 'I said *Cymbeline* to wind you up, Mum.'

'I knew that,' I lie.

'And cows.'

'That too.'

When the sonographer told Paddy and me that the little blob on the twenty-week scan was a girl, I was too happy to speak. I'd claimed I didn't mind one way or another, but whilst that had been true for Joe, this time I knew I wanted a daughter. She was my chance to get it right. I would pass on the wisdom of women, guard her against the masculine filter that would fix its distorted eye on her from childhood, spare her from her paternal grandmother's limited choices, maternal grandmother's bitter regrets, aunt's conflicted chippiness and my frustrated self-deprecation. My girl would thrive.

It hasn't quite unfolded that way, of course; a mother will learn more about herself by having a daughter than she'll ever be able to teach her. It's a lesson nobody tells us about.

Today I have learned that a precocious seventeen-year-old girl, even one I adore, is not an ideal boating companion for a woman currently fighting a physical sea change from top deck to old wreck. If I must have company, can't it be somebody my own age? An enthusiasm for crewing locks would be a bonus (Summer was never an eager volunteer), as well as a calming influence. And preferably somebody who doesn't lie conspicuously on the roof lifting an occasional leg to admire sparkly toenails. That's the company I crave, not a nubile reminder of my half-century-old decrepitude.

It's Paddy. I need Paddy. Fifty love. Every sight and sound of the river reminds me of him so acutely I half expect him to rise out of it like a merman with a windlass in one hand and a mug of strong tea in the other, calmly guiding me through the hazards.

Binton Bridge is almost upon us, my dry mouth reminds me, the first of the treacherous BBs.

Bowie's 'Fame' has replaced The 1975. That's more like it! Authentic seventies. I join in, my courage regrouping.

'You have a great singing voice, Mum.' Summer's head lifts in surprise and I give it my all until she ruins it by asking, 'Why did you tell us you were going to Leicester?'

'They found someone else,' I bluster too fast, thrusting the *Avon Navigation Guide* up at her. 'Look up Binton Bridge for me.'

'Why isn't Dad here?'

'He's working.'

'Does he even know you're doing this?'

'Let's not even go there.' I play back her line.

The butterfly glasses come off, a younger version of myself studying her older deceit. 'Just answer me one thing, Mum: this trip isn't a bucket list thing, is it?'

'Goodness, what makes you think that?'

'No Big C, you promise?' The tears are threatening again.

'Absolutely not.' I send up a quick prayer. (At my age, when cancer's picking off friends and idols like a terrorist cell, it's not something anybody can promise.) 'Summer, it's the small "c" I am suffering from right now, something most women endure sooner or later.'

'Tell me about it. Bloody cramps.' She leafs through the river guide. 'I am *so* premenstrual.'

(Oh, how I miss a hot water bottle pressed to my abdomen once a month. I never thought I'd mourn periods. And I don't per se, but I miss the trade-off: a seductive body, clear head, sex drive, sleep.)

'The *CHANGE*, Summer!' I remind her in a fear-laden gothic voice. 'It's not like I haven't told you about it.'

'That was ages ago; I thought you'd be over it by now.'

'Didn't they teach you about menopause at school?'

'I think it was covered in the reproduction module in like Year Eight, maybe? Isn't it just normal, though? Like puberty, only in reverse?'

'Imagine you're turning from a pony into a cow. At a pony show, with pony lovers everywhere. It's that normal.'

I started my first period during the end-of-year ballet showcase staged by Miss Ashworth's Dance and Drama Troupe in the local Baptist hall. I'd put the tummy pain down to pre-show nerves. We were messing around in the dressing room just before curtain up, seeing who could do the biggest high kick, when one of the little ones tugged at my hand and whispered *did you know you've pooed yourself.* The humiliation was absolute as I rinsed thin brown blood out of pale pink tights and a stretch-satin leotard crotch in the girls loos then held them under a ferocious hand dryer that scorched them to a lightly stained crisp. Too embarrassed to tell anybody what had happened, I performed with toilet roll wedged into my knickers and my knees glued together and was savaged afterwards by Miss Ashworth for not putting enough effort in.

My mother was sweetly sympathetic when I later admitted the awful truth, but I sensed her disappointment that this important step into womanhood had been the usual Eliza trip-hazard, whereas Jules had managed the transition discreetly. She'd talked us meticulously through the signs and gifted us our own supply of sanitary towels in anticipation, weird old-fashioned pads that attached to press-studs in special 'period knickers'. Jules, for whom puberty had started a year earlier, had already graduated onto the new adhesive sort and I wanted those too, but was told I had to serve my apprenticeship with the 'Nikini' to prove I was responsible (and not waste the supply I now suspect).

Periods remained my nemesis almost five hundred times over, a secret shame I never entirely accepted as natural, that felt like my body bullying me. And when childbirth proved the torture that showed me the curse was a blessed relief, menopause was lying in wait as punishment for wishing they would go away forever.

Summer's lying on her back again studying the *Avon Navigation Guide*, one twinkly-toenailed leg hooked over the other's bent knee. 'Imagine if Kwasi was waiting on Binton Bridge? I can't decide whether I'd forgive him like that,' she snaps her fingers, 'or scream "Go, Mum!" and we'll leave him looking at our bow wave.'

'We both know most people can walk faster than this thing moves,' I point out.

We're starting to pass the well-spaced private moorings of luxurious houses that mark an edge of Welford, a maypoled, three-pubbed showcase of an Avon village tucked in the bulge of the long river bend. Medieval Binton Bridge lies ahead, spanning two river islands where the water has been crossed and forded since the thirteenth century. A notorious challenge to navigate, it's the first road crossing since Stratford.

'Let's hope he can't walk on water then.' She closes the guide. 'He owes me that.'

None of the nineties bastards ever pursued me in that reckless love-struck way men do in books and movies. They were too cool, too self-conscious. So was I.

Paddy certainly never gave chase; it was the other way around until we were at least six dates in, which felt natural, given I was the more gregarious one with the bigger social circle, and then we chased each other.

Very occasionally, I still allow myself a wistful sigh that I'll never be wooed as an old-fashioned female object of desire in this lifetime.

The only time I can remember being persistently, adoringly shadowed by a love-struck admirer was at university when a fine art student in the year below got it into her head that I was the reincarnation of Tamara de Lempicka.

'STOP! *Fermare*! *Aspettare*!'

Matteo is on the mooring platform of the Four Alls pub

upriver from the bridge, his Ferrari parked at a rakish angle in the car park behind him. 'You must STOP, *cara*!'

Far from flattered by this fantasy fulfilment, I feel supremely put out because it is not how karma should work. It should be me on the roof of this slow-moving narrowboat for a start, champagne in hand, mildly amused by his fervour, not sweating at the helm while my nubile daughter – sunbathing like a fifties starlet – raises her head to say, 'It's that man you've never seen before, Mum.'

I want to shout back, 'Go away! Why are you even here? What about lunch service at Russo's?'

We go past sooo slooooowly. I keep as far towards the opposite bank as I dare.

He cups his hands to his mouth. 'Eliza!'

'Who *is* he?' Summer sits up, then gapes, open-mouthed. 'Is that a *Ferrari*?'

'Ignore him.'

'Sure.'

So, *so* slowly.

The stone archway with the arrow is set at a horrible angle of approach, the current making it a skilful procedure to get through even in low June water. Matteo makes his way up onto the bridge while I'm still angling *The Tempest*, shouting down, 'Eliza, listen to me, *bellissima*! Please stop this thing and talk to me!'

I pretend not to hear, although I am starting to wonder at his persistence. I know how much he wants this boat, but he can't have her. It was a cheap trick using all that prosecco-pouring Latin charm on me, and blackmail won't wash.

'You have my *cornicello*! My little hornet.'

'His *what*?' asks Summer, eyes wide.

'It's a lucky charm, popular in Italy.' Surely he hasn't followed me all this way to get his jewellery back?

'Is he...?' Summer's squinting up at him. 'OMG Mum, is he *Mr Vella*?'

'No!' I glance up too, then wish I hadn't. He's looking straight back at me, not at the boat or the beautiful girl on its roof, but at *me*. The smile is winningly wide, the brow pure Clooney as he throws his arms out and cries, 'Eliza, I have followed you all this way, please listen to—' His words are blotted out by traffic behind him on the bridge.

A bunch of canoeists have appeared in my path, forcing me off course. Now heading straight for a thick stone pillar, I have to throw the throttle into reverse to take another run at it. 'What does that bloody book say again about getting through this thing?'

Picking up on my fear, Summer reads from the navigation guide, '*Whilst not wishing to overemphasise the danger that appears at these bridges...* blah blah... *it's nevertheless necessary to indicate the danger that does exist.* Who wrote this? Just say IT'S DANGEROUS! OMG, we're going to hit it!' She covers her eyes as I go for broke and power through the arch.

It's all a bit of an anticlimax as we emerge the other side, engine glugging contentedly, a family of ducks parting to let us through.

'BRAVO, ELIZA!' Matteo has crossed over the road to applaud and shout down after me. '*BEN FATTO! Ti prego, possiamo parlare?*'

'I have no idea what he's saying,' I tell Summer.

'He said please can we talk.' (I'd forgotten she picked

up a smattering skiing in the Dolomites with the school.)
'Mum, are you and that man having an affair?'

'Absolutely not!' I snap. 'It's an Italian thing. He over-emotes.'

'But you do know him?'

'ELIZA! *Voglio scusarmi!*'

'He owns Grandpa's favourite restaurant and is obsessed with narrowboats.'

'Is he *stalking* you?'

'No! Although I have had Emma Thompson's stalker on loan recently,' I boast. 'Well, more of a superfan. Very polite.'

High on the bridge, Matteo isn't giving up. 'You cannot run from this forever, *bellissima!*'

Oh I can, I think furiously, my heart beating in my throat. I can run from all of it. Just not very fast.

'Joe has a friend with a stalker at uni,' Summer confides, losing interest in our heckler. 'Says he really grossed her out.'

'*Mia cara!*' Matteo's voice is fading behind us.

'This guy who stalked Joe's friend,' Summer confesses with a shudder, 'he sent her literally *thousands* of friendship bracelets made from pubic hair.'

'*Sei una donna fantastica! Non reisco a smettere di...*' Matteo's words fade away, the engine putter drowning him out.

'Was he very hirsute?' I ask distractedly.

'It wasn't all his own hair.' She jumps down beside me and lifts my dark glasses, sharp eyes gazing straight into mine. 'I demand to know everything, Mum. Does Dad know you have an admirer?'

The thought makes me feel a bit giddy and not at all like

the grown-up I pretend to be when I tell her in a serious voice the (almost) unexpurgated truth about Miles wanting to sell the boat and my inadvertent deal-brokering. And I explain that I'm trying very hard to put things right, even if it means playing along with a juvenile dare. 'Ed must have figured out what I planned to do. That's why he stole aboard. He also guessed you might need help en route.'

She looks away. 'I really thought Kwasi might follow us. I know I said he wouldn't, but...' Her nose wrinkles up. 'Fuck him. We're on the run. And we're being chased. This is a whole new side to you I never knew existed, Mum.' Her smile returns, bright as lightning, and I get another hug. '*Sei una donna fantastica!*' as the man on the bridge said.'

'Meaning?'

'You're one heck of a woman.'

Thrilled, I lift my chin, feeling like a female Indiana Jones pep-talking her youthful sidekick. 'It's just us three, the Avon and *The Tempest*, Summer. We *are* the river. Now let's have some more music. Put some Annie on, will you?'

'On it!' She picks up my phone from the roof. A moment later we're motoring through the water to strains of 'The sun will come out tomorrow... '

And it doesn't matter that she's picked *Annie* the musical not Annie Lennox, because we sing along at the tops of our voices that we love ya tomorrow. And today's starting to feel pretty good too.

21

Down Time

Back on the picnic blankets on the barge roof, Summer's now sitting cross-legged, paraphrasing the *Avon Navigation Guide* in an earnest voice-over that's a spot-on Stacey Dooley Investigates: '*Welford Lock is also known as the W A Cadbury Lock after the philanthropic Cadbury family who donated to the canal restoration.*' Her head tilts up. 'The chocolatiers?'

'The same.' I steer carefully past the weir towards the moorings. The lock being inaccessible from the village, there's thankfully no sign of Matteo.

'Is he here, your Italian admirer?'

'No man chases a woman four locks, Summer.' But I check again nervously nonetheless.

Welford Lock marks a big step down in river height. A cavernously unforgiving piece of engineering, I have been dreading it the entire way. It marks the navigational point at which I am totally beyond my comfort zone. I've crewed it for Paddy a handful of times and it's deep, fierce and murderously hard to operate.

It also needs setting. There's a small clutch of white Regatta Set cruisers moored above it, haw haw voices out of sight. Tying the narrowboat up opposite them, I jump off to set the lock, Summer reluctantly helping. The water gushes into the chamber with titanic force as I call instructions to remind her of the order in which we raise and lower the paddles to fill it ready for *The Tempest* to come in.

'I know all this, Mum!' She does some half-hearted windlassing before straightening up and smiling widely as an excited member of the Regatta Set bustles up.

'Let me do that for you, little lady!'

'Would you mind? That's so kind.' She beams, still playing it as Stacey, stepping back to let him take over and giving me a discreet thumbs up.

Soon offers of help are piling in from fellow boaters who hurry across from their moorings, a small army of chest-puffing manliness setting the lock in no time while I'm sent back to fetch *The Tempest* in.

Once again at the tiller, I am shouted to move her this way or that, tutted at (argh!) and criticised for my handling skills entering the lock, then given a lecture by a man with a very white moustache on the importance of keeping her forward of the 'cill', a ledge that can tip her stern up as the water goes down, leading to catastrophe. My only fan is an overexcited young cocker spaniel running up and down the bank, who jumps into *The Tempest* as we go down and wriggles upside down for attention, accustomed to being a boat hound, all matted river coat and lock-side flirtation. I appreciate his company until we're through the lock gates and alongside the landing stage to collect Summer, when I pick the little cocker up to offer back to one of her admirers on dry land.

'Give it to the wife, will you?' He waves me away before holding out his hand like Sir Walter Raleigh to help Summer aboard, eyes feeding lustily on her legs and backside.

A woman pants up, small and solid in Bermuda shorts and tee, eyeing my pearls suspiciously as she claims her dog back. 'You two ladies on holiday, are you?'

We both watch as her husband reluctantly lets go of Summer's hand and promises to call ahead to his friends downriver to make sure they help us at the next lock. 'Let them know a pretty girl is on her way.'

'You are such a gentleman.' She gives it the full Scarlett O'Hara.

It's only when he's out of earshot I hear her mutter 'Boomer.'

Age makes fools of us all.

Do I miss men doing practical things for me simply by virtue of my youth and sexual allure?

Admittedly, I never had as much of the latter as Summer – she has far more self-belief – but I had my fair share of assistance with flat tyres, blocked sinks and changing fuses during my temptress years; one male neighbour in London regularly and infuriatingly put out my rubbish and brought my post up.

The answer is no, I don't miss knights in shining ardour. Whilst hands-on help is wonderful from either gender, I often used to find myself waiting in frustration while a man did something I could manage perfectly well myself, then mansplained it and eyed my boobs. Which is not to say there aren't skills many men possess that I don't – Paddy's are plentiful – but while women might grow up being called the 'fairer' sex by men eager to step in and help, the dark secret is that we must still stir their loins to be fairest of them all, and that strikes me as not very fair on balance. It's either that or reminding them of their mothers.

The middle-aged hinterland between Damsel in Distress and Little Old Lady is full of women lifting heavy shopping into car boots unaided. Embrace the freedom, ladies.

Summer is on the roof channelling Stacey again as we chug through another Heart of Darkness stretch. 'The river is particularly attractive as it passes Hillborough Manor, Shakespeare's "haunted Hillboro". Haunted Hillboro's a Shakespeare Village, isn't it, Mum?' Her head bobs up. 'Grandpa taught us all the doggerel verse.'

'Remind me.' I search for the chimneys of Hillborough Manor on the north bank, but we're too deep in a twisting tunnel of trees and rushes, and I think the medieval house is still way ahead of us, while she chants:

'Piping Pebworth, Dancing Marston,
Haunted Hillboro, Hungry Grafton,
Dodging Exhall, Papist Exford,
Beggerly Broom and Drunken Bidford.'

Then she informs me that 'They used to have bar-crawl competitions. Shakespeare's squad won, and he got so caned he woke up under a plum tree the next day.'

'As you do.'

'Never.' She tilts her head and looks at me levelly, coming from that self-controlled generation with no great desire to drink (they prefer matcha tea or iced mocha).

'Getting trolleyed on Southern Comfort and lemonade was my clique's mission in life at your age,' I grumble.

She gives me a withering look. 'We take studying more seriously.'

'Ah, but will you ever understand rumbustiously bawdy Elizabethan comedy? And it was a crab apple tree Shakespeare fell asleep under.' I'm getting into my stride. 'What young scholar can hope to understand the rude mechanicals unless she's woken in a bath full of baked beans with a marker-penned moustache as your mother did as a student, Summer?'

I catch her giving me a thoughtful look, as if questioning how I could possibly have ever been young enough to be a student. Then I sense danger as the butterfly sunglasses come off.

'Better than waking up to find a video has been uploaded online of you having sex that you have no memory of whatsoever!' She sees my horrified face. 'Not me! It's a scenario, Mum. And it happens.'

'Must every conversation we have get so serious?'

'Date and drug rape are commonplace, Mum. And almost 70 per cent of the time, the drink that is spiked is alcoholic. Universities and music festivals are hotbeds for it.' She's speaking in short-fire TED Talk bursts again, a technique I suspect is my daughter's academic leitmotif, and I brace myself for a puritanical monologue on the dangers of drinking.

Instead, she tells me about a Year Thirteen girl in her

school who found out that the classmate she'd believed to possess the soul of a poet had shared sexual images of her online, and when she reported it, she was victim-shamed for being drunk the night they were taken. 'Her drink had been spiked as it turned out, but for weeks even she thought it must have been her fault because the evidence was out there for everybody to see and – are you even *listening*, Mum?'

'Yes!' Worried how shallow the river is here I'm trying to navigate to deeper water. 'And what you have to say is really important, Summer, truly it is, but I think the boat might be about to get grounded.' I wince as I hear the hull scraping on the riverbed, but we make it through.

Meanwhile, Summer starts complaining that older women are diffident on the subject of sexual coercion. 'You're continually seeking a greater authority to give you permission to stand up, which is why MeToo and TimesUp revealed the insularity of collective silence.'

'Just who was it that raised all you wokelets to be freethinking and unafraid to speak out?' I defend, and as I do I find myself visualising *Don't Flatter Yourself* man, my skin prickling.

'Yes, and I'm lucky to have the voice to speak out, Mum,' Summer says in her student debate tone. 'It's a freedom so many women throughout history have been denied: for centuries we were treated as property, prevented from controlling our own reproduction, legitimately *beaten*, disenfranchised, kept from top jobs and equal pay. And it's still happening all over the world, Mum. Sexually, women are routinely raped, mutilated, trafficked, harassed, exploited, assaulted. We can't blame *all* men, no more than we can simply blame white privilege for racial prejudice.

But we can call out those at fault, Mum. *One* by *one* by *one* by *one* if we have to.'

It sounds like something she's said before – the namechecks at measured intervals are a bit of a student debate giveaway – but it's still a magnificent, tub-thumping call to arms and I'm swept away, giving a cheer and letting go of the tiller to clap.

How does she possess so much self-assurance at her age? I was a political amoeba back then, red-flag-waving for the social life as much as the socialism, harbouring a naive belief that I was more liberated than my mother because I was on The Pill and had read most of *The Female Eunuch*. Or am I just listening to an updated version of myself thirty years ago, lecturing my parents' generation on nuclear disarmament, live animal export, the Falklands and the miners' strike?

'Maybe now you can understand why Kwasi is so special?' she says and launches into an impassioned description of his authenticity, his humanity and the gross prejudices he's encountered which leaves me in no doubt just how much she loves him. Then she ruins it by saying, 'People your age have no idea how hard it is being young, gifted and black in this country, do you?'

'Neither do you,' I point out gently.

'That's so typical, shifting the moral emphasis. Generation X's passivity and inaction is one big deafening silence.'

'And your mewling moralising is just white noise!' I snap.

She starts throwing more buzzwords around, but I'm too preoccupied handling the boat through shallow water to argue and, if I'm honest, deafening silence is my secret power when I find myself heckled by my children and their friends. What Summer has yet to realise is that, at seventeen, she's still encouraged to talk about race no matter her ethnicity, also about climate change, artificial intelligence and gender. At fifty, I've grown accustomed to finding myself aggressively muted because I've become the most reviled of Twitter memes in the witch hunt: a middle-aged white woman.

A Newcastle-born radio director I've often worked with is very fond of saying 'it's a Northern thing', particularly when other northerners are around, like a rallying cry. (This, despite living in Muswell Hill since 1992.) Whilst we can substitute 'Welsh', 'Scottish, 'Irish' with this fairly seamlessly – even 'Cornish' or 'Devon' – try it with 'Home Counties' and bathe in the awkward silence. Miranda Hart might be able to get away with it for comic effect, but not me. Not even if I gallop.

Similarly, an old drama school mate of mine who is mixed-race has traditionally started a great many sentences through her bright, funny and outspoken acting career with: 'Speaking as a working-class black woman.' And she can say that, it's her absolute right. She was born into it, grew up with systemic racism first-hand. It's a prefix that says 'don't argue with me unless you've felt my pain'. It's her identity, and during our thirty-plus-year friendship, she's helped educate me about it.

By contrast, I've always taken it as read that if I started a sentence 'Speaking as a middle-class white woman', I'd be lampooned. I'd never dream of doing it, of boasting my privilege. I was born into it, grew up with it, and soon learned to be ashamed of it, to seek change and use that education wisely. But now I'm over forty, and find 'middle-*aged* white woman' coined as a euphemism for ignorance and narrow-mindedness, I'm starting to wonder if there isn't something even more reviled than being born with my social advantages.

Perhaps, speaking as a woman, my age is the most offensive thing about me.

We're too close to the right bank, the hull still dragging hard against the riverbed, unseen stones and silt catching, pushing us off course. In a panic I pull the tiller the wrong way and her stern swings further to the reeds. Then, with a groan, the boat grinds to a halt. No matter how much throttle I give it, she's just churning up water. We are grounded.

I cut the engine.

'The propeller's got caught up in the weeds,' I tell Summer. 'No panic.' (I'm privately panicking quite a lot.)

'Sorry,' she clambers off the roof, 'is that bad? I shouldn't have distracted you. Can you fix it?'

She so rarely apologises nowadays, I'm surprised enough to look it. 'It's all good. I know what to do.'

'You're the best.' She smiles and I'm relieved to find I'm Mum again, not a hate figure.

While she goes below deck to tell Ed what's happening, I listen hopefully for an engine on the river, a passing bargee I can ask for a tow. It's silent, the splash splosh of waterfowl the loudest traffic this deep in the Heart of Darkness. There's nothing but impenetrable green riverbank around us, dense rushes and reeds giving way to flower-jewelled shrubs, overhung with willow, poplars and alder, a tunnel of waterside foliage. There's a long-abandoned wooden angler's jetty a few metres ahead, almost buried in the overgrowth, so there must be a path or track somewhere near – and we can't be too far from isolated 'haunted Hillboro' – but you wouldn't know it.

You can do this, I tell myself, trying to remember what Paddy does when grounded with a tangled propeller. Swears first, usually 'Fuckety fuck.'

I need to clear the prop so we can give her a push off with the bargepole. I step aside to pull up the trapdoor to the inspection bay. At the back is a heavily sealed watertight metal box – the 'weed hatch'; opened, it's possible to reach down through to clear the propeller of whatever's stuck round it. From memory, it's only possible to open the screw-bar holding its hatch firmly down with the aid of a lot of spanner-levering and kicking. Paddy usually swears even more at this point.

Summer reappears as I'm mid fuckety-ing. 'Ed's stuck on level seven. I just peed in the kitchen sink. Have you sorted it?'

'Almost!'

For the next five minutes, I kick, spanner and swear some more, but the thing isn't budging.

Summer is back on the roof, lying on her front so that she can watch and offer encouragement. 'Somebody'll be along in a minute who can help? One of the guys from the last lock, maybe?'

So much for female empowerment. (I sweep aside the fact that this was my own first option.)

'*You* could help,' I point out grumpily, but she's turned her head away to listen to something on the bank. 'Did you hear that?'

It's incredibly peaceful without the diesel engine putter: birds singing, a few duck quacks, river splashes and distant sheep bleating. 'Hear what?'

'A weasel maybe? Or a fox?'

We listen. Then we pick it out, a shrill barking from the riverbank out of sight.

'It's a dog!' Summer stands on the roof and calls. 'Hello? Anybody there?'

I give up trying to open the weed hatch. Perhaps if I can push her off the bank first and restart the engine, I might be able to get her moving and the prop can clear itself. Unclipping the bargepole from the roof, I swing it down into the water to find the riverbed like I'm punting, pushing with all my might. Nothing.

The dog barks again, closer now.

'Maybe the owner can help?' suggests Summer, calling again, 'Hey, helloooo, help! Anybody there?'

The dog barks once more.

And from inside the boat, we hear a muffled voice cry, 'Help! Super Mariooo Galaxy! Need a plumber! Luigi! She's taking on water! Maaamma-hoo-ha-hoo, wow-wow! I am GOING TO DROWN!'

When I was pregnant for the first time, an older friend, already a mother, said, 'Nobody can tell you how it feels to be willing to walk unhesitatingly through fire to save somebody until you have children.'

From the heart-stopping moment I turned to see Joe rolling off our sofa as a baby, to searching frantically for Summer when I thought we'd lost her in London Zoo, to picking Ed up from Reception, red-eyed and raw-kneed after being bullied, nothing prepared me for the fierceness of motherhood. It never leaves us, like a pilot light, requiring one click to ignite.

Water's gushing out from under the bathroom door, and Ed's having a Grade A meltdown, repeatedly shouting, '*Mario time!*', '*Mamma Mia!*' and '*Here I go!*'

'Stand back. I am going to break the door open, Ed.' I prepare to take a run at it.

'*Maaamma-hoo-ha-hoo, wow-wow!*'

I kick with all my might. The thing was designed to hold an army. My foot throbs. The door doesn't budge. More water races from beneath it.

Summer holds her hands up helplessly. 'Don't look at me!'

'Could you search for a crowbar maybe?' I kick the door again, my toes crunching.

'*Here I go!*' Edward wails. '*Mario time! Wake up Luigi! The only time plumbers sleep on the job is when we're working by the hour.*'

'He's a *fictional* plumber, Ed. We need a real one. And fast. Or at least a manual.' We've run aground in a mobile Not Spot, so I can't Google how to stop the supply pump forcing out the boat's stored water at such speed it's hammering against the bulkheads and rising fast underfoot.

'Ed, is it the shower?' I shout. 'Or a burst pipe?'

'*Here I a-go!*' keeps coming back at me through the door, along with, '*Mamma Mia!*'

'Stopcock!' I remember as I hurry through the boat to switch off the water beneath the well deck, then I wade back through the flood to address the bathroom door. 'Is the water still coming out, Ed?'

'No! *Babies!*' He laughs shrilly. '*Maaamma-hoo-ha-hoo, wow-wow!*' He's already sounding less stressed, although I can hear a lot of squelching and muttering. (Ed's always incredibly hard on himself when things break or go wrong, swiftly becoming non-sensical or non-verbal, which makes it hard to gauge how bad it is.)

'I've got a crowbar!' Summer hurries up wielding the big curved rod.

'NO!' comes a scream from the other side of the door. 'Do NOT touch the Ashwell's Patent Toilet Lock, *Luigi! Mamma Mia!*'

'Ooookay,' I promise cautiously, beckoning Summer into the saloon and whispering, 'Maybe we should let him calm down and focus on trying to get the boat going? We can stop downriver to try to get him out.'

There's another flurry of Mario catchphrases from the bathroom and the sound of a 3DS starting up.

Summer looks downcast. 'Sorry I was useless.'

Another apology. We are breaking records. I tell her she wasn't and give her a hug which she shrugs off.

'Things break in threes,' I tell her brightly, another saying brainwashed into me by Granny. 'Jammed door lock, snagged propeller, flood – so we'll be fine from now on.'

'You don't really still believe all that, Mum?' She raises the inherited ironic eyebrow far better than her grandmother or I could hope for.

I jump as I feel something cold against my ankle. The empty prosecco bottle's still on the floor. When I stoop to pick it up, I spot something glinting by the cooking range. It's Matteo's *cornicello*.

'Yes I do!' I snatch it up too, the gold charm digging into my palm, the memory of how it came to be here digging into my head, of how alive I felt. Mamma Mia, but I have to make things right again. Opening a kitchen drawer, I drop it in and slam it closed, repeating the phrase my grandmother often quoted: '*Luck affects everything; let your hook always be cast; in the stream where you least expect it, there will be fish.*'

'Who said that?'

'Doris Lessing, maybe?' I wrack my foggy brain for Granny's favourites.

'Ovid,' comes Ed's voice from the bathroom door. '*Mario Time!*'

Certain superstitions stick for life, I find, even if we dismiss them as hokum in adulthood. My maternal grandmother was responsible for most of mine, from counting magpies to pulling wishbones. She was basically Baba Yaga in a twinset and pearls, which is dangerous company for a slightly OCD overthinking grandchild; I was well into my teens before I could bring myself to pass somebody on the stairs or accept that faces I pulled wouldn't stick if the wind changed. I still hunt for four-leaved clovers, avoid treading on lines in the pavement, and of course it's a professional duty never to whistle in a dressing room or name the Scottish play in a theatre.

Paddy, who greets my irrational 'that will bring bad luck' moments with a long-suffering smile, takes great pleasure in breezing beneath ladders, putting new shoes on the table to be admired and spilling salt. There's just one superstition that has been handed down through his own family that he has always half-believed: it's bad luck to change a boat's name while she's in water.

Like rechristening *Lady Love* '*The Tempest*'.

I've managed to mop up the worst of the flood inside the boat and persuaded Ed to break off from his game long enough to throw all available towels on the bathroom floor. He insists he's fine, although he's now repeating '*so long, King Bowser*' and quoting Ovid.

'Keep him calm,' I tell Summer, going back up on deck to empty the pail of water over the side and make another attempt at opening the weed hatch, now using the crowbar.

It won't budge. Taking a breather, I can hear the same dog barking once more, but there's no sign of anybody around, the banks impenetrable. 'Hello? Anybody there?'

I try once more to push the boat away with the bargepole, finding it too heavy and cumbersome. It's no good, we'll need a tow-out if I can't get in the hatch.

Try the engine again. Maybe I wasn't using enough throttle. As *The Tempest* fires back into life and churns up water going nowhere, I feel something I haven't for years.

I am utterly out of my depth. I have no idea what to do. I'm entirely in the hands of fate.

I should want to cry, but it's so outrageously rejuvenating, I feel almost high. I've not felt like this in more than half a lifetime.

I hate to admit to biting off more than I can chew; it's not in my language. 'Don't ever give up' and 'keep dreaming big' are all amongst my well-worn phrases. That and 'No, I don't need any help, I can do it better myself!'

One summer job I had whilst at university was delivering flowers around west London in a rusty transit van nicknamed Wendy, back in the days when a standard driving licence qualified us to take to the wheel of everything from minibuses to Luton vans. A week in, Wendy and I set off to drop some zinnias in Chiswick – stereo blaring Old Skool courtesy of Kiss FM (Old Skool being a new sound then and Kiss a pirate station) – only to find ourselves hopelessly lost, the broken-spined London A to Z in 430 separate pages in the footwell. How I ended up at Reading Festival watching a band called Gaye Bykers on Acid is a long story involving a pair of Dutch hitch-hikers and a flat tyre, but I still remember just what it felt like, because I feel a bit like that now.

The difference between now and thirty years ago is that I found myself out of my depth on a fairly regular basis back then, the years between childhood and motherhood packed with uncharted oceans, whereas fifty is the shallow end of life, as I've just proven running a slow boat aground.

Not for the first time today, I feel a deep need for Paddy. He would have her back out on open water in seconds. In fact, we'd probably be hidden away in rushes alongside derelict Harvington Mill by now if Paddy was in charge, knocking back the champagne and laughing like teenagers.

But I wouldn't have proven anything to him if we'd done that, and he might still expect me to be trussed in a basque and Love Lubed in gratitude.

I need to do this myself, just as I needed to get out of trouble thirty years ago, when I left Björk and her band playing on the Mean Fiddler stage to find my transit and reassemble 430 pages of A to Z, plotting a route home via the doorsteps of half a dozen lucky west Londoners who woke up the next day to find bouquets waiting there.

(It goes without saying I lost my job, but my taste in music was revolutionised. Or at least until Joe's generation claimed it. And I found Annie again.)

After I've churned up the River Avon for several minutes going nowhere, Summer comes out looking victorious, carrying a piece of damp paper aloft. I cut the engine.

'Ed's told me how the flood happened. He's still being non-verbal apart from Mario and *Metamorphosis*, but we've been exchanging notes under the door. Look.'

On the paper is a conversation in smiley faces, one drawn in pen, the other in red lipstick (my own from the bathroom cabinet; I keep the same shade stashed everywhere for easy reapplication, another top tip I gleaned from a well-known actress, possibly Glenda Jackson). There's also a spider and a scream face – still strangely smiley – but I've no idea what the rest means. It just looks like Rorschach ink blots.

'He saw a spider in the washbasin and he tried to rinse

it back down the plughole,' Summer explains, pointing at the lipstick marks, 'but the tap came off in his hand and *whoosh*. See?'

Amongst Ed's many anxieties, spiders are top three, an arachnoid enemy he has no gameplay to defeat.

'Has the spider definitely gone?'

But Summer's not listening. She's pointing at the overgrown wooden jetty. 'Oh my God, look what's there!'

There's a very manky sheep watching us.

'It's a wild dog!' She ducks behind me.

'That's a sheep,' I dismiss. I'm not falling for that one twice.

'It's a fucking dog, Mum.'

'Sheep.'

It gives a deep-barrelled bark.

'OK, so it's a dog.'

It looks like a stray, poor thing, its matted coat in a terrible state. It's big – much bigger than Arty, more like a retriever or a labradoodle – and very hairy. And it's not there for us, I realise. It's looking down at something under the jetty, between the slats. It's trying to reach through there with a front leg, then its head.

And we hear a second bark, the shriller one we heard earlier.

'*Ohmygod*, it's got a little friend trapped under the pontoon, look!' Summer has leaned out of the boat to watch, gripping my arm tightly.

There is a second dog, she's right, much smaller, that's tangled up in some sort of netting and wire beneath the jetty. It must have come along to look at us and fallen through the broken slats. It's struggling to free itself, but the more it writhes, the tighter it gets trapped. The bigger dog is scrabbling frantically, barking again.

And then I notice, beneath its matted fur and mud and twigs, a row of enlarged milk teats.

'That's her puppy!'

'You have to do something!' Summer pleads, close to tears.

'Me?' I'm not certain a feral dog with its progeny in mortal danger is going to look too kindly on either of us wading across to stick an oar in.

'You're so practical and good at everything. You're a hero, Mum. Save her baby!'

The puppy lets out a terrified set of shrieks as the net twists tighter.

The mother urge is a fierce one, and my empathy is burning bright. Along with my ego. I'm a hero.

I hand Summer my watch, phone and pearls then slip off my shoes. The next moment I'm up to my waist in water as cold as an ice hole and riverbed weeds are trying to drag me every which way. The current's surprisingly strong.

The poor puppy is well and truly strung up. Getting close to it takes ages, my feet numb with cold, then I have to physically climb into the base of the jetty, mother dog still scrabbling overhead, flakes of wood raining down on me. As I struggle to unhook the caught-up netting, she pushes her head through the gap between the slats and I suddenly find we're nose to nose, her white-rimmed, panicked dog eyes inches from mine. She's close enough to bite my face.

Instead she just watches as I fiddle and twist and unknot with these gifts of fingers and opposable thumbs, the whimpering bundle able to wriggle around more and more until he's free and in my arms. And when he is, she licks him ecstatically, and licks my nose too.

The puppy is probably six or seven weeks old, almost entirely dirty white with just one black ear, cherubic curls and blue eyes. Even wet and scrabbly, he is adorable, a warm armful of gratitude and need.

He won't fit back up through the gap, so I have to take him round the long way, battling the wet undergrowth harder still with a precious bundle in my arms. As I flail around in the reeds, his mother waits on the edge of the jetty, ears pricked. Then I put the puppy by her side and I see that, deep inside the yeti coat, she's wearing an old leather collar that's worn a near-bald patch around her neck. An identity disk hangs from it.

'Who are you then?' I try to read it, but she picks her puppy up by the scruff of his neck and sets off purposefully.

Breathless, and with legs like lead, I clamber out to follow her up the bank, wishing I had a machete because it's like breaking through an untouched Amazonian rainforest as I track the dog through the thick undergrowth to a small shack hidden among the trees. It's probably the original angler's hut. In it are two more puppies, both female, one red and white, the other almost all black, both blinking at me shyly. I suspect I'm the first human visitor in their short lifetimes.

The mother looks at me anxiously but lets me come close enough to touch her, just lightly on her head. She shifts a little nearer. I stroke my hand gently towards her neck where her collar's rubbing. She cleaves to it, leaning into me, letting out a little groan, gazing up at me. It's Arty's eyes looking at me, that universal language dogs have when they have known human love.

I look at the tag on her collar. It's faded, but there's a number, a Birmingham code. She has a home somewhere, an owner. I can't leave her and her family here.

'Wait there!' I whisper.

But she and her puppies follow me almost as far as the jetty, from which I wade back to the boat, calling up to Summer to fetch me the sausage rolls from my suitcase and the big hessian bag from the boatman's cabin.

'Ohmygod they're adorable!' she shrieks when she catches sight of the three puppies with Mum on the bank, the noise making the little one-parent family disappear into the foliage again.

Back at the hut, mother dog and I trade sausage rolls for a fast friendship I'm not sure she's ready for. She's pitifully thin under the mad fur, but her puppies seem in good health, their eyes bright, their concerted attempts to make friends with me frustrated as Mum vies for every crumb.

Bribing her all the while, I gather all three puppies into the hessian bag and call her to follow.

She heels me, sniffs the bag, jumps up and barks a few times, bright-eyed with worry, but she lets me walk on, fighting my way free of the wooded bank. Holding the bag high, I drop back into the river and carry it across to hand up to Summer. 'Whatever you do, don't let go of that.' It's very heavy, noisy and animated.

After hesitating briefly at the edge of the jetty, barking frantically, mother dog plunges in to swim after me. I'm appalled how thin she is when I gather her up and post her onto the stern of the boat, pulling myself up after her.

We briefly look at each other, two fierce, wet mothers, before scrabbling apart to check our children are OK.

And I know, in that moment, I can let myself love a dog again.

My parents got their first dog the year I went to university, so Trinculo ('Trinkie') was always more of a weekends and holidays family friend to me. He was a West Highland Terrier just like Tintin's Snowy (they prefer small breeds) and he bit me more than once ('he's just playing, Eliza!'). I still have the scars. I don't think poor, cantankerous Trinkie ever really viewed me as family, as his pack, and I'm ashamed to say I didn't think much of him either. He had a permanently yellow-stained, pipe-smoker-ish beard, rubbed his anal glands along carpets like a self-stimulating Dyson, and growled whenever I hugged Mum, which she thought was terribly funny. I didn't.

Above all, he simply wasn't my dog. I wanted my own dog.

When we finally got Arty, I felt terribly ashamed for having not tried to love old Trinkie more, by then in his final embers of life, a steroid-pumped dodderer locked in jealous rivalry with a miniature schnauzer pretender. Because dogs thrive on love, not rivalry. Like humans. Like siblings. Like spouses. And mothers.

I go into the main berth to change into something dry while Summer finishes settling the big white dog and her puppies into a makeshift creche in the saloon, and on the way back

I address the bathroom door to excitedly fill Ed in on what's happening, promising him that we will try to release him as soon as possible to meet the new shipmates. 'It's just like that quote, *in the stream where you least expect it, there will be fish*. Except in this one there were dogs!'

It's greeted with silence. 'Are you still not talking, Ed. Ed? Is everything OK? ED?'

Hearing a faint, tinny rhythm, I realise he has his headphones on.

But just before I turn away, a soggy piece of paper is thrust out from under the door. In lipstick he's written, *Sorry I broke the bathroom.*

I look round for a pencil, write *I love you more than every bathroom in the world* and push it back under, ignoring a twinge as the mug of black tea I had earlier reminds my bladder it's coming through soon.

The paper is posted back out with a smiley face and *That is a ridiculously abstract concept.*

Love or that many bathrooms, I wonder, sending back a smiley face and a love heart. (As a twelve-year-old boy, I remind myself, both usually are alien, no matter where they sit on the spectrum.)

22

Rag Time

I'm standing on the roof of *The Tempest* trying to get a bar of reception so that I can call the number on the dog's collar. If I can get a signal, I may also be forced to call somebody to come and help get us moving again. Nobody has been past in either direction for almost an hour. The world could have come to an end for all we know.

Mum and pups have settled straight into their makeshift corner, walled in with bench cushions and lined with every blanket we could find in the cupboards. They have fresh water and an old rope toy of Arty's I unearthed in the boatman's cabin. Mum's polished off all my food supplies that don't contain dog-damaging ingredients, her litter sharing as well as suckling before all taking a nap.

Summer carries two mugs of weak black tea up on deck. 'That's the last of the water in the kettle. They are *so* cute. Can we keep them?' She puts the mugs down on the roof to jump up beside them, watching me wave my phone around.

'We need to find out if she has an owner first.' I step over my clothes that are drying in the sun. The only thing I could find to change into – apart from kinky basques – is an oil-stained blue overall of Paddy's. It's huge and far too hot and I'm just wearing crotchless panties underneath (it was that or nothing; I've added a strategically folded piece of kitchen towel). But I have my pearls, so I'm fine. I still want to cry a bit, but I'm fine. I'm *una donna fantastica*, so I'm fine.

'Why doesn't this bloody thing WORK!' I shake the phone and scream 'Bloody, bloody, bloody thing! I'm not trying to fucking stream a fucking movie. I just NEED TO MAKE A CALL!'

'Is this your hormones again?'

'No it's fucking technology!' And my hormones.

'Humanity can't be trusted with tech, I agree,' Summer says, launching into one of her TED lectures. 'We supersize it but we're too animal to control it. We'll always bring it back to survival and sex because we can't help ourselves. Face it, we're only on this beautiful big blue sphere to reproduce, period. That's why men have a gotta-fight-it, gotta-fuck-it urge. It's hardwired. Use it wisely and you have heroes. Digitise it and you have Twitter trolls and porn. Social media's turned us into gender propagandists.'

'What a comfort your mobile is still in your locker at school.' I'm standing on tiptoes beside her, and I have one miraculous bar! Argh, it's gone.

'My phone's not at school.'

'But your map avatar was still there when we picked you up.'

'Mum, I love it how Ned Ludd you are. The location tracker just records the point where I switched off my data.

It's right here.' She reaches up under her skirt. 'Lace garter iPhone holder. All the rage this year, according to the bridal shop.' She holds up her whizzy mobile, tapping the screen. 'I didn't want to look in case Kwasi hasn't mess— oop! He has. He is SO mad at me.' She presses it to her chest and closes her eyes. 'Can I stay on this boat longer? Like all week?' She's bright red.

'*You have a PHONE with a PHONE signal?*'

'4G on my network.' She looks at it again, finger flicking the screen superfast now. 'Do you want to borrow it? Can you wait until I've read all these DMs?'

Be a calm mother, I remind myself. Be strong.

'Yes and no and I pay the bill.' I snatch it up and call the number from the collar tag.

'*Don't* answer if Kwasi calls!' she pleads as a woman answers the call with a Black Country *Yuss?*

When I explain about the dog and her puppies, trying not to reveal how choked I am at the tearful jubilation to come, the phone is muffled instead and I hear the shout, 'Colin, I think somebody's found your nan's dog!'

Tearful jubilation is briefly delayed until Colin comes on the line wheezing emphysemically, 'Big white poodle, yeah?'

I suppose it's possible. 'She's been living as a stray a while. She has puppies!'

'Not my problem. I know it sounds harsh, bab, but Nan's in care now and she can't cope with Lady no more. We gave her to a fella with a narrowboat over Smethwick way who said he needed the company. Call him, not us.' The line goes dead.

'They don't want her back.' I return the phone to Summer, still in shock. 'She's a poodle called Lady.'

'That's suits you so perfectly, Mum!' She beams up, ironic eyebrow on overdrive. 'She's a Privileged White Dog!'

Paddy hated the name Artemis. He wanted to rename her Slinky after the *Toy Story* dog, which I vetoed on the grounds that Slinky was a) male, b) a dachshund and c) it's unlucky to change a dog's name. (Another one! From which we can deduce that it's unlucky to change any name except Reg Dwight, Marathon bars and Bombay.) We had a brief power battle through the first few weeks when I referred to her as Arty and he called her Slinky, but I won, control freak that I am.

'Lady' is a tough one. It doesn't really reduce – Lad? Dee? Ay? – and much as I loved the Disney movie, it's not a name I would ever give a dog. But she's been rescued by a boat whose name was once *Lady Love*, so maybe fate's trying to tell me something. If asked to list my top fifty dog breeds, poodle would not have featured.

Today is changing me.

I am already fighting for this poodle.

I stay on the roof, looking out for boats, stepping over both my clothes and a sunbathing Summer who has reclaimed her phone to read messages from Kwasi in forensic detail. It has now been an hour and ten minutes since we got grounded. The world has definitely ended. We'll all go savage again – which is handy, because the second mug of black tea is pressing down on the first and I may have to wee over-board soon.

'I could phone Dad?' Summer reads my mind.

'Not just yet. I need to think this through.'

'Like me with Kwasi,' she sighs.

'I'd hardly compare the two.'

'Yeah, Dad probably hasn't even got his phone *with* him.'

Flicking through her phone history, Summer has returned to her tech debate to lecture me on my generation's misappropriation of smartphones. 'You still see them as something to make calls on, like a digitised Filofax, which is totally antediluvian. They are personal space, a gallery of self, an ego-pod that we have the agency to curate.'

I try to tune her out while she's in TED-Talk mode. The river is serenely quiet along this stretch, deep in a channel of rush and canopy, slow as a trance. Except that now I can hear animated voices. Is somebody approaching? Maybe they can help us?

No, it's coming from Summer's phone. I pick up a few passing phrases: *Narrator of the Year... tell that to Vanity bloody Fair.*

'What *is* that?' I look down.

'Eight thousand views! They love you, Mum.' She holds it up.

I hear my own voice shouting from it, 'I'll wear double denim and drink Malibu for breakfast!'

I can rise above this, be firm, motherly, unembarrassed. 'Delete it.'

'Never!' She holds it to her chest.

'Hey! You all right, ladies?' shouts a cheery voice from the river. 'Need a hand?'

Salvation is paddling towards us in the shape of a kayak coming downstream, in it the sort of man who deserves music cued: 'Holding Out For A Hero'. His shoulders are Herculean, his chest a ship's prow tapering to the sort of lean midriff a woman just knows has every gym-honed muscle-pack add-on beneath that flotation vest. His tattoos are tribal, his smile could light a tunnel. Eyes as blue as the sky. All that and a plastic safety helmet with chin harness.

'We've run aground!' Summer sits up, tossing her hair.

He's on board in seconds. 'Let's get you moving again shall we, girls?'

I clamber down from the roof to explain the problem. 'Ran her too close to the bank in the shallow water, something round the prop, can't get the weed hatch open to clear it or push off the bank to get enough clear water to power it off.'

He tuts for a long time. *Tuts*. I *hate* tutting. 'Bet you're glad I'm here, eh girls?'

Directing his attention exclusively on Summer, who has dropped down beside me to admire his tattoos at closer range, he explains that narrowboat engines are very straightforward. 'A mate has one and we see this all the time, especially with novices like you out on day hires. I'll need to take a look at your prop, sugar lips. That's a *propeller*. It'll be in a hatch just down here. We call it the weed hatch.'

'Here's a house, here's a door. Windows 1 2 3 4. Ready to knock? Turn the lock – it's *Play School*!'

Like many fathers in the early seventies, mine kept such a low profile through my early childhood – working crazy long hours, as it transpires – that the first older male figure I strongly attached to was Brian Cant, presenter of the BBC's long-running show for Gen X tots, *Play School.*

'Ready to play, what's the day? It's Tuesday!'

That soft, kind voice, smiley face and thatch of red-gold hair were my comforters. I'd have followed him to the end of the rainbow through the round window, square window or, on very special occasions, the arched window. Humpty Dumpty, Big Ted, Little Ted and Jemima were soulmates. (Hamble the hard, rubbery doll with the fixed stare gave me nightmares.)

I was an early *Play School* junkie, hence a habit of recognising former presenters in vintage film and television plus a lifetime's soft spot for gentle golden-haired men with persuasive voices.

Our hero today is no Brian Cant, but he knows the tropes.

Treat a woman like a child and she will often behave like one: trusting, adoring, innocent.

One tap of a spanner and a double-handed manly twist is all it takes to get the screw-bar to release the lid of the weed hatch which he prises off to reveal a green rectangle of water. He pulls off his kayaking gloves and thrusts them at me. 'Don't lose those. Better have this too…' He pulls off a chunky gold ring.

I examine it while he's fishing around down there. I've seen a ring like this before, I'm certain.

He gasps as his tattooed right arm goes in. 'This water is *freezing*, ladies. Ah, Jesus!' He screws his face up. 'This is hard work, girls. This is brutal. I promise you. Good job you little ladies didn't try this.'

Summer and I obligingly reassure him he's being incredibly brave and strong, handing across a spanner and screwdriver when he asks, nurses to his surgeon.

'This prop is very badly compromised, I must warn you.' His voice is life-or-death serious. 'Get us a knife, angel pie. Great legs, by the way.'

'My name is Summer and I'm not interested in your opinion of my legs, thanks!' She fetches a serrated knife from the galley. From the glint in her eyes, I think she's quite tempted to plunge it between his shoulder blades.

While he uses it to free up and pull out handfuls of tangled reeds from the prop, followed by fishing line, plastic galore, frayed rope and rags, I get plenty of time to check out the tattoos on his right arm as it emerges each time: a barcode, a Roman numeral date and an Aston Villa lion.

Putting them all together, I'm back in the Picasso, being chased down by a Portaloo lorry. *You deserve to die, you mad old bitch.*

Surely not?

I look at the ring again. Is our kayak hero the driver who road-raged me? Or is my recall a bit woolly as usual? I can't be certain enough to call it, the memory fog too dense.

'There's something else... caught...' He's delving his arm deeper, the water up to his shoulder. 'Just need to free... GOT IT!' He pulls out a bra, still relatively intact, vamp red and big-cupped. 'Will you look at that beauty? I'd like to meet the bird who lost this.'

'If she's drowned in the river, maybe you'll get lucky?' Summer says with a maniacal little laugh.

'You're feisty, sweet cheeks!' He laughs too, not getting it, and asks her how old she is. 'Fourteen, fifteen? Legal?'

For once, Summer looks too outraged to speak.

'Is the propeller free yet?' I demand in a tight voice.

'As a bird, love.'

Summer and I catch eyes, feeling the irony.

Hatch closed, he pushes us off the bank with the bargepole as easily as an inflatable gliding through a swimming pool, and then manfully elbows me aside to start the engine himself and check she's running smoothly, telling me where I've been going wrong. 'Too much throttle through your turns, you see; my old lady did the same on the Norfolk Broads. Women drivers, eh?'

He takes back his ring and gloves and turns to give Summer a hot look, saying, 'All right, angel? How about I row alongside for a bit to make sure your mum doesn't ground her again?'

She glares at me and I realise she's still too angry to speak.

'That's really not necessary.' I manage another polite smile. Paddy would do no less to help a stranded boat than he has, I remind myself, and give him a bottle of the Moet in thanks, which he's thrilled about, paddling off with a shout to tell us that we've made his day. 'Especially you, baby doll! If Mum wasn't around you'd be in danger, beautiful!'

'Yeah, and you're a fucking sexist, teen-baiting DICK!' Summer screams after him, which spoils the moment somewhat, although he pretends not to hear it, paddling on.

'That was a bit ungrateful.' Following behind slowly in *The Tempest*, engine pitch-perfect once more, I'm jubilant to be on the move again. I've only lost an hour or so. I can still do this.

'Ungrateful!' Summer's still feeling unforgiving. 'His eyes were never off my body and did you hear him: "angel pie,

sweet lips, love, bird, baby doll"?' She turns to me furiously. 'Why did you give him champagne, Mum?'

'I was being polite. He helped us out of a tricky spot.'

For this, I get a kindly meant pep talk about my assertiveness. As an evolved Gen Z addressing the outdated X model, she says women like me believe ourselves to be self-assured because we complain all the time – about our husbands, our kids, our health (she doesn't mention menopause but I'm guessing that's a big whinge too), the service in restaurants, etc – and yet we're ultimately prissy nihilists. 'That man was openly sexist and a bit paedo, but you even *rewarded* him.'

I feel my deafening silence get louder. Summer is right, the kayaker did ogle and objectify her. And while that angered me, I dwelt more on being ignored and overlooked. *Don't Flatter Yourself. You deserve to die, you mad old bitch.* What a minefield this world has made for women.

'If I meet him again, I'll tell him just what I think of him,' I promise.

'That's hardly going to happen. We stand by our actions not our intentions, Mum. You *justified* his sexist language. I thought you had more balls.'

It came as a big surprise to me at school that French nouns are gendered into boy/girl. My vocabulary lists had separate changing rooms: windows and doors, female; floors and ceilings, male. It turned out the same was true in Italian and Spanish, and those clever forward-thinking Germans even factored in a third gender somewhere between the two. I now know Latin is the culprit of much of this, but I was spared that educational torture, partly because I attended a school that didn't require me to possess a mortar board and penis and partly because the eighties saw the introduction of the Modern Languages General Certificate of Education – O levels in old money – and Latin got phased out as a subject, much to my father's chagrin. (Chagrin come from the French noun, *chagrin,* which means sorrow or grief; it's male, *le chagrin,* as coincidentally is happiness, *le bonheur,* whereas madness is always female: *la demence, la folie, la rage.*)

The fact that English nouns are gender-free thrilled teenage me. Forget le, la, el, il, der, de, das. We say *the.* Neutral. Doors, windows, floors and ceilings can all party together in one big room of 'the'. It's gender-free, it's the, *the, THE.* Let's party!

But all too soon I saw that there is still a marked sexual divide in our lovely ungendered language. And that's fine when it's balanced, the ying, yang thank you ma'am/sir of girls and lads, ladies and gents. Women get referred to by more than 'lady' through our lifetime, however – tart, bird, cow, scrubber, bitch, to name just a few – and our body parts are coined to refer to both genders, none very positively: cunt, pussy, twat, tit. Barely skimming the surface there. I've never felt that cock, dick and bellend quite balance that up. And then there's balls. Balls are a good thing. Having balls is entirely positive. Hooray for balls! Except women don't have balls. Why can't we have a positive piece of our anatomy to represent being courageous and powerful in our own right? The clitoris, perhaps, or the ovaries – or if that's deemed too 'cis', then why not boobs? Yet 'it took boobs of steel to do that' somehow doesn't feel right; I can't see Ant Middleton shouting it at female participants of *SAS: Who Dares Wins.*

* * *

We're powering downriver. I have the tiller in hand, the wind in my face, and the desire for another loo break firmly in check.

Summer's inside, checking on Lady and her puppies and talking to Ed. I've asked her to tell him we'll stop at the next village to try to break him out of the bathroom without damaging the patented toilet catch. It's about two miles downstream, with two more locks to negotiate en route.

Alone on deck, I stifle yawns, roll my shoulders and swear a bit, punchbagged with exhaustion.

I've forgotten to switch my phone back to Do Not Disturb, and as soon as my network's signal reappears, it lets off a firework show of notification alerts in my boiler suit's pocket.

Lots of messages stripe the screen, the names making me highly anxious: Paddy, Jules, Lou and even the Agent-Who-Never-Calls – please let it be a casting call-up from Greg Doran and Erica Whyman! Others are from the estate agency, a couple of theatreland friends, my neighbourhood WhatsApp group. The real world is out there.

The first message from Paddy was sent three hours ago, informing me that the online grocery delivery has lots of substitutions and am I OK with short-date tomatoes? A second, within the last half hour, says New Neighbour wants him to go round this afternoon to quote for kitchen, but he's cleaning our windows first and can't find where I've put the indoor squeegee? Both are short and terse with battle tension, but also reveal he has no idea I'm here on the Avon, I realise with relief.

Nor does he know that Ed was sick on the school coach

– possibly deliberately – and stowed away. He doesn't know Summer ran away from a very fake wedding to join us.

The enormity of this deception daunts me. I send a terse reply: *Squeegee under utility sink. Slight change of plan here. More later. Ex*

My sister has sent a list of links to resources about the menopause. Lou has sent a dancing Bananarama GIF captioned YOU CAN DO THIS with *How's it going?* underneath. I send a hasty thumbs up back to both. The message from the Agent-Who-Never-Calls is a generic one with holiday dates when she'll be unavailable to clients (as opposed to just unavailable to me). The estate agency wonders if I'm free for more guided viewings (no mention of Matteo and the mill flat).

There's nothing from Miles at all, thank goodness.

A new message notification from an unfamiliar mobile makes me jump. Matteo doesn't have my number, I remind myself as I open it nervously, but it's just Lottoland reminding me that tonight's Euro jackpot stands at a hundred and twenty-three million pounds. Must buy a ticket.

This just might be my lucky day.

It's not that I believe I'll ever win the jackpot, not in my heart. But for that lapse of time between buying the ticket and *not* winning I like to let myself dream I might, allow myself to imagine I'll have no more money worries, indulge myself looking up properties we could buy, holidays we could have, charities we'll start up, the treats we'll give to friends and family. And to me, those few hours of fantasy are worth every penny. Paddy says it's a waste of money, but for the same amount he splashes out on one pint in the pub with his mates, I get hours and hours of happiness. I call that jolly good value.

'*Bidford Grange Lock (or Pilgrim Lock),*' Summer reads from the *Avon Navigation Guide* in a breathless younger-Royal gush as we approach it, '*was hand built with thousands of steel reinforced concrete blocks by the men from Gloucester Gaol.*' Her spoilt-brat voice is a superb pastiche and I realise (belatedly) that she is auditioning these descriptions to show off her range. '*Although the site was soft, floods frequent and avalanches commonplace, the resulting structure was effective and pleasing to the eye.* Oh my God! Floods and avalanches. So excited!' She pulls on her shoes ready to jump out to set the gates as we approach.

An elderly foursome are enjoying a tea break on folding chairs by a moored narrowboat, putting paid to my plans to nip behind a bush for a discreet wee. The menfolk predictably rush forth to help Summer, whose double standards annoy me. 'You are *so* super kind!'

Too tough for all that little-lady talk, I man the tiller, silent and brooding as *The Tempest* descends. The gushing water noise is not helping my two-mug-full bladder. I try to run a few pelvic floor exercises to keep it at bay, but it's not so much a floor as a mezzanine level these days.

Emerging through the gates, I nudge the lock landing to collect Summer who climbs back on the roof to sunbathe and study the Avon guide as we forge on downriver. Her next impersonation is Katharine Hepburn's clipped drawl: '*Bear left as the river splits. Barton Grange to our right was once the site of a grist and paper mill with lock and weir, but is now a golf club. I do so love golf.* Do you know Hepburn swung both ways?' She sets the book aside to look down at me. 'She was with somebody called Phyllis Wilbourn for three decades. I read it in that biography Granny gave you. She called herself Jimmy. Phyllis was her "secretary".'

Another deafening silence from me. Katharine Hepburn was one of my first idols, remains so, and her private life is fine kept private if that's what she wanted.

'All this reminds me a bit of *The African Queen*,' Summer is saying.

It's a running joke at home how often I still watch it, the classic movie in which a gin-swilling riverboat captain played by Humphrey Bogart is persuaded by Katharine Hepburn's straitlaced missionary to take his boat downriver in the Congo to attack a German warship. *African Queen* is one of my go-to movies; just the thought of it gives me a lift. As students, my housemates and I watched it so regularly we still quote whole scenes when we get together. The acting explodes through the celluloid in a film era when acting made chemistry, not the other way round.

I hardly think Shakespeare's Avon in June compares to the Ulanga River in wartime, but there is something of the puritanical Edwardian missionary about Summer. And I so adore the film.

I can't resist reviving Bogie's Charlie Allnut. *'I don't blame you for being scared, Miss, not one little bit. Ain't no person in their right mind ain't scared of white water.'*

Summer looks up from the book sharply. *'I never dreamed that any mere physical experience could be so stimulating!'* Her Rose Sayer is perfection. She knows the lines.

'How's that, Miss?'

'I've only known such excitement a few times before – a few times in my dear brother's sermons when the spirit was really upon him.'

'You mean you want to go on?'

'Naturally.'

'Miss, you're crazy.'

Letting out a shriek, Summer drops the book and starts clapping. 'Oh my God, you are so good at that, Mum!'

'You're better!' I clamp the tiller under my elbow and clap back.

I'm not quite sure what's just happened, but it's broken us both. We're a bit tearful and high. An old film script is the wormhole that's closed the short human lifespan separating our perspectives.

And it makes me bold enough to break my deafening silence. 'Just as you rightly told me not to live my life through you, Summer, you can't try to redirect mine, especially those years already lived.'

She nods, sobs, launches herself off the roof to hug me. When I hug her back, ribs are threatened. 'You drive me bloody mad, Mum, but I love you. I am so proud of you.'

'Entirely mutual.'

'Dad's your Bogie, isn't he?'

It's another moment that breaks us. It's not that Paddy is particularly funny. It is the word 'Bogie'. Shamefully silly. We try so, so hard not to laugh, but that reliable Finch family female giggling fit kicks in like a Heimlich manoeuvre; I have been gifted it with Mum, with Jules and now finally with Summer. It's so good it hurts.

★ ★ ★

Men who complain women aren't funny still don't appreciate that our humour works differently and yet with the same end destination, like charter and schedule flights. Their laughter is all too often a sex, drugs and rock and roll perfect storm, a single glorious endorphin kick: the fast-fire comic whose cocaine-line jokes make a room explode; the one-night stand joker, testosterone loaded and bought into en masse.

I used to make Paddy laugh a lot, and it was the best aphrodisiac in the world.

(And I can't deny being the one who has lacked humour in recent months, along with hormones.)

To share laughter with women connects us around the globe, no matter whether that humour is silly or sophisticated. We must see the funny side to survive. It has bonded us for millennia, this long haul of weeping giggles, funny bones and mutual adoration. It transcends language and knows no borders. When we laugh together, we can do so for a lifetime.

Somebody shouts from the bank that we're on the wrong side of the river. Pulling ourselves together, we jump to it. *The Tempest* is passing dangerously close to a line of moored boats and I steer her right.

Summer picks the book off the roof, her voice changing again, now Phoebe from *Friends* (which she and her gang are all addicted to). It's a very cute trick, and it occurs to me again that all this accent switching might be her trying to impress me rather than provoke me. *'To our left is Barton Moorings, and now we are passing several caravan parks. Is that like a trailer park? Why do they site them by rivers in your country?'*

'To give them a lovely view. A lot of people like to retire there. Maybe your father and I will.'

'Not so clever when ice caps melt and the sea levels increase and all their little metal houses float away because they've goofed up the planet, oh no.'

I ready myself to deflect another TED Talk, but she just smiles and continues reading from the book: *'Barton Lock (or Elsie and Hiram Billington Lock) is unusual in having three walls to enclose the lock island. The original wooden gates were salvaged from the Thames.* Hello!' she calls back as we're hailed by a group of lads in a day-hire barge, oy-oying Summer.

'Don't objectify my daughter!' I shout.

'Overdoing it, Mum,' she mutters. 'But I appreciate the effort.'

Then I almost steer into the weir by mistake as The Proclaimers start singing in my pocket that they would walk five hundred miles.

There's only one Miles.

'Aren't you going to answer that?' Summer asks.

I have started to sweat, the telltale hellfire of a flush rising.

'No. We've got a lock to get through.'

It's a busy spot, bargees and gongoozlers everywhere. I push my dark glasses higher, lower my hat brim and touch my pearls for luck, my eyes darting everywhere, almost surprised to find my brother's not waiting for us. We share the drop with another narrowboat heading off from its lunch moorings, my body pouring sweat, stomach grumbling furiously. It's past three.

As before, onlookers fall over themselves to help Summer and tell me where I'm going wrong.

This time, Summer tells them, 'We know *exactly* what we're doing and we don't need any help, thanks!' Which is unfortunate when moments later her phone rings with Vossi Bop and she dashes up the grassy bank out of sight to take the call, leaving me to do it all single-handed.

After a clumsy exit, I wait for her by the landing mooring, fanning myself and staring at my phone.

1 missed call. Miles hasn't left a message or tried again.

I open Paddy's messages to reread, my heart turning over a bit, knowing I must come clean.

But when I call there's no answer, and Summer is clambering back on board, looking furious and a bit teary. I give her a hug.

'Oh, Mum, he's been looking for us for hours. He thinks I'm with Joachim!'

'What did you tell him?'

'I told him that I love him and nobody else, but I can't handle how unhappy he makes me feel pretending this isn't a thing, and that I found today objectifying and difficult, and that I'm helping you take the narrowboat to hide it because of this dare you have with Uncle Miles, and that my brother is trapped on board, and that we found some stray puppies and got rescued by a sexist, and that you are going through this problem with your hormones, but we have had some really good chats including about him.'

'And what did he say?'

'Nothing. I think his battery ran out while I was talking about the puppies.'

★★★

The stretch of river that runs from Barton Lock to Bidford Bridge in a curving serpentine isn't long – five furlongs in navigation-speak, or just over half a mile – and houses with sweeping waterside gardens are already welcoming us on our right. We pass one I remember showing to potential buyers for the agency not long ago, a million-pound-plus des res with feature walls and a Jacuzzi.

Must buy that Lottery ticket, I remember. There's a pub mooring in Bidford where I plan to stop to ingest food and caffeine, use the Ladies, try to calmly break my son out of the narrowboat's bathroom and walk to the convenience store on the High Street beside the river to buy essential supplies and the ticket which will win us a hundred and twenty three million life-changing pounds.

My phone now lights up with 'Ain't Misbehavin" and Mum's picture.

I take the call.

'Everything's fine!' she says brightly.

'Does Miles suspect anything?'

'Not a thing. He's at the airfield all afternoon, so your father and I decided to come out for a little drive and offer our moral support. I hope you don't mind, but I told Daddy what you're doing. He thinks you're quite mad, darling girl. Where are you? We're in Bidford. We've bought a picnic so we can all have tea in Big Meadow and we're about to park. According to your little map app thing, you should be nearly here.'

'You can see my *location*?'

'On my telephone, yes. I wrote down the instructions so I'd remember what you told me to do.'

Eliza Ludd strikes again. It seems I've only stopped sharing my whereabouts with Paddy, but the rest of the family are still able to pinpoint me from anywhere on Earth. Meanwhile, having laboriously explained Google Maps to Mum so that she could track my whereabouts from Prêt a Manger on a recent trip to Bicester Shopping Village, she's used this privileged info to turn spy pro.

I'm steering the boat around the top of the serpentine bend, the medieval stone packhorse bridge coming into sight two furlongs ahead with its traffic lights at either end and the usual queue of cars. It's too narrow for two lanes of traffic, so motorists are obliged to take turns to cross in single file. The popularity of the riverside park, Big Meadow, means there's always a tailback. The sun glints off car roofs as they hurry across, an angry horn beeping as somebody nips through behind the others after the light's changed to red.

The same car beep echoes in my ear.

My parents are *on the bridge*.

'You'll never *guess* who we've just spotted!' Mum gasps. I can hear a snarly engine, which is odd because their Leaf is pretty much silent.

Then Dad's voice says, 'Bloody decent motor, that.'

In the background on the phone, a voice shouts, '*Cosa diamine stai facendo, eh?*' and Mum titters. 'It's Matteo from Russo's having a frightful ding-dong with a man in a van in front of us.'

Matteo Mele is also on the bridge.

'Has he seen you?'

'No, we're just turning into Big Meadow and he's crossing over. We'll park down by the day moorings where we all usually stop with Paddy. See you there!'

I hang up fast.

The bridge is still too far away to make out individuals on it. I put the throttle to reverse and give it a blast to kill our speed before clicking it to neutral, the narrowboat now at a stable enough standstill for me to dash into the saloon to dig out Paddy's birdwatching binoculars. Lady and her puppies watch me sleepily. Summer looks up from reading back through messages on her phone, her eyes suspiciously red.

'Granna and Grandpa have come to Bidford to see us,' I explain, 'and guess who is already waiting on the bridge?'

'Really?' she yelps.

I hurry back up on deck and scan the river ahead. I can no longer hear the Ferrari engine; it must have driven over and away.

Summer follows me. 'Can you see him?'

'No…' I keep looking, straining my ears. 'Can you hear a loud, snarly engine?'

'I can hear *lots* of car engines.' She concentrates. 'But he just has an old scooter, a Lambretta, I think.'

'Who has?'

'Kwasi.' She takes the binoculars. 'I thought that's who you meant? He's coming after me and Joachim, remember?'

'Why would he still believe you're with Pretend Ex when you told him about hiding the boat and Ed and the puppies?'

'Because I sort of let him think he was involved?'

'Why?'

'To make him jealous?'

'Summer, you have so much to learn!' I wail.

'If he thinks I'm with Joachim, he is going to literally go HAM, isn't he?'

After a pause, I'm forced to ask, 'As in cooked meat?'

'No, it's like really, *really* angry. As in Hard As Motherfu—'

'OK! I get it.'

My star-crossed daughter clambers on the roof, binoculars peeled. 'Why aren't we moving?'

'I think Miles might be onto us,' I mutter, thinking about the missed call. 'He might have persuaded Granna and Grandpa to double-cross us.'

'That's just paranoid, Mum. Or is that your hormones too?'

'Yes, it's all bloody hormones, Summer!' I throw the throttle into forward thrust once more. 'And mine make me feel HAM pretty much constantly.'

It seems Summer embellished the 'older lover' story *a lot* when talking about him to Kwasi, starting back in the days when it was all flirty fun, later using Joachim for creative inspiration at school whilst working alongside 'Mr Owusu', fuelling his already conflicted sense of outrage. If I thought Patch, the fictional red-and-white spaniel was a bit of an over-elaborate lie, it's nothing on erudite Joachim Conti, the acting coach who took her virginity so expertly at summer drama camp before returning to Teatro Español in his native Madrid, from where he has remained a Svengali and confidante throughout her later teens.

As well as possessing a back story that could make a six-part Netflix drama series, turns out, Joachim is just my type. Like mother like daughter.

'It was actually Jack who took my virginity and vice versa,' Summer confides from behind binoculars, information I had quietly guessed at and now don't know quite what to do with; should I say 'ah yes, I thought as much' or 'good to know' or 'mine was a Smiths' fan called Paul, I still have one of the mix tapes he made me'? I decide to use my deafening silence and a wise, salty look at the tiller.

The Tempest is soon eating up the two furlongs to the bridge at a good lick, following in the wake of another traditional narrowboat called *Romeo's Juliet* which seems fitting.

'I want you to understand that Kwasi isn't being possessive or controlling,' Summer says. 'He just thinks Joachim is an exploitative creep and he wants to warn him off big time.'

I try to imagine Paddy pumped over any of my bastard exes, real or imaginary. Nope. Not even when we first married. 'Why did you lie so elaborately?'

'It was a good story,' she shrugs, 'and I tell good stories. Truth is sometimes as much about authenticity of thought as arrangement of fact.'

'Nice try, but *you* should be the one to kill Joachim, Summer,' I tell her. 'Admit he's fake.'

'I have *tried*!' she pleads unconvincingly. 'You don't know Kwaz. He's all fire and passion. I'm amazed he hasn't figured out yet, especially when I uploaded that photo onto my phone. He was supposed to guess straight away. See this?' She holds it out, her face on screen beaming beside a familiar-looking man in blue surgical scrubs.

'Summer, that's you and George Clooney.'

'I know! How bad is that Photoshop? I did it in, like, one minute? And how can Kwasi *not know* who Clooney is? He's been around longer than Disney. *Granna* loves him. The original picture was taken *before I was born.*' She looks at me over the butterfly glasses. 'Are you OK, Mum? You look white?'

We're nearly at the bridge, motoring towards the furthest left of its eight arches, the current pulling us off course hard. Somebody is shouting down from the busy road above.

'Bit distracted. Who's that?'

'Ohmygod, Mum, it's him! On the top of the bridge! Go faster! FASTER!'

'Where?' Nobody looks familiar. The usual crowd of onlookers are crammed into the little step-aside spots where they must wait for single-file traffic to pass, some snapping and recording. Then I spot a big digital camera, a small afro and the face of a stone angel.

'Summer! Princess!' he yells. 'You don't have to fooking do this, beautiful!'

'He did it!' Summer cries jubilantly. 'He chased me four locks.' She turns to me. 'You said no man chases a woman four locks?'

I could point out that this is a bridge which means it's technically only been three locks since we said *hasta la vista* to the pretend wedding, but I don't want to spoil her moment.

'Summer Hollander, let them arrest me, I fooking love you!' he shouts down, sounding very Liam Gallagher. 'I'll fight anyone for you. And I'll wait for you.' He points down at me in my hat and dark glasses. 'She's MINE, you hear!

No old bastard is laying a finger on my princess!' Then he double takes. 'Mrs Hollander?'

I wave politely. 'Mr Owusu, hi!'

As we head under the left arch, Summer shouts up, 'I love you too! Please don't worry about Mum. Or Joachim!'

'I'll drop you off here,' I promise her. '*Talk* to him and tell him the truth. But go back home with Granna and Grandpa, understood?' We're puttering past the pub where I'd first intended to stop, now aiming for the public moorings further ahead on the opposite bank where Mum and Dad are waiting beyond the trees.

'PRINCESS!' comes a shout from the bridge.

'Will you really be OK without me?' Summer frets. '*Princess* is ironic by the way.'

The pub's car park is directly alongside the river, a Ferrari sitting conspicuously in it.

'We'll be fine,' I mutter distractedly, scouring the pub's decked sun terrace. A familiar figure is lounging at a table, nursing a tiny coffee cup. Our gazes lock for a long, long second before he stands up to shout, '*BELLISSIMA!*'

Summer spots him. 'Christ, Mum, do you owe him money or something?'

I look away, a marching drum in my chest.

I should not be flattered by this. Not, not, not. It's the boat he's after. Or his lucky charm. Or he's simply proving a point. Or he is a stalker after all. (Face it, Eliza, this isn't *Love, Actually*, and even if it were, now that we're all wise to that film's misogynist subtext – and realise Dame Emma is the only grown woman in it, which is why she makes us cry because she is desexualised into mothering everyone and wipes secret tears away while her husband wants to fuck his sexy young PA – you too would have a few witty one-liners and no sexy Italians chasing you whatsoever.)

Yet I *am* flattered by this. Because this man still looks me in the eyes, even across a river. And the jolt I felt realising that on meeting him is still jolting.

I am flattered because I am a grown woman, middle-aged mother, and competitive Finch whose daughter can't quite believe that a man could chase me four locks too.

Five, actually.

'SUMMER, PRINCESS!' comes another shout from the bridge.

'DARLING GIRL! *Bellissima*!' from the sun deck.

I focus on the river, my face on fire, wondering how I get out of this and praying Mum and Dad don't cotton on to what's happening.

'SUMMER!' From the bridge.

'CRAZY LADY! *DOLCESSA*!' The sun deck descants.

'HEY, FELLA!' Voice moving along bridge towards pub. 'Yeah, YOU down there. WHO THE FOOK ARE YOU, CALLING MY BEAUTIFUL GIRL A CRAZY LADY?'

Standing delivery from pub sun deck to bridge: '*Signore*, I do not know what you are talking about!'

'FOOK, YOU'RE HIM, AREN'T YOU?' Leaping over wall from bridge into pub car park (inadvertently landing on a car bonnet).

'*Oddio*, NOT the Ferrari!'

Running through car park. 'JOACHIM FOOKING CONTI!'

Summer shouts, 'No, Kwaz!'

I look back in alarm.

Matteo is standing on the sun deck, draining his tiny coffee. 'Do NOT use language like that in the presence of ladies, *basta*!'

Leaping over the rail from car park to sun deck, Kwasi storms, 'SAY THAT TO MY FACE!'

'Do not use that language in the presence of— ooft!' The first punch lands.

Summer shrieks, '*Do* something, Mum!'

'Just bloody well grow up and stop that!'

They naturally take no notice. As *The Tempest* keeps moving veeeeeeeeeeeery slowly past the pub on the river, all attention is on Matteo and Kwasi engaged in a wrestling match on the sun deck.

Summer's videoing it on her phone shouting, 'THIS WILL BE SHOWN IN COURT!'

I long to add, 'or Instagram slash YouTube slash Twitter,' but I can't risk our truce. It's mercifully not much of a fight. Kwasi's using the same bear hug tactic he used with the groom so Matteo can't throw a return punch, plus his camera's hanging from one shoulder like a handbag. They could be drunken slow-dancing until two burly men in bar aprons appear to separate them.

'THAT MAN ISN'T JOACHIM, KWASI!' Summer shouts. 'JUST SOME WEIRDO WHO KEEPS PESTERING MY MUM! Come back over the bridge! We're stopping!'

He sets off at a run, shouting a threat at Matteo I don't

catch. Meanwhile, Summer dives into the cabin to raid my handbag again, this time for cosmetics.

Wiping his face with a large white handkerchief, Matteo watches me warily over it, like a mask. That dark, intent gaze. The pestering weirdo line hasn't gone down well, I sense. I hold up a hand, hoping he will take it as a peaceful farewell gesture.

He dips his head, raises the handkerchief in surrender and smiles ruefully, then turns to walk away. I hate to admit it, because it's a very dignified response, but I'd expected a bit more drama.

I navigate across the river towards the mooring pitches on the opposite bank where I can see Mum and Dad's Leaf parked at the far end with their picnic table already set up, complete with flowered folding chairs, the Jack Russell lying in the shade beneath one.

I scour the area for Miles, but unless he's hiding up a tree, I don't think he's here.

'HELLO, TEMPESTUOUS ONES!' Dad is looking out for us, leaning heavily on his stick. 'Need talking in, Eliza? LEFT a BIT! Not so fast! Use the bloody bow thruster!'

The fight across the river was too far from earshot to have attracted their attention (not that Dad would ever hear it), this little pocket of riverside recreation a haven of vintage thermos and plastic plates.

'LEFT A BIT! MIND THAT OTHER BOAT! STRAIGHTEN UP!' Dad keeps barking useless advice. 'WHERE'S PADDY WHEN YOU NEED HIM, EH?'

'Cucumber sandwiches ahoy!' Mum greets us, hawking two plastic coolers round from the car boot. 'And seedless raspberry jam for Ed. What on earth are you wearing, Eliza? You look like a Kwik Fit Fitter. Never mind, you are doing *brilliantly* and we are *very proud* of you, aren't we, Peter?'

'Too headstrong and giddy for your own good, my girl! You look like you need cake.'

Oh God, they're so safe and staunch, so entrenched in life's tail-end kindness. I love them. I want to throw myself from the boat into comforting arms.

Summer bursts back on deck, kisses me, calls me a fucking legend, apologises for swearing, then leaps deftly across onto the mooring before hurtling up the bank. 'Hi, Granny and Grandpa! I'll be back. Can I invite my friend to have tea with us?'

'Of course!' Mum watches her running through Big Meadow towards the bridge. 'Why's she in such a hurry?'

'Love's light wings,' I sigh and Mum gives me a wise look. By contrast I feel like I have love's concrete overcoat on.

'Eliza…' Dad holds out a hand to help me off the boat to tie her up. 'All this nonsense is going to end here, yes? If you need money, we can lend you money.'

'No!' I stay stubbornly on board. 'It's nothing to do with that.'

'Stop it, Peter!' Mum snaps. 'We discussed this.'

'She's plainly exhausted and can't handle that thing.'

'She handles it a damned sight better than you ever did,' she snaps then smiles up at me. 'Don't give the children a second thought; we'll look after them both.' She lifts one of the plastic cool boxes with effort and hands it up to me. 'Now, I brought you some essential supplies, darling girl: just a few mini quiches and a bottle of chilled white Burgundy.'

'Thank you so much, Mum.' I feel even more choked, because she is so rarely my champion – especially when Miles is involved – yet today she is, complete with al fresco dining.

'Is Edward still locked in the loo?' she whispers worriedly.

'There's a crowbar here somewhere that I'm going to force the door open with.' I look round the boat's stern, then start with surprise to see a pair of familiar blue trainers with no-tie toggle laces, above two skinny legs in a school tracksuit.

'SHUT UP and LISTEN, people!'

Ed is on deck, outward-bound backpack strapped on like a turtle shell, bladeless multitool in hand. 'I have now completed my game including bonus levels, sealed off the tap in the bathroom and taken apart Ashwell's Patent Toilet Lock. I'm hungry and I find barging quite boring so I propose that I disembark here to have some of Granny's sandwiches.' He pats my arm awkwardly. 'Also, Mum needs a vacant bathroom because she has to urinate a lot.'

I'm still gaping at him. 'You broke out? Just like that?'

'I could always get out of there, Mum,' he explains in the fast, flat voice he uses when he's quashing extreme anxiety. 'It was a matter of being ready to do it. I needed to know that you would be OK. And I now think you are. *Mamma Mia!*' He presses the multitool into my hand before jumping onto dry land. 'You might have the thing that makes you barren and mad, but you are surprisingly good at navigating river locks.'

'Now get going!' Mum urges me, glancing over her shoulder and whispering, 'I think your father might have alerted Miles. While I was laying the picnic table, I caught him with his reading glasses on, holding his phone under his blazer and looking furtive.' Then she steps back and shouts, 'Show us all what you're made of, darling girl!'

An engine snarl makes me glance over my shoulder and I spot a red Ferrari crossing the bridge, drawing admiring eyes before racing south into open countryside with a fierce departing growl.

'Thank you!' I push *The Tempest*'s throttle forwards again. 'I bloody will!' Crazy lady is going all the way.

23

Time Immemorial

The Tempest's maximum speed is nine miles an hour – about the same as a leisurely cyclist – and that's going some on a river, not to mention the fact it's breaking the law, sending up a bow wave that would threaten to capsize every boat and waterfowl around us and drench bystanders. I risk six – the same pace you'd sprint for a bus – as we cruise away from Big Meadow, the village jetties on the opposite bank giving way to longer commercial mooring marinas, then out into open country.

The Avon is quieter here, no other river users in sight, the banks lush and protective. I'm bursting for the loo, forced to do a fidgety dance on the spot until I'm sure we're clear of any human life.

Then I put her in neutral, tie the tiller in position, grab the abandoned mop bucket to scoop water from the river and head down the steps to the boatman's cabin, through the bedroom berth and into the bathroom. Ed's left it very neat, the wet towels folded in the shower, Ashwell's Patent Toilet Lock dissembled in the soap holder, the basin cupboard open, its supply now switched off.

Oh, the relief of a proper toilet bowl! I use the river water to flush it, then make my way through the galley and saloon to the well deck to turn the diminished tank supply back on.

Lady watches me come and go while her puppies pounce on her wagging tail.

'I have nothing to feed you,' I tell her regretfully. 'You badly need a vet check and a wash and so much TLC.' I feel guilty for keeping them here, but I couldn't have asked Mum and Dad to take them.

The puppies attack their mum's tail with ever-more excited squeaks as the wagging speeds up. She looks at me intently. *This, to me, is more TLC than I've had in a long time*. I nod in understanding, and refill her water bowl, the kitchen tap now flowing again.

Then I remember the mini quiches.

In the chill box there's also cold meats and cheeses, various pasta and rice salads and leftover lamb from Sunday lunch. Dear Mum's determined I will run away with enough buffet food to host a small party on board. I feed Lady and her pups a selection. What was it Summer called her? Privileged White Dog? She is.

While I'm cramming the rest of the food in the fridge, the narrowboat lurches beneath me. The river current must have caught us up and made us drift. I hurry back up on deck, cursing myself for being fool enough to abandon the tiller. Another rookie error – she even has a river anchor although I can't remember how to use it.

I'm surprised how far downstream she's drifted. We

have run aground in shallow water again. This time *The Tempest*'s hull is lodged on a raised section of riverbed away from the bank. I put the throttle into reverse, grateful the propeller's not snagged. A few blasts of bow thruster and she dislodges into deeper water.

I consult the guide again. We're on the final furlong before the last of today's six locks, Marcliffe, which is hidden behind a sharp bend ahead of us. I've been on board very rarely when Paddy takes the boat this far.

My yearning for him spikes to fever pitch once more. Not because I can't cope on my own – the narrowboat was easy enough to get moving this time – but because being alone with *The Tempest* once again gives me that strange sensation of stealing something of his soul, of being in a world where he is here and yet not here, a strange grief-state that echoes the loneliness I've felt in our marriage sometimes, particularly recently.

Mr and Mrs Hollander are not what we were. The closeness has shifted, from one love to another over many years, from that abstract heart and soul intensity that Summer is just starting to experience to something more pragmatic we only rarely examine, usually in extremis.

My menopause is extremis, I have no doubt of it, but not one it's easy to communicate, least of all with a man.

It feels like failure, a loss of self and of control. In the same way his deep grief was locked into that part of him I cannot reach, this comes from a place that existed before we were us. Unlike marriage and babies and homes and jobs, this was always going to happen.

⋆ ⋆ ⋆

The weir is straight ahead, barricaded by floating barrels, the current pulling us towards it, the river's force stronger every mile downriver we go.

I steer left into a deep corridor of slab-sided engineering. I haven't checked with the *Avon Navigation Guide* as to how many prisoners laboured to create this lock, but it's brutally industrial amid all this bucolic greenery. There's nobody around to help. One top gate is open in welcome, thank goodness, a heron lifting off its rails as *The Tempest* enters.

I tie up and jump out to close the upper gate, grateful for the leg stretch, crossing and recrossing the footbridge, the shoulder-loosening focus of opening and closing paddles soothing me. Now that I'm alone in doing this, just as originally intended, I have a *que sera* sense of fatalism. Let Miles try and find me. I'll just keep pressing on.

Just occasionally, these maddening hormonal mood swings have a way of catching an emotional updraught that's close to an induced high. It's glorious. I can feel the tension drop away from me. Not just the tension of this single madcap day, but the days and weeks leading up to it, the constant irritation and stress and fear. My new-found serenity glows brighter than any hot flush, and I realise I can anticipate the cool welcome of peace of mind ahead. Not here and now perhaps, but it is out there, and I can sense what it will feel like, can hear Mum's voice reassuring me that it's wonderful to be out the other side.

Waiting for the lock water to lower, I check my phone for messages, feeling a nervous jump to see there's one from Paddy: *Hi love, hope book recording going well. Neighbour is stark raving. Thanks for that. Nets later. Will call after. Sorry we rowed. P.*

I could pick this apart in detail for hidden meaning but it's already making my chest hurt to try.

Feeling a bit teary, I reply: *Looking forward to it. I'm sorry too. Ex*

I then WhatsApp the Hollander Fam group with an animated sloth group hug sticker; cheesy, but I'm limited on choice and time here and I want to reassure the kids all is well. (I don't expect Paddy to read that one; he and WhatsApp stickers are never going to have a working relationship; simply mastering predictive text has almost destroyed his soul.)

I close my eyes and focus on the sound of water rushing from the lock, Paddy's theme tune. I feel grateful for him with a force that shakes me.

Why do I keep questioning my behaviour with him, my integrity, how much I once wanted to please him and act happy, when the truth is that I've often behaved that way simply because that's how he makes me feel? He's my travelling companion through a life in which I have a habitual need to perform to earn my passage, yet he's my free ride. *A wedding's just your ticket to love; it's marriage that's the journey.*

When I was an impoverished student with no car and a whopping overdraft, I hitch-hiked fairly regularly, usually with a mate but sometimes alone if I had to.

Tell people that now and they say things like 'Good God, you're lucky to be alive!' as though I stood in laybys with a handwritten card inviting passing motorists to enact a grisly murder in a handy industrial warehouse before distributing my mutilated body parts around dog-walking beauty spots. (Although since my children became teenagers, I've stopped arguing back that I was completely safe, and agree that it was pure madness.)

Thumbing a lift was entirely different to buying a train or coach seat amongst strangers and defending its priced-in solitude and silence with a Walkman and a book. Hitching a lift meant giving something back. Being a pretentious drama student, I sometimes made up characters, became a one-woman improvised show. I like to think retired lorry drivers still look back fondly at the hours they passed on the M1 with young Sadie the trainee undertaker from the Borders or Denise the Liverpudlian fire juggler.

Today, I've hitched a lift with a lot of different sides of myself, but there's one I haven't yet met, and being here alone in the boat has made me realise how much I'm looking forward to it, to introducing her into my life and to living that to the full. She's the person I'll be when menopause is over, when I have finished 'changing'.

The sun is lowering from teatime to cocktail hour, hot and unsympathetic as I pilot *The Tempest* through the Vale of Evesham. We've long since passed the rip in the riverbank where swift River Arrow cuts into the bigger, slower Avon and the holiday park at Abbots Salford over which news helicopters love to hover whenever flooding threatens, its tightly packed caravans like a shoal of fish viewed from above. To our left is the long ridge of Cleeve Hill, a low wrinkle in the vast, flat vale, constantly disappearing behind the thickly wooded riverbank.

With each change of landscape, I feel a little less paranoid that my brother will appear, waving from the riverbank, telling me I've lost the bet. There's nothing along this stretch bar trees and reeds and peace.

I need this solitude; I'm doing a lot of thinking.

Even though my craving for Paddy is reaching fever pitch, I *love* doing this bit on my own, feeling this connection with *The Tempest* without the constant well-meaning instruction, controlling something I've always dismissed as exclusively his. This old narrowboat is stitched into his life. I feel like I've borrowed his coat, just this once, to go out all by myself and, amazingly, it fits. She makes me happy too. Because Paddy makes me happy.

With Summer and Ed on board it was impossible to gauge the strength of this feeling, to know that it is still here, that no matter how many times it mutates and changes, it's my bedrock. And it is more than simply companionship or parenthood, physical desire or old-fashioned romance, more than shared memories or home, more than friendship into old age.

I don't even have a word for it (the Germans probably do because they have all sorts of clever ones like *Drachenfutter* for the guilty gifts we give to say sorry, as do the Japanese, like *Yugen* for a profound, mysterious sense of beauty in the universe). But in plain old British it's just plain old love. Just that.

Forget nets. I message him. *Look under your pillow, then look for me. Ex* I turn my location sharing back on and pocket my phone.

★★★

Fair-mindedness is a quality I have learned to value as the most precious of all human gems. It's no coincidence that I married a man who treats all his children equally, a quality innate to him.

Growing up, through my angstiest phases of self-doubt and sibling rivalry, I blamed many of my failings on my parents' competitive favouritism, on having a Daddy's Girl for a sister and Mummy's Boy for a brother. It's only through my own marriage and parenthood that I see how lucky I was, that we middle children have a rare balance, and that Jules and Miles had pressures of expectation far in excess of mine. I was the compensation: the arty daughter for Mum, the needy one for Dad.

I've sought balance throughout my life, the calm of equilibrium, of scales levelled by Lady Justice in her blindfold. My father and Jules, by contrast, like to quote American author William Gaddis: '*Justice? You get justice in the next world, in this world you have the law.*' And Miles doesn't care how poetic, rough or perverted in its course justice is, so long as it's in his gift, in which case his generosity knows no bounds.

But let's not forget that Lady Justice also carries a sword, too.

I hear it first: wasp-like, drone-like, only louder. Then I see it. A microlight: one of those ridiculous sewing-machine-meets-hang-glider contraptions only the maddest Baron von Munchausen adrenaline junkies ever try to master. Somebody like my brother.

What is he playing at?

My heart splutters with fear as I lift the binoculars to look closer. Take a moped and glue on wings and that's what is headed this way. With Miles in it.

My brother might have been learning to fly for weeks and can take solo flights for practice, but he hasn't passed his licence yet. If he has taken a microlight in search of *The Tempest*, it is unbelievably reckless, ill-thought-out and typical of him.

It's swooping closer. Miles is laughing his head off.

'Gotcha! Aarghhhhhhhhhhh!' he flies past.

'Miles, are you all right?' I shout up. But he's gone, disappearing over distant hedgerows.

There's a long, peaceful, river-cruising pause during which I wonder if I imagined it.

Then he's back.

'Eliza… Arghhhhhhhhhhh!' He flies by the other way.

'MILES!'

He crosses the river just ahead of *The Tempest*, dipping frighteningly close to the water before pulling up and turning sharply, banking right then vanishing behind a row of poplars.

Please let him be gone, I pray, please let him be gone.

Far from issuing an impossible dare, he always knew I'd take her. Nobody knows the child in me as well as my brother. I usually adore it that he does.

Not this evening. Not even close.

'Arghhhhhhhhhhh!' Miles is back, following the river path now, heading straight towards the narrowboat.

The family's sun king is out to eclipse me. Or should that be our Icarus? This is all the challenge was really ever about, I realise: an adrenaline rush for Miles is a lethal dose for anybody else. My little adventure is nothing to his great skyborne chase. He's loving this, whereas I feel duped and silly.

I can't possibly get away. There's nothing but reed banks to either side of me. Travelling at 4 mph there's no escaping the microlight at this close range.

Miles is still bearing down on us and shouting something I can't hear. His reflective shades glint in the sun. The déjà vu hits me between the eyes. All I need is some Donizetti and an eighties haircut. This is like Paddy's favourite scene in *Travelling Man* with the helicopter taking swipes at *Harmony*. Except that Miles looks terrified.

I put the boat in neutral and stop the engine. As I do so, the river goes eerily silent.

That's when I realise the microlight engine has stopped too.

'Arghhhhh!' My brother swoops closer. 'It's STALLED!'

I throw the throttle to neutral and then scrabble up onto the roof, channelling Lomax, grateful at least that we're not on Chirk Aqueduct.

'Aim for a field!' I scream. 'Land it! You can do it!'

Behind the aviator sunglasses, I can tell he's frozen with fright. There are tears. He passes overhead so close the updraft gives me a brief facelift. Then he veers right and loses height over a maize crop. Crows rise up, squawking furiously. There's a lot of swishing and clattering and swearing and then the microlight disappears from sight and it all goes quiet.

Not even pausing to take off the pearls, I dive into the river – total belly flop – and bog snorkel to the bank.

My heart is on fire, my head thumping with *please be OK, please be OK, please be OK*. My legs are already leaden, a stitch pinching. It's like fighting through hundreds of student yucca plants circa 1988, and the sodden blue boiler suit is now heavy as chainmail, but I put my head down and push, push, push toward the sound that I know to be my brother whimpering.

When I track him down deep in the maize, Miles is propped up against a remarkably intact, albeit upside down, microlight, and clutching his shoulder in a very WWII bomber pilot way, tears dried, pupils large, pale beneath the fake tan. 'Yay!'

'Are you hurt?' I rush across to check, aware he's in the early stages of shock.

'Not a scratch.'

I'm not First Aid trained, but I can confirm that he's suffered no obvious injuries. Yet.

'What the buggery fuck was that about, Miles?' (I'm never very articulate when I'm scared and upset, something I inherited from our father.)

'You sound like Dad.' He looks hangdog, glancing over his shoulder at the upended microlight. 'It's only my second solo flight and I may have veered a little off course. Then I ran out of fuel and the engine cut out.'

'We need to get help.' We're surrounded by walls of immature and green crop, already as high as my head. I clamber hurriedly onto the upturned microlight from where

I can just spot *The Tempest* alone on the river. Although I can hear the distant drone of the A46, there's no road in sight, not even a telegraph pole pointing to civilisation.

I sit down next to Miles, who is worryingly fix-eyed. 'You came after me?'

'The airfield's not far. Following the river is standard beginner navigation. I thought it was worth a look.' He pulls off his helmet and puts his head in his hands, shoulders shaking. 'That was bloody hairy.'

'Do you need me to call someone?' I grope for the phone in my sodden pocket. 'Emergency services?'

'I radioed into the team as soon as I made the emergency landing. It's fitted with a tracker so they'll come and pick us up.'

We're all being tracked, I think bleakly, like millions of little data dots.

'I can't believe what just happened!' He rubs his face in his hands, which are shaking.

I'm still mainlining adrenaline, and I'm very angry with him, but I hate to see my brother this upset, and I know how dangerous shock can be, so I sit down beside him and put my arm round him.

Then I realise he's laughing. 'I found the fucking boat! I won!'

I could hit him, but there's a manic tone to his laughter that makes me take a few deep breaths, heed Joe's words about his uncle being in a bad place mentally, and grip the shoulders more tightly. 'We're in a field of corn on the cobs, Miles. This is just us. Talk to me. What is all this really all about?'

'You're so wet, sis.' He shifts away.

'It's called emotional empathy.' I take my arm back. 'You should try it.'

'No, I mean you're soaked through. You swam across the river to save me?'

'It was more of a wading thing and no saving was required, but yes.'

'I can't believe you did that for me.' His pupils are even more dilated and otherworldly.

'I love you, Miles, of course I bloody waded for you.'

He starts to cry again. 'I've fucked it all up, Elz.'

'It's only your second solo flight.'

'Not that! Everything!'

At the bottom of the road on which we grew up was a short, steep hill we called Freewheel Mountain because it was great fun to fly down on our bikes. It finished with a humpbacked bridge and then a sharp right-hand bend that took skill to handle to avoid pitching into a berberis hedge outside a bungalow called Shangri La. The trick was to get up as much speed as possible going downhill, fly the bridge, land, peddle like mad and lean right to spit up gravel.

As soon as he came off stabilisers, Miles wheeled down it faster than either sister had ever dared, straight through the hedge.

He was cut to ribbons and his bicycle bent beyond repair, but he refused to cry because he was a boy and he'd been brought up not to.

It was only hours later, third in turn to use the bath water, that he started to whimper, the cuts stinging raw, the loss of his bike and pride humiliating.

When I blustered in to offer him my bike which was getting too small, he shouted that having a girl's bike was just as bad as having girls' feelings. I told him that it was OK for boys to be angry and hurt like girls, and that I sometimes cried in the bath too, at which he snarled, 'You're wrong! Only Mummy is allowed to cry in the bath because it's a *grown-up* thing!' Then he threw a soap on a rope at me and told me to go away.

I hated him for that.

Forty years must pass before I think to question why he was the only one of us to know that our mother cried in the bath. Like I cry in the bath. And it's only now I ask myself whether Miles still cries in the bath too.

I know for a fact he's still just as dangerous without stabilisers.

The trauma of the near miss has made Miles confessional and contrite; Joe wasn't wrong: his uncle is very down and deeply embarrassed about it. And just as I hugged him when he'd bloodied both knees at six, I hug him now and listen as he apologises, sobs and curses, promising he'll get a grip in a minute.

For a vain man, he can be refreshingly self-deprecating. He's a mess of insecurities, the glossy charm skin deep. Some days he can barely bring himself to get out of bed he tells me, others he hardly cares if he lives or dies. 'It's all so stale and fake, this so-called bloody life!' he groans, sounding like Hamlet had he lived to forty-seven.

I could point out that having a job might help, but he's now talking about Paddy, apologising for the family rift.

'I was such a berk, sis, and he was so uptight about it. I admit that's what selling the boat is about. To punish him.'

'For being awkward about your nineties crush confession?'

'God no! That's not why we fell out. I thought he'd have told you about it.'

'Come on, Paddy's a Fort Knox friend. He *never* betrays a secret.'

'It's not a secret. Lots of people know about it.'

'Know about what?'

Miles waves away a cloud of midges. 'It's history.'

This is one of his teenage catchphrases and it still drives me mad. I point angrily at the microlight. 'You could have just killed yourself here, Miles! Why? Because you want to win a bet? Life's precious. *Everything* matters, especially history. We learn more from the past than anything else.'

'Are you talking about your doll again?'

'You need to grow up, Miles!'

When he looks up again, eyes wild and bloodshot, I realise this isn't the best thing to say to a man in deep shock, and that I'm probably in shock too.

'Fuck, I really *could* be dead, couldn't I?'

The thought makes me feel sick.

'I'm a snivelling suicidal failure, and I'm nearly bloody fifty!'

'What's so bad about fifty?' (Hypocritical, I know, but I'm not taking that shit from a forty-something.)

'It's all right for you, Elz. You have everything you want! Your lovely home and solid marriage and adoring kids and award-winning job. You're the happiest woman I know.'

'Ha! Nice try, but according to Jules you all spent last weekend discussing my unhappy marriage.'

'I didn't say Paddy was happy, did I?'

That hit low.

'Don't tell me, he says I've changed?'

'How d'you know?'

'He's wrong. I'm chang*ing*.'

'Isn't that a fairy child brought up by humans?'

'That's a changeling.'

'I always thought I might be one of those.'

We can hear laughter from the river, a boat engine, an eighties anthem we both recognise: 'You Are My World'.

'Remember dancing to this as teenagers?' Miles nudges me.

I nod.

He sighs, reaching across to take my hand. 'Who was it said youth is wasted on the young?'

'George Bernard Shaw,' I squeeze it. 'He also said: "We don't stop playing because we grow old; we grow old because we stop playing".'

'I like that. I believe I just won our game, Sis.'

'Spoken like a true player.'

We watch the sun glinting off the microlight wheels.

'I wish I could make Paddy happy again,' I say out loud.

'He thinks you don't fancy him any more.'

'On Sunday you said he complained *nobody* fancied him any more?'

'I'm repeating myself? That's practically senile.'

'Miles, there's a big difference between "My wife, Eliza, doesn't fancy me" and "Nobody fancies me".'

'Stop being a paranoid dick, Elz. It's you. He loves you, it's always been you.'

I find I can't swallow.

Beside me, Miles snorts with laughter. 'We were like Statler and Waldorf from *The Muppet Show* on that narrowboat, all the old man grumbling we did. I miss that.'

I look up at the crows circling and cawing in an uninterrupted blue sky. Oh, poor Paddy. I've been so walled up in my survival bunker, feeling unattractive and dried up and rejected by a world whose gaze had moved on, I didn't pause to think how *he* felt about ageing. That he might feel less sexy than he once had, might blame my fading interest on his own physical failings. I wasn't the only one who started waiting for the other half to look away before undressing for bed last summer.

'So why *did* you two fall out?'

Miles lets go of my hand.

'I suggested we start up a boatmaking business together. He said no.'

As a young child, Joe loved playing at being a doctor or vet; for Summer it was dressing up as characters from her favourite books and films, and Edward's roleplay was inevitably machine-or-space-related, the more superhuman the better. The humanitarian, the entertainer and the engineer. Strangely, this mimics the young Finches a quarter of a century earlier, when Dr Jules, Dame Eliza and Captain Miles saved the universe from almost certain destruction on a daily basis.

Paddy once told me that his childhood was very different; while his sister played 'house', he had an imaginary boatyard where he did up barges.

'Fitting out narrowboats as weekend retreats, party pads and pieds-à-terre for hipsters,' Miles is explaining the business concept to me. 'It's pure gold. I've got a detailed business-plan, the right contacts, the perfect backers, a name even: Argy Bargy. Paddy's the secret weapon I can't do it without, but he turned me down flat. He said he won't risk putting you through what had happened last time.'

'That wasn't his fault! His dad died, his mum was ill, we had a new baby, my work dried up.'

'Tell him that. He says he can't do it to his family.'

I watch as my brother stands up with a groan of effort. 'Are you serious about this?'

'He loves those bloody boats. He could make them works of art.'

I sense how clever my brother's idea is, an entrepreneurial Miles masterstroke. And like him, I believe Paddy's skills and passion could make it work. But I also know prising him out of his workshop sanctuary wouldn't be easy. His confidence is very low, and he's dug in deeply with minimal overheads, very little pressure and a lot of cricket commentary. Plus trusting Miles is a tough call at the best of times; he has questionable sticking power.

I feel a competitive Finch spark. 'Argy Bargy's an awful name.'

'He said that too.' He offers a hand to help me up, then gasps with pain as soon as I take it, clutching his arm again.

'I think my collarbone's bust! Where's that fucking rescue crew?' Pulling out his phone, he presses a speed dial.

It's only now I'm standing up that I realise how cold I am.

Miles is on the phone, crisply British. 'Righty-ho. I'll do that.'

He pulls a small red flag on a metal rod from the cockpit and holds it above his head, like a tour guide. Squinting into the sun, he extends it like a radio aerial until the flag is above the maize. 'Be a love and put my shades back on for me?' He nods towards his top pocket. 'You know, I'm not sure flying is my thing,' he confesses as I balance them on his nose. 'I only took it up because my ground crew looks like a young Brando – that was him on the phone. Truth is, I'd much prefer cruising upriver with a sexy Italian.' The red flag dips to waggle at me. 'You have *ruined* my Russo's boating trip, you realise that? I got *distinct* vibes.'

'I hate to break it to you, Miles, but I don't think you're Matteo's type.' I clench my chattering teeth.

'I know that. The man's eyes were stuck fast to you last Friday. It's his nephew Massimo I'm after. A hundred and fifty pounds of Puglian muscle wrapped up in a compression shirt who cooks like a dream and loves live events. We've exchanged numbers.'

'What do you mean about Matteo?'

'Be careful there, sis. He's a hustler under all that charm. He knows what he wants, and he doesn't waste time.' A clatter of axles nearby makes him turn away, the Land Rover and trailer from the flying school crashing through maize. The driver is indeed a dead ringer for young Brando.

Miles retracts his flag, looking shamefaced. 'Here's my lift to a court martial.'

The microlight crewman is calm and professional, and far more concerned with checking out Miles's shoulder injury than attaching blame. I stand by and start to shiver with cold.

'I must get back to *The Tempest*,' I interrupt eventually, my teeth castanets now. 'I'll return her to Stratford for you, Miles. Matteo's offering a good price. I'll square it with Paddy somehow.'

'What are you talking about?' He turns to me. 'I can't see a boat.'

'But you said it: you found her. You won.'

'Can you see a narrowboat?' he asks Brando Instructor, indicating the maize.

'No, I can't see a narrowboat,' Brando says obligingly.

'Turns out I found something far better.' Miles smiles, eyes glistening at the edges. 'And you *have* changed, Elz. I remember you like this.'

'Can I just clarify what you're saying?' I check anxiously.

'Talk about ruining a moment. Keep the change. Keep *The Tempest*. And please try to talk that stubborn man you're married to into thinking again about the business idea.'

Kissing him gratefully, I run back through the yucca plants and out onto the riverbank.

But I can't see a boat either.

She's gone.

24

Together Time

There's a public right of way that runs alongside the entire length of the river called Shakespeare's Avon Way which follows its course, alternating from bank to bank and using existing footpaths and bridleways to allow those on foot to stay as close to the riverbank as possible.

Along this stretch, it's on the south bank.

I am on the north bank, listening to a Land Rover roaring away out of sight.

There is no path. There are crops and hedges and barbed wire and livestock. And despite the dry weather, there's also mud; a lot of marshy, gloopy, sticky riverside mud. Even so, I think I'm probably moving faster than a drifting narrowboat.

Where is *The Tempest*?

My phone is stubbornly blank.

I am criminally irresponsible, leaving an emaciated dog and three puppies adrift. But even without the anchor down

The Tempest shouldn't have drifted this far out of sight, should she?

I have visions of her upside down in Harvington weir, a tragedy unfolding: the blue lights and police tape and media furore, the mourning grief, the British public catching hold of the story and swirling into an angry online hate mob: *'There were puppies on there! Little puppies!'*

I deserve to be locked up. Throw away the bloody key.

What was it Jules said, that women are more likely to inflict death upon themselves or others when they are menopausal than at any other stage of life? Well, she's right.

There's a canoeist coming upstream! That means he will have come through Harvington Lock. Surely he must have seen *The Tempest*?

I scrabble my way to the bank to shout for his attention.

Red helmet, glinting ring, tattoos.

It's the Kayak Sexist on his return leg.

He draws alongside the bank. 'Fuck, what happened to you, love?'

'Fell overboard. Have you seen my barge?'

It takes him a moment to register who I am. 'Oh, trapped up against the weir walkway down at Robert Aickman.'

She's drifted as far as the next lock, where I was planning to hide out by Harvington Mill.

'She's stuck in the reeds; you'll need to clear your prop again. You left the cute young brunette in charge I take it? Women drivers, eh!'

'Actually men cause four times as many driving offences as women,' I quote a recent Sheila's Wheels' ad campaign.

'Avoiding you lot.'

'Or chasing us along dual carriageways to shout insults.'

'Come again?' He looks at me as though I'm insane.

I feel slightly insane. 'You road-raged me last week.'

'Tell it to someone who gives a shit.' He makes to push off from the bank with his paddle. But I grab it.

'What are you doing, you mad old bitch?'

'It's mad old bitch again, is it?' With all my strength, I wrest it off him and start clambering back up the riverbank, shouting at him, 'I'm leaving you up a creek without a paddle, you bigoted bastard!' Summer's voice in my head, making me add, 'I hope this will help you address your innate sexism, ageism and bigotry on a personal level!'

I make it to a field fence and throw it over first, then climb after it and sprint in the direction of the lock.

Which is demonstrably mad and quite bitchy, but also positively childish, I'd say. In fact, I'm not feeling old at all.

I'm three fields further along with a bad stitch before I relax enough to slow up, confident the kayaker isn't chasing me on foot.

Creeping closer to the water's edge, I can't see Sexist Kayaker on the river either.

Up ahead a tributary stream feeds into the river and I'm trapped at the point of a triangle. I'll have to find a way across the stream, but the far bank is an impenetrable-looking six feet wall of bramble and nettles that I don't think I can hack through with a kayak oar. It's that or crossing the river again.

The whine of an outboard motor makes me turn and look

upstream. A flash of orange draws closer. A little inflatable launch is buzzing along the river at speed. I know it straight away, having edged my way past it on numerous occasions to get across the garage, cursed it, hauled it on and off its trailer and once famously overturned it on a Cornish creek losing a picnic for five.

Standing up, tiller in hand, is the unmistakeable shape of my husband.

He is wearing his suit.

Paddy never made any secret of the fact he's old-fashioned enough to want to pull out chairs, foot restaurant bills, open doors and mend things. We wrangled a lot about it in our early days together as chairs were scraped back and forth between us, bills split, doors slammed and I hid the things I clumsily broke.

Over time, as I hid the broken bits of myself from him too, and lay awake anxiously wishing he footed more of the big bills and opened more of the metaphorical doors in life for our children, I realised Paddy had stopped holding out chairs for me. And I experienced that contrary pinch of sadness women do for the dying art of chivalry.

'Need a lift?' He says it with such cool, I feel like I've stumbled back into an *Avengers* episode, which was where today's mission started, but this time it's the *New* ones, with Gambit helping Purdey into a speedboat, my boiler suit and pearls look and his suit bang on vintage. Less convincing is the way I clamber aboard and almost fall straight out, inflatable wobbling madly, or Paddy trying to get me to wear a child-size life jacket.

'*The Tempest*'s up ahead at the lock,' I tell him, hoping she's still safely stranded where Kayaking Sexist saw her.

We buzz on towards the weir, Paddy in surprisingly good spirits, joking, 'Brought your own paddle, I see?'

'I'm oar-struck,' I joke. 'How did you find me?'

'You shared your location.'

'But my phone got drowned.' I take it out of my pocket and realise that thanks to the wonders of modern wizardry, its waterproof boast has held true and it's back in business, a screen message telling me that dampness has been detected in the charging port.

There's dampness in my charging port too at the sight of Paddy, chin high and heroic. And the little tingles and shivers going on down there are something I've not felt in a very long time.

'This is quite some anniversary surprise.' He doesn't look at me.

I open my mouth to tell all, but I don't genuinely know where to start or how I'll talk around the grateful lump in my throat, so I adopt a Purdey-ish enigmatic pose and say, 'That was the idea.'

'You're beautiful, you know that?' He smiles down at me.

Whilst clearly not true at this present moment in time, I'm owning that compliment. Perhaps unadvisedly I tell him, 'I'm wearing the crotchless knickers.'

He almost ploughs the inflatable into the riverbank.

★★★

The gregarious hosts of the fortieth birthday party we went to all those years ago in their riverside garden are great characters. A quantity surveyor and his private caterer wife, they are can-do people, absolutely the sorts you'd want on your side in a crisis. Which makes it handy they live opposite a river lock where so many day trippers in hire boats get their propellers snagged on the weeds by the weir.

These intrepid sorts think nothing of rowing across to help and it gives them something to dine out on that month. Like the day they saw a marvellous old barge rammed against the weir walkway. 'Turns out to be the *Marie Celeste* of narrowboats. Not a crew member in sight! Inside, there's the most darling puppies imaginable and a terribly sweet poodle Nigel befriended with a Werther's Original.'

'Only one thing for it, wasn't there, Sooz darling? We whisked them all back across the river for a bowl of Chum.'

'Yes, barely sat back down with a fresh round of Pimm's when a couple appeared in an orange dinghy and boarded the old barge. *Quelle surprise* if it wasn't the actress I knew yonks ago and her husband. They came to a party here once; he hardly said a thing and she didn't stop talking, danced a lot, drank like a fish and even went over to the old mill with Nigel and his ghost hunters.'

'I was all for rowing straight across to help them out, but sometimes a little voice tells you it's best to wait, doesn't it, Sooz?'

'Too right it does! What I actually said was: "Don't even go there, Nige darling. Can't you see Eliza Finch is perfectly capable of handling this situation herself? This is *her* moment: she's a true English rose like Rose from *African Queen* and now that she's in full bloom, she's unashamed to be middle class and middle-aged and menopausal because she's *living life* as a great mother and a good wife and loving daughter and sister and fantastic friend and a proud feminist! What's more, she risked *everything* to save the boat her husband loves, and she did it all *in pearls!*'"

(OK, I'm imagining all this because I can't hear a thing over the roar of the weir, but I do spot them waving and pointing at Lady and her puppies stretched out in the sun looking blissed out, and I wave back with a thumbs up and nod and smile at their 'drink?' gestures, and thumbs up again, grateful that they haven't changed a bit, and looking forward to laughing it all off later.)

The first thing I must honourably do is confess to Paddy about the bet with my brother.

But when I do, he just nods and says, 'Yeah, he told me.'

'You *knew*?'

He pulls open the trapdoor on the stern deck and jumps into the bay to open the weed tank.

'I phoned him as soon as I'd dropped Ed off this morning. I wanted to try to talk him out of selling her.' Taking off his suit jacket, he hangs it on the tiller and rolls up his shirt sleeves. 'Miles told me about the bet. He never thought you'd do it, but I did. That's when I discovered the *Navigation Guide* was missing from the bathroom and the spare boat keys had gone.'

'And you didn't try and stop me, follow me, take over?'

Great handfuls of twisted brown rush leaves are coming

out. 'I didn't think you'd want me to. I wanted you to have a chance to do it for yourself, to feel a bit better about yourself.'

'I did.'

'Besides, Tesco.com were due and the neighbour wanted a quote for a kitchen,' he smiles up at me, shaking the water off his arms and straightening up to close the prop hatch. 'That should do it. I'll use the bargepole to hold her away from the walkway and you can get the engine started. You're still skipper.'

I don't move, hanging onto my paddle. 'I loved taking her downriver, even the bastard bridges. I was going to hide her here, near the old mill's dry dock.'

'Good plan. Let's do that.'

'There's no need now I've won the bet is there?'

'Well, you've come all this way,' he steps closer, 'and we have champagne.' That slow smile emerges. Is he thinking about the crotchless panties, I wonder? I don't mind if he is; I'm thinking about them too.

'Still awestruck?' He nods at the paddle which I'm holding like a Masai warrior's spear.

I am a bit, but I put it down. What I long for him to say is that he's proud of me and that he thinks I was brave and brilliant and that I'm forgiven for being grumpy and sweaty and not wanting sex much, and that while today's adventure might just be a few hours' cruising downriver for him, he appreciates that for me it was a life-affirming challenge, life-changing even. Because he knows that I did it for him. For us. For love. And, Eliza my darling, my beautiful girl, *Bellissima*, that's *amore*.

But he doesn't do that. And that's OK because we've been

424

married for twenty-two years and I know Paddy doesn't say stuff like that.

What he does do is kiss me. And it's that kiss. That kiss which flips something upside down inside. That.

By the time we've manoeuvred *The Tempest* into the old mill dock, a secret passageway overhung with willows, we are gripped with unspoken lust.

Only for a moment do I hesitate before we hurry below deck. Given that having sex is an ambitious undertaking for us nowadays – and we've only managed it twice in the past year, both times with the lights out after I'd consumed a bottle of wine to get in the mood (and still wasn't in the mood) – on a boat in daylight, stony sober, it's high risk. Surely we have more debriefing to do before these crotchless enticers come off?

It seems not. Because Eliza Finch *is* in the mood for sex today, and Paddy Hollander is taking full advantage, flagpole already aloft and no need for blue pills.

I usually hate myself naked, and haven't really looked closely at Paddy unclothed for a while, but today I find us beautiful, the shared intimacy of ageing that has taken us from such careless young perfection together to this, familiar bodies whose combined age is over a hundred, our mutual attraction springing from a far deeper well.

I should go to the bathroom to clean up a bit. But Paddy is looking at me so lovingly, as though I'm Venus de Milo (only with arms, a pulse and insect bites) that I can't bear to lose his gaze.

'I couldn't love you more,' he says, which for Paddy is

absolute poetry and I'm frightened I might cry and ruin it. But as we look at each other, we start to laugh instead.

Because it is ludicrous, us two naked in a canal barge on a weekday. It's not even our anniversary. Yet we are so hopelessly, hugely turned on. There's no overthinking, over-drinking, performance nerves or deadly silence. The fluffy cuffs stay firmly in the drawer and there's just lots of laughter and a bit of gasping and grunting, and compliments and endearments, and all-important shuddery joy as we remember we used to be really quite good at all this once.

Then we open a bottle of champagne and talk about Miles's business idea and Summer's complicated romance (me championing both) and all the places we can take *The Tempest* together when we're old empty nesters (Paddy championing Shropshire). We're so engrossed, it's only when we hear barking and music from the garden across the river that we remember we've been invited for a drink and that Paddy hasn't yet met Lady and her little family.

So we grab a second bottle of champagne and jump in the orange dinghy to row across the river and toast enduring friendship and puppy love.

Above all, we toast the fact there's life in these old dogs yet.

25

Celebration Time

'To Argy Bargy!'
  'It's now called Dream Boats, Dad.'
  'To Dream Boats!' everyone choruses, glasses clinking. I touch rims with my sister beside me, can tell from her fixed smile that she hates this new name too. It sounds like a male stripper troupe.

We are in Russo's, where my parents are treating the extended family to lunch to toast Miles and Paddy's new enterprise, which is already on its fourth name change – I've a fiver says it will end up as Hollander and Finch. Name aside, Miles has certainly done his groundwork: market research is in, business model posing prettily, projections good enough to float investors' boats.

Miles has already signed up an old venture capitalist friend for the lion's share and, somewhat alarmingly, our host and genial restaurateur Matteo Mele is also coming on board. Nothing awkward in that. I will look him in the eye when I am good and ready. Possibly next year.

We're in the restaurant's wine cellar, a part of which is a new private dining suite, working our way through a taster menu that showcases the all-new, authentically Puglian dishes. Convivial as ever, Matteo is alternately sitting with us, fetching food and wine or checking on the kitchens as lunch service carries on in the main restaurant above us. This is the first time I've seen him since he and Kwasi were separated like rutting deer as we glided past aboard *The Tempest*.

Summer originally wanted to invite Kwasi here too, but until 'Mr Owusu' officially leaves the school's payroll at the end of term there's no way Paddy's endorsing the relationship; Kwasi is of the same opinion. I'm quietly hopeful.

It's a gourmet tour de force, or *giro de forza*, with tongue-tinglingly sweet mussels, aged ricotta, softest slow-cooked lamb and nothing is overcooked or too hot. Antonio never cooked like this.

The cousins, all gaggled together at one end of the table, are stuffing themselves with high-class pizza and playing a boxed trivia quiz that Jules brought from London because she's a proper grown-up parent.

Here at the adults-only end, Miles is holding court sporting a big sling (it turns out he suffered hairline cracks in both his collarbone and humerus in the microlight crash). Right now, he's talking up his plans for the business. '*Slow* is a disrupter buzzword on the horizon. Narrowboats deliver a perfect capsule of authentic, personalised slow.'

He's a man transformed, restored to making-things-happen glory, the foppish sarcasm nowhere to be seen, his enthusiasm infectious. I don't think any of us realised how unhappy he was until he had something to focus on. His mood lifted overnight.

The false wall behind him is made of old wooden wine crates installed as part of the Russo's refit. Multiple rectangles have been cut from it in front of which hang a mosaic of ornately gilt-framed screens like a gallery, digital back projectors creating a clever bit of media trickery. A discreet sign offers diners the chance to curate their own slideshow of images. It's so new even Miles didn't know about it. Today we're being treated to a slideshow of the Cotswolds, the pictures dim against the light spilling from the chandelier over the table. I feel like I've seen Bourton-on-the-Water and Blenheim Palace from every angle. Russo's definitely needs a better image library.

Reece asks Miles about his plane crash, which he's happy to describe, now beefed up to include a tailspin, ducking-and-draking along the river, rolling through the crop and a small explosion.

I catch Paddy's eye. He isn't saying much as usual, but he looks happier than I've seen him in a long time, the easy smile quicker, the future a place he wants to go to. Our gazes keep tangling all the time, which I love. He's not wearing his suit today because I 'forgot' to pick it up from the cleaners, but thankfully we're still aglow from having sex twice last week, something I'm hoping will last him a while.

Talking Paddy round to the idea of giving Miles's boat-fitting business a go was surprisingly easy – having my blessing was the push he needed to reconsider his decision. Besides which, the prospect of designing New Neighbour a kitchen made him realise his heart is no longer in bespoke butcher's blocks and larder cupboards. In fact, he was so relieved when she turned down his quote, he opened another bottle of Moet. 'It's all about resale at the end of the day, isn't it?' she'd explained when she popped round with Death-stare Baby on her hip last weekend to break it to us that she's decided to go with the big-name designers at twice the price, adding that as a gesture of neighbourly goodwill they're dropping the solicitors' action, which she hopes means we're cool with the trade vans that need to park across both sides of the drive while her new kitchen is being fitted? We said that was fine. I've parked wantonly ever since.

'You have adopted a rescue dog, I hear?' Jules leans across to me. 'With *puppies*?'

'Three.' I can't help smiling widely every time I talk about Lady and her poodly brood. 'The vet thinks they're not even six weeks. The mother and her son will stay on with us,' I glance at Paddy again, the infectious smile shared, Lady's blue-eyed, black-eared boy his sidekick from the moment they met. 'Our friends Nigel and Susie are taking one pup when it's old enough and,' I miss a beat, 'Matteo's having the other.'

'Is not greyhound, but the story break my heart.' Our host swoops between us with fresh glasses and a new wine to try. 'This Pinot Grigio is *spettacolare*. Like a kiss on a mountain top, eh?' I sense his eyes on me.

I don't look at him. I stare at his necklace instead, dangling level with my gaze, the *cornicello* pendant glinting in the candlelight.

It was Paddy who offered Matteo one of the puppies. After just one evening in this cellar talking boats, he, Matteo and Miles are already a bro-trio, like the Three Musketeers,

Ghostbusters or Kirk, Spock and McCoy. I fear manly misadventures ahead...

There's an 'ooo!' from my parents as pictures of Stratford Upon Avon are projected on the little picture screens: Shakespeare's birthplace, the river, lots of swans.

'There's the Gower Monument!' Jules points out.

'Ah, this is good!' Matteo is still crouching between us. 'This is for you Eliza, yes?' he tells me before turning to Jules. 'Your sister tell you about her superfan?'

'Her what?' Jules looks amused.

'Last week a visitor from Japan came into Russo's for a coffee before he flew home, leaving a gift for our most famous diner. He was kind enough to copy his camera card files onto a flash drive as a memento of the day he and Dame Emma Thompson posed together by Shakespeare's statue.'

I lower my fork. If revenge is a dish best served cold, I am eating it.

On screen I'm laughing. I look happy. Really happy. Sexy happy. Walking beside me, Matteo's laughing too, although half his head's cut off, making him harder to identify, his pendant catching the light with a lens flare.

'There's Eliza!' Mum points out in surprise.

'Is that Paddy with you?' whispers Jules.

I mop my sweaty brow with my napkin. My mouth is dry. I knock back the wine in one, feeling like I've been kissed on a mountain top.

All the family – especially Miles – think this is hilarious. 'He didn't *really* think you were Emma Thompson, did he?'

I watch Paddy, who is laughing too. He was livid when he thought I'd tried to sell Matteo *The Tempest* that day, but we've put that misunderstanding to bed (twice) and he has no fear or suspicion of Matteo. Why should he? There's nothing to fear. The road-raging man who crossed his arms and watched when I tried to save a life on a hard shoulder was hardly somebody I could ever feel attracted to. Could I?

The slideshow has moved onto the photos Matteo took when handed the camera. They're artfully composed, and even though I can see I'm sweaty and embarrassed, I'm sharing the joke with the camera.

'Very flattering.' Jules sounds surprised.

'You look gorgeous, Mum!' Summer whoops. 'When was this?'

And it's now I realise that my tourist friend isn't in any of the frames. Just me. The me I remember from years ago. This woman has none of my affectations. If I gave these to the Agent-Who-Never-Calls, she might call.

I'm acutely aware that Matteo is across the table from me now, filling Dad's glass and telling him about the riverside apartment and the offer he's put in. I don't look at his face, but I catch the *cornicello* twisting and glinting.

That necklace got caught on my sleeve when we kissed, and I later picked it up from the boat's galley and put it in a drawer. Why isn't it still there? Has he got a replacement? I can just make out two engraved Ms.

There's a lot of sniggering with Summer and Ed, phones and games consoles out. A moment later the screens are all hijacked by live video of their faces filtered with bunny ears, noses and whiskers and weird anime eyes.

'Your children have hacked my media wall!' Matteo wails.

'Actually the screen mirroring link is right there.' Ed points to the discreet sign inviting private dining guests to share their images. A moment later we witness Sonic the Hedgehog power flexing. Next it switches again to a group of boys doing a Carpool Karaoke mash up of TV theme tunes on their way to school, their new driver joining in. She's called Manpreet and is boundlessly cheerful, although Ed's already complained that she uses third gear too much and has a poor understanding of box junctions.

'This is even funnier!' he announces. 'This is Mum being super embarrassing!'

(*Please* don't let it be my Mr Vella confession again, now at 10,000 likes, not that I'm checking more than once a day.)

But the picture onscreen is of me in a baseball cap. I'm looking over dark glasses and in through *The Tempest*'s porthole to give Ed a double thumbs up and a goofy smile at Luddington Lock when he was trapped in the bathroom. He caught me at a bad moment – one eye half-closed, the other seemingly missing an iris, my mouth hanging open – yet it's still so very me, I rather like it.

'That picture is hilarious, Mum!' Summer snorts from the end of the table. 'What is the filter on that, Ed? Is it fishbowl? It makes her head look super weird.'

'There is no filter.' Ed is looking at me anxiously.

Everyone else in the cellar is chuckling, including Paddy.

I don't care if I look super weird; I still like it. When younger, I would have wanted it destroyed but I'm now wise enough to recognise a photograph I'll look back at in twenty years' time and be grateful for. Because that day on *The Tempest* changed me. Just a few hours escaping

433

downriver transformed the way I see everything, the way I view my marriage, my strengths, my womanhood, its invisibility, the Change itself. *Those who travel, live twice.* It turns out, you don't have to go very far at all, just out of your comfort zone.

This photograph is special. *Through the round window...*

Then the screens all abruptly switch to luscious shots of authentic Puglian ingredients bearing Russo logos. The kids groan, realising the game is up and Big Brother has intervened, but the gelato has arrived at their end so they hardly care.

Matteo swoops round the table as we all get busy with a taster menu of desserts, and this time when he dips beside me, I look at him.

Bugger.

He can still hold a gaze.

'Everything OK?' he asks, lowering his voice. 'I make ugly photo go away.'

'Was it ugly?'

He laughs, drinks in my eyes a moment longer, then helps Jules and me to dessert wine 'that is like kissing in a Tuscan peach orchard'.

My family are talking boats, theatre, business, music, holidays, sport and law. Dad's voice is loudest as always, Reece in competition, Miles in descant. I push my untouched pudding plate towards Paddy who lifts his fork in thanks, rapt as Dad discusses this year's Ashes. Mum looks at me and winks, then digs around in her teeth with a nail.

Is that me in twenty-eight years' time?

I'm hot and anxious and a bit tearful. I can feel myself start to vanish again. I hurry upstairs to visit the Ladies,

434

passing invisibly through the tables of lovely young things and the ghostly old in the main restaurant.

My familiar cubicle sanctuary is a small safe-zone of comfort.

I take out my phone and send Lou a GIF of shark-infested waters. *Family lunch!*

She responds with a sticker of a life raft that inflates to reveal her Bitmoji in a bikini, speech-bubble popping up to say *You Float My Boat* (I can guarantee Lou didn't watch it through to the full bikini message before sending, which is why I love her).

Bladder emptied, thin hair tousled and lipstick reapplied, I regard my reflection steadily. Here is Older Me with her younger eyes staring out, still in here; I blink slowly, feeling the two unite again. Together we pull the porthole face, one eye half-closed, thumbs up. It's so immensely cheering, I do it again. Twice. Me, myself and I.

I say 'carpe diem!' and 'fuck them!' into the mirror and feel a lot better. I now believe Mum when she says how heavenly life gets after menopause, and I'm holding that thought.

When I come out, Matteo's waiting in the corridor, lounging against the wall, all louche creased linen. He steps in front of me, a smile stop sign. 'You are ignoring me, I think?'

'How did you get your charm back?' I point at it.

'I have never lost my charm, *bellissima*, it's my looks and hip joints that have gone to the dogs.'

I'd forgotten all the fun in his eyes; their cleverness; their challenge.

'I won't give up on you, crazy lady,' he says quietly. 'This feels like the beginning.'

'It isn't,' I tell him. And I want to add something profound like: *This is my life, my midlife, and I may be more than halfway through but that's not half the story.*

But I don't think of anything remotely clever like that. Instead, I pull the porthole face and give him a double thumbs up, and his bark of delighted laughter is reward enough. I feel strong. Incredibly strong, and cheerful, and defiant as I march back through the restaurant, chin high, sensing all eyes on me, Eliza Finch: wife, mother of three, jobbing actor, cake-baker, wine-drinker and a changed woman.